Praise for *The Floating Feldmans*

"When Annette Feldman decides to celebrate her seventieth birthday with a family cruise, drama—and hilarity—ensue."

—*People*

"Family reunions can rock the boat. This one does it on a cruise ship. When the Feldmans hit the high seas for their matriarch's seventieth, a lot of drama and laughs come out in tight quarters. Think *This Is Where I Leave You* meets *The Family Stone*."

—theSkimm

"*The Floating Feldmans* is a hilarious romp on the sea that is perfect for your poolside reading this summer! I read this book with a wide grin, and I know that you will too! Highly recommend!"

—Catherine McKenzie, bestselling author of *I'll Never Tell* and *Spin*

"Friedland uses multiple perspectives, witty dialogue, and complex characters that are incredibly relatable to deliver a funny, astute look at the family dynamic and the relationships shared within. Whether on a cruise or taking a staycation, contemporary readers will want to have *The Floating Feldmans* on deck."

—*Booklist*

"*The Floating Feldmans* is a fast, funny, surprisingly heartwarming ride on the high seas."   —Shelf Awareness

"Friedland creates vivid characters with distinct voices, from the outwardly critical matriarch to the insecure teenager. . . . A fun look at family drama on the open seas."   —*Kirkus Reviews*

"*The Floating Feldmans* is a story about an estranged family's wild vacation. This book is so dramatic that it might actually make your fam feel normal . . . even if you're losing your mind on day five of your own trip."   —*Cosmopolitan*

"Take a big, dysfunctional family, reunite them for the first time in ten years on a Caribbean cruise ship they can't escape, and add endless buffets, blindfolded pie-eating contests, and impromptu conga lines on the sundeck. What could possibly go wrong? Both cruising fans and skeptics alike will get a laugh out of this story of a family trying to stay afloat." —*National Geographic*

"Friedland's well-executed and smartly structured novel features chapters from each character's point of view. The simple but clever premise lets the author explore the complicated tensions of family relationships in a compressed and directed way . . . there is dry humor and a certain sweetness as well." —*Library Journal*

Praise for *The Intermission*

"The snappy dialogue makes this an effortless page-turner, almost a movie treatment more than a novel . . . intelligent commercial fiction." —*The Wall Street Journal*

"*The Intermission* is a thoughtful look at the complexities of marriage, delivering deep truths about how we share a life with another person. It will have you wondering: How well do I really know my spouse?" —PopSugar

"A multifaceted look at the difficulties and rewards of marriage." —*Kirkus Reviews*

"Entertaining marriage saga. . . . Friedland insightfully dissects motives, lies, and love in this engrossing deconstruction of a bad marriage." —*Publishers Weekly*

"Expertly paced and eerily realistic, this novel will make readers think twice about the line between deception and mystery in any relationship." —*Booklist*

TITLES BY ELYSSA FRIEDLAND

Love and Miss Communication

The Intermission

The Floating Feldmans

Last Summer at the Golden Hotel

Last Summer at the Golden Hotel

ELYSSA FRIEDLAND

BERKLEY • *New York*

BERKLEY

An imprint of Penguin Random House LLC

penguinrandomhouse.com

Copyright © 2021 by Elyssa Friedland
Readers Guide copyright © 2021 by Elyssa Friedland
Excerpt from *Most Likely* copyright © 2021 by Elyssa Friedland

BERKLEY and the BERKLEY & B colophon are registered trademarks of
Penguin Random House LLC.

Library of Congress Cataloging-in-Publication Data

Names: Friedland, Elyssa, author.
Title: Last summer at the golden hotel / Elyssa Friedland.
Description: First edition. | New York: Berkley, 2021.
Identifiers: LCCN 2020046445 (print) | LCCN 2020046446 (ebook) |
ISBN 9780593199725 (trade paperback) | ISBN 9780593199732 (ebook)
Classification: LCC PS3606.R55522 L37 2021 (print) |
LCC PS3606.R55522 (ebook) | DDC 813/.6—dc23
LC record available at https://lccn.loc.gov/2020046445
LC ebook record available at https://lccn.loc.gov/2020046446

First Edition: May 2021

Printed in the United States of America
1st Printing

Book design by Elke Sigal
Map illustration by Muriel Smith

For Jason, who loved a good joke

"It's not the changes so much this time. It's that it all seems to be ending. You think kids want to come with their parents and take foxtrot lessons? Trips to Europe, that's what the kids want. Twenty-two countries in three days. It feels like it's all slipping away."

—MAX KELLERMAN, *DIRTY DANCING*

"Everything old is new again."

—PETER ALLEN

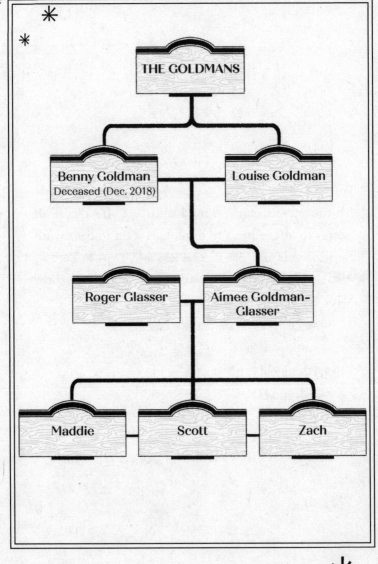

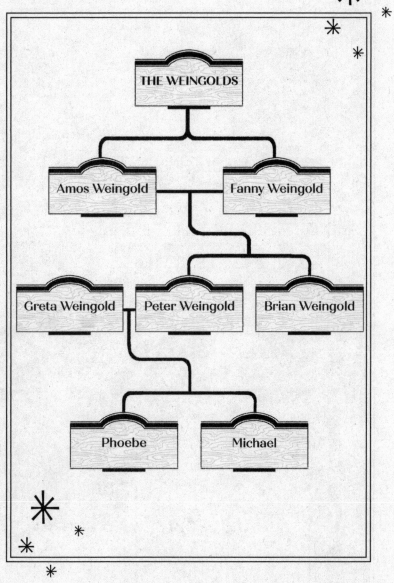

THE WEINGOLDS

Amos Weingold — Fanny Weingold

Greta Weingold — Peter Weingold — Brian Weingold

Phoebe — Michael

Prologue

WINDSOR, NEW YORK, 1981

As was tradition, Louise Goldman took the stage after the appetizer course was served at the final banquet dinner of the summer at the Golden Hotel. Her dress, beaded, formfitting, and floor-length—always a gown for the last night—dazzled as she mounted the steps and walked slowly toward the podium. The crowd of four hundred looked at her from their round tables, upon which white-jacketed waiters were setting down heaping portions of steaming brisket, dimpled mashed potatoes, and braised carrots. Goblets of thick, glistening gravy were placed alongside the meat in silver vessels, and waiters who dripped on the white cloths would escape rebuke that night, but only because it was the last night of the summer, and tips were already sealed into tidy envelopes. Such was the joy of closing out a successful season at the Golden Hotel that even Marty, the captain of the dining room, who kept watch over his "boys" like a general in a foxhole, would let things slide. How could anyone not feel at ease in the warm, wood-paneled dining room of the Golden Hotel, which played summer palace to so many returning guests year after year? The place was steeped in tradition and memories, each room a waffle of nooks and crannies that meant something different, but of equal sentimental value, to everyone who paid a visit.

From her perch behind the microphone, Louise watched her family. They were seated at the traditional "owners' table." Louise's daughter, Aimee, a cherub of a twelve-year-old, full-cheeked with a pink complexion, was seated next to Peter Weingold, and next to Peter, his twin, Brian, who was hitting his brother repeatedly with a slap bracelet. Rounding out the table were Amos and Fanny Weingold, partners to the Goldmans and parents of the twin boys. Amos had been best friends with Louise's husband, Benny, since they were old enough to sit alone on the stoop of their adjacent Lower East Side brownstones. "You play jacks?" Benny had asked Amos. Amos had said yes, and from that point on, they were inseparable. They went to Brooklyn College together, drove cross-country together, worried their mothers together, and—eventually—opened the Golden Hotel together. What if Amos hadn't liked jacks? Louise sometimes shuddered when she considered that affinity could have dictated the course of a life.

"Hello, dear friends," Louise purred into the microphone. She knew just how to make her voice sultry without sounding salacious—the trick was to pull from the lungs, not the throat. A few hundred heads murmured hello back, ready to delight in her song. "I can't thank you enough for helping to make this perhaps our most memorable summer ever at the Golden Hotel."

Louise said that same line every year, but guests happily absorbed the compliment anyway, even the repeat customers, who must have heard her say it at least a dozen times by now. But maybe the line was true. Maybe the Golden Hotel was like a cabernet stored in oak, improving with age, every additional summer layering the place with more character and depth. She tried not to think about the fact that for the first time in longer than she could recall, the hotel was not at capacity for Labor Day weekend. Close to, but not at full occupancy. Benny had started to tell her the specific numbers, but she'd told him a hairdresser appointment beckoned. Louise had wanted to stop by Roberta's on the lower level to have her raven locks teased before dinner. With any luck, Janet, the hotel's resident makeup artist, would also be available to touch up her makeup. Janet knew the best colors to bring out the green and gold specks in Louise's hazel eyes; she'd trained at the Chanel counter in Lord & Taylor. Besides, Louise didn't want to hear upsetting news, not when the final banquet was hours away. She had never been able to handle disappointment well.

"I can't remember a more exciting Gold Rush than we saw today—congrats, Rosenblum family; you certainly earned your place in history." Louise gestured to the plaque on the eastern wall of the ballroom, where winners of the annual obstacle course competition held on the last day of summer merited a spot of honor. "I just wish you hadn't had to push the Friedmans into Lake Winetka to clinch your victory."

Polite laughter from around the room. Benny flashed a thumbs-up. Fanny wasn't paying attention. She was trying to keep her teenage boys in order, especially Brian, who seemed to be the cause of most of Fanny's gray hairs. Why didn't she color them, like Louise did? The Golden Hotel had a fine hairdresser on premises, a Frenchman they'd stolen away for the summer from a Manhattan salon. And why did Fanny have to wear that awful dress on such a festive evening? It wasn't even floor-length. And it was a sallow beige, the color of Aimee's cheeks when she was under the weather. The guests could go and upend the formality that made the Golden Hotel special, but the relaxing of the dress code shouldn't come from the owners. She'd just heard that Brown's had done away with jackets for the men on Friday nights. And Grossinger's was allowing bathing suits at the breakfast buffet. Louise planned to speak to Benny about it tonight. He listened to her best when she put on her silk nightgown and rubbed his back.

From the stage, Louise watched Amos and Benny chatting animatedly. Their unblemished friendship over so many years was a marvel. If only she and Fanny could click the way their husbands did. Aimee was busy staring at Brian Weingold instead of watching her mother, and Peter Weingold was staring at Aimee. It was a love triangle that would concern Louise if the kids were a little older. For now, she'd just keep an eye out. Her daughter wasn't going to become a Weingold. Not with Louise the doyenne of a luxury resort that hosted the finest families from Long Island, New York City, and New Jersey; no doubt highly eligible sons would be presented to Louise and Benny on silver platters in due course. Aimee was pretty and bright, with clear blue eyes that didn't come from her or Benny. Perhaps a recessive gene. Perhaps . . . well, there no sense thinking about that now. The point was, Aimee would have her pick of suitors. The lone child of the Goldman family needed a suitable mate, and that person wasn't going to come from the owners' table.

"I know how excited everyone is to dig into their last supper—I know, we're Jews, but we can have a last supper, too." More laughter. How those giggles sustained Louise. Echoes of them rippled in her ears all the way through to November. "And of course, you're all looking forward to the fireworks. So without further ado, let me bring out our master of ceremonies, Alfie De-Bruce, who will accompany my song on guitar. After, Jimmy Jones and the FreshTones will take over, and we invite everyone onto the dance floor." For the final evening of summer, staff pushed the tables to the perimeter and laid down a temporary parquet floor for fox-trotters and waltzers to swarm.

An elderly man in a full white tux and tails came from behind a red curtain to join Louise and saluted the audience. He struck the opening chord on his guitar, and Louise led the crowd in the Golden Hotel's anthem. In 1965, when the hotel had seen its fifth consecutive year of growth, Benny and Amos had commissioned a famous songwriter to write a ballad about the hotel, extolling its virtues. The songwriter was contractually obligated to mention the magnificent lake, warm vibe, breadth of activities, and of course, the scrumptious and abundant food. His fee was astronomical—but a newly married Benny was persuaded by his bride, who knew a lot about business from her father. Louise Goldman, née Frankfurter, was from one of the wealthiest Jewish families in Montreal. Originally from Paris, the Frankfurters had made their way to Montreal in the 1930s when they sensed the political winds shifting. Her father had made a fortune in fur, then lost a fortune gambling, but in between, Louise had picked up scores of business acumen. She knew you had to spend money to make money. Fast-forward several decades, and the anthem of the Golden Hotel was a lullaby parents sang to their children months after decamping to the city, where instead of songbirds providing backup, truck horns blared and subways rattled by.

As usual, Louise ended the song with an a cappella solo, the crowd knowing when to quiet down and let the mistress of the hotel have the final word. There were only so many years left that she could do this—already she could see Aimee shifting uncomfortably. Her daughter would soon be a teenager, when nothing Louise could say or do would be right, and certainly coming on stage to lead a crowd in song would be on the no-no list. Louise intended to embrace the tradition while she could. The crowd rose to its feet in enthusiastic applause when she concluded, and Louise made a swooping curtsy and kissed Alfie on both cheeks.

"*Bonne nuit, beaux gens*," Louise purred, another last-night tradition the crowd adored. She bowed like a wilting flower. "*Je vous aime.*"

When she returned to the table, Benny threw an arm around her and whispered in her ear: *You were marvelous.* She looked at her husband tenderly. She hadn't married the man for his looks, but as the years wore on and their marriage weathered its early troubles— so many excited doctor's appointments, so many bassinets put on hold never to be purchased—her husband's face had morphed from something once only tolerable into something more dashing. She loved Benjamin Goldman of the Lower East Side more than she'd thought possible. More than she loved her father—before he'd ruined their family, anyway. More than her gang of brothers combined. Her love for Benny was tied only with her love for Aimee, and that was something biologically driven, not something she'd chosen. Because she had *chosen* her husband, even though many from her generation had not exercised the luxury of finding their own mates. Louise saw these ineluctable pairings happen every summer at the hotel: parents trading their children like cattle at a livestock auction. "I'll give you one JD for nice legs; I'll give you over six feet tall for family money." It made her uneasy, these forced couplings. She wouldn't coerce Aimee, just offer mild suggestion.

"Kids, start eating," Fanny said, and Louise watched as she took the leanest slices of brisket and piled them on her boys' plates, leaving gelatinous blobs for the rest of them.

"Leave some for us," Louise quipped, and Benny shot her one of his looks. Nothing she wasn't used to and certainly nothing she couldn't handle. She could play her husband like a fiddle, which wasn't to say anything derogatory about him. He was simply an instrument she had mastered, but it was one she loved to play. Did Yo-Yo Ma tire of his violin? She should think not!

"The meat is gross," Brian said, stabbing at a thick piece with his fork. The boy had no manners. Louise saw his cloth napkin crumpled into a ball next to his water glass. His sandy hair, worn too long in Louise's opinion, flopped in front of his eyes. Aimee, on the other hand, was cutting her food into small bites the way Louise had carefully instructed her ("about half the size of your thumb"), the same way her mother, Celine, had taught her.

Amos chuckled. The man had a guttural laugh, and his whole body shook when he was amused. He was by nature more serious than her husband, but when he laughed, it had a way of elevating everyone's spirits. Peter had the same laugh. He was a quiet, re-flective boy, but when he cracked up—usually in response to his numbskull brother's antics—Louise could actually understand why Aimee followed those boys around the hotel everywhere.

"When you kids own this place and we're six feet under, you

can serve anything you like," Amos said. "Chicken fingers, for all I care." He beamed with pride. Turning over the keys to the Golden to his boys was something Louise sensed he was eagerly awaiting. She needed to make sure Aimee never got pushed out. Deliberately or inadvertently. Sometimes Louise worried that with all of the time Benny spent charming the guests and being the public face of the hotel, Amos might be cheating him right under his nose. Not that she had any proof. And when she told her husband to be careful, he balked.

"Bigger waterslides!" Peter called out.

"French fries at every meal!" Aimee said predictably. Her daughter did love to eat. It was another thing that would have to be watched carefully. Maybe she'd get her to do a Jane Fonda tape the following morning before they packed up. Or take a class with Julie, the sweet aerobics instructor the men loved to ogle on their way to the golf course. Aimee was awed by Julie's rainbow assortment of legwarmers. Rumor had it she'd tied a golf caddy to the bedpost with those legwarmers in staff housing, but it wasn't Louise's place to spread tales.

"A movie theater," Brian contributed. "With only R-rated movies."

"But don't forget tradition," Benny chimed in, lifting his wineglass to his lips. A few dribbles of the kosher cabernet dotted his angular mustache. "There's a reason the guests keep coming back here year after year when so many of our competitors are flopping."

Louise, Amos, and Fanny all nodded. It was something they could agree on. The Raleigh, Kutsher's, The Round House . . . they were all suffering despite making changes to entice a younger clientele. "Cooking light" classes for the moms, skateboarding lessons for the teens, a game room with an Atari. Meanwhile, the Golden Hotel still held true to its origins: shuffleboard tournaments, a simple card room where the men played bridge until all hours of the night, a diving board for belly flop challenges, Saturday lunches of cold cuts and borscht soup. And the reservation book was full. Almost full.

"To tradition," Amos called out, lifting his glass. Fanny raised her Diet Coke. She was a teetotaler, rarely letting her hair down (though with those gray roots, why would she?). Even with her puritan ways, Fanny was asked to join the gals for mah-jongg and canasta while Louise was sidelined. It was probably because everyone assumed Louise was too busy with her hotel responsibilities, but the exclusion stung nonetheless.

"To tradition," Benny, Louise, and Fanny echoed, and even the kids joined in, lifting Shirley Temples dotted with juicy maraschino cherries. There was so much about the place their children loved: the Memorial Day opening barbeque that featured packaged Twinkies and Ding-Dongs, the Friday night trivia parties, the comedy shows they snuck into after bedtime, the Gold Rush relay race—which, as the owners' children, they were prohibited from winning, but still, they kept records of their personal bests.

The Weingolds and Goldmans clinked glasses, seven arms outstretched to join in the center of the table, and Louise delighted in the moment, her favorite of the whole summer. As was tradition, the families who'd stayed with them over the summer would meander over to their table to say their goodbyes and thanks as the evening wore on, and after the main course was served and a twenty-foot-long Viennese dessert table rolled out and the last wedge of apple strudel cut, the guests would congregate on the front lawn for fireworks, already pining for the next summer.

STORIED HOTEL COURTED
BY POTENTIAL BUYERS

The Golden Hotel May Be Shutting Its Doors for Good
June 2, 2019

By Frank Loomis

Windsor, NY—Famous for hosting entertainers in residency like comedian Sid Caesar and singer Brenda Lee, for its never-ending babka loaf on Saturdays, and its once-immaculate 1,800 acres of landscaped grounds, the Golden Hotel may be ending its reign as the preeminent Catskills destination after nearly sixty years in business. The co-owners, the Goldman and Weingold families, who built the hotel and have owned and operated it since 1960, have confirmed that they are in serious talks with a Texas-based company that wants to purchase it.

It's no secret that the tradition of families spending summers in the Catskills, either renting a bungalow for the entire summer or settling into a hotel room for a week or two, is on the decline. While the Golden Hotel once boasted a waitlist for its eighty bungalows and four hundred rooms—rumor had it if you could beat Benny Goldman at poker, you could get ahead in the queue—now the reservations desk has confirmed to the *Windsor Word* that the hotel is never above fifty percent occupancy. A refusal to modernize with the times could be to blame, as could the availability of more exciting options in the area. The effect of travel review sites, such as TripCritic, could also be among the sources of the Golden Hotel's woes.

The two families who control the hotel, with a fifty percent ownership stake each, wouldn't get into specifics about the offer and the timeline for a potential sale, but it's believed by several who spoke off the record that the potential purchaser is hoping to turn the hotel into a casino. "I just hope it doesn't become one of those weird places where people pay to meditate and milk their own cows," said Horace Fielding, owner of nearby Fielding's General Store. He was likely referring to Y-1, a yoga retreat and wellness center that stands on the grounds of the former Kutsher's resort.

Benny Goldman, who along with his wife, Louise, was considered the face of the Golden Hotel, died six months ago due to complications from a heart transplant. His famous pink 1968 Cadillac has been seen in the driveway of the Golden Hotel; it's believed that his widow is currently in residence. Amos and Fanny Weingold have been spotted in town as well, so it appears the older generations of both families are on hand to discuss the offer and decide the fate of the beloved summer home of so many families.

"We weren't the inspiration for the movie *Dirty Dancing*," Benny Goldman once told the *Windsor Word*. "If we were, it would have been called *Dirtier Dancing*." He was referencing the common misconception that his hotel served as the inspiration for the iconic movie starring Patrick Swayze and Jennifer Grey. It was, in fact, the competing Grossinger's resort upon which the movie was based.

"I hope they have dollar slots," said Bobby Winter, owner of Winter Garage and Gas, who believes the area would be enhanced by a new casino resort. "Foxtrot's table minimums are too damn high." Foxtrot opened in 2018 on the premises of what was once the Sunny Mountain Bungalow Colony. (It's believed that the phrase "Bungalow Bunny," referring to the women who loosened their morals during the week while their husbands worked in the city, was coined there.)

Lacey Lovett, who owns the Motel Matilda along with her wife Sharon Timbale in neighboring Liberty, NY, said she'd be excited if the Golden Hotel was taken over.

"Long gone are the days where the little woman hightailed it to the country while her husband went to work," Lovett said, noting that she did hope the new owners wouldn't directly compete with the Matilda's fleet of services. The motel is known for its craft-beer-for-women-by-women classes and tantric yoga workshops.

As for the hotel employees, many of whom have spent their entire careers doling out Golden-crested towels at the pool and balancing gigantic trays of food on their arms, feelings about the future of the hotel are mixed.

"I want to serve matzo ball soup until the day I die," said Abe Futterman, one of the dining room's captains known for his good humor and lightning speed in bringing food from the kitchen to the guests.

But concierge Larry Levine was less emotional.

"I don't really care what happens to the Goldberg Resort," he said. "I always planned to retire in 1980 anyway." Why he misnamed the hotel or the year is unclear.

Despite numerous requests for further comment, hotel CEO Brian Weingold, son of co-founder Amos Weingold, could not be reached.

Whatever the future of the Golden Hotel, it will be the home of many beloved memories for thousands of families who played bridge in its oak-paneled game room, partook in the famous Sunday bagel and lox brunches, lounged in the heart-shaped hot tub, were regaled by some of the country's top artistic talent, or simply cozied up with a good book in the well-stocked library. No word on whether other members of the second- or third-generation Goldmans and Weingolds will return to "campus" to help decide the fate of their childhood summer home.

Chapter One

Brian

Brian put down his copy of the *Catskills Crier* and grimaced. First the *Windsor Word* and now the *Crier* were turning their attention to the hotel. When he'd replaced all the mattresses with Tempur-Pedics (1,200 beds!) and renovated the golf clubhouse, it had been crickets from the reporters. Brian had emailed photos to the editors in chief of both publications and not even gotten a response. But suddenly the local papers were sniffing around, and he had six voice messages and nine unanswered emails asking him to comment on the offer.

He took a swig of bitter coffee from his thermos and stared blankly at the line of phones at the hotel reservation desk. There was very little about the day ahead of him that he was looking forward to. He didn't necessarily want to feel the jolt of caffeine, but sitting behind the reservation desk would surely put him to sleep otherwise. The phone had rung about a half hour earlier and had shocked his eyes into an open position, but when he'd answered, "Good morning, the Golden Hotel," a confused voice on the other end had responded, "Sorry, I must have the wrong number."

Historically, this weekend—the third week in June—would kick off the busy season. His father and his longtime business partner had built the hotel as a summer destination for those wishing to escape the hot city, boldly joining the ranks of many more seasoned establishments doing the same. But over the decades, they had expanded it to an all-year-round facility, with a modest bunny hill for skiing, an outdoor skating rink, fall foliage excursions, and spring gardening classes. Still, summer would always remain the peak time, not only because occupancy was at its highest—in its heyday, the Golden's summer reservations booked up more than a year in advance—but because its historical roots lay in the summer season.

Photos ornamenting the hotel documented the "hot" season from the early years. Brian loved to study them, to let the history envelop him as he passed framed pictures of ladies in the modest swimwear of the sixties, children licking Popsicles, men playing bridge under umbrellas. He made his way to Memory Lane now, the nickname of the hallway that housed the majority of the pictures. He eyed a large print of the canteen, which still served cold beers and hot dogs all day long, and the kidney-shaped pool, affectionately called the Nugget, where the bobbing heads of children looked like pinheads dotting the surface. A recent guest had complained that the curvy lines of the pool made it difficult to do laps. Replacing the pool with the more modern rectangular shape now in fashion would cost a fortune, and Brian didn't quite know where that ranked on the list of desperately needed renovations.

After the bedbug crisis, he'd had no choice on the mattresses. And when the golf clubhouse had suffered a devastating flood, it had meant new everything. There was simply no budget for discretionary improvements. Not if they were going to make payroll. To pay the insurance premiums. To keep up bountiful platters of food.

"This look okay, boss?" came the voice of the hotel's long-standing social director, Larry Levine, aka the Tummler. Hired by Benny and Amos in the late 1960s, Larry was the kid from their neighborhood who could always stir up a good time. On the sizzling streets of downtown Manhattan, he hosted egg-cracking-on-sidewalk competitions, organized stickball tournaments, and was the first to pull the plug on the fire hydrant. When it was clear the hotel needed a full-time minister of fun, there was one clear choice. If the Golden was going to compete with the other giants in the area, a top-notch entertainment master was needed. Fifty years later, Larry was still the activities director. As he approached, Brian noticed he had on two different shoes.

Larry handed over a printed sheet of paper with a list of the hotel's daily activities. Brian's heart sank as he perused it. Combined with Larry's bizarre comments in the newspaper, it confirmed what he'd suspected for the past six months. And it meant he couldn't put off a call to Larry's wife any longer.

"Larry, this is an activities list from December 1983. Look here. It says ice skating show at ten; ski hill opens at eleven; snowman-building competition after lunch. Rubik's cube demo in the pagoda. Look outside, Larry. It's sunny. It's June, Lar. We have water aerobics, the walking club, outdoor checkers."

Larry stared at him for a beat, then glossed with the sheen of embarrassment.

"Right. What was I thinking? Let me go print up the correct schedule," Larry said, shuffling back to his office. These kinds of episodes were happening with more frequency. Larry would be unaware of his surroundings or say something totally out of time and place, but would recover moments later. Brian clung to those flashes of clarity, hoping that whatever was ailing Larry was transitory. He could ask Larry directly, but he didn't want to shame the man, who was clearly trying to cover up whatever was going on. This was common with dementia patients, according to Brian's Google search. The more prudent course of action would be to call Sylvia, Larry's wife. There was no reason he shouldn't do that today. It wasn't like the phones were ringing off the hook.

Brian took in the faded salmon of the lobby carpet, the mysterious stains on the wallpaper, the threadbare sofas with cushions permanently sunken from the weight of guests fed three decadent, diet-be-damned, all-inclusive meals a day.

Twelve million dollars.

The number had echoed continuously in Brian's brain since the formal offer had come in. "Twelve mil, huh?" his father had repeated when Brian had shared the news. "I have to tell Louise."

The Goldmans and the Weingolds were fifty-fifty partners, so that meant six million for his family, which he would split evenly with Peter. Technically the proceeds of a sale would go to his parents, but they'd already made it clear they intended to pass their share down. There would be taxes and legal fees, but he'd probably be left with more than a couple million dollars at the end of the day. To Peter, it would be pocket change. His brother was a partner in a fancy law firm in Manhattan. His house in Alpine, New Jersey, had cost nearly three million dollars. Brian had looked it up after his sister-in-law, Greta, had gone off the rails when he'd kept his shoes on and tracked the faintest trace of dirt onto the white silk rug in the palatial living room. Who chose white for a rug? Nobody with a hospitality background, that was for sure. Only someone with money to burn. Unlike Peter, to Brian anything north of a million was an impossibly large sum to consider. How would he spend it? Would he have anyone to share it with? Maybe Angela.

Angela Franchetti had been his on-again, off-again girlfriend for the past eighteen months. She was a local girl; his parents would call her a townie. She'd practically grown up in the hotel; her father, Vinny, was a full-time employee and in charge of the seasonal waitstaff. He was famous among Golden guests for his recommendations. The thick-accented Italian could be heard three tables over saying things like, "The gefilte is heaven tonight," or "Too much salt in the soup in my humble opinion." To Angela and the other children of staff, Brian, Peter, and Aimee were royalty, pint-sized nobility waiting to be handed the keys to the castle. And Brian had the Kennedy looks to go along with the Camelot image, or so everyone told him. Thick sandy brown hair that was just now going gray, blue eyes, cheekbones that Janet, the cosmetics vendor, wanted at. "If I could swipe bronzer on those babies . . ." she would kid him, to which he'd put up his hands in a karate defense.

His twin, Peter, took after their parents in the looks department. He was short, like their father, and had the same mousy hair and eyes that were mostly pupil with only a narrow ring of brown as their mother. It was such an unfortunately mundane collection of features that his face was hard to place. He was frequently reintroducing himself to people outside of the hotel.

Brian may have cannibalized the attractive genes in the womb, but Peter had gotten the lion's share of the brains and ambition. While Brian was causing mischief in the hotel, making out—and often much more—with the daughters of guests and staff, Peter was completing math workbooks and tracking the stock market because he'd invested his bar mitzvah money in blue chips hand-picked by some of the hotel's Wall Street clientele. And when his brother wasn't studying his portfolio and talking GDP with the old men playing pinochle, he was staring at Aimee Goldman.

Aimee Goldman. What would she think about selling the hotel?

The last time Brian had seen her was six months earlier at Benny's funeral. She'd looked good, considering the occasion. Up-scale suburban mother was a style she wore well. In contrast, Angela was a messy-bun-and-jeans woman, but to be fair, there weren't many places that demanded formal attire in their neck of the woods, where BYOB could mean bring your own BB gun. Aimee had never really been his type when they were growing up. She was serious—not quite as much as born-middle-aged Peter, but she'd definitely needed a little extra convincing to be naughty. They'd had a sprawling resort as their personal playground, and yet Aimee and Peter were such sticklers for the rules, worried they'd mess up the furniture or get caught stealing ice cream from the industrial freezer. The irony was that after so many years of being reckless with his future inheritance, he was the one overseeing the place, while his brother and Aimee barely gave the Golden a second thought.

He supposed Aimee was nominally involved as Special Advisor. Or was her title Creative Director? When she came with her family for the last two weeks of summer, she would stop by Brian's office and ask for an update. How were reservations looking? Was the town still making trouble about the garbage dumps by the highway? How serious was the racetrack odor problem? Brian didn't resent reporting to her—if anything, talking to Aimee about the business was invigorating. The staffers cared, but there was nothing like speaking to a fellow owner, someone born at the Golden, who carried its essence in their blood. When Aimee would leave with her family, it would reinforce just how lonely Brian was in Windsor without the company of his brother and childhood friend. He was never supposed to be here for this long.

When Brian had agreed to take on the CEO role, it had been understood to be a temporary move. He'd had wounds to lick, and the Golden seemed like a safe place to do so. If anyone was going to take over the hotel permanently, it would be his brainiac brother or artistic Aimee. Peter was a numbers wizard and Aimee was visually gifted, and he—well, he was good-looking and charming, but that was only a fraction of what was needed to run an empire. Melinda had actually said that to him when he'd mused about who would take over for Amos and Benny.

Brian had met his ex, Melinda Roth, at the hotel. It seemed everything in his life could be traced back to the Golden. She was the first and only woman Brian had ever had to chase. Melinda had been staying at the hotel with her aunt and cousins for a week while her parents were overseas. Long hair the color of wheat spilled over her muscular shoulders, and she liked to keep her light green eyes hidden behind oversized sunglasses. She was from California. It was the first time Brian had ever met someone from the West Coast, and she might as well have been from another continent: That was how exotic someone from outside the tristate area appeared to him. Instead of being impressed that he was a Weingold, like most people he encountered, she rolled her eyes and said something snarky. "So you're just gonna take over this place instead of doing your own thing?" What could he do after that? He was hooked.

Brian liked the challenge she presented. If Melinda was initially attracted to him, she hid it well. Eventually, his charms and relentless pursuit wore her down. He flew her out to the hotel the summer after they met and did everything in his power to impress her. A famous magician was performing in the ballroom, and Brian arranged for Melinda to be sawed in half. He filled her room with roses. He had the chef deviate from the typical menu to create a health-conscious California menu. He regaled her with decades of the choicest hotel gossip: Melinda knew who *shtupped* who and where and when, and which guests paid their bills in cash and who never paid at all. When he proposed a year later, she said yes.

Melinda and Brian settled in Brentwood, a thirty-minute drive from where she'd grown up in the Valley. Fanny had cried for days when he announced their plans to move west. By this point, Peter had already made it clear he was going to law school, and Aimee was engaged to Roger Glasser, who was in medical school in the Midwest. Nobody from the second generation was stepping up to run the hotel. For heirs apparent, they were a pretty apathetic lot, though Brian never had any guilt about shirking hotel management. What would he be able to contribute, especially while his parents and the Goldmans were still vibrant? His father talked a big game about wanting to pass on the Golden legacy, but he and Benny were resistant to any suggestions from the younger generation. Snowboarding, happy hour, a rock wall—these were just a sampling of ideas shot down without genuine discussion.

After they married, Brian took a job working for Melinda's father, who owned a string of car dealerships in Southern California. Dick Roth was all about Brian learning the business from the bottom up, so he put Brian on the showroom floor for a year. It wasn't glamorous work—as a Weingold he felt more employer than employee—but he obliged to please his father-in-law. Besides, the back seats of the roomier SUVs had ample space for daytime snoozes. Shortly after settling into a new home and job, Brian discovered that Melinda was pregnant. He found the double-line stick at the bottom of their kitchen garbage pail when he was looking for a bill he'd accidentally tossed. He was surprised she hadn't told him, but what did he know about women? Melinda was the first woman he'd ever truly loved. Everything else was just quick one-nighters at the hotel and sloppy sex in his college dorm room. He'd figured she planned to share the news over a special dinner. Maybe she'd hint at it with a meal of baby carrots and baby lamb chops. Not that she ever cooked. Fanny didn't care for his wife's lack of domesticity. And Melinda didn't appreciate her mother-in-law inspecting her pantry and freezer and then sending three large boxes filled with prepared meals packed in dry ice, with notes explaining how to warm them up and suggesting side dishes.

The hours on his feet at the dealership could be grueling, and one day he left work early because of a splitting headache. He hoped his father-in-law wouldn't find out. The man was about as enthusiastic about Brian as Fanny was about Melinda. On the West Coast, the Weingold name and the Golden Hotel just didn't have the same cachet as in the tristate area. Melinda's family were the big shots here. If Dick Roth liked you, he could get you a brand-new Mercedes C500 before it hit the showroom floor. Brian wondered sometimes why he couldn't have fallen in love with one of the girls from New York or New Jersey who were pushed at him, like Peter had. He'd married a girl who hung around the hotel from the less affluent bungalow colonies in the area. Greta was suitably awed by Peter's pedigree and liked the idea of joining a family that would score her a front-row seat at the Rodney Dangerfield performance.

Melinda's car had been in the driveway when he arrived, which made Brian happy. She was rarely home during the day when he called—always running to an exercise class or shopping. He took the stairs to their bedroom two at a time after he couldn't find her on the ground floor.

"Oh, shit" was the first thing he heard when he pushed the door open. Melinda's bare back, with its constellation of freckles, told him everything he needed to know. She was straddling somebody, but Brian couldn't see who. It didn't matter. Even in that moment of discovery, he'd realized the identity of Melinda's lover was irrelevant. His wife had hopped off and wrapped herself in a sheet, suddenly concerned with modesty.

The man in bed with his wife turned out to be Randy, the muscly contractor who had been doing some kitchen renovations for them. Brian had just given the guy a few extra bucks because he was pleased with how quickly the work was progressing. Now he understood why Randy was the first contractor in history to actually report faithfully to his job. Later, at a dive bar, Brian babbled to a sympathetic bartender that if only someone at the Golden had put out, his father wouldn't have had to bribe and chase down the plumbers, air-conditioning repairmen, and pool guys.

"Let's talk in the kitchen," Melinda said while Randy fumbled for his clothes. Brian followed her wordlessly downstairs as Randy called out, "I'm really sorry, Brian. By the way, the countertops will be in next week."

"What about the baby?" Brian asked the minute they were alone. "I found the test in the garbage."

"It's not yours." She said it with so much certainty that he'd known it to be true.

A month later, he was in divorce proceedings, unemployed, and homeless. Amos and Fanny sent him a ticket home. He spent a month feeling sorry for himself in his childhood bedroom, listening to Paul Simon and smoking cigarettes out the window, until his father told him it was time to get his act together. He'd put on ten pounds from inertia and letting his mother feed his heartbreak.

"I could really use your help at the hotel," Amos said. "The bungalow crowd is sneaking into the shows at night. And you know we always look the other way when guests fill their pocketbooks with food, but lately they've been coming to breakfast with empty suitcases. Come up for a few months and help me straighten things out."

They'd both known it was a lie. Amos and Benny were in their prime. Occupancy was high, but well managed with a large and capable staff. Amos was meticulous about keeping the grounds and physical plant tip-top, and Benny had been well connected with the talent that kept the guests entertained in the lounges nightly. It was true some of their competitors had been starting to struggle, but since the Golden had been built in 1960, decades after its peers, it had had a genuine competitive advantage. The facilities had been fresher and the clientele younger. Brian had been about as needed as an appendix. But he'd gone. What else was there to do? He had no other skills.

Would his parents have ever encouraged him to work at the hotel if they'd foreseen its eventual demise? Could they even see it coming, or was it like missing the aging process on your own body? Each new gray hair hardly stood out; an extra wrinkle barely made a dent.

But Brian saw it all.

Mrs. Shirley Schoenfeld sitting in her usual spot, her wheelchair parked next to a potted plant she claimed offered nice shade. Next to the soda machine, Archie Buchwald, skin crinkled like linen, reading the newspaper upside down. Sal Rosensweig was telling one of the maintenance crew in his usual boom that his grandchildren were coming up for the week. In addition to suggesting to Sal that he adjust his hearing aid, Brian had the unfortunate task of relaying that Sal's grandchildren had just emailed to cancel their visit.

"Brian, you wanted to see me?" Lucy Altman said, appearing at the check-in desk. Lucy was an intern from the Cornell School of Hospitality, which seconded a junior for an internship at the Golden every summer. Aimee had been the one to suggest the program, which she'd discovered when college touring with her daughter, Maddie. When Brian had asked Maddie if she planned to attend the Hotel School, as it was commonly known, she'd said, "I don't think young people should specialize so early. I'm seeking a less vocational education." It had taken a lot of restraint for Brian not to audibly groan.

Lucy was no better. She talked about how "cute" and "quaint" the Golden was and how she just loved "rural America," while simultaneously twisting her nose ring and using Snapchat. She was still arguably the most qualified person to have applied to work at the hotel in ages. Her résumé didn't have a single typo and had come attached to an intelligent, if not overly inspiring, cover letter. Lucy had written how eager she was to work at a place with "a retro vibe" and to "make a real difference," as though the hotel were a charity organization and not a for-profit business. It didn't actually turn a profit, but that didn't mean that wasn't the goal.

"Hi, Lucy. There's going to be an owners' meeting this weekend. I need your help getting the place shipshape. Please make sure my parents' room is in perfect condition, and Mrs. Goldman's cottage as well. Aimee Goldman might be coming with her kids, so please make sure she has two of the best connecting rooms, and put some fresh flowers in there, too."

"And your brother?"

"I'm not sure yet," Brian said. Peter hadn't texted him back, which was infuriating. Why did the care of the entire hotel have to fall on his shoulders alone?

"Is this about the casino offer?" Lucy asked. That was another thing about millennials and Gen-Zers. They had no boundaries.

"The families meet regularly to discuss the hotel," Brian said firmly. "Usually we do quarterly phone calls. This time, well, looks like everyone just missed the place."

"Okay, because a lot of the staff is really nervous. I mean, everyone knows the Golden Hotel is the last of its kind still standing, and you know how these people rely on—"

"Lucy," Brian stopped her. "I know all about it. Tell everyone to relax. Now, we need to duct-tape some of the sofas in the lounge before my parents and Mrs. Goldman arrive. Do they make duct tape in clear? Also, I'm told only three of the toilets are working in the ladies' room. And I know it's going to be a scorcher this week, so let's get the AC units cleaned out and—"

"Brian," Lucy interrupted him. "It's going to take a lot more than duct tape to get this place spick-and-span. You said Aimee's kids might be with her?"

"Yeah, why?"

"Um, they probably aren't going to be happy that the Wi-Fi is out."

"Really? When did that happen?" Brian asked.

"Three weeks ago," Lucy said. "I put a sticky note on your desk."

Lucy used a rainbow-colored sticky notepad. There were so many colored squares on Brian's desk that together they resembled a Mondrian.

"I'll have to look into that," Brian said, trying to remain calm. "Or maybe you can handle it?"

"Sure. Also, one of the bungalow folks said nobody has cleaned the goose poop in the pool for at least—"

"I'm aware of the goose excrement situation." He was not actually aware. "I'll get maintenance on that."

Lucy appeared embarrassed on his behalf, suddenly very interested in her Birkenstocks. *Don't they teach you goose poop cleanup at Cornell?* he wanted to ask.

Brian checked his watch. It was almost lunchtime. He wanted to speak with Chef Joe to make sure all of his parents' favorite foods were on hand for the week. If there was one thing he was certain of from a lifetime at the Golden Hotel, it was that thorny matters went a lot more smoothly on a full stomach.

He also needed to check the dishes and glasses to make sure the chipped ones weren't served at the family meal. Showboating for his own family—sad but necessary. He thought about something he'd once read in the newspaper. Theater producers would give out free tickets to fill the audience when investors were attending the performance. Where could he find a set of likely Golden guests to fake high occupancy? He imagined renting a few Coach buses and filling them with residents of nearby old-age homes.

"That's all for now, Lucy," Brian said. She gave him a tentative thumbs-up and backed away.

A new email pinged on his computer screen. A message from his brother.

"Oh, for fuck's sake," he said aloud.

Chapter Two

Aimee

While walking through the automatic doors that slid open to the Scarsdale ShopRite, Aimee Goldman-Glasser squeezed her eyes shut for a beat and said a silent prayer: *Please let me not run into anyone.* She pushed a wobbly cart through the produce department, not bothering to check the apples for bruises or the melons for firmness before slotting them into plastic bags. So far, she'd made it past the vegetables and fruits and the specialty salad dressings and dips without seeing any of the mothers from around town. Aimee had been strategic about her timing. Instead of grocery shopping at her usual hour, 9:30 a.m., after barre class and coffee klatch, she'd waited until the late afternoon, when most of the women she knew were either wrapping up social lunches or at home starting to think about prepping dinner. Others were still at work, shielded by cubicle walls or the thick glass of a windowed office. How Aimee would love to hole up in an office and never come out. Not for meals. Not for fresh air. Not for anything. She did "work"—but remotely—and if she was honest with herself, the consulting she did for the Golden Hotel averaged about three hours a month, hence the air quotes.

She swung her cart in the direction of the refrigerated dairy section, grateful for the blast of cold air. Aimee was sweating through her thin silk blouse. It would need to be dry-cleaned, like the bulk of her fancy wardrobe necessitated. It seemed the more expensive the label, the more care had to go into maintenance. It should really be the opposite. Well-made threads should be able to withstand a simple spin in the washing machine and a tumble through the dryer. Their household dry-cleaning bill was the kind of ridiculous expense that was absurd if she thought about it in isolation, but wasn't so large as to cause her to change her habits. Until now. Now she might be forced to reconsider many things she'd once taken for granted, like the name-brand grocery items she was carelessly adding to her cart without giving the generic versions a second glance.

Aimee gently added two cartons of organic eggs (cage-free chickens blessed by a shaman, three dollars more than the Shop-Rite brand) and a container of Almond Breeze. She and her husband, Roger, were off cow's milk since he'd returned from a medical conference a few years back declaring that dairy was the devil. She held her doctor-husband in such high esteem that it hadn't occurred to Aimee to prod him on the details. He'd said something about increased risk of diabetes. Or was it Alzheimer's? The nearly full container of 2% had gone down the drain of their stainless-steel sink, and she'd stocked up on dairy substitutes. Roger Glasser, internist with a five-star rating on Health Grades.com, treated half their hometown of Scarsdale. He even had a drop-in clinic in a less affluent area about an hour away, where patients traveled to see him. What did she know about health and wellness compared to him? She didn't feel like she knew much about anything beyond after-school soccer clubs and yearbook meetings, not after more than two decades of parenting had turned her once sharp mind into sludge.

In the pantry aisle, Aimee shuttled past the colorful cereal boxes and nearly forgot to grab a box of Honey Nut Cheerios. Well, technically, they were Nature O's, the artisanal substitute that was twice the price and another sign of her privilege. Her children were coming for the weekend and would want their usuals. It was a sign of how distraught she was that her children's wants and needs weren't front and center. In theory, she craved a sliver of life to call her own—to not spend every waking second worrying about whether Zach ever washed his sheets in college, if Scott was remembering to eat, or whether Maddie was holding her cell phone too close to her ear—but this wasn't the way she wanted to get there. Not by crisis.

Traditionally, for Father's Day weekend, the five nuclear Glassers celebrated the Hallmark holiday with a decadent brunch at home, a round of golf for Roger and the boys, then dinner at Szechuan Palace. When it had been her turn to be feted a month earlier for Mother's Day, Aimee's life hadn't yet capsized. Two mimosas at breakfast had made her giggly and extraordinarily affectionate, then she'd fallen into a nap during the massage the kids had gotten her, and at dinner she'd been so jolly and rested, she'd indulged in multiple heaps of lo mein and fried rice. Now Aimee could barely get a yogurt down without running for the toilet. At least the bomb Roger had dropped on her would be good for her waistline. After continuous and only moderately successful dieting for four decades, this was a genuine silver lining. Aimee wished she'd been born with her mother's petite frame, or even her father's athletic build, but instead she had thicker limbs and a lazy metabolism. "Try no carbs," her mother would say. "Stop eating after seven p.m." Louise Goldman was full of suggestions—did the woman ever keep an opinion to herself?—but nothing she could offer would quell this crisis.

Maddie, Aimee and Roger's eldest child, was planning to drive to Scarsdale from the West Village with her boyfriend-almost-fiancé, Andrew Hoff, tomorrow morning. Maddie was counting the minutes until she got a ring on her finger, scouring the apartment she shared with Andrew in search of a velvet box. "I even looked in the toilet tank," she'd confided in Aimee. Maddie was twenty-nine and one of those women born with a life plan: work hard, go to a good college, choose a career that will allow for intellectual satisfaction but with flexibility to raise a family, and find a good man to marry before turning thirty. If it was possible to push out 2.5 kids (one boy, one girl, one unicorn), her daughter would figure it out. Maddie had emphasized what a big deal it was for Andrew to spend Father's Day away from his family, missing the hoopla at their club. Andrew came from a ridiculously wealthy family in Palm Beach—because after a certain number of zeroes in your net worth, it did become ridiculous. His family had been Jewish once upon a time, but traditions gently stripped away with each passing generation—first the mezuzah disappearing from the doorpost, then the menorah getting lost, and finally the "stein" falling off their last name like a weak tree branch. Aimee knew Patsy and Bick (those names!) didn't love that their son was in love with a girl with Borscht Belt roots. Still, Maddie claimed a ring was imminent. If she was right, it meant Aimee would be mother of the bride before long. It seemed impossible. One minute she'd been spreading Desitin on her first-born's diaper rash; the next she'd been discussing oval versus cushion-cut engagement rings with her.

Scott, her middle, was flying in for the weekend later that night. He was in his second year of medical school at the University of Chicago, Roger's alma mater. The news would hit Scott the hardest. He was the most sensitive of her trio, and he idolized his father. After years of struggling to figure out his place in the family (if Maddie was the hyper-focused all-star and Zachary the adorable baby—they didn't call him Wacky Zacky for nothing—where did Scott fit in?), Scott knew middle-child syndrome was real. But by high school, her boy had figured out that following in his father's footsteps would be his calling card. Scott could focus for hours and was a whiz at chemistry. He was the only one of the Glasser kids who ever asked to go to work with Daddy. Maddie fainted at the sight of needles, and Zach preferred video games to everything else, but Scott would spend as much time as he could "assisting" his father in the office. Roger knew the extent to which Scott worshipped him. That alone should have prevented her husband from being so stupid! That . . . and the threat of jail time.

Zachary, sweet Wacky Zacky, was back living at home. Just a month earlier, he'd finished off five years at the University of Vermont—the "extended plan," she and Roger called it. He'd graduated with no job or career path—at least, none that he'd shared with his very curious parents. "Failure to launch?" her nosy next-door neighbor Betsy Lehman had asked when she'd orgasmically watched the youngest Glasser moving back home. She was always peering over the fence that divided their properties. "Just weeding," she'd say whenever Aimee caught her snooping. "Weeds are on the ground," Aimee would call back with forced levity.

She'd been complaining about Betsy's fake weeding to Roger one night when Zach had come into the kitchen to retrieve a pint of ice cream. "Did someone say weed?" he'd asked. Her son was not entirely without passions.

Betsy's inquiry had nettled her precisely because it was on point. Zach had only declared a major after repeated letters from the dean warned him he wouldn't graduate otherwise. He'd finally chosen geography, which sounded more like an elementary school class than a university discipline, and it was a subject in which Zach wasn't particularly strong. On the long car rides to the Golden, the Glassers would play a geography game to pass the time. One person would say a place, and the next had to follow with a new place that started with the last letter of the old place. Zach, as the youngest, had already been at a disadvantage. Still he refused the hints Aimee and Roger had whispered in his ear, choosing instead to follow "England" with "Doodie" and "Frankfurt" with "Tushy" and, for no reason at all other than a spelling handicap, "Orlando" with "apple." He'd thought cartography was the study of go-karts.

With hushed conversations and the TV on to occlude the sound, thus far she and Roger had managed to keep the impending crisis away from Zach. It helped that their son was a low level of stoned all day. She wanted to tell Zach not to smoke in the house, that if he was going to live under their roof, he had to abide by their rules. But what rights did they have anymore? Her authority was a phantom.

Zach, Scott, and Maddie were about to find out their father was a criminal. Not just any criminal, either. Roger had, *allegedly*, violated four federal and six state statutes, and faced up to fifteen years in prison. The children would learn their comfortable, cushy, name-brand-everything lives were based on a lie. The man they'd cuddled with on the couch to watch Monday night football and who'd taught them to ride their bikes safely and never without a helmet had put hundreds of people in harm's way. These chilling thoughts returned to Aimee for the millionth time as she stood at the bakery counter, studying the blueberry Danishes that were Roger's favorite. For the past twenty years, Aimee had gone to ShopRite once a week to stock up, always making sure to pick up her husband's preferred indulgence. This time she couldn't bring herself to pull a number from the dispenser on top of the display case. It wasn't much retribution, withholding an item from the grocery list, but Aimee would grasp at whatever small victories came her way. Roger's food choices would be far grimmer in prison, if it came down to that. Their lawyer wasn't sure yet. A deal was a possibility; a plea bargain that would strip Roger of his medical license but would spare him criminal sanctions. Keeping everything quiet and away from their children, the thing Aimee cared the most about, still seemed impossible.

A "pill mill." That's what her husband had been running out of his secondary medical office for the past decade. Unbeknownst to Aimee, their lavish lifestyle was funded by Roger doling out OxyContin scripts willy-nilly. She wondered if patients even feigned pain, or if his laxity and greed were so profound, they didn't need to bother. Her husband was what the pharmaceutical company who manufactured the painkiller called a "whale," because he was one of their biggest distributors of product. Hooking people on Oxy had apparently paid for their kitchen renovation, annual trips to the Bahamas, their BMWs, even Zach's extra year of college. The list of what the drug money had paid for went on and on. Her silk shirt. Their twice-weekly housekeeper Marcia's salary. Scott's debt-free medical education. Everything they had was tainted; she could no longer enjoy a single one of her possessions. Aimee had Googled what Oxy pills looked like. They were no bigger than the Advils she popped after a frustrating encounter with Betsy, and they came in a rainbow of pastels depending on the dosage. Now the nubby throw on their living room couch reminded her of the sea green eighty-milligram pill. A mustard-colored vase in their kitchen was the same color as the forty-milligram. Aimee threw them both out.

For all these years, Aimee had believed Roger when he'd explained away their largesse. He'd said he'd stopped accepting certain insurance plans, which meant more full-payer patients. He'd said his practice had expanded to offer holistic services, including nutritional counseling and wellness treatments, which were all out-of-pocket. It wasn't like Aimee was oblivious to the fact that most doctors didn't live the way they did. She suspected Roger ordered a couple more tests than absolutely necessary, maybe accepted kickbacks from the physicians he referred to. But hooking innocent people on a debilitating drug that wrecked millions of lives? No, that she'd never imagined. Her brain wasn't that creative; her imagination stopped at adding pecans to cranberry sauce. Just a few months earlier, a memoirist had come to speak at the town library where Aimee volunteered. The author had told the local audience about losing her life savings because a boyfriend had hoodwinked her. Aimee had nodded sympathetically while thinking, *I would never be that stupid.* And now, karma. She cringed at her naïveté. Had she always been this foolish and trusting? Gullible, sure. The pranks Peter and Brian used to play on her . . .

As Aimee moved on to the checkout lanes, she spotted Betsy Lehman unloading her cart. Betsy was just one of many women in town who would secretly delight when the scandal broke. Aimee narrowly managed to avoid her neighbor's detection by swerving into a different lane. She paid for her food so absentmindedly that when the cashier asked if she had any coupons, she responded, "I'm fine, how are you?" After loading the trunk, she collapsed behind the driver's seat of her X7. The weight of this secret was exhausting—literally. Because Aimee hadn't wanted to worry Zach, she was letting Roger remain in their bedroom. But sleeping next to him was miserable. Roger even snored like a guilty man. She had barely gotten more than an hour of consecutive sleep since Roger had confessed.

A knock on her window startled her. Aimee begrudgingly rolled down the window.

"Hi, Betsy."

"Hi there, Aim." Aimee hated the nickname, especially when it came from someone she preferred to keep at a distance. The only shortening she tolerated was "A" from Roger, and he knew better than to use it these days. "I just saw you sitting there and was wondering what your plans are for this—"

Aimee's cell phone rang. She eyed the name on the caller ID. *Thank you, Maman.*

"Sorry, Betsy, it's my mother. I've got to take this." She rolled up the window so quickly Betsy's chubby fingers barely escaped getting caught.

Since Aimee's father had died last year, her mother's interest in her only child's life had reached new peaks. Louise and Benny, a mismatch in the dawn of their marriage, had been that rare couple that seemed to grow closer as the decades wore on. Over the years, they'd met in the middle on so many things—Benny had agreed to expensive piano lessons for Aimee and to ordering silk frocks from Paris for both his wife and his daughter; Louise had agreed to an anniversary tradition of Nathan's hot dogs and a ride on the Cyclone at Coney Island. When Benny had died, it hadn't so much seemed to Aimee like the loss of a distinct person, but rather that her mother had been halved. Because of this, no matter how busy Aimee was running household errands, responding to stressed texts from Maddie, or keeping track of her boys, she answered her mother's calls. Even now, with tears pressing against the backs of her eyelids and Scott's rocky road melting in the trunk.

"Bonjour, Maman," Aimee said. Louise's antennae were angled with such precision that any angst in Aimee's voice was difficult to mask. She braced herself for questioning.

"Oh, darling, thank goodness you picked up. This is terribly important."

In spite of everything, Aimee smiled.

Louise Goldman, mistress of the Golden, with her predictable flair for the dramatic. It occurred to Aimee that it would have been nice to include her mother in their Father's Day plans. But her head was spinning with other concerns: protecting Scott, siloing Zach, wondering if the Hoffs would let their blue-ribbon boy propose to the daughter of a criminal. Louise had slipped through the cracks, another piece of collateral damage left in Roger's wake.

"I'm here. What's up?"

Out of the corner of her eye, Aimee watched Betsy wheel a shopping cart toward her smug eco-friendly Prius, a casual sway in her hips. Aimee envied the lighthearted way she moved, unloading the groceries to the beat of some invisible song. Aimee had once been that happy woman who went about her daily chores with a rhythm that propelled her, though it already felt like a lifetime ago. In reality, she'd been that person just two weeks earlier—right up until the moment she'd come home from her afternoon shift at the library and found Roger with a drink in his hand, a grave expression knitting his eyebrows together and shadowing his jaw. "There's something I have to tell you," he'd said. She'd braced herself for the revelation of an affair, followed by a request for a divorce. Aimee remembered sitting down opposite him, prepared for the sort of betrayal that ran freely through their affluent suburb. If only her problems had been that commonplace! There were so many things she would have preferred to hear. *I got a stripper pregnant. I'm secretly gay. I'm running away to the circus.* Pretty much anything was better than *Hey, I'm a drug dealer and might have killed some people.* Not that Roger had the balls to put it that way. He'd tried to tap-dance around it until she'd asked him point-blank: *Do you deal Oxy?*

Louise's voice summoned her back.

"I don't suppose you read the latest issue of the *Windsor Word*? I hear they've put it online," Louise said. Her "they" referred to the entire universe of people under age fifty.

"No, I haven't," Aimee said.

Guilt blossomed in her chest again. She could've been a heck of a lot more active in the nominal role she held at the hotel that entitled her to a monthly paycheck. Instead she devoted herself to the care and well-being of her family and tended to the hotel only in fleeting moments of spare time. There was just so little of it. Roger's white coats needed to be cleaned and pressed, dentist appointments made for the whole family, the pantry kept stocked. Her children's needs were bottomless. Every task ate away at her waking hours. Scouring for the best sneakers, researching educational summer programs, landing the best SAT tutor ($200 an hour): These were the generous slices of the pie chart that was Aimee Glasser.

She had just been thinking that, with her children grown and flown—two-thirds of them, anyway—it could be a good time to get more involved in the Golden. At times, the fantasy of seizing a professional life for herself had been so appealing that she'd tooled around with business cards on the computer, staring at the neat type that read, "Aimee Goldman-Glasser—*Creative Director, The Golden Hotel.*" She had ideas for an updated hotel logo that she wanted to show Brian. But if she was really honest, hadn't she been partly relieved when Zach moved back home? She hadn't exactly encouraged him to spread his wings when she'd left snacks on the counter and done his laundry. It didn't matter now anyway. Her empty nest quagmire had been before the Roger deba-

ELYSSA FRIEDLAND

cle. What Roger had done topped any of the sordid tales she'd grown up hearing around the hotel. Her life was reading like a salacious novel.

Aimee pictured the *Windsor Word*, square and pink, inky pages that left smudges on the hotel furniture. It was the weekly paper that came out unreliably on Thursdays in the area of the Catskills where the Golden was located. For many years, Louise Goldman had edited its arts and entertainment section, which was her way of making sure that the concerts, plays, and comedian acts at her hotel were listed first. Rivals said Louise Goldman had put the B in Borscht Belt, but if that chatter ever got to Aimee's mother, she would have assumed B stood for beauty.

"Well, a few weeks back, some hotshot reporter came sniffing around," Louise said. "He'd heard there were some maintenance issues at the hotel. Now, with the racetrack nearby, some of the more crotchety guests are complaining about a manure smell, but with the potpourri we put in every room, you really can't even smell it. And then last winter our generator failed—remember that huge storm in February?—and anyway, you get the idea. Well, this article made it seem like we were having financial problems and couldn't keep the Golden afloat. Of course, they tied it to Daddy's passing. Everyone knows he was the brains, not Amos."

"Go on," Aimee said to her mother. When Louise got hysterical, it was critical to throw in the occasional "And then what happened?" or "Really?" because otherwise she might accuse you of not listening.

"Well, within three days of the article coming out, Brian got called by some operators of a casino. You know those dreadful

42 ·

places off the interstate? They want to buy the Golden and turn it into a cheap card trick parlor with slot machines. It'll bring lowlifes to the area. But . . . they are offering real money."

"What do you think?" Aimee asked, pondering just how little emotional space and time she had to deal with this.

"I think it's a real offer, and we need to consider it," Louise said. "It's not only up to me, though. You know that. The place isn't the same without your father. I could never imagine letting it go while he was still alive, but now . . . Anyway, I'm just so grateful that I can always count on you. I swear, if you had problems, I simply wouldn't . . ."

Aimee's stomach lurched.

"Darling, are you there?" Louise asked. "Can you imagine selling the Golden?"

Aimee pictured the peeling wallpaper and the aging waiters, thought of the bedbugs that had ravaged the place a few summers earlier, and exhaled. Her father wasn't the only thing missing from the hotel. Robust management that spread the weight of responsibility across more than just one person's shoulders, a complete reno, a younger staff and clientele: Those were also among the key ingredients missing. Still, it had never occurred to her that the hotel wouldn't remain part of her family forever. The thought was so startling, she wasn't sure if it filled her with sadness, nostalgia, or relief.

"Brian has called for an emergency meeting," Louise said. "Starting this Sunday. I'd really like you to be here. I don't want the Weingolds to bulldoze me now that I don't have your father by my side." Louise had always been suspicious of the Weingolds skimming, particularly Amos. Her theory was that, with Benny

schmoozing the crowds, warming up the audience before entertainers took the stage, joking with the waiters and the bellmen
and slapping backs all around, he wouldn't have felt it if his pocket
got picked by Amos in broad daylight. She brooded about this to
Aimee regularly.

"What does Brian say?" Aimee asked. Brian Weingold was
running the place day-to-day. If anyone needed the lights to stay
on at the Golden, it was him.

"He's just asked us all to meet at the hotel," Louise said. "I
don't know his position."

They both fell silent for a moment. Aimee fished in her bag
for a bottle of water. She was terribly parched. Anxiety did that
to her, made sandpaper of her throat.

"I really can't get away, Maman," she said after a long swig.
"You go up without me, but send me any documents you want me
to review. But it's just a terrible time right now. I mean terribly
busy, not terrible in general." Aimee bit her bottom lip to stop
rambling. She wanted to unburden herself, to say out loud that
her life was like a ball of yarn unraveling down a staircase. That
inside her chest, she felt a balloon inflating. But she couldn't, especially not to her mother. Not now, with Louise counting on perfect Aimee staying that way. Louise had never been fully on board
the Roger train. She had had bigger dreams for her daughter
("Look, there's Senator Javits's grandson on the tennis court," she
would say, and shove Aimee in the bucktoothed, prematurely bald
man's direction). Aimee typically delighted in showing Louise
just how well Roger had done over the years. Louise could no longer throw a *Just an internist?* jab at Aimee after they'd bought
their six-thousand-square-foot home in the nicest part of West-

chester, with bathrooms where the marble climbed all the way up the walls and a basement finished in polished oak. All three children skied with private instructors out west, and Aimee's upgraded engagement ring could take someone's eye out.

Louise was quiet. Her mother's silence could slay her more swiftly than a harsh word. Aimee felt terribly squeezed. Being in the sandwich generation, having to weigh her parents' needs against her children's, had her feeling like jelly spread too thin, leaving both slices of bread forlorn. But in the competition for the scarce resources that Aimee Goldman-Glasser had to offer, her offspring came first. And if there was ever a time her kids needed her full attention, it was now. She had a sudden image of pulling into a prison parking lot, carrying a see-through purse, her children shuffling behind her looking mortified. Having seen every season of *Orange Is the New Black*, Aimee was something of a prison expert. God, would she bribe prison officers to get cigarettes to Roger, putting coke bags up her you-know-what? Aimee shook her head back to reality. Roger didn't even smoke! Or maybe he did. There were clearly things about him she didn't know. She checked herself again with a pinch to her thigh. This had to be what losing it felt like.

"I'm really sorry, Maman. But I gotta go," Aimee said, and tossed the cell phone onto the passenger seat.

She drove home without seeing the streets or the cars in front of her. It was a miracle she didn't crash. Selling the Golden? It was strange that Aimee had never considered the possibility before. The family camp thing in the mountains was a tough sell to teenagers who depended on super-speedy Wi-Fi for their existence. Certainly her children did, even begrudging the annual family pilgrimage for Labor Day weekend to close out the season. So many of their competitors had shuttered—Kutsher's, the Raleigh, the Concord, Brown's in a devastating fire—why had Aimee assumed the hotel would remain in her family forever, going on and on like the Energizer bunny? Or at least preserved like a treasured heirloom, though it was a lot harder to mind a hotel than a ring in a vault. When she turned onto her street, Aimee pushed the hotel into the compartment of her brain labeled *Deal with Later.*

In her driveway, she saw a police cruiser and a black SUV parked one behind the other. Zacky! She felt her heart leap out of her chest and crash to the ground. If she was breathing, she couldn't tell.

"Zach!" she screamed, the house key still wobbling in the keyhole as she pushed her way inside.

"He's fine," came Roger's voice.

"What the—" Aimee said, looking around at the state of their home. Her collection of first-edition books, scattered on the ground. Her watercolors, tossed carelessly off the walls. The contents of the desk in their living room, spilled everywhere, pages torn and crumpled. The glass from a framed wedding photo on the mantle was shattered. Shaggy, their golden retriever, barked furiously from under the piano bench.

"I'm sorry, ma'am," said a uniformed police officer, appearing behind Roger. "But we have a search warrant."

Roger looked down at the floor. Things were clearly even worse than he'd told her.

Zach appeared at the top of the stairs, crying. When was the last time she'd seen her boy shed tears? The youngest Glasser would fall off his skateboard, skin split like a banana peel and requiring twenty stitches, and still remain composed. She wanted to strangle Roger. It was only the presence of the police that stopped her. The children didn't need two parents in prison.

"What's going on, Mom? They broke some of my stuff. I'm really freaking out." Zach wiped his cheek with his ratty T-shirt.

The long, elm-lined driveway of her family's hotel flashed before her eyes so strongly, it was like she was having a stroke. She summoned strength she didn't know she had and looked at her boy.

"Honey, everything is fine. Pack a bag with a week's worth of clothing. Bathing suits, sneakers. Don't forget something to sleep in. We're going on a vacation. Today."

"We are?" Roger asked, finally meeting her gaze.

"You're not. The kids and I are. If you need us, we'll be at the Golden."

To: FamousAmosWeingold@aol.com; Fanny@thegoldenhotel.com;
phoebe@free2bphoebe.com; Louise@thegoldenhotel.com;
AimeeGoldmanGlasser@gmail.com
CC: mweingold@student.harvard.edu
Subject: POTENTIAL SALE OF GOLDEN

To All Concerned Parties:

I regret that I cannot join everyone in Windsor to discuss the
potential sale of the Golden Hotel (hereinafter, the "hotel") and meet
with the prospective buyers. I will be sending Michael in my place to
represent the Peter Weingold interests. Phoebe will accompany him.
Michael has just completed his sophomore year at Harvard and is an
economics major, as I believe you all know. As such, I think he will be a
genuine asset to any future negotiations. I know that I have the most
business experience in this group. Thus, I expect to be in touch with
you during the week to answer any questions and provide counsel. I
URGE everyone to remember how special the hotel is when exploring
offers. I tasked a junior associate with pulling some comparables
("comps") and we are the ONLY waterfront parcel of 1,000+ acreage
within twenty miles. Futterman's, which I suspect will be used by the
buyers as another buyout target, is in FAR MORE DISREPAIR and has
had three citations from the alcohol and tobacco board for violations.
I also want to remind everyone that Windsor, far from being a sleepy
town away from the city, is now becoming a rather hip destination with
many boutique day spas and roadside motels opening.

Best of luck this week and please avail yourselves of Michael's
business acumen.

Yours,

Peter

PS: Greta regrets that she can't accompany the children but she will be undergoing a minor medical procedure. She sends her love.

To: Mom Weingold; Dad Weingold; Brian Weingold
CC: mweingold@student.harvard.edu
Subject: IMPORTANT

Once again, I apologize that I can't get up to the hotel this week. The promotion to managing partner has been more taxing than anticipated, but it is rewarding. I write separately to you because I do not want Louise Goldman to make you feel sorry for her, playing the desperate widow card. While the hotel is likely the main asset that Benny left her, Louise's (née Frankfurter) parents surely left her a comfortable sum when they passed. Will Aimee be in attendance? She is usually a voice of reason and I think will be a productive member of the team, though hopefully Roger will stay out of things. I have found him to be something of a blowhard.

Love,

Peter

Chapter Three

Zach

"Mom, you're going to have to tell me what's going on eventually," Zach said, chewing feverishly on his fingernail. "The police tore our house apart, and you think I'm not gonna ask questions?"

"I told you, it's nothing you need to worry about. It's just a misunderstanding," Aimee said, crouching on the front steps of their house and fighting with a stubborn suitcase zipper. "And please lower your voice. I don't want to worry your sister."

Maddie had arrived early that morning. Their father was ashen, as he had been since the police had come, so the cover story of his stomach ailment was easily corroborated by his complexion. Maddie needed no convincing to stay away, even as she quipped, *I'm just one stomach flu away from my goal weight*, from *The Devil Wears Prada*.

Zach looked toward the car, where his sister was already in

the back seat, FaceTiming. Probably with her dipshit boyfriend, Andrew Hoff. Zach had met him last month at his University of Vermont graduation. He'd been seething when Andrew had said that the University of Vermont seemed like a cool place, but that he'd only considered Yale because he was a third-generation legacy (and then had mumbled "Go Bulldogs" under his breath). Zach didn't even get why Andrew had been at the graduation—even his own brother had missed it because he had finals. Zach's parents rolled out the red carpet for Maddie's boyfriend in a way they never had for *his* significant others. Sure, Sarah, his freshman-year girlfriend, had lifted a few pieces of silver and uncorked his father's 1987 Château Lafite without permission. But the others were nice. They were "quality," to borrow a word his mother would use.

"Maddie's not listening, trust me. But seriously, please tell me. I'm not a kid anymore."

His mother stood up suddenly and swiveled around to face him squarely.

"First of all, you will always be a kid to me." She stood on tiptoe and planted a kiss on his forehead. It reminded him of the time his mother had spontaneously wept at the pediatrician's office when Dr. Layhem announced he was five feet five, making him officially a half-inch taller than his mother. "But this is between me and your father."

"How can it be a private thing between you and Dad and also a big misunderstanding? If it's a misunderstanding, you can just tell me." He knew his prodding wouldn't get him anywhere. When his parents made up their minds that a matter didn't concern their children, no amount of nagging made any difference.

Predictably, his mother didn't bother answering. She hoisted a duffel in the air and motioned for him to take the rest.

"Be careful with the orange bag. And Zacky, not a word of this to Maddie or Scott. Please. I'm begging you." Fat raindrops fell unexpectedly from the sky, as if the universe was helping his mother avoid his questions.

"Let's hurry," Aimee said, and they hustled into the car. As they pulled away, Zach looked back at their house. His father was staring at them from the window in his office, expressionless. Zach faced forward again, slipping on his Beats.

"Mom, I cannot sit next to Zach for another minute. I can hear his music so loudly," Maddie said, shooting him a daggered look. They had been on the road for five minutes.

"You're chewing like a cow," Zach shot back, and felt gratified when, after Maddie stuck her tongue out at him, she slipped her wad of Trident into a tissue.

"Andrew said Dad should drink ginger tea," Maddie said.

Zach cued up his most obvious eye roll in response. What kind of know-it-all gives a doctor medical advice? The guy dressed like a Vineyard Vines model, had an IQ in the range of a bad bowling score, and tied sweaters over his shoulders unironically. And he could never just say he was from Florida. He had to make sure everyone knew he was from *Palm Beach*. Zach wasn't thrilled with the last-minute redirect to the Golden, but he was happy to avoid a weekend with Andrew.

"Mom, just so you know, Maddie has been texting Andrew the entire ride that you're acting batshit crazy," Zach said.

"Don't look at my phone," Maddie snapped.

"Don't call me gross," Zach said.

"Mom, how much longer—"

"The next person to start a sentence with 'Mom' is walking the rest of the way," Aimee said, her tone sharper than normal. "And seriously, for people so desperate to be treated like adults, I can honestly say you sound exactly the same as when you were both in the back seat in elementary school."

"I'm sorry," Zach said quietly.

And he was. His mother had been catering to him since he'd moved back home, making his favorite enchiladas twice a week and cleaning his room on Marcia's days off. He couldn't understand why all his friends were in such a rush to get places of their own. He was a forty-minute drive to Manhattan and could see his buddies if he felt like it. In the meantime, he had a comfortable free room and three meals a day, and he never had to change out of his pajamas. Did he really want to share some dirty walk-up apartment and fight over the PlayStation remote?

"Can you please turn up the AC back here? It's stifling. And does Shaggy really need to sit in the front?" Maddie asked, dramatically peeling off her sweatshirt. Zach snuck another glance at her phone while she did so. She had texted a Bitmoji of herself with a single teardrop and written to Andrew, "Off to the Golden. Wish I was with you instead." Andrew had responded, "Watch out for the bedbugs," and inserted a vomit emoji.

At hearing his name, Shaggy barked and poked his head out the open window.

The golden retriever was the latest addition to the Glasser household. Bucking the trainer's advice, their mother had cradled Shaggy like a newborn for the first six months of his life.

"You know he can't sit in the back. Shaggy gets carsick, don't you, boy?" Their mother nuzzled the soft reddish fur on the back of the dog's neck. Zach saw her hand shaking as she looped a finger through Shaggy's collar. Whatever was going on between his parents, it was rattling his mother to the point that Zach hadn't seen her eat since the police had left their house the day before, and yet there had been an empty wine bottle in the trash this morning.

After the cops had departed, his father had straightened up, returning books to their shelves and collecting scattered papers. Meanwhile, his mother had called Maddie to tell her about an offer to buy the hotel and the need to change the Father's Day plans so they could discuss it with the Weingolds. It was the first Zach had heard of any such offer. "Best if Andrew spends the weekend with his own family. I don't think the Weingolds will want a stranger around while we talk business," she'd said.

That comment had led to a fight between his sister and his mother about how anyone dared call Andrew a stranger. By the time the call had ended, Zach couldn't ever remember seeing his mother look quite so exhausted. He'd wanted to ask her if they had pizza in the freezer—she'd forgotten to make dinner—but instead backed away quietly to his room, where he resumed a fruitless Google quest to figure out what the hell might be going on.

Despite doubling his normal pot allowance before bed, he still hadn't been able to get to sleep. Conjectures of why the police had come to his house had swirled around his head, growing wilder as the hours ticked by. By midnight, he'd been sure it had something to do with tax evasion. A father in Zach's high school class had gotten in trouble and had had to pay a massive fine to the IRS that necessitated the family selling their house and moving to an attached condo near the train station. He remembered when the mayor had made headlines for paying the family housekeeper off the books. How did they pay Marcia? By 2 a.m., Zach was wondering if his father could be part of an international spy ring. He desperately wanted to trade theories with Maddie, but his mother had been adamant. And whatever he told Maddie would get to Andrew; there was no more sibling trust he could count on. He could call Scott, but everyone in the family always made such a big deal about not bothering him while he studied. "Turn that down, Scott is taking a practice test," his mother would bellow if he dared play music.

"Mom, what are we going to do at the hotel?" Maddie asked as they passed through Tuxedo, site of the long-defunct Red Apple Rest. Before it had shuttered, their family would stop there for burgers and milkshakes. Now it was a McDonald's. "Is it really up for sale?"

His mother didn't answer. She was fiddling with the radio, trying to get away from the fuzz. The stations on the approach to the Catskills were the worst. It was either talk radio, where people called in to complain about their gas bills, or oldies music.

"Mom?" he repeated. He watched her head snap to attention.

"Well, we're going to have fun, for starters," she said, trying way too hard to sound cheerful. It was the same voice she used when she coaxed him to study more. *I'll test you. We'll make it fun,* she'd say. "And there's going to be a meeting with the Weingolds about the hotel. Probably a series of them. The hotel wasn't put up for sale, but yes, an offer did come in." Clearly defeated, she turned the radio off. Shaggy slumped in his seat, pawing at the seat belt.

"Do you guys have any thoughts about it?" she asked, looking back at them for a beat. "I know you have so many memories there."

Even though they went for only a few weeks every August, Zach and his siblings had many happy memories of their own. Maybe not quite at the level of their mom, who would giddily point out to them all the nooks and crannies in which she'd used to secret herself with the Weingolds. But they had their share of fun. They would raid the kitchen at night, Maddie and Scott taking cookies, while Zach would drop whole sugar lumps onto his tongue until he had so much energy that he literally had to run up and down the stairs to burn it off. Zach had had his first kiss at the hotel. Scott had conquered his fear of crowds when their parents had made him present the Gold Rush plaque. Maddie had snuck into the salon and colored her hair orange with stolen hair dye, maybe her single act of rebellion ever.

"Andrew says the Catskills are over," Maddie said. *Andrew says. And if Andrew said it was raining on a sunny day, would you walk around with an umbrella?* Zach wouldn't even mind his sister's worship of her boyfriend if she wasn't so dismissive of everything *he* had to say.

"Are all the Weingolds coming?" Zach asked.

"Oh my God, you are so into Phoebe Weingold," Maddie said, flipping her head to smirk in his direction. "You were, like, gaping at her during Grandpa's funeral. Honestly, when they handed you the shovel to put dirt on his grave, I thought you were going to fall into the hole because she was standing on the other side."

His cheeks burned. Had he been that obvious? It was just that seeing Phoebe had really taken him aback. For years, their two families had spent weeks at the hotel together, and Phoebe had never sparked much interest for him. She was a couple of years older and had spent most of her time flirting with the lifeguards. The last time he'd seen her before Grandpa Benny's funeral, she couldn't have been more than fifteen years old. He'd been thirteen, had just suffered through the embarrassment of his bar mitzvah—why did getting up on stage to chant from the Torah and make a speech have to exactly correspond with the time when his voice was cracking and he had raging acne? She'd been awkward herself, flat-chested and also smeared with pimples. At the funeral, Zach had seen an entirely new person. Her tan skin glowed, and her hair, which she'd used to wear exclusively in a braided ponytail, was long, wavy, and the shiniest brown he had ever seen. From her tight black sweater, he could see her flatness had given way to perky, full boobs. He'd had to think about the Holocaust to cool his erection.

"I am not," he said.

"You are, too," Maddie said. "She seems vapid."

"Oh, yes. And Andrew is just the deepest. I love when he talks about his job working for his daddy like he's Elon Musk."

"Shut up," Maddie said, and elbowed him in the ribs. "Hoff Global is a major company."

"Ouch," Zach said, clutching his side. "Not all of us have padding there."

"Mom, Zach just called me fat."

"Quiet down, both of you," their mother said, twisting herself around to shoot them another warning look.

"I was just curious. I hadn't really spoken to her or Michael in years," Zach deflected.

Phoebe's younger brother, Michael, was wicked smart, always with his nose in *National Geographic* and memorizing vocabulary words instead of playing Marco Polo with the rest of the hotel brats. The kid never removed his rash guard, even on a cloudy day. It was like he was literally hiding under layers. Maybe he'd changed, too. The Weingolds and the Glassers hadn't overlapped at the hotel in ages.

"Do you follow her stupid Instagram feed? Free2BPhoebe, I think it's called," Maddie said. "Like, who is stopping her from being Phoebe? What is that handle supposed to mean?"

"Peter mentioned that she's something of an accomplished photographer," Aimee chimed in.

"Um, if you call taking selfies and pictures of avocado toast photography, then sure," Maddie said.

Zach took offense on Phoebe's behalf. She had one hundred and fifty thousand followers on Instagram, and he was pretty sure she got paid to wear certain things and take pictures of herself in them. It wasn't like his sister had some unbelievable job. She was a real estate broker in Manhattan and spent most of her time trying to convince people that it was totally normal for a kitchen to double as a bedroom. If Phoebe could make money just for wearing a certain T-shirt and tagging a brand, he didn't think his sister should be so judgy about it.

"Phoebe's an influencer," Zach said. "It's a real thing. And her pictures are good. I mean, I've only seen a few, but they've been good." And by a few, he meant he'd studied every single post of hers until his eyes felt like they were going to bulge from their sockets.

"The jobs of your generation," Aimee mused. "I'll never understand them. You guys know I worked at the hotel for a bit before I got married, right? Reservations, activities, human resources. And your father, he killed himself in medical school, then residency. I swear he never slept—" She broke off inexplicably, her voice faltering. "Anyway, yes, Phoebe and Michael are both coming, but not Peter or Greta."

"Have they realized Michael is, um—" Zach asked. At Grandpa Benny's funeral, he'd worn a suit that looked like a straitjacket on him. *A straight jacket.* Ha! He wanted to share the joke out loud, but his mother was squeezing the steering wheel like Sandra Bullock in *Speed*, and Maddie was back to texting Andrew.

"Let's not gossip about the Weingolds, please," his mother said. "People in glass houses shouldn't throw stones."

What the hell was that supposed to mean? Who was gay in their family? Scott wasn't gay, though being in love with medical textbooks definitely counted as non-hetero. His mother's cryptic message must relate to the police search, to the muffled fighting between his parents, to the reason his dad was being left behind on Father's Day weekend. But fuck if Zach could even guess at what was happening. And he wasn't even stoned. Whatever their father had done, he needed his mom to let it go. He couldn't imagine losing the Golden Hotel and his parents getting divorced in one summer.

Defeated, he slipped his Beats back on and let the White Stripes lull him into a trance. He knew they were approaching the mountains when his ears started popping. Zach flicked his eyes open and stared out the window at the rolling foliage until he saw the wooden sign for the hotel, with its white-painted letters in a loopy script. Under the name were three carved green leaves, a logo his mother had designed that had been added to the welcome sign when she was a teenager. How long had the capital H in "Hotel" been missing? That seemed like something that should have been addressed. Was this an example of what Grandma Louise was referring to when she complained the hotel wasn't being properly run?

Before he could ask, Maddie said, "'Ello, welcom' to the Golden 'Otel! We got mutton and lager for yas." Zach sometimes forgot how funny his sister could be when she took the stick out of her ass. He felt a trace of excitement for the week ahead, and not just because he would be in close proximity to Phoebe.

"Look, I think that's Peter's car," Aimee said, pointing out the window. A Land Rover with a Harvard bumper sticker on the back was pulling into the driveway of the hotel at the same time, approaching from the opposite direction. The driveway leading to the main building was a semicircle surrounding a stone fountain with two entrances off the main road that converged into one superlong road lined with tall elm trees. It was majestic, like driving into a fairy tale.

Zach peered into the passenger seat, where Phoebe had her bare feet up on the dash. He could make out bright blue polish on her toes. He checked his phone covertly, looking at Free2BPhoebe's feed. Under a picture of the Golden Hotel, a black-and-white one from the 1960s that she must have dug up from the internet, she'd written: "Retro week begins. Stay tuned for pics of me chillin in the skilz old-school style." Normally Zach would roll his eyes at that sort of thing, the silly hashtagging and overuse of emojis so beloved by his friends, but when Phoebe did it, it was adorable. He found basically everything she posted appealing, whether it was snaps of her visit to an ice cream museum, a live clip of her getting another tattoo, or her sampling organic beers. Not that he ever commented or liked her posts. She probably wouldn't notice if he did, anyway. Her last post, a close-up of her latte where the barista had made a music note design with the foam, had garnered 1,700 likes and 400 comments.

"Is Dad going to come up if he feels better?" Maddie asked. She'd already asked their mom the same question at the rest stop an hour ago.

"No, he will not. There'd be no point. I don't think he's that invested in what happens to the Golden."

"Isn't that where you met?" Maddie asked. She got this droopy look in her eyes. "He was a bellman, and you tripped over a suitcase because he'd left it in the driveway, right?"

Their mother nodded absentmindedly. At this point they were already at the front entrance. Maddie tapped Zach and made the universal sign for crazy, a swirling pointer finger by her ear. Zach shrugged. Maybe he *should* tell his sister about the police. He wasn't equipped to deal with problems of this magnitude on his own. But he also didn't want his mom to be angry with him for disobeying her. God, he was such a little kid still. It didn't help his manhood that he was crammed into the back seat of the family car and had asked his mom to stop for snacks twice on the ride.

A valet dressed in a maroon vest and pants with a braided gold detail approached their car. Grandpa Benny used to say that he and Amos had scoured every fabric store on the Lower East Side to get enough gold thread from the bargain bins to detail the uniforms. "Makes the guests feel like they're arriving at a palace when they see all that gold," he'd said. By the looks of the hotel now, its welcome mat faded and torn, the stone façade crumbling, it was more like a visit to a haunted house.

"Good afternoon, Aimee, Maddie, Zach," the valet said, bending toward the rolled-down passenger side window. "Oh!" he said, startled when Shaggy reached out his head and licked him.

"Otto still works here?" Zach whispered. "Isn't he like a hundred and six by now?"

"Shush," Aimee said, but Zach noticed a little smile creep across her face. Otto had to have been old when *she* was a kid at the hotel. He thought he remembered a story about her and the Weingold boys playing tricks on him, pretending guests were identical twins and that he was sending bags to the wrong rooms.

"Hello, Otto," she said, stepping out of the car and giving him a hug. "Why don't you let us carry our own bags?"

Otto didn't object.

"We're so excited to have you and the Weingolds in house at the same time," Otto said. "It sure has been a while."

In the distance, Zach saw Phoebe snapping photos of a flopped-over white flower in a small garden bed to the side of the hotel's front door.

Two minutes later, he checked Instagram.

"Oh, the cycle of life," she had captioned the photo. It already had sixty-five likes.

Chapter Four

Amos

It was a funny thing to feel grateful for macular degeneration, a condition that made Amos feel like he was seeing everything through layers of cellophane, but as he watched his grandchildren pull into the driveway, followed by Aimee and two of her kids, he was happy that his vision wasn't sharp. He felt almost surprised when Peter's Land Rover and Aimee's car stopped at the main entrance of the hotel. He was half expecting them to step on the gas and blaze right through the front doors, bulldozing his life's work before they even sat down to a family meeting. And was that a goddamn dog he saw, getting pulled on a leash by Maddie?

He wondered if Louise was watching this scene from her cottage window and thinking the same thing. He would ask her later at dinner, once she eventually made her way to the table. His partner's wife loved to make an entrance. He couldn't remember ever sitting down to a meal where she wasn't the last to arrive, sauntering toward their table with a sashay in her hips. Benny would look at her admiringly, never seeming to tire of her luster. Amos himself wouldn't have known what to do with a woman like that. Fanny was just right for him. A sturdy, dependable, behind-the-scenes kind of gal, content to feed and clothe her family and cheer them on from the sidelines. It niggled him every now and then that Louise dropped so many comments about her and Benny being the "public faces" of the hotel, but Amos wasn't delusional enough to deny she was right. She just didn't need to say it so often and make Fanny feel less than. Besides, a younger Fanny had hardly been a shrinking violet when the lights were out. Far from it. Heat rose to his face at the memories.

Fanny was noticeably glum because Peter wasn't coming. Amos was, too, but he was hardly surprised. Their older son—older than Brian by six minutes, but it might as well have been six years—had never taken much interest in the hotel. As a teenager, his favorite movie had been *Wall Street*. He'd even slicked his hair like Gordon Gekko. Now he was managing partner of a major law firm in Manhattan, possibly headed toward becoming the first person in history to say on their deathbed they wished they'd spent more time at the office.

Amos *was* surprised that Greta hadn't come along with the children. When money was concerned, his daughter-in-law was typically all ears. At family meals, when Amos and Brian would side-chat about mundane items, like which porter needed to go and whether they should change meat suppliers, Greta rarely lifted her gaze. But if they mentioned the taxes going up due to increased land value, her fork would clatter to her plate. "You said the land is worth how much? Does that include the additional acres with the hiking trails?" And Brian, saint that he was, would patiently answer her questions, while Peter was off in another room on one of his endless conference calls.

It had to be the "medical procedure" Peter had referenced keeping her away. Greta was surely having something lifted or tucked. The woman had more stitches in her body than a needlepoint blanket. Now the poor thing was probably fretting from her hospital bed that she had to leave the fate of the hotel to her children and the Goldmans. He still remembered overhearing Greta's grandmother, a pushy bungalow gal fond of sneaking into the shows by thrusting her bosom at the bouncer, pushing her to chat up Peter. "Brian's cuter," Greta had protested. "Brian's going nowhere," Lillian Bauman had responded. Amos had never told Fanny what he'd overheard. She was fiercely protective of the boys and wouldn't have been as capable of overlooking the slight. Besides, Amos wanted to encourage Peter receiving the attention of a young lady. Greta was one of the more attractive single gals, with an endearingly crooked nose and an elfin chin that suited her petite frame and yellow curls perfectly. Early into their marriage, both of those imperfect features had been corrected with Peter's sizable earnings. At the time, Greta had been just what Peter needed to divert his puppy dog worship of Aimee, who couldn't seem to take her eyes off Brian. That was never going to happen, Fanny and Amos knew with certainty. Their younger son gave most of the girls at the hotel whiplash when he came into a room. They worried one day he'd give somebody's daughter more than a stiff neck. And Louise Goldman wasn't taking a Weingold for a son-in-law. So from both ends, that was a nonstarter.

"They're here?" came Fanny's voice. She rolled up to where

he was standing at the window. The wheelchair was new, and Amos was still getting used to the ambient sounds of their coexistence. The motorized hum of her chair startled him when he heard the approach. Before Fanny's stroke took the feeling from her legs, she had padded around in terry cloth slippers that made a pleasing swoosh when they rubbed against their carpeted bedroom. A sound that for years made him reach for a Viagra.

"Yes. Phoebe and Michael arrived at the same time as Aimee and the kids. No Roger. Or Scott. It's probably better. There will already be enough cooks in the kitchen."

It was a familiar joke. Whenever one of the owners checked in on food preparation—because preparing two hundred gallons of matzo ball soup at a time was no easy feat—Chef Joe would respond good-naturedly: *I don't need more cooks in the kitchen.* He was a master of his domain, not unlike the superheroes that prepared the food on cruise ships, but lately he'd been slipping. Early on in their entrepreneurship, a proprietor of a beloved restaurant, now long-shuttered, in the town of Liberty had told Amos and Benny that the key to proper seasoning was that you should never be able to detect the presence or absence of salt. Lately, the food at the Golden was tasting like it had been prepared in Dead Sea water. Only useful if you needed to clean a scrape with your soup.

"Have you spoken with Brian about this yet?" Fanny asked. She had positioned herself next to him at the window. He watched her face soften as she took in the forms of her grandchildren. Phoebe was a beauty, a cross between what her mother had looked like when she was young with her strawberry blond hair and button nose, and her uncle Brian with the piercing green eyes. Michael, their brilliant grandson, was a cipher, fiercely private whenever Fanny gave him the third degree.

"Only a little," Amos said, putting a hand on Fanny's. She no longer wore the wedding ring he had given her more than sixty years ago. The medications she took swelled her joints. He'd offered to buy her a new ring, but she refused. "I'm wedded to the past," she said, and Amos wasn't sure if she caught her own pun.

"Well, you should," said Fanny. "I'm worried about him." *You know I can only be as happy as my least happy child*, Amos completed her thought. He wondered if Brian was less happy than Peter. Just because Peter checked more boxes of a so-called successful life didn't mean he had any more satisfaction than his twin.

"I will. We've just gotten here, though," Amos said, and rubbed his eyes to signal that he needed a break from the discussion. It was a subject he'd already turned over in his mind dozens of times since Brian had told him about the casino offer.

The hotel had saved Brian at a time when his life was in shambles. It had enabled him to return to the place where he'd been the golden boy and to feel like a man again after Melinda had eviscerated him. Amos and Fanny had both thought he'd work there a few years and move on—maybe to New York City to pursue a career in sports management, something he'd shown an early interest in back when the Golden had hosted celebrity athletes. Having interests was never Brian's issue; his problem was follow-through. He was an all-hat-and-no-cattle kind of guy, and if running the hotel had taught the senior Weingolds anything, it was that nothing could replace good old-fashioned hard work.

When Brian had come to work at the hotel, Amos and Benny

had still been young men, relatively speaking. They'd been robust, swimming laps and playing doubles with the rotating cast of sports stars who trained there. Benny, to his great credit, had never once complained or showed a trace of resentment when Brian arrived hat in hand. They'd put Brian on the payroll and had started handing off responsibilities to him. To have a child in need was a delicate thing; Benny had recognized he was lucky that Aimee was so well taken care of by Roger—it had been something he spoke of often. Any income from the hotel that accrued to her was gravy. The same went for Peter, who needed the Golden riches the least of the second-generation kids. Amos wondered what Louise had said privately to Benny about Brian taking on a leadership role, but if she'd complained, Benny had never let on. That was not something to take for granted. The competing interests of families in partnership led frequently to lawsuits and vitriol; so far, they had been spared. It helped that Brian wasn't the power-grabbing sort. If anything, power was being foisted on him as a life preserver. It was easier to stomach sharing a steak with someone you knew to be anemic, and after the Melinda episode, Brian was as deficient as they came.

"I just hope these meetings go smoothly," Fanny said. "It's a lot of pressure for Brian." She rolled backward toward the closet, and Amos winced as she struggled to weave between the furniture.

He and Fanny had only arrived from Florida the day before, and it had taken quite a bit of effort to settle in with Fanny's new mode of getting around. The steps outside their cottage presented an insurmountable challenge, so Brian had set them up in one of the larger guest rooms, where they could avail themselves of the hotel elevator. It felt strange to be anywhere but their cottage, where framed family photos covered every horizontal and vertical surface and the boys' childhood projects still hung on the refrigerator with magnets from local businesses.

"I will try to grab him before we're all together tonight," Amos added, watching as his wife bumped into the bedpost. There were so many ways he wanted to help Fanny. To get the cardigan out of the closet for her; to lift her into bed; to bend down to get the reading glasses she perpetually dropped. But she was resistant to showing weakness. At least she'd asked him to speak to Brian. Calming Fanny's nerves was a small way he could be helpful.

"Good. I'm going down to see the grandchildren," Fanny said, and the motorized buzz of her wheelchair sounded again as she went out the door.

"I'll be down soon," Amos said.

He could use another minute to collect himself before he faced everyone. He missed Benny more intensely now than when he'd died. Walking through the hotel, with an offer to sell pending, Amos could feel his best friend and business partner's presence everywhere. Benny's bellowing laugh sounded when Amos entered the comedy hall. He thought of Benny's ferocious appetite when his favorite apple turnovers were in the dining room. Benny's shadow loomed when Amos stared at the wooden sign in the rec room posted above the pool cues that said: RESERVED FOR BENNY G. Benny sounded with each bouncing ball on the tennis court and every splash in the pool. Echoes of his friend were in every inch of carpeting; one of their closely guarded secrets stashed behind every piece of plywood.

Even the worst of their problems took on a hazy afterglow when Amos reviewed them in hindsight, including the worst of their fights. In the hotel's first decade, there had been a college-age tennis instructor named Daniel, single and the son of prominent guests of the hotel, who was rather fond of giving lessons to the young girls. The *very* young girls. His hands wandered during serves; he never missed a chance for hands-on teaching. A more robust Larry brought it to their attention. Amos wanted to tell Daniel's parents; Benny wanted to rough the kid up but good. It was the kind of scandal that could have destroyed the hotel if anyone found out. In the end, they planted drugs in Daniel's cabin and fired him that way, but not without Benny giving him a swift kick in the nuts and Amos threatening the life out of him. Then there was the kosher meat scandal from 1975, when they found out their supplier was using nonkosher meat from the same source that delivered to the nearby penitentiary. Another mess that would have sunk the hotel—they were only saved by outrageous payouts to keep certain mouths quiet.

To think there was a chance the entire building would be razed and turned into a windowless casino, dimly lit on the inside, the chorus of the guests' laughter replaced by the ding-ding-ding of slot machines. He wondered if the tree where he and Benny had carved their initials would survive a change of ownership. Would he appear overly sentimental if he stipulated in the contract that it couldn't be chopped down?

He wasn't a fool; his head was not in sand. Amos knew the hotel was on the decline. Not a single one of its competitors was still standing. Kutsher's was now a flaky wellness resort; the Concord was a casino where busloads of retirees were dropped off to part with their Social Security checks. Amos meant to drive over and see it for himself. It was called Resort's World, and it advertised with a massive, blingy sign on the highway. Grossinger's had been demolished just a few years ago. In the seventies, Benny and Amos had had it out with the matron herself, Jennie Grossinger, for stealing away some of the bigger stars on their talent roster, including Joan Rivers and Andy Kaufman. After that, Amos had secretly wished their hotel would suffer an outbreak of food poisoning during peak summer season. But when he'd read the news about Grossinger's being destroyed because the family couldn't afford to maintain it, Amos had wept for his old rival.

But even with the guest book filling at a snail's pace—the Golden used to go through three thick, leather-bound books in a single summer—Amos never imagined a time when the hotel wouldn't be there. Keeping it alive was about more than providing his son with a sense of purpose. It was about preserving memories for the thousands of families who had come through the double doors with carved G's for handles, wearing the weight of the city on their faces, dragging their luggage hazily until they could hand it off to a waiting bellhop. After a week or more of entertainment and nonstop eating, of shuffleboard tournaments and Ping-Pong rallies, of schmoozing with the other guests and making matches for their children, the families had left transformed. They'd been lighter. Not actually—a week at the Golden was good for at least three pounds—but their energy had been buoyant by comparison.

The hotel still had its regulars, the families for whom the Golden tradition was so important that it kept the lights on. The Cohens from New Jersey came back every year to defend their title in the hot dog eating contest. The Felbers of Flushing returned because it was Grandma Ruth's favorite place on earth and the only place she wanted to celebrate her birthday. (In fairness, it had once been reported to him by her family that Ruth had never been on an airplane.) The Glicks, the Rosensweigs, the Paulsons: They all had their special reasons for returning. But what about the Richmans? George and Estelle had been bridge partners with Amos and Fanny for years, but all at once it seemed they'd gotten fancy and had started to vacation in Europe.

He walked over to the phone on the desk and dialed the bellman station.

"Otto speaking. How can I help you?"

"It's Amos. Just wondering about some families. Have the Prozans been here recently?" They were the reigning champions of the ballroom dance competition.

"Oh, no. Not for at least five years. They claimed they saw mouse droppings and never returned. Brian inspected and said they were pencil shavings, but we didn't see hide nor hair of them again."

"What about the Simon family? The ones from Connecticut," Amos asked. They used to take room 604, a king suite with a soaking tub and balcony, for all of August.

"Moved to Vancouver ages ago," Otto said. "Anyone else, boss?"

"Nah. Thanks, Otto." He settled the phone back into its cradle and scratched his chin thoughtfully. There was a whole group of families from South Jersey who used to travel to the hotel en masse every summer. It was a barely kept secret that the couples were known to toss their room keys into a bowl on the last night and play mixed doubles off the court. This had gone on successfully for nearly a decade, until the divorces started. The hotel had lost the entire group rapidly.

Nostalgia was not a sufficient raison d'être. That was the thing with co-owning a hotel with another family, and probably why it was always best to have outside investors. Decisions couldn't be made on heartstrings alone. And Winwood Casinos had made a very tempting offer for the property. Twelve million dollars to acquire all 1,800 acres. Amos didn't have to ask if they planned to repurpose any of the existing buildings. He'd been on Winwood's website and seen their other flashy establishments. Without question, if they handed over the title to them, the bulldozers would storm the gates. The comedy hall where Jerry Seinfeld—before he was Jerry Seinfeld—had cut his chops would come tumbling down. The iconic kidney-shaped pool where Amos had taught the boys to swim would be filled in to make way for another casino building—because these fellas who ran the gambling joints didn't want guests spending too much time outdoors. Amos put his hand to his chest, feeling the tightness. Was he having a heart attack? No, this was just what it felt like when your life's work hung in the balance, like your ventricles were squeezing together trying desperately to hold on to something.

He traced the underside of the desk and felt a thick layer of dust collect on his fingertip. He blew it off and watched the dust mites sparkle in the light streaming in from the window. It was time to face the music. Amos headed for the lobby to greet his family.

On the stairs leading from their second-floor room to the lobby level, Amos paused in front of the portrait of him and Benny posed in front of the clubhouse at the nine-hole golf course. It was from the baby days of the hotel—early 1970s, if Amos remembered correctly. The boys had just been born and were the hit of the hotel—somebody, maybe it was the bridge instructor, had nicknamed them the Tweingolds. Amos used to joke he should charge the guests to hold them. In the portrait, he and Benny were both in argyle vests, long shorts, and dark socks hiked up to their knees. It wasn't like the two of them to be self-aggrandizing, but there was a terrible crack in the wood paneling, and Benny had suggested it would be cheaper to just hang a picture over the crack instead of repairing it. Years later, through several rounds of renovations, contractors would come through and ask about patching the wall behind the picture. Benny and Amos would always answer "Nope!" in unison. Some things deserved to remain, even when their original purpose was obsolete. It was like a metaphor of aging. He and Fanny had been at their best when they were parenting small children, cleaning scrapes, and helping with homework, but just because those days were a distant memory didn't mean they should be put out to pasture. That was kind of what life in Florida felt like, like being in God's waiting room. Being back at the Golden was like having his body greased with WD-40. The Catskills air always did that for him, made him feel healthy and strong, as it had for the thousands who'd sought refuge there to fight off tuberculosis near the turn of the century. Maybe he and Fanny should return to Windsor full-time. Though he knew before he let the idea really sink in that Fanny's wheelchair would be a disaster to manage in the snow and that the hilliness would make even his daily constitutional impossible.

Amos stared at the portrait for one last beat. *Why'd you have to go and die on me, Benny?*

Chapter Five

Aimee

She should have just powered off her damn phone. She had five missed calls from Roger. She'd hit decline every time— and who knew how many times he'd tried to get through while she was driving through the numerous dead zones en route to the hotel—but after his sixth attempt to reach her, she caved. This was after Roger texted: **You are with two of my three children. Please pick up.** He'd added a Memoji of himself with prayer hands. It was the pathetic-ness of the overture that made her relent.

"Yes?" she'd said, making sure not to mask the clipped tone of her voice. She was in the middle of zipping up the dress she'd planned to wear to dinner, but it was still too tight. She'd eaten so little in recent weeks, she'd thought it might fit. Irritated, she let the dress puddle at her ankles and combed through the rest of her suitcase. Couldn't Roger's betrayal be good for anything? "Betrayal" wasn't a strong enough word. It was a *crime*. She attempted to say it out loud. The dull monosyllabism stuck in the back of her throat like a dry cracker.

"Aimee," Roger said, his relief plain. "Thank you for answering. We need to talk."

"This is a terrible time. I'm about to go to the dining room to see everyone," she said. "I'll call you when I have time."

"Aimee, please—" Roger begged. She wondered where he was in their house. At the kitchen table, hovering over a pint of ice cream? Roger was an eater when he was stressed, the opposite of her. Or maybe he was in the den, combing through the family photo albums and wondering how he could have been so insanely stupid.

"Just listen. I know you said this is a bad time, but I spoke to my lawyer this morning. He gave me an estimate of what the legal fees are going to be to defend this. Aimee, I know how much the Golden means to you and your family—but the proceeds from a sale could really help us out. They could keep me out of jail. Please think about us. Our family."

Us? Us! Had Roger been thinking about "us" and "family" when he'd agreed to peddle drugs that were destroying entire communities, making people horribly sick? Losing their families. Dying in droves. People were actually *dying* because of what Roger was giving them. How could she ever share a bed with him again?

"I can't do this now," she repeated as a reel of the past thirty years of their lives together started playing in her mind. She wanted to press pause, but it was like the button on the projector was stuck. She saw the day they'd gotten married in the gazebo by the lake at the Golden, when it was sweltering and Roger pulled off his bow tie during their vows. She relived walking across the threshold of their home three times with newborns in infant carriers. Heard the sound of Roger singing Frank Sinatra at the top of his lungs in the shower while he shaved. It would be a lot to throw away—not that ending her marriage would erase all those good moments, but they would take on a different character. She recalled advice from her mother: *Fighting with your husband is like picking at a pimple. It always leaves a scar.* Louise had probably been cautioning her not to yell at Roger for leaving the toilet seat up or putting back a nearly empty container of milk. Louise could never contemplate the magnitude of this marital rupture. Her sixty-year marriage to Aimee's father had been nauseatingly perfect. They'd kissed and cuddled well into their seventies. She and Roger had never been like that. Hell, sometimes she pictured Brian Weingold when they were having sex, and then she'd feel so guilty at how aroused she got that she'd lose interest altogether.

"Aimee, I really need mon—"

"Where's all your drug money? Can't you use that?"

She heard him sigh.

"My accounts have all been frozen. It has to come from you."

"Goodbye, Roger," she said, and tossed the phone onto the bed, where it bounced off and tumbled onto the floor.

"Jesus," she moaned, bending down to retrieve it from under the minibar.

One of Brian's innovations had been to add minibars to the guest rooms. "People need more than Manischewitz if they're going to be stuck with their families," he'd quipped on an owners' conference call. The margins on alcohol were great, especially when you included the absurd minibar upcharge, so everyone had acquiesced, even though Louise had said she didn't understand the need to get drunk in the room when they had plenty of wine in the dining room. Maybe if her husband had faced up to twenty years in an orange jumpsuit, she would have understood the impulse to do a shot or two in private.

Aimee opened the fridge and took a mini Belvedere down in one long swig.

A text message beeped in her hand. Scott this time. That was why she didn't power off her phone. Because she was still a mother, and mothers didn't get the luxury of disconnecting.

Everything okay? her boy had written. **You were so weird on the phone yesterday.**

Scott had been about to set out for the airport when Aimee had stumbled onto the scene of the police tearing up their house. Mercifully, she'd had the presence of mind to call and stop him from coming. Her middle child lived in the library at the medical school and usually had his phone set to silent. Luckily he'd picked up, and she'd mumbled something barely comprehensible about needing to get to the Golden and that he should stay put in Chicago.

He'd clearly been taken aback. But she'd also detected a note of relief. Not having to come home for the weekend meant he had more time to study. Or maybe he didn't want the family time. Wasn't their not going to the Golden more often also because the kids had outgrown the nuclear bubble?

What should she say to him now that a day had passed? You could more easily pull the wool over Zach's eyes than Scott's. The trouble was, the vodka was already hitting her. She had to correct numerous typos before she was able to respond: **Yes, yes. All**

good. Miss you! *Your dad is the Pablo Escobar of Westchester,* she added silently in her head.

A knock startled her as she was buttoning up a blouse she knew reeked of schoolmarm. If only she hadn't had to pack so quickly. Everything besides the one dress that was too tight made her look like a hausfrau with a lifetime membership at Chico's.

"Mom, you in there?" Oh God, Maddie. More collateral damage from her husband's terrible judgment. The more she thought about it, there was no way the Hoffs were going to let their son marry the daughter of a criminal. They barely approved of the Glassers to begin with. Sure, Maddie's father was a doctor, but it was nothing compared to the snobs they hobnobbed with in Palm Beach, titans of industry whose net worth had seven zeroes. The pictures of Benny and Louise dining with the likes of Jackie Mason and Rodney Dangerfield did not impress the senior Hoffs. They prided themselves on getting into social clubs that traditionally excluded their own kind. Meanwhile, the Catskills flourished as a mecca for those excluded from other hotels. A GEN-TILES ONLY sign that Benny had found at a yard sale hung ironically in the management office.

For different reasons, the idea of a Hoff-Glasser marriage had never sat entirely well with Aimee, either. Andrew just didn't seem like his own man, and her daughter was so fixated on fulfilling THE PLAN (she worshipped at the temple of to-do lists) that Aimee wondered if she would accept a ring from a houseplant if offered at the right time. Aimee worried her daughter was so impressed with Andrew's family and background that she'd lost sight of how special her own upbringing was. *You're a Goldman, goddammit,* she'd want to say. *Your grandmother hosted Eleanor Roosevelt! She was invited to the Montreal and Lake Placid Olympics because so many of the athletes trained at the hotel. Your grandfather was invited to the Oscars by Tony Bennett! So what if the Sullivan County Health Department gave our kitchen a C last year? We were once in the* Guinness Book of World Records *for smoking the largest sturgeon in history!*

Despite her reservations, Aimee didn't believe it was her place to discourage her daughter. If the relationship was bound to unwind, it should be because of what the kids wanted, not because of something out of Maddie's hands entirely—like a federal crime committed by her father.

So Aimee kept her mouth shut, even as reservations bubbled inside her veins. Louise had meddled in her love life, and it had driven Aimee crazy. Any boy Aimee so much as chatted with, her mother demanded a full recanting. *Are you "interested" in this boy?* she would ask, studying her manicure to feign nonchalance. *Where do his parents live? Is he in graduate school? Is he a serious type, or one of these wild fellas just smoking grass with the staff?* "Why don't *you* date him?" Aimee had once suggested after Louise had thrust a pre-law bachelor in her face, and Louise had balked. "Now you're just being nasty. Can't a mother worry about her only child without it rising to the level of a federal crime?"

A federal crime, Aimee thought. *We've got that covered now!*

Instead of testing her parents with a struggling artist or poet, Aimee had dutifully fulfilled their expectations. Roger was perfect on paper and just as charming in real life. A University of Pennsylvania undergraduate on his way to University of Chicago Medical School—a Jewish mother's orgasm. And yet Louise hadn't rejoiced at their coupling. When Louise approved of something, she couldn't mask the pleasure on her face. There was nothing opaque about her emotional spectrum—all the staff at the hotel were terrified of her facial expressions. A nose wriggle could send a waiter reeling. She had a crippling eyebrow raise that made you feel you'd never made a good decision in your life. When Aimee had told her mother she was going to marry Roger, Louise had pursed her lips, and through them had slipped out, "If you're sure." Then had come a perfunctory hug and double kiss. Tears had followed, but it hadn't been clear if they were the joyful kind.

It was terribly cliché, but Aimee didn't want her mother to find out about Roger's crime, because she didn't want her to have been right all along. To have any reason to say *I told you so*. Because, historically, Louise had been right about so many things. Aimee did look better with the blond highlights Louise had suggested. Their kitchen in Scarsdale did look bigger when they'd blown out the wall between the pantry and the den. Maddie *was* putting on weight in high school and needed to cool it on the carbs. Zacky's arm *was* broken when he fell playing softball in the Gold Rush game, even though Aimee had been certain he was faking. The list of things her mother had been right about was excruciatingly long.

That childish impulse not to give her mother the satisfaction was not the only reason for her secrecy. Louise was a new widow, her sorrow a cloud that followed her everywhere. And she had to make a major decision about the hotel without her partner. She was an eighty-four-year-old woman who deserved some peace. So it was twofold why Aimee didn't open up: to spare her mother and to spare herself. Mothers and daughters. Was there any other relationship so achingly complex? It seemed, despite her best efforts, that she and Maddie were destined for a similarly complex future.

"Yes, just a second," Aimee said when her own daughter knocked again. She quickly put the drained Belvedere bottle in the wastebasket and covered it with some crumpled tissues.

"Hi, honey," she said, giving her daughter a peck on the cheek. "Ready for dinner?"

"Yep," Maddie said. She was pouty, lower lip jutting out as if to dare Aimee to ask what was wrong.

Maddie had confided a while back that she thought Andrew might ask them for her hand in marriage over Father's Day weekend. "He's chivalrous like that," Maddie had said. "And when he does ask, you'd better tell me the proposal plans so I can make sure I have a blowout."

Roger and Aimee had laughed at the time. The idea that anyone in the millennial generation was still asking for permission was a joke. They were all so entitled and did whatever they felt like doing anyway. If enough people liked it on social media, it was sanctioned.

"Mom, that shirt. Seriously?" Maddie squinted, eyes clearly assaulted by the floral print of Aimee's blouse.

"That bad?" Aimee tugged at the top button self-consciously.

"Florals aren't really my thing. I guess it's good for your age." Maddie plopped on the bed, picking at a cuticle. Did these children have any idea how awful they could sound? "So, my room smells like mothballs."

"I'll buy you an air freshener." Aimee went to the bureau mirror. The shirt wasn't that bad, was it? Maddie's top was white, with holes where the shoulders were meant to be, so Aimee took the criticism with a grain of salt.

"Where? The general store in town sells, like, batteries and stamps only." Maddie, twenty-nine, could so often sound like a pubescent teen. If Aimee closed her eyes, sixteen-year-old Maddie would manifest, Jansport backpack at her feet, chugging a Diet Coke while complaining about something or other. She may have her shit together more than Zacky did, but at least Aimee's youngest was always kind and appreciative. He'd wanted to move back home, or at least hadn't balked when Aimee suggested it.

"We'll get one from a gas station, then," Aimee said. She could use an air freshener, too. When she opened her top drawer to put away her undergarments, a moldy cheese smell escaped.

"Like, today, please!" Maddie rolled onto her stomach and began tapping out a text.

Aimee frequently marveled at how different her children were despite being raised by the same parents, loved equally (that was absolutely true), and given the same opportunities. As an only child, Aimee was the single sheet of Play-Doh molded by her parents. She wasn't just the first pancake, the lumpy one with burned edges; she was the only pancake. She ought not to be surprised by her children's differences, having grown up alongside the Weingolds: Peter, so serious, often described as fourteen going on forty. Brian, mischievous, the boy who never grew up. No matter how devoted a parent was, at best you were making a difference around the margins.

"Yes, today. I'll ask Brian. Let's get down to dinner," she said, maybe a bit too harshly. She could show her daughter more compassion after springing a Golden weekend on her, separated from the object of her infatuation. None of the Glasser kids had shown much interest in the hotel in at least a decade. How could they enjoy the simple pleasures of the Golden when their father had spoiled them with Four Seasons and Ritz-Carlton amenities? They found the place ceaselessly dull—if only they knew all its saucy secrets. But who was Aimee to tell them about all the illicit affairs, the payoffs to the staff to keep things quiet, the pregnancies that had bloomed between staff and guest and the wrong Mr. and Mrs.?

Aimee would love to blame her children's apathy entirely on Roger, but that wasn't fair. They brought down the average age by fifty percent, and her children didn't even have the Goldman last name. When they signed up for activities at the hotel using Glasser, nobody fawned all over them the way they had over her. It was on her to impart family pride, and she'd botched it. Maybe it wasn't too late. But as a swell of optimism tingled her fingertips, she remembered the reason they were all gathered together.

She wondered if Peter's children felt differently, and she made a note to observe Phoebe and Michael over the next few days. Had she failed her children by not instilling in them enough pride in their roots? She'd once overheard Scott say to one of his friends that his grandparents owned "some random hotel upstate," and she hadn't even bothered to correct him. To tell him and whatever shit he was talking to that the Golden Hotel was a vital piece of their heritage, the resort where thousands of families had bonded, shared laughter, made memories. It had a Wikipedia entry that was three pages long, for God's sake! But it wasn't the Atlantis in the Bahamas, where Roger booked them every Christmas break, with its sprawling water park, trapeze camp, and snorkeling expeditions. Yes, you could take out a canoe at the Golden, but there was a good chance you'd get a splinter from the seat and the boat would have at least one patched-up hole.

She and Maddie were almost to the dining room when Aimee asked, "Have you chatted at all with Phoebe and Michael? I feel like I barely know those kids since we stopped coming to the hotel at the same time . . ." They both fell silent, Aimee at least thinking back to the night that had eroded the tradition of joint family stays, a July Fourth barbeque ten years prior that had gone terribly wrong. Amos and Benny had missed the whole thing. They'd claimed they were fifty meters away, dealing with a busted speaker. It could have been a cover to avoid meddling in the family drama. Had Fanny really dropped a blueberry pie in her mother's lap? Had Louise really said such critical things about Brian out loud? Had Peter called Roger a jerk-off? Aimee was positive she'd seen Phoebe trip Scott with her jump rope. If the fireworks hadn't malfunctioned, setting off a blaze that forced an evacuation of the hotel and destroying the waterfront pavilion, the two families might have parted ways for good.

After that summer, the families took separate months at the hotel. The Weingolds came in July and saved August for traipsing through Europe. The Goldman-Glassers attended local day camps in July and spent the last two weeks in August at the Golden. The separation had saddened Aimee at first, but she'd reminded herself that it was different than when she was a child. Her kids had one another; so did Phoebe and Michael. They didn't need to play Brady Bunch.

"I talked to Michael a little. He's also put out about the mothball stench in his room and concerned the smell will cling to his cashmere. Phoebe is taking pictures of literally everything and posting them with moronic captions," Maddie said.

"I guess she's excited to be here, then," Aimee said, now definitely feeling like a failure.

"Uch, no. She just has to let her followers know where she is every thirty seconds or they'll put out an APB."

"Hm," Aimee said, but her mind was already elsewhere. Out of the corner of her eye, she saw Brian Weingold standing with the maître d', reviewing a diagram of the room. He was tapping various places on the seating chart with the eraser side of a pencil. She felt the flutter in her stomach that seeing Brian always gave her, from the first awareness of her sexuality to today. At her own father's funeral, she'd had to will herself not to look over at him, knowing her thoughts wouldn't be appropriate for the occasion.

Why couldn't Brian deteriorate with middle age like the men in Scarsdale, with thinning hair, pasty skin, and a paunchy waist? Brian had perpetually tan skin, which the sun kissed instead of scorched, the opposite of Roger, who covered himself in SPF 100. Not that protecting oneself from melanoma was unsexy; it was more that striping one's nose with zinc oxide to go from the car to the inside of a store was major overkill. Brian had little scrapes on his forearms and calluses on his fingers that she assumed were from doing manly things like cleaning the gutters or fixing the roof. Again, Roger was the opposite. When something broke in their home, his answer was always to call in a professional.

Today, Brian was wearing perfectly fitting jeans with a blue button-down tucked in. His salt-and-pepper hair hung over his eyes. Aimee chastised herself for feeling so giddy in his presence. She was a premenopausal mother with three grown children, married for more than thirty years. It wasn't becoming to act like a schoolgirl around Brian, who wasn't even much of a friend anymore. They rarely saw each other, spoke only a few times a year on the phone about the hotel, and were tied together only through a business interest. Moreover, they were together this week to face the hotel's existential threat, not for her to flirt.

At that moment, a middle-aged waitress with bright red hair pulled up in a clip approached and whispered something in Brian's ear. He laughed and squeezed her elbow. Aimee looked away.

"I'm starving," Maddie said. "Look, Zacky's already at the table. He looks really upset. Do you know what's going on with him? He barely spoke on the ride up."

Aimee froze. She was being forced to lie to so many people. She'd lied to Zach about the police. She'd lied to Scott about Roger being sick. She was about to lie to Maddie about her brother. She would lie to her mother when she inevitably asked where Roger was. If she were Pinocchio, she'd be due for her second nose job. Thank goodness she'd had the vodka. Aimee hated to think what this kind of deception would feel like sober.

"Oh, probably something with a girl. I wouldn't worry," she said, and then, overreacting, put a protective arm around her daughter's shoulders. They were rarely physically affectionate anymore, and Maddie just kind of stared at the hand on her arm like it belonged to an alien.

"All right, I'll go sit with him and see if I can dig up some info," she said, and slipped out from Aimee's hold. Her children might bicker, but they cared about one another.

Aimee's eyes scanned the dining room, where more than a hundred tables were set with the same carnation pink tablecloths that had been used since her childhood, white napkins fanned on top of white china plates with a green fleur-de-lis design. She did a quick count—maybe only thirty tables were occupied. Around the perimeter, uniformed waiters stood at attention. Aimee recalled the time when the workers hired by her father and Amos had had to perform physical strength tests in order to get the job, like firemen. They'd needed to balance round trays, thirty-six inches in diameter, stacked with at least ten full plates topped with aluminum lids while still making it to the kitchen and back from the farthest table within thirty seconds. The waiters flanking the dining room were probably those same fit boys, only thirty years had passed since their last fitness test. There was one particularly wobbly-looking one at the end of the line whom Aimee wouldn't trust to handle soup.

She followed Maddie to the owners' table, positioned in the same spot since the hotel's opening summer. Benny and Amos believed in sitting together at every meal, so that no family felt jealous if they chose to join one party over another. They'd chosen the back corner of the room, the table closest to the kitchen, so that they could make quick stops to check on operations, and so what were arguably the worst seats in the dining room didn't go to a paying customer. Their table for two had become a square when they'd gotten married, then they'd expanded to a round one when the children had come along, then to a long rectangle that could accommodate three generations. They'd been fourteen all together. Traditionally, Benny and Amos sat at opposite heads, but because they'd shared a language only they understood, they could often be heard shouting down the long length of the table to each other in what sounded like gibberish to the rest of them.

When she approached, Aimee thought she noticed Amos avoid her gaze. She hoped the decision about the hotel wouldn't turn into a Goldman versus Weingold fiasco. Next to Amos sat Brian, and across from him were Phoebe and Michael. On Brian's other side, a chair had been removed so that Fanny could roll up to the table in her chair. There were empty seats where Peter and Greta would normally be, and of course there was the empty seat next to Aimee that Roger would typically occupy, next to which was Scott's empty spot. Then there was Benny's chair at the end, the most gaping hole of all. As if their table were a microcosm of the entire hotel—emptiness where there once was fullness, awkward silence where boisterous laughter used to reign.

Shortly after Aimee had settled into her chair, Louise made her entrance, circling the table and greeting everyone. Then she sat in Roger's empty chair instead of her usual spot.

"Need to appear united," she whispered knowingly in Aimee's ear. Louise smelled strongly of Chanel No. 5 and Pond's face cream.

Brian, who had joined, dinged his fork on a water glass and cleared his throat. The guy even ahemed attractively. She thought about what other noises he made. Did he grunt in bed? Whisper dirty talk?

Focus, Aimee. She pinched her thigh. There were so many things more important than how sexy the scruff on Brian's jawline looked.

"It's great to see everyone. My brother regrets that he—"

But Brian was interrupted by George, the loyal head waiter

for the past forty years. His waistline seemed to grow with each year he gave to the job, like a tree whose age could be measured by the girth of its trunk. He didn't so much walk over to their table as waddle.

"What a treat to see everyone," George said, swooping in with a large tray. "Chef has prepared all of the hotel specialties for tonight."

"Pass it all down here," Zach said. Her son was always hungry. She suspected it was the pot. He couldn't still be growing, could he? Neither she nor Roger was naturally tall. Not like Brian, who was . . .

George started lifting silver lids off platters with elaborate gestures. Steam rose and fogged Aimee's reading glasses. She quickly slipped them off. How could she have forgotten to remove them before dinner?

"For the first course, may I present the following: kippered salmon spread, pickled herring in heavy cream, traditional borscht soup, and gefilte fish. And, of course, everyone's favorite—fried liver in schmaltz."

Aimee watched her children's faces go white. Even her own stomach was gurgling at the thought of eating those foods, especially together. It was like a heart attack on a tray. Rendered chicken fat as a cooking ingredient really ought to be illegal.

"Do you have anything vegan?" Phoebe asked from her end of the table.

"I'm Paleo," Michael announced. "And fried liver is a chess opening, not a meal."

"Smart-ass," Phoebe said.

"Michael is a master-level chess player," Fanny interjected.

"We're going to gain a million pounds," Maddie whined.

"Well, I'm not," Phoebe said. "I'm not eating any of this." She pulled out her phone and snapped a close-up of a particularly gelatinous-looking herring. "You guys like 'Herring today, gone tomorrow'?"

"I'll try something," Zacky said.

"You will?" Phoebe asked him, wrinkling her nose.

"'Course not. I was joking," Zach said, pushing away his empty plate. Oh God, Maddie had been right. Why did crushes have to be so dehumanizing? Decades earlier, Aimee had wanted to display her paintings in the hotel art exhibition, but Brian had called the event lame, and so she'd crossed her name off the list and stashed her watercolors behind her bed.

"I'm sorry, Uncle Brian, but this looks nasty," Michael said. He pulled an energy bar from the man-purse thing he'd been carrying around since arrival.

She watched Brian redden, color rising through the stubble on his cheeks.

These kids! They were all spoiled brats.

"Well, I for one am ready to dig in," Aimee announced, pushing up her sleeves like she was going to eat Medieval times style. She took two slices of gefilte, a large scoop of kippered salmon, and three helpings of fried liver.

"Should you be eating all that?" Louise muttered at her. "Your blouse is already pulling in the back."

Aimee swiveled around in her chair and signaled for George to come back.

"Got anything stronger than Manischewitz lying around?"

Chapter Six

Zach

"Mom, Brian is talking to you," Zach said, embarrassed by how quickly his mother was swilling the wine. Since when did she drink this much?

She looked up, a wild flare in her eyes.

"Oh, sorry. What did you say?"

"I was just asking if everything was all right," Brian said.

"Yes, yes," Aimee said. "Just lost in memories. I was thinking about the time Maddie fell into the fountain during Miss Golden Girl and her white dress became see-through—"

"Mom!" Maddie yelped. "Seriously?"

What the hell was wrong with his mother? Zach needed to steer things in a different direction. He looked at Phoebe, hoping she might inspire conversation. She was sucking in her cheeks and had her arm outstretched, phone in hand.

"The lighting here sucks," she said, now swiping furiously with her index finger. Zach looked up at the ceiling. About a quarter of the bulbs in the dining room were burned out, and the crystal chandelier hadn't worked for years. "None of the filters are helping."

He tried his luck with Michael.

"How do you like Harvard?" he asked. "You just finished sophomore year, right?"

"I love it," Michael said. "I'm in a new play. We're going to perform this summer in Cambridge. A bunch of the drama majors got together and rented a black box theater in Harvard Square. We're doing *The Boys in the Band.*"

"That's great, Michael," Aimee said. "You'll have to send us a recording." Finally, his mother seemed to be returning to herself and had switched to water.

"Your father said you were majoring in economics," Fanny said.

"I changed," Michael said, fumbling with the wrapper from his bar.

"Well, I don't see how being a drama major will help you find employment," Fanny said, jabbing Amos with her elbow. "What happened to law school?"

"I want to be an actor, Grandma. So being a drama major should be pretty useful," Michael said. He spontaneously did an aggressive version of jazz hands, which made Maddie and Phoebe laugh while confusing everyone else.

"An actor?" Amos asked. "Since when do you have talent?"

"He comes alive onstage," Phoebe said, looking up from her phone.

"Thank you, sis," Michael said. "And may I say that your post about inversion therapy was just divine?"

Phoebe hopped up from the table and did a spontaneous head-stand. Her pants, sheer and loose, fell past her knees and revealed a large cactus tattoo above her right ankle. Why a cactus, Zach had no clue, but it was cool. Maybe he should get a tattoo. But what? Whatever he chose would be lame like a month later.

"Another tattoo?" Amos asked, leaning back to put in eye-drops. "Phoebe, why are you treating your body like it's a canvas? You want to do art? I'll buy you some crayons."

"Do your parents know about this . . . this . . . plant on your leg?" Fanny asked, palming her cheeks like the kid in *Home Alone*. "We need to call Peter."

"Dunno," Phoebe said, plopping back in her seat. "If they follow my Insta, then yeah."

"Should we, um, talk about the offer?" Zach asked. It didn't feel like it was his place to bring it up, but it was really weird no one had mentioned the whole reason they were together.

"You mean the hideous casino company that wants to destroy our ancestral home?" Grandma Louise said, dabbing at the corners of her mouth with a napkin. "Benny is rolling in his grave."

Ancestral? Hadn't his grandfather built it from scratch in 1960?

"They may not raze everything," Amos said. "The golf club-house is new. Wasn't that countertop stone imported from Italy, Brian?"

"Does anyone else think it's weird that 'raise' and 'raze' sound the same but kind of mean the opposite?" Michael asked.

Zach appreciated Michael's attempt at levity but seriously questioned his timing. That could be a bit of a problem for an actor.

Fortunately, George swept in at that moment with another heaping tray.

"Chef Joe wants you to try his new kugel recipe. He's always innovating in the kitchen," the head waiter said, doling out small plates with square wedges of kugel on them.

Brian looked down at his piece, jiggly in the center and burned at the edges. "What's different about this?" he asked.

"Normally it's just apple cinnamon. Chef added raisins!"

"It's delicious," Fanny said with a mouthful.

"How much are they offering again?" Zach asked. "Do we have a term sheet to review?"

When everyone just stared back, he added, "What?" and shrugged his shoulders. "I took some business classes in college."

"Sweet," Phoebe said, and snapped a picture of him.

Chapter Seven

Brian

Brian awoke Sunday morning in Angela's bed with a jolt. He didn't normally wake feeling anxious. If anything, it was the opposite. He tended to leisurely let his eyes flop open, then work his body through a series of relaxing stretches. Finally, he'd swing his feet to the ground and make for the coffee machine. He almost never set an alarm.

Angela had to be at work for the breakfast shift most days, so she served as his wake-up call on the nights he spent at her place. After she left, he'd usually flip open his laptop and search through his favorite porn site for new posts. Angela satisfied him—she was pretty adventurous and rarely said no—but there was something deeply satisfying about going it alone, especially in the mornings when he had the place to himself. But this morning, he was out of bed before seven, drinking coffee and without giving porn a passing thought.

Dinner the prior evening had not been enjoyable. He'd missed having his brother there, even if his absence had come as no surprise. Peter worked himself to the bone in a soulless corporate tower all day and night. To what end, Brian couldn't understand. To gift Greta another handbag made from an endangered species? The last time she'd been at the hotel, his sister-in-law had made a stink about the uneven cobblestone paths that connected the buildings because she'd said they were ruining her Louboutins—his niece had told him those red-soled shoes cost more than a thousand dollars a pop. When Brian had heard that, all he could think was that each pair could make a sizable improvement to the health care plans they offered their employees. Or combined, assuming she was the Imelda Marcos of New Jersey, the money could mean a new swimming pool. The floor of the existing pool was so rough and gravelly, the hotel medic was routinely called to remove chunks of plaster from bare feet. Brian knew it wasn't his twin's job to subsidize the hotel, but he couldn't help fantasizing about all the ways Peter's money could improve the Golden.

At the very least, Brian was glad that Peter had sent his children. Phoebe was as millennial as they came, but at least she was cashing in on her egocentricity. And Michael, he was such a smart, quiet boy—Brian yearned to know him better. The actor announcement had come as a shock to him, and apparently to everyone else, too. What else did they not realize? Fanny used every opportunity to work the dining room at the Golden to find matches for her grandchildren, and she certainly wasn't asking any of the guests if they had any nice boys for Michael. Even the wheelchair didn't slow her down. The night before, she'd rolled up to several tables inquiring about single girls, even after Michael had mentioned that he'd gone into New York to see *Angels in America* on Broadway three times.

Brian thought the stroke might have rejiggered Fanny's brain chemistry, but having a brush with death had made her even more intent on seeing her family settled. And not just settled, but settled in the way becoming of a Weingold: married (to someone of the opposite gender), proper job (one that required an advanced degree, preferably), nice house (minimum one acre of land in a fashionable suburb). He tried to cut his mother some slack, especially in her present condition. It pained him to watch how cumbersome her movements were, the clunky and inelegant way she moved around the place that used to feel like a second skin. Still, he wished she would relax. Times were changing, and she wasn't on board.

Having his father around was a mixed bag. With his parents spending more time in Florida, Brian finally felt a genuine independence in leadership that simply couldn't manifest under his father's watchful eye. Yesterday, in the presence of Amos, he hadn't been able to escape the scepter of judgment. Amos had asked him why he wasn't booking midweek entertainment. Brian had seen Amos chastise the waiters for not refolding the napkins when a guest went to the restroom. He'd spotted his father studying the daily list of activities with a critical eye. Having his parents back on campus was eroding his confidence. And what had he been thinking with that menu last night? His parents didn't eat like they used to—they were on low-sugar, low-salt diets, and the kids wouldn't touch anything that wasn't triple-certified organic. Popular hotels were serving farm-to-table cauliflower "steaks" and farm-raised branzino with sautéed kale in malted beer jus. At the Golden, they were adding raisins.

Officially, Amos and Benny had given Brian the run of the place ten years ago, a titular shift at first. Chief Executive Officer had been slapped into his email signature, with little else changing. But gradually they'd allowed more slack on the rope. Brian had developed a feel for hotel management and didn't shy away from those innovations he could get Benny and Amos to approve. Still, the hotel had faltered.

So much of the decline of the Golden had been out of Brian's control, and had started long before he took over. It was the three A's that had sunk the Catskills, reporters and historians said. First came air-conditioning. With AC available in the city, urban dwellers didn't feel the need to flee to the mountains in the summer. Then came air travel, which was constantly getting cheaper. Just last night, Brian had gotten a pop-up ad on his phone advertising a $69 flight to Iceland, a stunning Nordic blonde beckoning him to the Blue Lagoon. That was certainly a more exotic way to cool off in the summer than a visit to the Catskills. Finally, there was assimilation. Jews were no longer forced to barricade themselves into the hotels that welcomed them.

Brian had been so exhausted by the evening's end that he'd virtually crawled into Angela's bed and let her pat his head gently until he'd fallen asleep.

"Family will do that to you," she'd said when he'd come into her condo bleary-eyed.

Now she was at work, and Brian contemplated the day ahead. The first official meeting of the families was due to start in a couple hours. Dinner had been a warm-up, and not an auspicious one. He reached for his cell phone and found a message from Howard, the president of Diamond Enterprises, the holding company that controlled Winwood Casinos. *What now?* Brian thought. Howard knew the families were meeting this week. And he'd promised they had until Labor Day to make a final decision.

Nobody knew this, but Howard had approached Brian a full three weeks before he'd shared the offer with his family and the Goldmans. He'd told himself it was because he needed to run numbers, that when he presented the offer, he wanted to have answers to the obvious questions: Is the purchase price fair? What will the profits be after taxes? Should we seek out other buyers? But the thinly veiled truth was that Brian just couldn't face what he perceived as the inevitable. He was going to lose his job and the only home he'd known since he'd found Melinda in bed with another man. Running the hotel had saved him, even if it felt sometimes like he was captaining the *Titanic*. When he thought of moving into the future without the hotel scaffolding him, he got weak in the knees. In the back of his head, he thought how much easier it would be if he had just told Howard "thanks but no thanks" and gone on with his life. Nobody had needed to know.

Because there were still times, on sunny days when the pool rippled in the breeze and the lawn shone verdant, that he brimmed with hope. At closing time, once he was done reviewing payroll and meeting with the dining captain and the head of the maintenance crew and he'd approved yet another room rate reduction, Brian would sit in the swivel chair in his office and prop his feet on the desk. In that comfortable position, he imagined scenarios where the hotel became the vibrant, bustling center of culture and amusement it had once been. The problem was that he wasn't sure how to get from point A to point B; he had a million ideas and no clue about execution. The interns from Cornell were good, especially Lucy. But as quickly as they arrived, they were gone, and Brian was left alone to follow through on their "action items" lists and stare at their "inspiration boards."

The voice mail from Howard asked that he call back immediately. Damn. He hadn't even had coffee yet.

"Brian, the dillydallying about our offer's gotta come to an end," Howard said by way of greeting. His Southern drawl made it sound like their negotiations would end with a saloon duel. "We've located another property nearby that will suit our purposes just fine. Now, we like the history of y'all's place. And I gotta say, there's something real nice about turning gold into a diamond, but y'all gotta be ready to play. This other site is mighty nice. Same acreage. And we don't need to bulldoze any structures."

"Bulldoze." Did Howard need to choose such a visceral word? How about "renovate" or "remodel," to soft-pedal it? It almost made Brian want to tell him to take the offer and shove it up his cowboy hat, but it wasn't his decision to make alone, not once he'd let the cat out of the bag.

"So what does that mean, exactly?" Brian asked. "You know I said we have a complicated ownership structure and would need time to discuss. You said we could have the summer to think things over. I said by Labor Day—"

"I'm a man of my word, Bri. But the situation has changed. Y'all have five days to decide. I'll need an answer by Friday or we're going to buy the other property," Howard said.

Brian was left holding the phone in shock. He had to tell everyone that a decision would need to be reached in five days. The fate of sixty years of history condensed into a five-day discussion. It was unthinkable, and yet it was reality. Brian had thought that even if they decided together to sell at the end of this week, a successful season could unseal the decision. If the reservations picked up, if Brian could get Seinfeld back, if, if, if . . . So many ifs, and with every one came a glimmer of hope. Now it was futile to even consider a turnaround. Friday. Damn, that was soon.

He climbed out of bed and reached for his wrinkled button-down from the night before, wishing he'd had the foresight to keep a clean set of clothes at Angela's. Not that he needed to dress up for the meeting. The Golden wasn't run like a fancy corporation, operating documents housed in a corporate glass tower like where his brother worked. Ownership was simple, despite what he'd told Howard. The hotel had been owned fifty-fifty by Benny and Amos. When Benny had died, his stake had passed to Louise, with the understanding it would pass to Aimee eventually. There was the matter of the board, though. About ten years ago, a lawyer who was a frequent guest had caught wind of how informally the hotel was run and insisted he'd help set up a corporate governance structure. Under the terms created, a sale would need a sixty-six percent vote. All family members had been given board seats. Because Louise had inherited Benny's shares, she had two votes. Everyone else had one, including the grandkids. Brian prayed the decision would be reached via amiable discussion, though he could easily picture them lobbying for votes, forming alliances like contestants on *Survivor*. They'd had minor scrapes along the way, but the two families had coexisted without a single lawsuit. Even the July Fourth dustup from years back had been swept under the rug out of respect for the deep friendship between Benny and Amos. With Benny gone, the balance of power was at its most fragile.

Their last "reunion" had been at Benny's funeral. After the

burial, both families had settled in the cocktail lounge and reminisced for hours. Each Benny story begat another, and it had been nearly sunrise when they'd parted ways. This gathering had a different character. For one thing, Peter wasn't there. His niece and nephew appeared uninterested (maybe he shouldn't have fixed the Wi-Fi), Louise was tense, and Aimee seemed distracted, bordering on distraught.

What *was* wrong with Aimee Goldman that she was chewing furiously on a hangnail and her knee was shaking so hard that she'd rattled the dinner table the night before? A flush had filled her cheeks every time he'd spoken to her. It was the same reaction he remembered from their childhood. A young Aimee had tried to hide her crush on him, very deliberately looking between him and Peter in even increments, making sure she alternated whom she sat next to, but it was obvious nonetheless.

Was she still reeling from her father's death? Worried about her kids? Maybe it was the potential loss of the hotel. The three of them, Peter, Aimee, and himself, had been the princes and princess of the empire back in the day. They'd always believed themselves to be special.

More likely, with her lavish lifestyle, Aimee considered the hotel a waste of her efforts. Why bother with the shabby inn beyond hope?

No matter which way she was leaning, it was still surreal. Each time a peer hotel was leveled, it was like learning an acquaintance had cancer. You paused, you took notice, you expressed pity, but you never thought for more than a fleeting second that it could have anything to do with you.

But how could they fool themselves into invincibility when the reviews told a very different story?

COMMENT CARD—JULY 6, 1967

Dear Benny, Amos, Louise, and Fanny:

We cannot thank you enough for a most marvelous stay! From the 4th of July fireworks, the comedy evening (that one about the rabbi and the monk . . . still cracking up!), the show tunes evening, the sumptuous meals (must get Chef Joe to give up his brisket recipe!), to the campfire sing-a-long, we couldn't have asked for a more special time for our family. We love the new billiard lounge and card room. There's no place like the Golden in our book! We'll be back to close out the season. Harvey and I are getting in shape for the Gold Rush, though we know we don't stand a chance! Another superb vacation for the Heller clan.

Fondly,

Harvey, Barbara, Jenny, and Sammy Heller

P.S.—Fan, see you at the Temple Beth Am canasta tournament!

COMMENT CARD—AUGUST 1, 1983

Dear Weingolds and Goldmans,

What a lovely stay we had at the hotel. This is our tenth summer, as you surely know. The food was bountiful as always. We are returning home in elastic pants. The father-son tennis tournament was a lot of fun and our daughter really enjoyed the mah-jongg for teens evening. As we love the Golden dearly, we thought it might be worthwhile to pass on a few (minor!) suggestions. Consider some lighter options in the dining room. The rooms would also benefit from

a refresher. Our kids would have loved more offerings on the
television than the five local channels and the bathtub was a tad
grimier than we would have liked. See you next summer! Unless
Barry wins salesman of the year—then we're headed to Costa Rica all
expenses paid!
    Fondly,
    The Millers

WWW.TRIPCRITIC.COM

August 22, 2020

THE GOLDEN HOTEL, Windsor, NY (6,902 reviews)

Service: ★ ★

Property: ★ ★

Overall Experience: ★ ★

How likely are you to recommend this Golden on a scale
of 1-10?   3

    We were truly disappointed with our stay at this
hotel. Upon arrival, we found the bellman asleep on a
luggage cart and had to lug our own bags. Our
reservation couldn't be found because the computer
system was down. The "concierge" handed us an
activity sheet at least two decades old. The water
pressure in our shower was barely a drizzle and the
sheets gave our youngest child a rash. The website
advertises an ice-skating rink and ten har-tru tennis
courts, but we found both closed with dubious

"under renovation" signs on them. Our families have spent many summers at the Golden Hotel and we were excited to return after a ten-year hiatus, but this has been a real letdown.

The Stein-Waltmans

Chapter Eight

Louise

In their Central Park West apartment, Louise and Benny had slept in different bedrooms since the day Aimee had moved out. Benny snored loudly, which was the prime reason Louise suggested he take over the guest room, but there was more to it. On the surface, they were the perfect couple, the host and hostess with the mostest. But they had their share of issues.

When she and Benny needed to have it out, which was far more often than their public faces let on, they told Aimee they were going for a walk. Their daughter was sensitive and a worrier—it came with being artistic. And Louise was acutely aware that Aimee didn't have a sibling to turn to, the way she did with her brothers when their parents fought. In their building's back alley, shielded by the ambient noise of the city, they would brawl. Louise knew about the women who threw themselves at Benny; she was less sure how tough his resolve was. She didn't like the way the color girl in the salon looked at him, fingering his grays and encouraging him to stop by for a "touch-up." These flirtations were among the top sources of their fights, and Louise might have pushed harder if she didn't have secrets of her own.

Sleeping apart from Benny was never necessary at the Golden, even after Aimee became Mrs. Roger Glasser and moved her things to a permanent suite in the main building. Louise chalked it up to the mountain air. The breeze cascading through the open windows and the crispness that could only be found in the Catskills lulled her into a stupor that Benny's orchestral blasts couldn't shatter. But even if Benny had sounded like a trumpet all night and she couldn't sleep a wink, she wouldn't have slept apart from him at the Golden, where rumors swirled like honey in tea.

Louise's generation cared about keeping up appearances. Nowadays, women were running around in yoga pants and no makeup—and they were deemed "brave" for it. Couples were sharing bedroom problems with their friends. Social media made privacy a relic. She didn't understand the need to break down these barriers, and she never would, no matter how many times the grandchildren tried to convince her otherwise. "Get Facebook, Gram," they would badger her. Why? So she could look up all the women who used to throw themselves at Benny? So she could feel bad about the way her sagging chin looked in photographs? No thank you.

Unfortunately, the mountain air had not worked its usual magic last night. She'd kept reaching for Benny in the dark, her hand meeting only emptiness and cool, dry sheets. She had been forced to dip into her emergency stash of Klonopin in order to rest. She felt her husband's absence the most acutely when she was at the hotel. He was like a ghost that haunted every inch of the place, and she had stayed away since the funeral.

A Canada warbler beat its wing against her windowsill. Louise studied its beautiful body. It was a common sighting in their neck of the mountains, but the bird always made Louise smile. Benny had once said its feathery coat reminded him of her. Its top half, the backside, was a beautiful gray, but the bird had a stunning bright yellow color stretched across its belly. Under its neck were a series of spots resembling a necklace of pearls. "Like you, Weezee." He'd sometimes called her that. "Elegant fur coat on the outside, bright dress underneath. And jewelry." She watched mournfully as the bird flew away.

Louise couldn't believe she'd accepted a date with Walter Cole a few days earlier. She was in no state to entertain suitors. Walter was a widower who lived three floors below her in the San Remo, and she'd caught his desiring eye the moment Benny had arrived back from the hospital with a full-time attendant at his side. While once Louise had criticized the widows and widowers who swarmed like flies at a shiva, she had more empathy after Benny's passing. Loneliness was a shadow. Sometimes it loomed large, other times small, but it was impossible to shed entirely unless you submitted to total darkness. But being back in the hotel solidified for her that she wasn't ready. She had to call Walter and put off the date. He probably didn't even like her. Just wanted a nurse with a purse, like all the other geezers.

She stood in front of her closet and pondered what to wear to the morning meeting. It was Sunday, Father's Day, and while they would be meeting in the boardroom, she knew she ought to sweep through the main dining room and wish her best to the families that were still choosing the Golden to celebrate holidays and special occasions. She selected an ivory linen dress and topped it with a thick coral necklace. She had a matching lipstick that would complement it perfectly and beige wedge heels that were forgiving of her bunions. Louise believed firmly that the minute she refused to wear heels, it was all over. She might as well check herself into an old-age home and eat dinner at 4:30 p.m. To think Aimee flitted through life in flats. She wasn't even tall, and her calves could use elongating. And what about Maddie? She was in sneakers. Sparkly, ridiculous-looking high-tops in the main dining room last night. Louise hoped Aimee had the sense to make sure Maddie never appeared so casual and sloppy in front of her future in-laws. She remembered fondly searching for the perfect ribbons for Aimee's every outfit and combing her hair until it shone.

When Maddie was born, Louise had been so happy the baby was a girl. "There's nothing like a daughter," she'd whispered to Aimee, holding her granddaughter in her arms for the first time. Aimee, in the fog of anesthesia, had said, "Yes. But I'm definitely having more kids. Would hate if she had to be an only child." The comment sliced Louise regularly.

She went to the mirror to apply her makeup, checking the time on the thin gold watch that Benny had given her on the thirtieth anniversary of the hotel's opening. It was a sign of how much he'd cared about the place that they'd tended to celebrate the hotel's milestones before their own. A common joke, one that had sometimes hit too close to home, was that Benny had been having an affair—with the Golden. If he'd bought his "girlfriend" something special, like a new roof over the sports pavilion, then he'd have to buy something even nicer for Louise to assuage his guilt. That was what accounted for the bulk of her jewelry collection, every gemstone and link of precious metal correlating to another facilities improvement.

She applied the last of her face, trying not to dwell on how long it took her to be presentable. Each decade was good for another ten minutes in front of the mirror, another millimeter of pancake. If she made it to ninety, she might as well not plan anything before lunchtime. She had thought by now she'd relax her aesthetic standards, maybe take a page from Fanny's book; Fanny rarely bothered with more than lipstick, even at special events. But even as Louise's liver spots multiplied and her veins bloomed to the surface, she refused to leave the house without rouge and her hair set in its signature waves. She rejected the platters of dessert ordered "for the table" and stuck to berries. If she could maintain dignity with cosmetic products and a lean diet, Louise considered herself one of the lucky ones.

Content with her appearance, she stepped outside into the sunshine and set out on the path toward the main building. She did her best to record the dilapidation, to study the ways the Golden had lost its luster. But it was true what they said—it was hard to see your own hunchback. The hotel was so bound up in her conscience, and her memories of summers there so vivid, that she simply couldn't see the changes. Sure, she saw that the guest book on the check-in counter was only a quarter full, but somehow it didn't register past the superficial part of her brain. The part of her brain where feelings were stored could still see a guest book torn at the seams from overuse, overflowing with "best place on earth" messages.

Aimee, though. She would rely on her daughter to be her eyes. Aimee, who was attached to the hotel, but not with the same fierceness. She could see its flaws. The grandchildren, too, but Louise wasn't particularly interested in their criticism. Zach was wearing a T-shirt with Che Guevara on it, though Louise doubted he knew who he was. Or at least she hoped he didn't; not that she intended to get into a political debate with the boy who'd needed an extra year to complete a geography degree and who probably couldn't find Cuba on a map. Though he had given them all a shock when he'd inquired about the business terms of the offer. That was more than Maddie had had to offer. She had blathered on about mothballs for most of the evening.

"Sweetheart, I was just thinking about you," Louise said when she bumped into her daughter in the corridor leading to the boardroom. To her surprise, Aimee had traded last night's flats for a kitten heel, and she looked rosy for the morning summit. Was that bronzer on her cheekbones? *Bravo*, Louise wanted to say. Aimee's dress was a black cotton with a small daisy design, belted at the waist, a modern take on an older silhouette. She was happy to see a return in fashion to celebrating feminine curves. Those androgynous outfits some women wore . . . they made Louise shudder. Imagine, a woman wearing a tuxedo to the Oscars and all the critics cheering her on! Unthinkable, truly. Andy the Blouse Man, who came to the hotel on Tuesdays, was the person who had first taught Louise the importance of cinching at the waist. He taught many of the women at the hotel about a heck of a lot more than just fit. When his trailer door was shut, it signaled a "private showing" to a good customer.

"What's wrong with my outfit?" Aimee asked. She looked over her shoulder as if checking for a trail of toilet paper.

"Nothing," Louise said. "You look lovely."

Aimee seemed distrustful. "Oh, um, thank you. So do you."

Why did her daughter automatically assume she was being critical? If she studied Aimee's appearance for a beat too long, analyzing her hair color, pondering her chin cleft, well, she had her reasons. And they weren't close to what Aimee thought they were. Historically, Aimee had whined that Louise could only find her faults. They had had one particularly brutal blowout at one of Aimee's art shows. She'd been exhibiting her paintings at the 92nd Street Y, and Louise had been horrified to see that Aimee hadn't brushed her hair for the event. Louise had yanked Aimee into the bathroom and done the best she could with the pocket comb she carried everywhere, all while Aimee sobbed that she was hurting her. It had taken weeks for the two of them to move past that incident. But was it not a mother's job to help a child look their best? She'd paid for the fancy private school so that Aimee could get the finest education. She'd researched tennis instructors and found the best speech therapist so that Aimee didn't choke on her L's, so why was helping with her appearance off-limits? Nobody else would tell Aimee if she had lipstick on her teeth or if her bra straps were showing. People were jealous of them. They were the Goldmans. If they didn't look out for one another, no one would.

"How's Roger?" Louise asked. They were outside the closed

boardroom door. She felt sorry he'd been abandoned over Father's Day weekend, though she appreciated her daughter putting Goldman business first. Aimee, like so many children of her generation, could view family obligations a little too à la carte.

"Why do you ask?" Aimee said.

"I ask because he's your husband and the father of your children, and it's Father's Day and he's home alone with a stomach bug." Goodness, Aimee could be so up in the clouds.

"Oh. He's fine. Feeling much better. The kids will call him later. Shall we go in?"

"Yes, in a second. Any news on . . . ?" Louise tapped Aimee's ring finger, where she wore her much-upgraded engagement ring.

"Huh?" Aimee asked. "Oh, you mean Maddie. I think soon. Certainly she hopes so."

"Well, all right, then. Gown shopping will be upon us," Louise said.

"Probably not. Kids these days don't do the whole black-tie wedding bit all that often. I mean, the Hoffs are showy, but even with that, I doubt you'll need a gown. Let's not jinx it, anyway."

"You're right. Pooh pooh," Louise said, pretending to spit. "It can get muddy up here, and a gown could get destroyed." She observed her daughter's raised eyebrow. "I know what you're thinking. Maddie isn't getting married here if we don't own the hotel anymore."

"Maman, Maddie isn't getting married here even if we still own the hotel," Aimee said, putting a patronizing hand on Louise's elbow. What did her daughter mean by that? Why wouldn't Maddie want to get married on a sprawling, majestic property that her family owned? Only a chosen few were lucky enough to even have such an opportunity.

She would never understand kids these days.

The boardroom was freezing when they entered. Brian was against the far wall, fiddling with the thermostat. Louise tightened the cardigan around her shoulders.

"Morning, Louise. Morning, Aimee," he called out to them. "Sit anywhere around the table. I thought we'd keep things casual."

"Good morning, Brian," Aimee said softly, tucking a strand of hair behind her ear and smiling coquettishly. Louise appraised her daughter's dress and heels again anew. Aha. The four-decade infatuation lived on.

"Fanny, Amos," Louise said formally, and took a seat across from them. She gestured for Aimee to sit next to her. She preferred a two-against-two setup.

Fanny's chair made her sit taller than the rest of them. Louise wondered if that made her uncomfortable, or if she liked having a presence. After Fanny's stroke, Louise had sent flowers and a Zabar's platter over to the Weingolds, and visited a few times. Fanny's body was paralyzed on the left side from the waist down. Still everyone kept saying how lucky she was. Louise marveled at Fanny's positive attitude, with a sinking feeling that she wouldn't handle things nearly as well if the stroke had befallen her. Fanny would never dance in the Golden ballroom again or stand in photographs next to the talent. She wouldn't walk down the aisle at her grandchildren's weddings. And yet she seemed so grateful to have made it through the stroke with her mental faculties intact.

It had made Louise envy Fanny, and not for the first time. "I can still play mah-jongg and canasta," Fanny had said, her face forming a smile that was bookended with two deep dimples. Those dimples, deep ravines, were the only physical trait she had passed on to Brian. They made her look youthful, even as she sat in a wheelchair, silver hair hanging limply over her eyeglasses.

"Morning, Louise," Fanny said. "Aren't you all dolled up for this?"

Louise grimaced. She hated digs masked as compliments.

"Sleep all right?" Amos asked. What was making him ask that? Hopefully she'd remembered to put concealer in her handbag.

"Not too bad. I do not like the new sheets at all," she said, unable to resist the jab at Brian's management. "Where are the children?"

She wasn't in the mood to waste time with pleasantries, discussing whether the hydrangeas would bloom in blue or white this year. Not a single member of the third generation had arrived, and it was twenty past ten.

"Um, let me text mine," Aimee said, fishing for her phone just as Zach and Maddie stumbled in together.

"Everything all right, darlings?" Louise asked, hoping they noticed her deliberate clip.

"Yeah, why?" Maddie asked. "We're on time."

No, you're not. But Louise held her tongue. Because at least her grandkids had beat the Weingold kids.

"I think we can start," Brian said. "I'm sure Peter's kids will be along shortly."

"We're here, we're here," Phoebe said, bursting into the room with Michael behind her. They were both red-faced and panting, dressed in athletic clothing.

"We went for a jog," Michael explained, removing a sweat-band. In her lycra, Phoebe physically resembled the hotel's long-gone aerobics instructor, Jenni. "Stick out your tail," Jenni would say in class, singling out Louise, who could never seem to master a butt-blaster. Jenni had no trouble sticking out her own tail. That woman had used the straddle stretch for more than just her muscles, leading to her eventual termination after Glenda Perl found Jenni "lunging" with her husband, Sam Perl.

"It was so beautiful. I, like, totally forgot how gorgeous it is up here," Phoebe said, plopping into a seat next to her grand-mother and planting a kiss on Fanny's cheek. The familiar flare of jealousy bloomed in Louise's chest. Why didn't Maddie and Zach hug her? She knew she had a formal carriage—they'd called her Grammy Fancy when they were little—but that didn't mean she didn't want to squeeze their cheeks.

"I'll go with you next time, Phoebe," Zach said.

"I bet you will," Maddie chimed in with a smirk.

"Now that we've all discussed our exercise plans," Brian said amiably, "why don't we get down to business?" He passed out pack-ets. Louise took hers half-heartedly. The cover page said ABOUT DI-AMOND ENTERPRISES. She didn't care a fig about Diamond Enterprises and its management team. The CEO, Howard, looked like a buffoon with that silly bolo tie. The hotel was either going to remain in their families or be sold. This wasn't like giving a dog away and making sure you were passing your pet on to a good home. If the Golden was sold, that would be the end of it. She hated to think of it becoming a casino—especially since she had watched her family's coffers drained in the underground card rooms of Montreal. Gambling was such an ugly business. Louise's stomach would turn when she saw the men playing bridge for money in the card room. It brought back the worst memories of her mother crying at the kitchen table, begging her husband to stop. "Think of Louise," she would moan in French. "Think of Louise."

She feigned interest while everyone else started to leaf through the packets. Underneath the one about the buyer was a thicker packet with graphs and spreadsheets that made her head spin. She had a nose for business, but it was less informed by calculations than driven by an innate sense of what worked and what didn't. She trusted her instincts over any calculator. Benny had been like that, too. Amos was the stickler for running numbers. All science and no art, that man. What business did he have in hospitality?

"You'll see lots of important figures in the second packet. Our occupancy rates over the last five years, operating expenses, marketing budget, demographics. It's a lot to take in, and I don't think this first meeting is the time to make any decisions. We should be talking, asking questions, seeing what page everyone is on," Brian said.

"Thank you, Brian," Aimee called out. "This all looks very useful."

"I have an email from Peter that came in last night," Brian said. "I thought I would read it out loud." When no one answered, Brian produced a folded piece of paper from his pocket.

To All—

I have had some associates at my firm pull some numbers and I think we can ask Diamond to come up to fourteen million reasonably. Can share my data if needed.

Yours,

Peter

"So I guess that's a vote to sell?" Aimee said.

"Not necessarily," Amos said sharply. "I think Peter is just saying we should get a better offer before we decide."

"Well, if he could have made the time to be here, we would know what he wanted," Louise said, her hands fluttering to her mouth. She was normally composed to a fault. Her mother had schooled her that way. Even when their family had had to give up their six-bedroom house in Westmount and move to the third floor of a triplex in Côte Saint-Luc, Celine Frankfurter had scavenged thrift shops to dress Louise in fine frocks and would give her a good slap across the cheek if she saw her using the wrong fork or forgetting to lay a napkin on her lap. But the Weingolds could unhinge her, unleashing a sharp tongue she normally kept in check.

"Peter runs one of the biggest law firms in Manhattan," Fanny said predictably. As if to threaten Louise, she rolled her chair closer to the table so she could rest her fists on it. Unmanicured nails, naturally. And there was a salon in the hotel, where owners received treatments without charge.

"Guys, chill," Michael said. "I've been in touch with my dad, too. He's on it. We're all in this together. Let's take a moment and breathe."

"Are we just thinking sell or keep, or are we also thinking of ways to cut costs and change things up?" Maddie asked. Louise gave her an approving nod. "I mean, when Hoff Global is looking at a company, Andrew's family doesn't just think about whether they can sell it or—"

"Exploit the workers and get richer?" Zach asked. Phoebe laughed, apparently multitasking as she typed furiously on her phone. The nerve of that kid. She had her dirty sneaker propped up against the table.

"Shut up," Maddie said, obviously kicking her brother under the table, because Zach jolted and shouted, "Ouch, Fattie." It was his cruel former nickname for his older sister—"Fattie Maddie."

"Mom!" Maddie.

"Mom!" Zach.

Aimee was staring out the window. A sliver of mountain was visible through the gap in the curtains. Louise remembered choosing the taupe damask from which all the curtains at the hotel were made, nearly six decades earlier.

"Aimee!" Louise said, waving a hand in front of her daughter's face. "Your children are about to kill each other. You might want to chime in."

"Sorry, sorry. Kids, knock it off. I mean it. Brian, what are your thoughts? You know this place on a day-to-day basis better than any of us. Is there a chance we can turn things around?"

"Well, I have thought of several measures that could help our bottom line." He shuffled through his papers. "We could switch to silk flowers on the dining tables. We spend approximately two thousand each week on arrangements."

"Ralph counts on our business. This would kill him. Benny was very close to him, too," Amos said, knowing that bringing up Benny would earn Louise's sympathy vote. But she was already against Brian's suggestion. Fake flowers were gaudy. What would come next, plastic cutlery?

"I have other ideas," Brian said. "We could cut out afternoon tea service and save on labor and food."

"No!" said Louise, Amos, and Fanny in unison. Food was at

the heart of the Catskills hotel experience. Most guests would rather give up their pillow than a meal.

"I have a thought," Aimee said, hunched forward on her elbows. Louise hated when Aimee slouched. "Why don't we cut back on some of the free programming? It seems reasonable to charge for the dance and canasta lessons."

Brian nodded. "I like that. Since when is anything free these days?"

Louise exchanged glances with her fellow senior statesmen. Their children just didn't get it. They were missing the beating heart of a Catskills summer. You put your wallet away and enjoyed, leaving behind the daily acts of commerce in the city, along with the traffic and smog. She hoped Amos or Fanny would speak up so she wouldn't have to contradict her own daughter, but Fanny was now crocheting some hideous scarf, and Amos was twirling his pencil in circles.

"No offense," Phoebe said, though it was obvious something offensive was coming. The air-conditioning kicked on, and she waited patiently for the rattle to quiet before continuing. Zach was staring at her in wonder, waiting to receive whatever pearls she meant to impart, like Moses receiving the Ten Commandments. "But all these ideas suck. You'll save some money but just piss off the guests. You're putting a Band-Aid on things instead of making real changes. Like this brand I did a project for, RePoached—they sell water bottles made out of elephant tusks that have been confiscated from poachers and then donate the—"

"Honey," Fanny said gently. "We all appreciate you taking an interest in the hotel, but we have to make a very important decision, and time is of the essence."

Since the stroke, Fanny's speech had borne remnants of the brain trauma, and she pronounced "decision" like "decishin" and "essence" like "eshensh." Louise wanted to strangle her grand-children when she saw them stifling giggles.

"Mom, let's hear her out," Brian said, pushing his papers aside.

"Thanks, Uncle Brian," Phoebe said, crisscrossing her legs on the chair. "As I was saying, these water bottles just weren't selling well no matter what they tried, even with me as the brand ambassador. And then one day it occurred to them: They should add insulation and sell them as green juice thermoses."

"Meaning?" Amos asked, his patience visibly wearing thin.

"Meaning you need bigger changes. You need to be hip and modern, and seriously, the Golden needs to be at least remotely cool. No offense, but nobody young would come here if they weren't forced. It's like a place you get dragged to by your grand-parents. But, like, with some major changes, this place could to-tally be a hipster paradise with a waiting list for a room."

"She could be on to something," Brian said. "There have been articles recently about the Catskills being in vogue again. The small changes aren't going to add up to a hill of beans when we're this much in the red. I mean, sure, we can change our laundry service or our soap supplier—"

"Speaking of soap, actually, there's a really cool bee pollen soap sold in my neighborhood that I think would be awesome to have in the guest rooms," Maddie said, eyes wide. It was refresh-ing for Louise to see her granddaughter enthused about some-thing that didn't start with the phrase "Andrew says."

"I love bee pollen facials," Michael said. Louise shuddered. She hated when men were precious about their appearance.

"That may be, but our guests hate bees," Amos said. "You know how much money Benny and I laid out to those damn exterminators over the years to get rid of wasp and hornet nests, and how many complaints we got about bees swarming the outdoor buffets? We're not *bringing* bees to the hotel."

"The bees won't be here, Grandpa. It's their pollen," Phoebe said, laughing. "You're so cute. Although . . . we could have an apiary."

"That sounds awesome," Zach added. He'd once had a girlfriend who was into stuff like that. Sheep's milk hand cream and beetle juice massage oil. She'd brought a whole basket of the stuff when she'd come to Louise's for dinner. *Ever heard of flowers?* Louise had wanted to ask, but instead she'd said, "Oh my, how lovely," and dumped the whole basket in the trash after the girl had left.

"Wait, OMG, I just had an even better idea," Phoebe said, now on her feet. She assumed a ridiculous pose where she had one arm stretched in front, the other in back, her knees in plié. "Two words: GOAT. YOGA."

"What?" everyone seemed to say at once.

"Here it is!" She presented her phone to the table.

"I see a woman contorting her body with a goat climbing on her back. Such things are expressly forbidden in the Bible," Amos said.

"This is a Jewish hotel!" Fanny was averting her eyes.

"On that note, actually, Andrew says that the Golden is way too—" Maddie started.

"What happens when the goat has to go to the bathroom?" Aimee asked, squinting at the screen.

"I'd try it," Zach said.

"I think we're maybe getting ahead of ourselves," Brian said sensibly. Louise looked at him thoughtfully. Why had she always thought he was a disappointment? Could it really be just that she was jealous Fanny had two children and Brian was so devastatingly handsome, it was hard for Louise to handle him being intelligent, too? Other people's misfortunes did have a way of boosting her just the slightest, of making her own struggles manageable.

"I do agree modernizing is a good idea," Brian said. "We can start by having a social media presence. I should have gotten on that ages ago. I'll ask Lucy."

"Already done," Phoebe said triumphantly. "I set up @Golden HotelCatskills yesterday on Instagram and Snapchat."

"And?" Amos asked. "Is that like the Facebook?"

Even Louise was embarrassed on behalf of her generation. "It's just Facebook," she said quietly. Walter had asked her out on Facebook actually, via a direct message.

"And it's off to a solid start. The Insta account has three thousand followers in the first twenty-four hours." Phoebe shrugged. "I know, I would have liked to hit 5k, too. I'll do a bikini shot at the pool and get us there."

A knock came at the door, and Otto poked his head in.

"Pardon the interruption," he said, folding himself into an awkward bow that nearly knocked the visor off his head. "Guests are lining up for the Father's Day brunch, and everyone is asking for the owners."

"Why don't we call it quits for now?" Amos said, standing.

"Actually, there's one more thing," Brian said. "I received a call from Howard Williams this morning. Diamond Enterprises is considering another property—a piece of land not far from here, probably part of the Ratzigers' farm. We have until Friday to make our decision."

"What?" Louise felt her chest tighten. "We need the summer to think this over. That's unreasonable."

Amos slapped his hand down on the table so hard, the water glasses shook.

"We're not just a piece of land. We have eighty thousand square feet of hotel property, spread out over ten buildings. We have tennis courts, a pool, ballrooms, a kitchen that can feed a thousand people at once. How can they compare us to a piece of land?"

Brian hated to have to say this to his father, the man who had designed every inch of this place, breaking his back bent over blueprints. He had gone hat in hand to bank after bank for construction loans and visited at least fifty other hotels to learn the business. He'd weathered lawsuits from slip-and-falls, suffered through two recession cycles, survived scandals that might have sunk another hotel, and still come out with a pulse.

"Dad, that's all we are to them. A piece of land. They're going to raze everything."

Nobody spoke for a moment. Even Phoebe put her phone down.

"Listen, I'm as sorry about this as anyone. But we now have only five days to decide the future of the Golden Hotel."

@GoldenHotelCatskills
Goat yoga, bee pollen facials, green juice smoothies,
and a zero-waste program might be coming your way.
Follow this account and tag three friends to enter to win
a chance for a free overnight stay at the sickest resort in
the Catskills.

Chapter Nine

Aimee

Aimee was searching for Zach and Maddie. After the meeting had broken up, she'd spent a couple of minutes talking to her mother, and when she'd turned her back, her children had vanished. She'd checked the recreation room, the pool, the golf clubhouse, the tennis courts, the half basketball court, even the library. There was no sign of either of her children, and the clock was ticking.

If the Glassers had been in Scarsdale for Father's Day, as planned, Aimee would be pulling a twice-baked French toast casserole out of the oven and stirring homemade lemonade. Roger would be whistling "The Star-Spangled Banner" or "America the Beautiful" in his armchair, an annoying habit of his that she'd ignore in deference to Father's Day, and the kids would be spread across the leather sofa watching *Master Chef* or its television programming opposite, *The Biggest Loser*. Their household would hum with merriment, laughter, and a few spats to keep them humble. The comforting smell of cinnamon swirled with vanilla would throw a warm cast over it all. She would have that tingly feeling she got when all five of them were under one roof. Instead, she was in the Catskills, with two-thirds of her children. Aimee suspected none of them had even remembered to call their father, even with the yellowed HAPPY FATHER'S DAY banner hanging over their heads in the lobby. She was still waiting for the self-centeredness of her children to reach its tipping point. Not that she hadn't helped them get there, making sure Marcia ironed Zach's boxers and shipping home-cooked meals packaged in dry ice to Scott once a month.

During the meeting, she'd made up her mind that she would remind the children to call Roger. No matter what, he was still their father. She'd believed him when he'd said he'd done what he'd done to make their family life better. What was impossible to reconcile was that he'd chosen to destroy other people's lives in order to better their own. She didn't want to accept that she'd married someone who could be that selfish or have the capacity for such egregious tunnel vision. Part of her attraction to Roger had been that he was a doctor, and not for the reasons that made the yentas at the Golden push their daughters toward the medical students working as waiters and bellboys. It was because he said things to her on dates like, "I've just always wanted to help people." When she'd inquired why he'd chosen internal medicine as a specialty, he'd said, "Because I want to treat the whole person." Roger had an answer for everything, and it was usually a confident one that made Aimee respect his self-assurance—not unlike the way Maddie looked at Andrew, she thought now, alarmingly.

Call your father, she texted the kids, and sank into a leather chair in the lobby that reminded her of the furniture in Roger's first medical office.

She recalled the day he'd signed the lease. The office in the town center hadn't been anything special, just a simple waiting room with dated furniture in 1960s orange and an exam room that barely fit a doctor, a nurse, and a patient at the same time. Roger would sometimes have bruises on his back from knocking into the medical scale. His first nurse, Caroline, was one of those pint-sized, perky women whom men adored. Button-nosed, naturally blond, and always with a tooth-bearing smile.

But Aimee had never genuinely worried about them getting into trouble together, even though Louise had had a fit when she'd gone to see Roger about a rash and met the pretty nurse. "I know my husband, Maman. He's not the type," Aimee had reassured Louise. "If you saw everything I've seen at the Golden, you might not be so sure," Louise had retorted. Aimee didn't know Roger at all, it turned out. Maybe it was impossible ever to know someone else, which made watching her daughter contemplate binding up her life with another person terrifying.

She and Roger had set up the office together, and when it was complete and they were exhausted and sweaty and dreaming of a cold glass of white wine as a reward, her husband had turned to her and said, "It's missing something." She'd immediately gone into caretaker mode, running through the mental checklist of what they'd thought he'd need: pens, paper, printer, computer, files, file cabinet, magazines, magazine rack. Check, check, check. It was all there.

"What?" She must have looked nervous, because Roger said, "Relax. It's nothing like that. I just feel like the walls could use something. Would you paint something that I can frame?"

"Oh, Roger, I'd love to. But I'm not a real artist," she'd said. "We can get you a photograph or something from a gallery that will look much better. I know a woman who can give us a good price on—"

He'd put his index finger to her lips. "I want something you make. You're talented. And even if you weren't, I want to see an Aimee Goldman-Glasser original every time I come into the office. Like at the Golden."

Behind the registration desk at the hotel hung one of her first paintings. It was a watercolor picture of the Golden's front lawn, the tree swing in the foreground. Roger loved it. Everyone who came to the hotel did. She had been about eight when she'd painted it, and had signed her name in bubble letters. "Paint the hotel again," Roger had requested, and he'd hung her much-improved version of the lawn in his waiting room. It was the first time she'd picked up a paintbrush in years, and she'd been surprised to find the strokes were familiar. Emerald green mixed with a dash of white had given her the exact color of the leaves she would pull from the trees; brown with traces of yellow had rendered the shade of the swing.

Goddamn you, Roger. He had so many good parts. He wasn't a straightforward villain like the bad guys in the superhero movies the boys had dragged her to when they were younger—the ones that had given them nightmares but still they'd insisted on seeing. But what he'd done was unforgivable. She couldn't stay with him. Could she? Maybe spouses overlooked all sorts of bad behavior. Her mother certainly alluded to plenty of antics in the Catskills that weren't aboveboard. The problem was that family secrets, the really bad ones, were kept under lock and key, and so it was impossible to measure just how bad hers was.

In private moments when she had time for more than a minute's reflection, she blamed herself for being in this predicament. If she hadn't fallen into the path of merry housewife and made her entire world about her husband and family, this would be less crushing. If she had pursued art meaningfully, or worked at the hotel more diligently, certainly she would feel more confident that she could navigate life without Roger. She hadn't really understood the working moms who came to school plays in high heels and were constantly checking BlackBerrys and dashing off. Now she envied their sense of self. These women were like earthworms. If you cut them in half, they would regrow the necessary parts to stay vital.

Aimee stood up and was walking toward the elevators when she heard Maddie's voice around the corridor.

"I feel like Andrew is upset with me that we're not together this weekend," her daughter was saying. "I mean, we do live together, but he has to go to Palm Beach a lot for work, so we're apart more than we'd like to be. But, like, Andrew really isn't into the Catskills. It's nothing personal. He just gets carsick easily. And when I told him that we wouldn't be seeing my dad this weekend, he said he really ought to go see his father. Mr. Hoff is getting honored by the hospital anyway Tuesday evening. I feel like I should be there. What do you think, Grand-mère?"

Grand-mère? Maddie turned on the French when she wanted Louise's approval. Since when were they so chummy? If Maddie was that put out about coming to the Golden, she could have just said so to Aimee directly.

"Of course, my love," came Louise's voice, gravelly with age but still strong enough that it carried clearly around the bend. "If you feel you need to be with Andrew, then go."

"But what about Mom? She said she really wants us here this week to help make the decision. It's about the future generations, blah blah blah. But, like, Phoebe had some smart things to say, much as it shocked me. And Zacky's here. I know he's not exactly a brain trust, but he does represent our interests. And apparently has taken a business class. Who knew?"

"I'll deal with your mother," Louise said. "You're going to be building a life with this young man. He has to be your priority. Pack your things, and I'll have Larry get you a car service back to the city. Then you can get down to Florida easily. Trust me, what happens to the Golden will mean nothing if you're not happily married. You need the stability that finding the right man can provide."

Maddie squealed as Aimee cringed. She held on to the wall for support.

"You're the best, Grandma! I'm going to get my things." A smooch sounded.

"You need the security that only a marriage can provide?" Aimee hissed at her mother, once she was sure she'd heard the elevator snap shut with her daughter inside. "Did I accidentally stumble into a time warp?"

"*Mon Dieu*, Aimee! Where did you come from?" Louise asked. "You're all flushed. I share your sentiment; this morning's meeting was startling. Five days—"

"I'm not flushed because of the—"

"I mean, Phoebe and her goats. Brian suggesting cutting back on food. I feel like I don't even know this place anymore, and I am sure your father is rolling in his grave. Anyway, I'm glad Brian cut the meeting when he did, because I have to get to the beauty parlor before my roots get any worse. My regular girl is gone, and I know I'm going to have to explain everything to the new gal."

Aimee inhaled sharply. Three counts in; four counts out. That's what the website she'd Googled had said to do when a panic attack was coming on.

"Maman, before we start talking about whether you should stick to Ravishing Red or experiment with Glamorous Ginger, I'd like to discuss you giving my daughter permission to leave the hotel to go see her boyfriend in Florida without even checking with me."

Louise's eyes bubbled with tears unexpectedly. This wasn't what Aimee wanted at all. She was spoiling for a row, but tears, no thank you.

Her mother dabbed at her eyes with one of her signature white linen handkerchiefs. Kleenex were gauche, along with paper cups and toothpicks. Roger had a touch of that old-school in him, too. It was one of the things about him of which Louise approved. He'd make the kids transfer Chinese takeout onto china plates. He never saw patients without his white coat, unlike the "newfangled" doctors that treated Aimee's parents from time to time, who went to work in jeans. "I don't know if we can trust him," Louise had said of Benny's cardiologist. "He was in dungarees."

"I'm sorry if I crossed the line. You seem so absentminded since you've gotten here, I thought you might appreciate if I helped you out. Besides, I thought you trusted my judgment."

She did trust her mother. What niggled Aimee wasn't so much Louise acting in loco parentis, but the antiquated garbage she was feeding Maddie. It was one thing to call a suitcase a valise and refuse to use a to-go coffee cup; it was quite another to teach a twenty-nine-year-old woman she needed a man to be happy. Of course, Aimee was particularly sensitive on this point now.

"I just didn't love all that stuff you were saying about Maddie needing a man and having to run to be at Andrew's side."

"Oh, goodness, is that it?" Louise paused to check her makeup in her compact, smacked her lips together after applying a fresh coat of lipstick. It was like she was trying to emphasize that there was nothing wrong with being old-fashioned. "I believe Maddie *will* be happier when she's settled. You've said yourself that she's always been a girl with a plan. And surely you want the same kind of security you have with Roger for your own children."

Oh, God. They couldn't discuss this. Not now.

"Think the beauty parlor has room for me, too?" Aimee asked, smiling at her own diversionary tactic. A salon stop was a good idea anyway. That waitress she'd seen Brian acting chummy with had the kind of hair that looked its best natural and windswept. Aimee was not so lucky. A blow-dry would go a long way toward feeling some semblance of control over her life. She heard the commercial playing in her head: *Can't tame your children or husband? Tame your curls instead.*

"Of course. We'll kick someone else out of a chair if necessary." Louise looked giddy about the mother-daughter beauty excursion.

Once upon a time, Roberta's, the in-house salon, had been the most bustling spot at the Golden. Wash-and-sets had been booked weeks in advance. Women had fought over appointments with Maria, the best of the nail technicians, known to whittle cuticles into nonexistence and lacquer nails that wouldn't chip for a full week. It was also the best place to collect gossip. There was an unwritten rule that anything could be said from under a hair dryer dome. Engagements had been busted up during dye jobs, reputations destroyed during bang trims.

"By the way," Louise said, looping an arm through Aimee's and steering her toward Roberta's. "Before I ran into Maddie, I called over to Roger's office to make my appointment for the shingles vaccine. You know he's the only one I trust to give me my shots. The girl who answered said she doesn't know when he'll be back in the office."

Aimee froze. Of course her mother would figure out something was up eventually. She had eyes in the back of her head, in Westchester, in the Weingolds' living room, and all over the hotel. If the woman had a network of spies reporting to her, Aimee wouldn't be surprised.

"His stomach thing is getting worse. I just didn't want to worry you," Aimee said. She didn't have to fake her panicked expression. "I guess he doesn't know when he'll be well enough to work."

"And you're sure you don't need to be with him? I hope I didn't pressure you too much to be here with me while we negotiate against the Weingolds."

"No, no. I'm sure. I'm staying," Aimee said. She didn't bother nitpicking her mother's phrasing. *Against* . . . like they were getting divorced from the Weingolds. "Let's get beautiful. Larry said there's a good comic tonight doing the late show. We can get dressed up."

Suddenly Aimee didn't really give a damn anymore if the kids called Roger. She wanted her hair done and a stiff drink.

Chapter Ten

Zach

Zach desperately needed weed.

His mother had rushed them out of the house so quickly on Saturday, he hadn't had time to grab his stash. He'd also forgotten underwear, but he was more upset about the bag of sativa he'd left behind. There was surely a hookup to be had in the Catskills. Woodstock was only an hour's drive away. And the guy behind the counter at the gas station in town had definitely been high on something, though that could have been fumes. He'd return to the Shell station if he got desperate enough. First, he figured he'd try his buddy Wally from college. That guy could locate marijuana on a deserted island.

After the family meeting had broken up, Zach had texted Wally and gone outside for air. He'd thought about asking Maddie to play bocce, but she'd disappeared the minute Brian had ended the meeting. He'd found a group of guys about his age on the outdoor basketball court, and they'd played three-on-three for a good hour. When he'd asked if they were staying at the hotel, they'd laughed like it was the funniest thing they'd ever heard until one of them said, "No, man, we just sneak in to play ball and steal food." Zach prudently decided not to share that he was an owner.

"Hey," came Maddie's voice after he and the guys had said their goodbyes. He was shooting free throws, annoyed Wally hadn't texted him back yet.

"We need to call Dad," she said, approaching with her cell phone pointed toward him.

Father's Day. Right. Normally he blamed his spaciness on the weed.

Maddie dialed from her cell, and Zach heard his father's voice spill out after two rings. "I'm feeling a little better . . . miss you guys . . . Shaggy all right? . . . Love you, too." Maddie handed the phone to him.

"Hey, Dad, Happy Father's Day." Zach was keenly aware of his sister's presence next to him. He might have pushed for information if she wasn't hovering, waiting for her phone back.

"Thanks, Zacky. Listen—I wanted to ask you, how is everything—"

A different cell phone ring sounded in the background—the opening bars of *Für Elise*. What the hell was happening? Did his father have a burner phone? And if so, who set the ringtone of a burner phone to classical music?

"You know what, son, I have to go. I'll call you back later." The line went dead before Zach could protest.

"Got that done," Maddie said lightly, taking back her cell

phone from Zach. "You okay, Z? BTW, I was maybe wrong about your girl Phoebe. She's not completely without worth."

"Uh-huh," he said, hearing that ringtone over and over. "She's cool. And yeah, I'm all right."

"She's cool" and "I'm all right" weren't exactly accurate. Zach's Google search history told the real truth. In his cache: *Is Phoebe Weingold dating anyone? Reasons why a police search is conducted. Where to buy weed in the Catskills.* And then a string of *Roger Glasser AND police AND crime.*

"I'm gonna head in to shower," he said.

"Wait," Maddie said. "I may be getting out of here. Andrew's dad is getting honored, and I think I'm going to go to the ceremony."

"Okay," he said with a shrug. Was he supposed to care? At least he could stare at Phoebe more freely.

"Anyway, I just wanted to know what you think about the hotel before I leave. Like, do you care if Grandma and the Weingolds decide to sell?" Maddie fiddled with her bracelet as she spoke. If Scott were here, she'd be discussing it with him. Scott was more like Maddie, a man with a plan. He was going to be a doctor; Zach couldn't remember a single Halloween that his brother hadn't dressed up in a lab coat and scrubs, a plastic stethoscope dangling from his neck. Maddie had always held Scott in high esteem, asking him advice about school and dating, even though she was older than him. In Scott's absence, apparently he was Maddie's best option. Zach straightened his spine and sank a three-pointer that he tried to make look effortless.

"I mean, yeah, I care. I love this place. I know I never come, but I guess I thought I would maybe bring my own family here one day." Zach pulled his baseball hat lower to shade his reddening cheeks. "But I also understand selling. I mean, my sink water was brown this morning. I had to dry-brush my teeth."

"My closet door fell off the hinge and landed on my foot," Maddie said, gesturing toward a welt on her ankle. "But we have a lot of memories here. Remember when we hid in the laundry bin and then we got rolled all the way to the pool hut?" His sister burst into hysterical laughter, tears pooling in the corners of her eyes.

"Of course. What about the time Scotty had that allergic reaction to the cashews and started coughing during Golden's Got Talent, and Grandpa Benny got so mad at him for ruining the performance?"

"Oh my God, that was terrible. And classic Grandpa." Maddie imitated his stern baritone. "Kids, do you know how much it cost to build this set? Do you know how much I'm paying this MC to be here? You will keep quiet or else." She narrowed her eyes the way he used to when he wanted to appear threatening, which was often.

Sometimes Fanny would feel sorry for the kids when Grandpa Benny lost it at them. She would whisper, "Remember, silence is *golden*," and slip them their favorite strawberry sucking candies with the soft centers. Fanny was really nice, come to think of it. It was crappy seeing her in that wheelchair.

Maddie looked at her watch. "Shoot, I gotta go. Text me updates, okay? I do want to know what ends up happening." She surprised him by standing on tiptoe and hugging him. He had at least six inches on her. With regret, he watched her go. If there had been an opportunity to tell his sister about what had happened back home, he'd missed it the minute she left the court. A police toss of their home wasn't something to casually drop over text, especially while she was with Andrew.

Zach tucked the basketball under his arm and headed toward the main building. He checked his cell for the twentieth time for a message from Wally, but nada. When it rang, he jumped. Wally never called, only texted.

"Hey, Dad," he said, looking at the caller ID and instinctively moving out of earshot toward one of the walking trails.

"Son, sorry about before. You got a minute now? Maddie just texted me that she's leaving."

"Yep. Dad, what's going on?" He lowered his voice. Half the guests were deaf, but just his luck this conversation would be overheard. "I know you and Mom said everything is just a big misunderstanding, but I'm not a moron. I didn't want to ask on the phone before when Maddie was there."

"Zach, I will tell you everything. But not today. You need to focus on your mother and grandmother—make sure they make a sound decision. How are things going over there? Any decision yet?"

Zach didn't like the tone of his father's voice. The hotel had never concerned him much before, so why was he suddenly so interested?

"Not yet," Zach said. "It's hard to imagine selling this place. Maddie and I were just reminiscing about the times—"

"Listen, Zach, the memories won't evaporate if the hotel gets sold. Honestly, the place is a dump. Can you imagine having to go there instead of to Atlantis? You didn't seem to be that upset when I got you private scuba lessons in December. Let's be real. Push a sale, Zacky. That's money that could end up yours one day."

Zach was suddenly very uncomfortable. He looked at his feet. A pile of green leaves had clustered on the ground from where he'd been pulling them off a tree.

"Yeah, I guess so. Listen, Dad, I gotta go. Mom needs me to walk Shaggy." He didn't wait for his father to say goodbye before dropping the call. It may have been Father's Day, but Zach wasn't feeling much goodwill toward the man at the moment.

Where was Shaggy, anyway? Zach hadn't seen their dog since yesterday. Maybe his mother had locked him up, which she hated to do. Amos hadn't been happy yesterday when their family had arrived with a canine, and he hadn't done much to hide his displeasure.

"That mutt's gonna urinate all over the place," he'd griped at dinner when Zach's mother had asked their waiter for a bag of table scraps.

"Dad, with all due respect, there is already urine on the furniture. And it's of the human variety," Brian had said. Everyone had squirmed a little after that.

Zach decided not to head in for a shower after all. He needed a walk, some time to sort things out without distraction. He started on one of the easier hiking trails, marked by green arrows painted on tree trunks. The path helped him avoid passing the rebuilt auditorium, which he couldn't see without feeling pangs of guilt and remorse. The weight of that secret gnawed at him whenever he was within fifty feet.

He was about a half mile away from the hotel's main building when he felt something like a rock hit the back of his head.

"Jesus," he said, putting his hand to his skull. "What the—?" He looked up at the canopy of treetops.

"Shit, sorry," came a voice he knew all too well from hours of watching her Instagram stories. "I was just trying to get your attention."

Zach spun around until he located Phoebe perched on the tin roof of the maintenance hut, at least twenty-five feet up in the air and dangerously close to the edge. He startled when she stood up and started walking around the roof's perimeter, barely looking down.

"Phoebe, what are you doing? Don't jump. Please." Zach's heart was pumping; he wondered if he could catch her if she plunged.

She started to laugh maniacally. "I'm not suicidal, silly. I'm trying to get a decent Wi-Fi signal. Uncle Brian said it was fixed, but I can't upload a video file no matter what I try."

Relief flooded his nervous system. "So you scaled a building?"

"I had to," Phoebe moaned. "Or else the Chinese will kill me."

The Chinese? First policemen tossed his house, now Phoebe Weingold was worried about the Chinese coming after her. Thank God he wasn't stoned. He couldn't handle an ounce of mental impairment.

"I think you should come down," he said, feeling ridiculous when he instinctively extended an arm to her. Even if she crouched down, there would still be ten feet between them. And he'd never be able to catch her, light as she was. His muscles were puny, and even the friendly basketball game earlier had sent him gasping for air. He imagined her toppling him, both of them flopping to the ground like overturned trees in a storm.

"Not until I get this post done," Phoebe said. "Michael took the car to go into town to track down some loser barista guy."

"So you guys, like, know he's gay?" Zach asked, feeling bad

for yelling it out. It was the first time he'd heard a Weingold mention the elephant in the room. Even his mother had shushed him and Maddie in the car when they'd talked about it.

"I think the guy at the tollbooth driving up here knew Michael was gay," Phoebe said. "That doesn't mean my parents do. I mean, my mom probably does; she's pretty much with the program. But for my dad to know would mean he would have to spend time with Michael. And that can't exactly happen when you live at the office. My grandparents, of course, have no clue. That would give Granny another stroke."

"Uh-huh," he responded, because he was a blathering idiot who didn't know how to formulate intelligent sentences.

"Anyway, back to my situation. I have like three hours and seventeen minutes to get this thing posted or I'm out five thousand dollars. Have you heard of EarBeats?"

He had, and nodded. Zach desperately wanted EarBeats, the best noise-canceling headphones on the market, but they cost five hundred dollars. It was one of the few things he desired that made him wish he'd followed his friends into jobs instead of moving back home to play *Call of Duty* in the basement. He could ask his parents for them for Chanukah, but Chanukah was six months away. And he wasn't eleven years old.

"The company that makes them is paying me to post a picture of me using them. But it has to happen today or I'm in breach of contract."

Hearing Phoebe say the phrase "breach of contract" was surprising and intoxicating all at once.

"I think I can help you if we can get you down," he said. "I'm pretty good with computers. At the very least I can drive you to town, where you'll get a signal." He didn't expound on why he was so good with computers as the freshman year memory flooded his brain. He and his roommates had needed access to quality porn, but the good stuff was all behind a paywall. One of his buddies was a computer science major and had led the all-nighter effort to successfully bypass YouPorn's payment page. The challenge had unlocked a latent interest in Zach; not just an interest, a talent. In fact, when Scott had lost all of his notes from his first semester of medical school when his laptop had fallen into a fountain on campus, it was Zach he'd called to work his magic to retrieve them. He wondered if Maddie knew that story. He did good, useful things when asked. He was not a loser.

"I can get down the same way I got up," Phoebe said, and before he could ask how, she flung her arms and legs around a skinny beech tree and shimmied her way down with the ease of a chimpanzee.

"Next time I do this, I'll wear pants," she said, gesturing to her inner thighs, where the jagged bark had scratched her. Prickly heat flowed through him. How was he supposed to look at Phoebe Weingold's inner thighs and stay cool?

"All right, Wall-E, help me out," she said, and handed over her phone. He pressed the home button to bring it to life and was surprised to find that her screensaver was a picture of her, Michael, Amos, and Fanny sitting around the fire pit at the Golden. She registered his surprise.

"You'd understand if you met my other set of grandparents. Nana and Papa Bauman are, like, the worst. Besides, I love the hotel. Michael and I have been exploring all our favorite spots since we got back here. Michael had this huge crush on one of the tennis pros last summer, and we found this place to set up our lawn chairs where we could watch him all day and he couldn't see us. And I took my first real photograph—like the first one I was super proud of—of Lake Winetka at sunrise. I had been out all night with one of the bellboys and ended up on that tiny stretch of beach where the rowboats are kept. Anyway, he woke me when he had to start his shift, and I saw the most amazing orange and pink sunrise I'd ever seen in my life. I took a picture on my phone and he, like, made a huge deal of how great it was. I showed it to my mom later and even she kind of freaked over it."

"That's really cool," he said. "It's cool being back together here—our two families. I feel bad sometimes about that fight at the barbeque. Like it was all my fault. I'm the one who said something about the roller rink falling apart, and then everyone looked at your uncle Brian, and then—"

Phoebe shrugged. "Our grandparents have been partners for sixty years. An argument was bound to happen. They made up; that's what's important. The dry cleaners got the blueberry pie stains out of your grandma's dress, I assume?"

He laughed, though he hadn't been laughing the night it happened.

"Luckily the fire shut everything down anyway. And nobody got hurt," Phoebe added. Zach bit his lip hard.

He wondered if Phoebe's nonchalant attitude meant that her grandparents didn't regularly trash his grandparents, the way Louise did the Weingolds. Better not to ask. If there was one thing he was learning from getting older, it was that most thoughts were better kept inside his head.

"Password, please," he said, handing the phone back to Phoebe.

"I should be able to get a Wi-Fi signal from the hospital down the road. Walk and talk?" He lifted his arm in the direction of the hospital and caught a whiff of his BO. "I'm really gross from basketball and need a shower. Sorry you're seeing me like this." He tugged at his jersey sheepishly. It swam on him mockingly, practically begging for muscles to fill it out.

"You look cute," she said, and looped an arm through his as goose bumps stormed his flesh. "Walk and fix, though, would be better." She rubbed her thumb against her other fingers, the universal symbol for money. "I need my yen."

"That's Japanese," he said. "You mean yuan."

"Why do my parents say Scott's the brain in your family?" Phoebe said, looking genuinely puzzled. "You know a lot for a supposed dummy." She was obviously joking, but the remark stung. Zach made a note to speak up even more at the next family meeting. He wasn't dumb. He had some attention deficit issues, and he found many things infinitely more appealing than studying, but he was pretty sure his IQ was above average.

"Thanks, I guess," he said, counting the pebbles on the path instead of meeting her gaze.

Phoebe broke free from their pretzeled arms and said, "Race ya to the gatehouse." Before he knew it, he was sprinting to catch up to her.

I owe you big-time," Phoebe said. They were seated on a bench in the town center eating ice cream after Zach had successfully uploaded the video.

"It was nothing," he said, wondering how Phoebe could manage to eat her chocolate cone neatly whereas his mint chocolate chip was melting everywhere. He wondered if she'd noticed him discreetly pop the Lactaid pill in his mouth while he was "grabbing napkins."

"You have a little something on your face," Phoebe said, and used her index finger to wipe away the green dribbles on his chin.

"Thanks," he said. "It's melting so—"

"Wait, you have more," she said, leaning in closer. "Just kidding." Then she planted her lips on his and parted her mouth gently. He tasted chocolate and the mint of his own breath, and perfection. When they finally pulled apart, Phoebe looked at him with a glint in her eye.

"Good. I've been wanting to do that since dinner last night."

Chapter Eleven

Amos

R ug! The rug!" He heard Larry Levine's voice booming from behind the concierge station. *Always a tumult from the Tummler*, he thought.

"Amos, the rug! *Your* rug!" Larry's voice was incessant.

Amos's hand flew to his head. What was wrong with his hairpiece? He had just used his pocket comb to tame flyaways a few minutes earlier. Amos still hadn't adjusted to his newest accessory. He'd been bald for at least a decade and never really fretted about it, even when the hairs had started collecting in the shower drain at an astounding rate. He cared a heck of a lot more that his back creaked and his knees were arthritic. Fanny was perfection in many ways, but a beauty contestant she was not, and Amos didn't feel pressure to keep up. Though he'd run a summer resort for nearly six decades, the work mostly kept him indoors, shaded from the sun's punishing rays. But in Florida, where his days were far too empty and taking up golf was a requirement of declaring residency, suddenly his baldness was presenting something of a problem.

"Wear a hat," Fanny had chastised him. "I can get you a nice sun hat right at the Publix on Collins Avenue." But he didn't want to wear a hat like the other geezers on the golf course. He wanted his hair back, especially now that he had retired to an over-sixty-five community in Boca Raton and was feeling his age more than ever before.

Suddenly Larry was in front of him, awash in panic.

"What's wrong with it?" Amos asked, wondering why the guy had to yell "your rug" so loudly. Also, did he need to call it that? Sure, that's what he and Fanny called his hairpiece jokingly, but not publicly.

"It's on fire!" Larry yelled, moving with surprising speed across the lobby toward the coffee and tea station. Amos was momentarily heartened to see the old guy move so quickly. Earlier that day when Amos had wished Larry good morning, he could have sworn the Golden's lifelong concierge had responded, "I think Mondale's really got a shot."

Realizing, finally, that Larry was not referring to Amos's head and was running toward a spot on the actual rug, Amos followed his eyes to where a group of bellboys were dumping water on a burst of flames smoldering on the lobby carpet.

It was then that Brian came dashing into the room, grasping a walkie-talkie.

"Call the fire department," his son yelled to no one in particular, though Amos could see the flames were already extinguished.

"It's fine," came a chorus of voices from where the fire had erupted, and Brian swept his forehead in relief.

"I got this, boss," called out Victor Herbert, the head of the maintenance crew.

Brian put up praying hands in Victor's direction. "You all right, Dad?" he asked, putting a hand on Amos's back.

"Yes, totally fine. Not sure what happened."

"Me either," Brian said. "Guess this might be Diamond Enterprise's problem, though, not ours."

"Not necessarily," Amos said, though he wondered if that morning's meeting had just been for show, to make the old folks feel like they had a say.

"Yeah, yeah, I know. Just when I see all the problems, sometimes I think it could be nice to wash our hands of this place."

Amos looked around. He didn't like discussing business around prying ears.

"I suppose. The place really isn't what it used to be, is it? I don't see how we can compete with the fancy-schmancy hotels with the Netflix and the coffee gadgets in every room. Those things never used to matter to our guests."

"It's not Netflix that's the problem. And we have a crazy coffee maker, too. It even starts small fires," Brian said, smiling broadly.

Amos took pleasure in his son's good looks. Such a handsome boy, who always seemed just a bit lost. He and Fanny had been beyond grateful when it had seemed his life was settling into a predictable rhythm—marriage, a job with his father-in-law he couldn't screw up, children likely. They'd felt so much more relief when Brian had married than Peter, who they'd always known would land on his feet, if he ever decided to leave them at all. Though seeing the hours Peter put in at the office, how he always had those white things sticking out of his ears so he could participate in never-ending conference calls, didn't fill him or Fanny with satisfaction. They worried about both their boys. Maybe it was the plight of parents generally, but it did seem like their two were an especially big handful. They worried Peter would keel over dead at the office, and they worried Brian would fall into a deep depression, and that was before they even got into their worries about their two grandchildren. Michael was going the struggling actor route? And was he missing the obvious when his grandson had brought a "friend" to the hotel last year and declined a second room? How would Fanny react if his suspicions were correct? Then there was Phoebe, whose job existed only on her cell phone. By his granddaughter's age, Amos had already been engaged and a business owner. What was this generation waiting for?

Amos lowered his voice to a whisper.

"Brian, I'm worried about *you*. If we sell the hotel, what will you do? Your mother and I are in Florida now almost all the time. You'd be welcome to come down there if you'd like. A lot of young people like South Beach."

Brian looked wistful as he tugged at a loose thread on his shirtsleeve. Amos wondered if Fanny was still sending Brian clothing from Bloomingdale's sales.

"I think it's time I figure out the next steps on my own. Without your help. But I love you and appreciate you both." Brian rose and moved in the direction of where a small crowd was still gathered by the scene of the fire. Amos thought to join him. There was still life in his bones. He could figure out how to hide the damage in the rug, and where they could get a replacement coffee urn quickly. But as he went to lift himself up, he felt the weight of his legs keeping him down, like he had ankle weights working as resistance. It was as though his body was telling him to rest, that running a hotel was a younger man's game. Self-consciously, he scratched at the rug on his head. Who was he kidding? He took nine pills each morning and swallowed a bottle of antacid each night.

"Take this at least," Amos said when Brian returned, pulling two crisp hundred-dollar bills from his wallet. "For the fire inspector."

"Dad, it doesn't work that way anymore," Brian said, pushing away the money.

It doesn't? He and Benny had handed out bribes at least once a week. They'd practically put the police chief's kids through college.

"Besides, the Golden will be just fine," Brian said. "We're going to have bee pollen facials at the spa. Oh, wait, we don't have a spa." He flashed his killer dimpled smile again.

"Well, at least we have a working fire extinguisher," Amos said, remembering Benny and their shoestring days. They had purchased the fire extinguishers secondhand. He remembered the twinkle in his best friend's eyes. "Something's gotta be used. It's these or the towels."

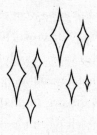

Chapter Twelve

Brian

Even though he'd given the all clear to the staff, Lucy had gone and called the fire department anyway. "It's protocol," she'd said, actually putting the staff handbook under his nose. "Rule 3.1 states that in the event of a fire, including an 'only smoke' incident, the fire department must be called, even if the situation is able to be controlled by hotel staff."

Brian was liking Lucy less and less. She was clearly embarrassed that she hadn't come up with the idea of putting the hotel on social media and therefore had taken to criticizing all of Phoebe's posts. *She made the pool look so small. The grass looks brown with the filter she used.* Meanwhile, the hotel was up to six thousand followers, about two thousand of which had entered the giveaway for the free stay.

The firemen had insisted on inspecting the entire property, which had led to an astonishing number of "This isn't up to codes" and "We'll be backs" from the fire chief. All this headache because, as it turned out, Shirley Schwartz had set up the memorial candle for her late husband next to the tea kettle and coffee urn. Why she had to mourn Herb in the lobby was a mystery to Brian, until he heard her saying while being comforted after the fire, "This was my Herb's favorite spot in the hotel. Right next to the Sanka."

At the end of the day, Brian should have been exhausted mentally and physically, but instead he was wired. He didn't feel like going back to Angela's place, and had sent her a text saying he needed to work late. She had responded with a simple, **No problem. I'm not really feeling great anyway.** Angela was easygoing, which Brian wanted to appreciate, but he sensed it was because she felt lucky to be with him and not because she was that way by nature. And what did that say about him, that he sought out relationships in which he'd have the upper hand? He'd be lying if he said he got butterflies when he saw her, that he thought of ways to impress her like he had Melinda. If anything, the pleasure he took from their relationship was that she seemed to view him as though he were the Earl of Windsor.

Was he still that wounded from Melinda's betrayal? It had to be that. Otherwise, he wouldn't bother studying her Facebook profile. She'd actually gone and married the contractor. They had three children. What was Brian lacking that the other guy had? God, he needed a drink before this self-reflection went any deeper. The Catskills provided a far too perfect landscape for contemplation, and right about now the last thing Brian wanted to do was think. He headed downstairs to the jazz lounge and nearly shed a tear of joy when he found the bar open past its usual time. There were a few stragglers perched on stools and one staff couple canoodling in the corner. He didn't have the energy to tell them to take it to the boiler room like the rest of the employees did.

"What can I getcha, boss?" asked Paula, the brassy bartender who doled out drinks nightly at the Golden.

"Scotch. A double, please," he said, sliding onto a stool and cradling his head in his hands.

"That kind of day?" she asked, placing a glass with one large ice cube before him, just the way he liked it. "I heard about Mrs. Schwartz and the fire. I can make it a triple if you want. On the house." It was one of Paula's familiar jokes. He gave her a smile he knew was too feeble. The problem with anything being "on the house" was that the house was crumbling.

"I'm going to let the first shot kick in, and I'll be back to check on you in a bit," Paula said, moving to the other end of the bar with a wet rag. Brian followed her with his gaze. Paula had probably been on the Golden staff for a good decade by now. She'd cut her chops as a bartender on a cruise line. After handling the drunken masses partying until all hours of the night, serving cocktails to the tame accountants and lawyers from the tristate area was a breeze—not that the collared shirt set weren't just as wild when no one was looking. Paula gave herself over to the job, keeping track of the way Mrs. Cohen liked her martinis with extra olive juice and remembering that if Dr. Mondshine asked for a whiskey neat, what he really wanted was a double but didn't want Mrs. Mondshine to realize. If the hotel closed, Paula would be one of many casualties. Some, like Larry, needed to retire. Quite a few of the waiters, lugging trays since the sixties and seventies, were testing the limits of their balance and strength. But Paula was in her prime. It wasn't like in the old days, when the seasonal staff came from the best colleges and graduate schools to earn cash and find a match. Those guys had been temps—the longest stint was no more than three summers. Nowadays, the staff were locals who counted on their salaries desperately. When Brian's eyelids fell, all he saw was a conveyor belt of faces he'd need to fire. Which was why he needed to stay awake.

Out of the corner of his eye, Brian spotted a lone familiar figure sitting at a booth for two, nursing a glass of wine. He rose from his stool to join her.

"Aimee," he said, catching her by surprise. "Want company?" He motioned toward the empty seat opposite her.

"Um, sure," she said, moving her sweater off the chair to make room for him. He sat down and took a long pull from his drink.

"Looks like we both needed a little help this evening," he said, lifting his nearly empty glass.

"I sure did," Aimee said. She clinked her wineglass against his Scotch and took a sip that outsized his.

"You okay?" he asked. "I've never seen you in a hat before." She was wearing a straw sun hat, even though they were indoors and it was past 10 p.m.

"Yeah, well, I'm not really a hat person, but . . ." Her voice trailed off. "There was an incident at the beauty parlor."

"An incident?" he asked. And just a few minutes earlier he'd been thinking about how great a hire Anna, the newbie, was. The ladies seemed to love her "modern" styles, and the salon business was finally ticking up after years of operating at a loss. His father and Benny had once suggested closing it during a particularly bleak meeting of senior management, and Louise had all but forced them to get second circumcisions for their audacity.

Aimee slowly removed the hat, and Brian felt his eyes widening despite his attempt to appear nonplussed. Hadn't her hair been straight and past her shoulders at the meeting that morning? Now she looked like a standard poodle.

"I got permed."

Even Brian knew that perms had gone the way of leg warmers and shoulder pads. An entire section of Memory Lane captured Golden guests in peak eighties style.

"It didn't help that the fire department evacuated the salon during my appointment, so the solution was on my hair for an extra thirty minutes," she added.

"That's Lucy the intern's fault," Brian said. "I kind of want to fire her, but she works for free and is remarkably good at organizing the payroll, so—"

"You manage a lot here," Aimee interrupted. "I'm sorry that I didn't really step up more over the years. I guess it was easy to busy myself with the kids and just assume you had everything under control. But there's really no excuse."

"You've got a lot on your plate. Three kids! A husband," Brian said. "And for what it's worth, I think you have the kind of face that can pull off any hairstyle." What was he saying? Why was he flirting with Aimee Goldman? It had to be the Scotch. And the mood lighting. And the fact that she really was a lot prettier than he'd ever realized. He was starting to notice what his brother had seen all those years.

"Ah, yes. My husband, Roger. The asshole." She polished off the last drips of wine in her glass and signaled for Paula to bring her another.

"Excuse me?"

Aimee shook her head. "I'm sorry. I've had too many of these." She pointed to her empty glass. "Or not enough, depending on how you look at it. I came down here planning to get so drunk that I stopped caring that I look like Marcia Clark."

"Ooh, the O. J. movie was so good. Did you see it?"

"So good!" Aimee took a handful of pistachios from a bowl and began shelling them. "I think I'd better start trying to sober up. Did I just tell you my husband is an asshole? He is, I just didn't mean to blurt it out."

"You did," Brian said. "But I've already forgotten it. Unless you want to talk about it."

"I don't want to talk about anything. Well, we can talk about true crime movies. I've always been partial to dramatizations of the Menendez brothers. You?"

"I like a good Robert Durst documentary," Brian said. "Anything that makes my own family seem normal makes for perfect entertainment."

"I feel the same." He could see in the crinkles around her eyes that she meant it. Had her eyes always been that lovely shade of green, or had she gotten color contacts? And how had he never noticed her ample chest? This was not the same body he'd grown up around. If that was what childbirth had done to her, he was certainly glad she'd become a mother.

"I could maybe have another," he said, eyeing his empty tumbler suggestively. "Were you serious about sobering up?"

"Does it still look like I got electrocuted?" she asked.

"Kind of," he said.

"Then bring on the booze," Aimee said, her body unfolding itself like a paper airplane. He didn't take the time to think about the consequences when he slid over in the booth so that he was next to her, so close he could smell her shampoo.

Paula had way too many years of experience behind the bar to even cast a second look at them when she brought over the next round. And the next. And the next.

THE WINDSOR WORD

FIRE SWEEPS THROUGH CRUMBLING HOTEL

Will this be the final flame for the Golden?

By George Matsoukis

Hotel guests were terrified late Sunday afternoon when a raging fire broke out in the main lobby of the Golden Hotel. Four fire departments from the area responded to the scene and were able to extinguish the flames, but not without significant damage to the building.

Sources from hotel management could not be reached for comment, though as the *Windsor Word* has previously reported, all owners are on-site this week. It is believed they are gathered to discuss selling the hotel to casino operators Winwood Holdings, a subsidiary of Diamond Enterprises.

The source of the fire could not be verified, and some tongues are wagging that this was no accident. Others are insisting the blast came from an overturned memorial candle.

"Normally we wait for the end of summer for the bonfire," quipped Sunny Bowman, the longstanding groundskeeper at the hotel. In a sign that the hotel could be winding down operations, Mr. Bowman said he has not planted any perennials this year even though co-owner Louise Goldman is a known begonia lover.

ELYSSA FRIEDLAND

The cutbacks could also just be evidence of a general belt-tightening. Several hotel guests were overheard complaining that the gefilte fish was from a jar instead of homemade.

This is not the first time a fire has ravaged the Golden. Nearly a decade earlier, fireworks on July 4th got out of hand, destroying the auditorium and smoldering at least half of the front lawn.

There is no word yet on whether the current fire will have an impact on the offer from Diamond Enterprises and what steps will be taken to remediate the damage. Among the items damaged by smoke were a signed photograph of Jackie Mason and a baseball bat used by Willie Mays. The extent of the damage is not yet known.

It is far too easy to view this fire as yet another sad episode for a hotel and region facing tremendous pressure to stay robust and relevant.

Chapter Thirteen

Aimee

Oh. My. Fucking. God. What had she done?

She rolled over slowly and quietly, hoping not to wake the sleeping body next to hers. Or the one she thought might be next to hers, based on her recollection of the prior evening. The sheets were ruffled, evidence that what she thought happened hadn't been a dream, but nobody was there. That made things easier. She returned to her back and stared at the ceiling, feeling the pulse of her hangover with every breath. The ceiling fan was spinning, or was that just in her mind? She was too old for this feeling. As if to second her opinion, Shaggy barked from his dog bed.

Aimee sat up slowly and stared back at her golden retriever, certain she saw judgment in his eyes.

"He's done far worse to me," she said out loud, likely trying to convince herself more than her puppy. Shaggy didn't even like Roger, which should have been her first clue that her husband was no good. Dogs sensed things more acutely than people. One whiff and they knew who deserved a menacing growl. Shaggy sniffed her butt regularly and couldn't get his face away from her children's crotches, but he either ignored Roger or gave him the death stare. Proof positive.

Still, no matter how terrible Roger was, and how carelessly he'd pushed their family off a cliff, that didn't mean she should go sleeping with Brian. Somewhere in deep storage there had to be dozens of notebooks in which she'd scribbled the monogram AWB in loopy cursive. When she'd still been into sketching, she'd even attempted to draw their likenesses together, like they were sitting for a wedding portrait. But that was when she was a hormonal, shit-for-brains teenager whose crushes felt like hot lava running through her veins. Now she was a premenopausal woman who had a daughter on the verge of marriage; Maddie could even have a child within a couple years. That would make Aimee a grandmother. Grandmothers didn't have one-night stands. Grandmothers didn't get so drunk that they suggested sneaking into the cabaret lounge to belt out the Golden anthem at 2 a.m. Grandmothers knitted. They played canasta. They did not act like Aimee Goldman-Glasser had last night.

She eyed the alarm clock on the night table. It was the size of a matchbook and didn't have any of the features she was used to in the luxury resorts Roger insisted on: a docking station for her phone, ocean waves to fall asleep to, a wireless connection to the coffee maker. It was 9:47 a.m. When was the last time she had slept that late? She felt like Zach, finding herself horizontal at this hour. The families were due to gather at ten thirty to continue discussions. Thank goodness she hadn't overslept and been forced to stumble in looking like she'd been hit by a Mack truck.

She was suddenly grateful to Louise for dismissing Maddie yesterday. Her daughter would sense something. She remembered overhearing Maddie and her friends giggling about how sex had a smell, and that was how they could tell who among their friends had been up to what. It had made Aimee terribly self-conscious around her children, as though they would pick up the scent of her and Roger's lovemaking. Zach, she wasn't too worried about. He was far too enraptured with Phoebe to notice much else.

Yikes, she thought. She had slept with Brian, who was Phoebe's uncle. This was all feeling very soap-opera-like. *Next time on* The Golden Hotel: *Will Aimee's affair with Brian complicate Zach's chances with Phoebe? Tune in tomorrow to find out. Now, a word from our sponsors, Happy Family Dishwashing Liquid.*

She forced herself out of bed and wriggled into her only pair of blue jeans and a thin linen button-down. It was an outfit casual enough to communicate that she was feeling cool about what had happened. It was the exact opposite of how she felt, but she didn't need her clothes to scream, *I'm freaking out!* Sex with Brian Weingold. She was so shocked that it had happened (*Adultery! Her! Longest-serving PTA president!*) that she hadn't yet reveled in what it had been like to be with him. His hands were rough, his kisses were tender, and his body was the perfect size to envelop her. She remembered him asking, after he'd groaned with satisfaction, "Have you? Can I?" with the consideration of a man that recognized sex was a two-way street. Roger wasn't a bad lover, but he used his distinct advantage of knowing that Aimee had no one with whom to compare him. She had been so young when they met. Why hadn't she banged half the waiters and lifeguards at the hotel like most of her friends had? Why the hell was she so fearful that her parents would find out? Everyone bed-hopped in the Catskills. It was a form of cardio.

So now Roger had . . . competition. Or did he? Would she ever sleep with either of these men again? Aimee didn't know the answer to that any more than she knew what the hell they should do with the Golden. There was a good part of her that wanted to just flip a coin. Like the way she used to resolve conflicts between Scott and Zach. *Whose turn is it to use the PlayStation? Let's let a nickel decide.*

The boardroom was full when she arrived, with one extremely noticeable absence. Her mother charged right over, leaving Aimee little time to wonder where Brian could be.

"I've made a call," Louise said dramatically. "Diego will be here tonight to fix this." She pointed with a red-lacquered nail at Aimee's hair. "He was all set to go to Fire Island for the weekend, but I explained to him just how dire the situation was, and he's driving up as we speak."

"You seriously called your hairdresser from the city to fix my hair?" Aimee was incredulous. Or she wanted to be, but actually, there was very little surprise in what her mother had done.

"Yes, and you could express a little gratitude. He's going to charge something astronomical because of the house call and the driving, but I'll cover it. Whatever is going on between you and Roger—because I am no fool—coming back from the Golden with your hair looking like fusilli isn't going to help."

Aimee seized on everything she couldn't say to her mother: that Roger didn't love her because of her hair, that what was wrong between them wasn't reversible like a perm. Instead she muttered, "Thanks," and took a seat in between Zach and Amos.

At least this way Brian couldn't be next to her, where the thump of her heartbeat would definitely be audible. It was already drumming loudly, each beat whooshing in her ears like ocean waves.

"Mom, Phoebe and I got to talking more last night. We have some really good ideas that can save the hotel," Zach said. Aimee nodded feebly. She was feeling the alcohol way too much to talk substantively about the hotel, but she noted something in her son's beautiful blue, but normally glazed, eyes that she'd never seen before. It sounded cliché, like something that would only be expressed in writing, but there was a definite spark there. Maybe it was because of Phoebe and her pheromonal tug on him, but her son was undoubtedly excited about the prospect of work. Aimee felt a double pang of guilt now. How could she fairly assess the fate of the Golden when her husband needed the proceeds of a sale to stay out of jail, but her son was actually eager about being productive for the first time ever? As if sensing her allegiances shifting, Roger texted at that moment.

Any news? Lawyers say sooner we can get them a first payment the sooner they can get to work. Catskills over. This is for the best for everyone.

She flipped her phone to silent and thrust it back into her purse.

Brian entered, a folded newspaper in his hand. He looked at everyone before taking his seat, and Aimee felt his gaze on her for an extra beat. She hadn't flirted or been flirted with since her teenage summers at the Golden, younger than her own children were today. But she sensed that flirtation could reignite with muscle memory. At least it had for her last night, sitting next to Brian in a dimly lit room, laughing like fools about their childhood memories at the hotel, inching closer together with each story.

"My brother loved you," Brian had blurted out at one point. "I probably shouldn't be telling you that."

"It's okay. I already knew," she had said, lightly grazing the inside of Brian's forearm. "Do you like Greta? Are they happy together?"

"Greeda? She's all right, I guess. Phoebe and Michael are nice children, and I don't think you can come down too hard on a person if their children turn out well. I know I don't have any of my own, but I've come across enough families at the hotel to draw that conclusion confidently. Besides, nobody really knows what goes on in another person's marriage. I didn't even know about my own."

That was maybe the truest thing Aimee had ever heard anyone say.

"I'm sorry about Melinda," she had responded, and instead of saying thanks, Brian had slipped his hand under the table and squeezed her thigh.

"It's ancient history," Brian had said, and Aimee wondered if such a thing truly existed.

"So I assume many of you have seen the article in the *Windsor Word*?" Brian said now, laying the newspaper flat on the table.

"That reporter is a moron," Fanny said. "Horace over at the General Store told me that same reporter ran a story about how he was always out of stock in everything, but that he never even came into the store to see for himself. Or called for comment. Brian—why is there no nosh set up for this meeting?"

"Really, Mom?" Brian said. Aimee bristled on his behalf. To be the top dog and still get chastised by your mother for not providing pastries. Besides, Aimee didn't think Fanny needed any more food. At yesterday's gathering, she'd filled a plate with at least a dozen rugelach. Since she no longer had the ability to exercise, all those calories were going to go straight to her, well, fanny.

"Zach and I have something we want to say," Phoebe said. Five sets of eyes swiveled to look at her. She was dressed in a crop top and jean shorts and wore a hat that said PRAY FOR SURF. It wasn't what you'd call a "dress for success" ensemble, but still, she commanded everyone's attention.

"So yesterday Zach saved me from jumping off a building. Kidding, kidding. I was just on the roof of the maintenance shed to get better Wi-Fi. Uncle Brian, seriously, WTF with the slow connection? Anyway, we ended up walking around the hotel for like three hours in the evening and came up with a whole list of ideas to turn the Golden around. And we'd like to share them." She turned to include Zach. Aimee suspected she was smart enough to realize it would be helpful to have a Goldman on her side. Phoebe was proving the whole don't-judge-a-girl-by-her-crop-top thing.

"We do," he said, rising to pull a laptop from his backpack. She hadn't realized he'd brought his computer, but of course he'd need something for gaming. "Brian, can you set us up with a projector?"

"We don't have that kind of capability," Brian said, clearly embarrassed. "No one's ever asked for that."

"That's because this is a place to relax," Louise said, coming to his defense. "The whole purpose of coming to the Catskills is to unwind. We used to say Benny and Amos were the only men working around this place."

"Exactly," Amos seconded. "We want people on the links. Watching shows. Eating. You don't come to the Golden to work." He shook his head, looking to his generational counterparts for support. "We only put in a business center so that we could get an extra star."

"Things don't really work that way anymore," Aimee said softly. She didn't want to make Brian feel worse, but she knew the children were correct. "Work doesn't stop in the summertime. It's a twenty-four-seven thing these days. Roger's patients text him at all hours. On Christmas. Yom Kippur." Oh God, she thought as she said that out loud. She had once believed his connectivity was a sign of how much he cared. But were his calls actually customers reaching out for refills, like he was a street hustler? No, that couldn't be. She chided herself, recalling dozens of conversations between Roger and his patients where he'd soothed them for as long as they'd needed, asking patiently, "When did the rash begin?" and "Can you hold down any liquids?" And sometimes, "Yes, I think you should call an ambulance. I'll meet you over at the hospital so that you're not alone." *Nobody is all bad or all good*, Aimee thought. There was a world of gray; a place that was once as lustrous and now lackluster as the Golden proved the point. The hotel, like her husband, wasn't obviously primed to be dumped. Would she drop him if he was an alcoholic? Certainly not. A compulsive gambler? Aimee's grandmother Celine had never left her husband, even when the creditors took everything away. There was such a thing as loyalty.

"So can we present?" Phoebe asked. "We'll do it without the screen."

"Sure," Brian and Aimee said simultaneously, perhaps both feeling their obligation as the middle generation to mediate.

"Great," Phoebe said, popping out of her chair. Her stomach was smooth and taut, and her legs were shaped so perfectly, Aimee imagined them popping out of a mold. It was insanity to compare herself to a twentysomething who had barely birthed a complete sentence, let alone three children, but still Aimee imagined with horror the puddles of cellulite and maze of veins Brian had worked his way through last night. Though he hadn't seemed turned off. He'd been into it, panting, squeezing his eyes tight with pleasure. Or had that been to avoid looking at her? No, that was absurd. He kept his eyes closed during sex because he wasn't a psychopath.

"Zach and I came up with a list of ways to make the Golden great again. I know, I know. Sounds very MAGA, and we're obviously not going for that." Phoebe stuck her finger down her throat. Aimee cringed. She was no fan of the man in the red hat, but the last thing she wanted was for generational World War III to break out by throwing a political debate into the cauldron. Benny called anyone who wanted to raise taxes a socialist; he'd nearly punched a helpless teenager visiting the hotel last summer for wearing a Bernie Sanders T-shirt. Restrained by Brian, he'd instead sat the boy down and subjected him to an hour-long lecture about why he, an honest, hardworking citizen, shouldn't be forced to subsidize lazy people with his hard-earned dollars.

"We don't expect to do all of these things, but we decided the most important move is to modernize. We have to make the Golden cool if families are going to return," Phoebe continued.

We decided. Was every millennial destined to be an entrepreneur? Was nobody an employee anymore? Aimee felt like the weight at the base of a pendulum, pushed from Team Grandparents to Team Grandchildren and back depending on who made the last good point.

"I mean, it's fine to, like, try to cut costs by getting rid of fresh flowers or only changing the sheets every other day—which is totally environmentally conscious, so that's good. But it's gonna take more than that." That was Zach, apparently also an expert in hospitality. The boy whose feet had a stench so bad, it trailed from his room down to the basement.

"We're listening," Brian said. He caught Aimee's eye and winked at her. A bona fide we-had-secret-sex wink. This time, there was no mistaking it.

"I just emailed everyone a list of our ideas," Zach said. "If you all check your phones, you'll have it waiting in your in-boxes."

"My phone's broken," Fanny said.

"Grandma, your phone isn't broken. You haven't charged it in like a month," Michael said.

"We can share," Amos said, scooching over.

"Can't see a damn thing on this screen," Fanny said, squinting.

Aimee pulled out her phone, hoping Zach and Phoebe had used a large enough font that she wouldn't need to put on her damn reading glasses.

Phoebe and Zach's Ways to Make the Golden Great Again (but not in the bad way)
1) Goat yoga
2) Zero-waste program
   a. Composting station a MUST

3) Farm-to-table dining—all farms/orchards/cattle identified on menus
   a. Gluten-free
   b. Paleo
   c. Sustainably raised
   d. Non-GMO
4) Meditation classes (with the possibility of silent retreats)
5) Build an organic, naturopathic spa specializing in Reiki and tattoo refreshers
6.) Escape room
7) Ugly sweater knitting club
8) Mountain rappelling
9) Bee pollen products in all rooms (revisit apiary idea)
10) Coffeehouse on premises (no more free coffee) with gift shop featuring local artisans
11) Pop-up museum (styled for Instagram)
12) Selfie stations throughout the hotel
13) Concierge app on phone
14) Hashtag feelings mural wall
15) Llama petting zoo
16) CBD everything
17) Cryotherapy tank

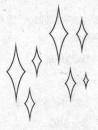

Chapter Fourteen

Amos

"What are you going to wear to this ridiculous outing?" Fanny asked him once they'd returned to their room. "I never thought I'd be grateful to be handicapped."

Amos sat on the edge of the bed and hiked his socks over his bites. The mosquitoes were vicious this week, but Phoebe went apoplectic when he spritzed bug spray. *That has Deet*, she yelled while holding her nose and covering her mouth.

"I'm wearing whatever I'll feel comfortable burning after. I wonder how much they charge for this. They should be paying us to go."

"What did you think of Phoebe and Zach's list?" Fanny asked. "I didn't understand half the things on it. What is CBD, and why do we need it in everything?"

"Apparently CBD is grass. But legal. I said to the kids that if that's what they have in mind, they're in the wrong part of the Catskills. Woodstock is an hour away, and they are welcome to use my car. The other suggestions were even more ridiculous. A silent retreat? Go tell our guests to shut up for five minutes and we'd have blowback. And everything connected via the phone? The whole point of coming to a place like this is to disconnect."

"It used to be. You know, I don't think Peter has picked up one of my calls in ages. It's only email, email, email. And then all he'll write is *I'm tied up in a meeting.* What happened to our little boy?"

"He needs Brian," Amos said, though of course Fanny already knew that.

Frick and Frack needed each other. Brian was the risk-taker, and Peter kept him from ending up in the local precinct for random mischief; Peter would have moved into a textbook if it wasn't for Brian bringing out his lighthearted side. Their boys were better together. Alone, they became more exaggerated versions of their natural selves, and it didn't benefit either of them.

"What about Greta?" she asked. Amos noticed she didn't use their usual nickname for their daughter-in-law, which meant this was a serious conversation.

"She serves her role. And we know Peter's a pleaser. He knew she liked nice things, and he wanted to give them to her. But just like when he was little and decided to memorize the map of the world and the periodic table of elements, he took it a step too far. She's probably very lonely, especially with the kids gone."

"I think you're right," Fanny said. "I can date her first plastic surgery to Michael's first year at Harvard." Her chair approached him from behind, and she put a hand on his waist. "Amos Weingold, you are a very intelligent man."

"You don't run a hotel and observe thousands of families and not pick up a thing or two," he said. Lord knew he wasn't book smart. His teachers at P.S. 110 used to chase him down the hallways for his assignments. He'd learned to slip into the boys' room at exactly the right moment to avoid discussing a C on a math test. He'd found a loyal girlfriend to cheat off whenever he could. In this way, he and Benny had been alike—though he'd taken on more of the number crunching than Benny, who'd thought they could run the place on charm alone. They'd been students of life, not Algebra II and Civil War history. This seemed to be the case with many entrepreneurs. Peter's unbroken string of A's had always been a marvel to Amos. Brian's report card, which had had a more diverse representation of the alphabet, was more familiar territory.

Fanny licked her index finger to flatten the few stray hairs that stretched across the canvas of his bald head.

"I'm glad you got rid of that hairpiece. I like you just fine the way you are." His wife kissed him on the cheek. She knew better than anyone what this week was doing to him. To hear his life's work callously referred to as "dated," "tired," and "irrelevant," to name a few choice words that had been thrown around, and to see decades of history, laughter, and memories—the stuff of legend, really—distilled to a bottom-line number was nothing short of heartbreaking.

"And to answer your question from before, they charge a lot to do this goat yoga business, but we're going for free. Because our granddaughter is going to post a picture of herself hugging a goat, and apparently that's worth the price of five free spots in the class," Fanny said.

"Five? Who's not going?" Someone had been able to opt out of this and it wasn't him? He was in his eighties! He didn't even know what yoga was, even though his doctor had recommended it to help his back and knees. What Dr. Browning didn't realize, as a man in his late forties, was that you hit a wall around age seventy where you simply refused to try new things, and you didn't feel bad about it, either. Amos didn't actually intend to participate, but after Aimee had spontaneously given a rousing speech about how everyone should be open-minded and willing to listen to other people's ideas, he'd felt he didn't really have a choice about coming along.

"Brian said he needs to work. Plumbing contractors coming in to deal with the brown water situation. And Michael's staying back. He said he doesn't feel well. Which concerns me, because the Rothsteins are leaving tomorrow, and he hasn't even gotten Sarah's number yet." Fanny pouted. "I need to stay alive to see at least one of my grandchildren married. He'd better not tell anyone about this drama major stuff or nobody will let their daughters go out with him. Though I suppose Peter has enough to support another household."

Amos smiled to himself. Fanny could win the Powerball and immediately fret about how complicated the tax forms would be.

"I wouldn't give too much thought to Michael and the Rothstein girl, truly." He watched for a flash of understanding, but nothing. "Fanny, are you sure you want to come? You can just rest while we go putter with the goats." His wife looked tired. But then again, she always did. Apparently Louise had once told her that Bloomingdales bags were smaller than the ones under her eyes. This in an attempt to let the hotel makeup girl make over Fanny.

"There is no way I'm missing the sight of Louise Goldman

on her hands and knees while a goat climbs on her," Fanny said, and rolled to the door. Amos could swear it was like she had set her chair in superspeed mode.

"You're right. That's not something to skip," he said, and opened the door for her. "Let's go be hip. Good thing I got a new one last year."

Yogi Land Farm was about a forty-minute drive from the Golden, but it might as well have been on a different planet.

"What is this area?" Fanny peered out the window in wonder, the way the twins used to when they took long car trips.

Amos shared in her amazement. Along the road they saw one hippie-dippie shop after another: local jewelry, local apples, local candles, local e-cigarettes, and the kicker, a general store called the Locavore anchoring a strip of smaller boutiques. He rolled down the window and discovered the whole street stank of patchouli.

"Did being local change its meaning since we were young?" he asked rhetorically. Local had used to mean "from the neighborhood," and it certainly wasn't a label you'd slap on a product to help it sell.

"Mr. Weingold, the farm is just up ahead," said Carlos, who was behind the wheel.

The driver was Brian's doing. His son was being impossibly cautious, not letting Amos drive himself even though he could see perfectly well with the eyedrops. That lamppost from the accident a year ago had been in a blind spot! And he drove a hell of a lot better than these yokels texting in their Priuses.

But there was no point in fighting with his son, so he'd acquiesced to having one of the gardeners drive him and Fanny to the yoga class. It turned out being a passenger wasn't too terrible. He and Fanny had sat in the back together, and Carlos had run ahead to open the doors for them. It reminded him of the fancy building Benny and Louise had moved into on Central Park West after fleeing the suburbs, where the doormen flailed around to serve the tenants, flinging themselves into traffic to hail taxis and relieving their hands of grocery bags. He wouldn't have minded the gilded life, but Fanny was insistent they stay put in their split-level home on Long Island. *We're different*, she'd insisted. Why did being different mean he had to plunge his own toilet and replace the burnt-out bulbs when Benny could just call downstairs to his super? But Amos had never pressed too hard. He wanted to keep his wife happy, and Fanny wouldn't have liked living in a place where the women lived at their cosmetic dermatologists and lunched in fine restaurants. She wanted to play cards and see her grandchildren. And that, Amos could give her.

"Good grief, thank goodness you drove us," Fanny said as they approached Yogi Land. She was right. There wasn't a space to park. Solar-powered cars and pickup trucks plastered with bumper stickers were double-parked for nearly a mile.

"I'll be right here when you're done," Carlos said, jumping to help Fanny out of the car and into her wheelchair. "Look over there. I see Mrs. Goldman and her daughter."

Amos made out Louise across the road. She was hard to miss in the neon pink jumpsuit and matching visor. He wondered if she was trying to attract the goats or scare them off.

"Looking good, Grandma," called out Zach's voice, and Amos turned to see the pockmarked boy standing with Phoebe a few paces back from Louise. Those two were getting awfully cozy. Amos wasn't sure what Phoebe saw in him, though he was proving to be less of a dolt than previously assumed. He wondered what Louise thought about their pairing, assuming she'd even noticed.

Louise had not been herself since losing Benny. They'd been lucky sons of bitches, he and Benny, finding wives they were so compatible with. The downside was a small price to pay—immeasurable sorrow when your partner went before you.

"Grandpa," Phoebe squealed. "Thank you so much for giving this a chance. We got so lucky there was a class this afternoon. I tried to go in Brooklyn a few weeks ago, but the Health Department shut it down. Anyway, you're going to love the goats. They are adorbs." She linked her arm through his and kissed him on the cheek. He had missed that feeling, the warmth of his grandchildren. He would play soccer with donkeys and swim with pigs if it meant his granddaughter would show him this kind of affection on a regular basis. He looked over at Fanny and saw she was thinking the exact same thing. Weingolds came with dimples, and Phoebe's were epic. Still, she didn't often smile enough to bring them out to their full potential, but today she did.

"I brought mats for everyone," she said.

"They don't provide mats?" Fanny asked, shaking her head in obvious bewilderment. The notion was as absurd as telling Golden guests to bring their own towels to the pool.

"No, Grandma. It's not sanitary! Zach, come with me. I have to introduce myself to the teacher and get some good photos." She bounded off to where at least seventy yoga mats in a rainbow of colors were lined up on the grass. And if his macular degeneration wasn't acting up on him, weaving between the mats were the goats. Bleating, grass-eating, pooping goats roaming freely, climbing over people who had willingly paid for this experience.

"Are you really doing this?" Aimee asked Louise loudly. "I have to. For Zach. But you totally get a pass."

"I'm not dead yet, darling," Louise said, and Amos watched as she headed toward a spot in the front row, purple yoga mat tucked under her arm.

"Baa-maste, everyone," the teacher called.

You're okay! It's okay! It'll come out. I looked it up. Goat excrement is totally washable," Phoebe was saying, flailing in a mad dash to locate paper towels. Many of the yogis had whipped out cell phones from their spandex and were recording.

"Water, water. I need water," Louise was saying. She had collapsed onto a lawn chair someone had miraculously produced, and was fanning herself dramatically with a stack of Yogi Land brochures. Zach had appeared with wet napkins and was dabbing at the pile of poop that had collected on Louise's pants.

"Please recycle those when you're done," said a random passerby in a trucker hat and Birkenstocks.

"Excuse me," Louise said, waving a finger at Trucker Hat. "Did a goat unload his waste on you today?"

"Listen, lady, climate change is real. It's more serious than cancer."

Uh-oh, thought Amos. Louise's eyes went wild. He had a sudden urge to duck and cover.

"Have you lost any friends to cancer?" she asked, rising from her chair.

"Um, no, but—" the man stammered.

"Well, I have. Many. So I will decide what's more serious than cancer. And I am not 'lady.' I am Mrs. Goldman, and I made the Catskills what they are before you were even born."

"Maman, that's enough," Aimee said, casting an apologetic look at the stranger.

But Louise was right. Amos wanted Aimee to stop apologizing on behalf of their generation. He was getting awfully sick and tired of the Gen-Xers and millennials and the Z's—basically anyone who had been on this earth for less than six decades—telling him what to do. Life experience had to count for something. When he looked back on what he'd known in his twenties, it didn't amount to a hill of beans. It was enough to build a hotel, but he'd made plenty of mistakes along the way. It was something he and Benny used to joke about—the tomfoolery of their younger years. "Remember the time we paid the washing machine repair guy up front and then he never came back with the parts?" "Remember when we double-booked comedians and then both of them refused to go on stage?" Their mistakes could fill a hundred guest books, but they became fewer over the years. Experience was the most valuable teacher, and now he, Fanny, and Louise were being directed by people who'd never held a steady job.

Well, Amos wasn't going to take it for another minute. He met Louise's gaze, forging an unspoken pact.

"Your mother is right to be upset," he said to Aimee. And to Mr. Climate Change, he simply said, "Beat it before I get angry."

Chapter Fifteen

Brian

"Brian, you got a few minutes to chat, pal?" Howard Williams asked him.

It was just before five, and Brian was heading to the dining room to speak with the maître d' about the evening's theme meal (A Night in Morocco) when the president of Diamond Enterprises called.

"Uh, sure, yeah," he said, ducking back into his office. He knew what was coming. Another shakedown. Howard would tell him that a third possible tract had been identified or that the board was demanding a lower purchase price. He groaned internally. "What's up?"

"Well, this is a little bit delicate, but I didn't see how I could not tell you. After reading about the fire, I had my guys do a little more due diligence on your property. Checking on the insurance policies, safety inspections—you know, usual stuff. One of

my guys—young analyst from Princeton—he's real sharp. He
went over all the numbers again and found something a bit off."

Off? Brian sank into his desk chair. He reminded himself this
was probably another tactic employed by Howard to knock a few
bucks off the purchase price.

"What did he find?" Brian asked.

"Y'all said your family and the Goldmans were fifty-fifty
partners, right?"

"Absolutely," Brian said. "Split right down the middle. Like
Solomon."

Howard cleared his throat.

"Darlin', could you freshen my whiskey for me?" He was speaking to someone else, and Brian was growing impatient. What time
was it in Texas? "Sorry 'bout that. Anyway, I hate to be the bearer
of bad news, but looks like your father's partner, Benny, was trim-
ming a little bit of fat over the years. Well, a lot of fat. Do you get
what I'm saying?"

"No, I don't," Brian said. His voice was firm, but his insides
were quaking. He pictured Aimee, sweet, warm, naked in his arms
the prior evening. She worshipped her father.

"What I'm saying, Mr. Weingold, is that your father's partner was stealing from him. Big-time. Now, in light of this discovery, we're going to have to take another good look at the books.
I'm sure you can understand. Let me give you an example of what
my young fella found. In 1993, Mr. Goldman took out a mortgage
against the property without your father's signature. I'm not even
sure y'all own the property free and clear to sell it. Do you want
to hear more?"

But Brian had already dropped the phone.

Chapter Sixteen

Aimee

S he still couldn't believe she hadn't seen Brian alone since their evening together. She'd been more than relieved when he hadn't joined the goat yoga excursion. Not that he hadn't seen every inch of her already, but she honestly thought she might look better butt naked than with the clingy pull of exercise pants and a sports bra. Lycra was like a sausage casing; it sucked you in, but the fat had to go somewhere. Which meant a muffin top and bulges of back fat, in her case.

After everyone returned from the ill-fated excursion, they dispersed to their rooms to shower. It wasn't just her mother desperate to rinse off. Aimee had been in the midst of savasana when a baby goat had come over and licked her face.

After freshening up (i.e. intense scrubbing with a loofah), she headed to the dining room, but found only Zach and Phoebe at the family table. It was fitting to find them there; those two were certainly acting like they already owned the place.

Moments later, Fanny, Amos, and Louise came in together. Her mother looked to have regained her composure since the incident. Fanny was fretting that nobody had seen Michael since the morning.

"Where's Brian?" she asked, trying to sound casual.

"He's dealing with hotel business," Amos said. "First it was toilets, now there's some staff issue. I'm sure he'll be in soon."

Aimee had no choice but to accept Brian's absence and trudge her way through Chef Joe's attempts at putting a Jewish spin on Moroccan classics, though she didn't think matzo balls had any business floating in chickpea stew.

Who cared if Brian was avoiding her? She wasn't a teenager waiting to be asked to the Golden Gala. Whether Brian "liked" her or "like-liked" her was irrelevant. Relevant was taking care of her children. She really ought to check in on Scott. And make sure Maddie had made it to Florida all right. Relevant was taking care of her mother, who was still on edge post goat incident. Relevant was behaving like a wife. Relevant was seeing that a sensible decision was made about the hotel, one that was fair and didn't rely too much on the competing interests of her husband and son. *SELL! BUY!* She imagined Roger and Zach yelling like stockbrokers on a trading floor.

"Brisket vindaloo?" George offered, appearing at her side with a tray.

"Why not?" Aimee said, defeated.

When Brian finally showed up during dessert, he took a seat at the opposite end of the table and didn't look her way once.

Tuesday morning arrived in a most unpleasant fashion, the sound of a jackhammer drilling in the room next door. She was going to call down to the front desk to complain, only to realize after sitting up that the noise was coming from inside her own head.

She had slept like total crap. The Ambien she'd taken had been no match for the dangerous combination of wine, spicy food, and Brian's face appearing before her on a repetitive loop. It was after nine already. She had to meet her mother at the salon shortly. Diego, true to his word, had confirmed arrival at the hotel yesterday. Louise had promised to be there to oversee Aimee's makeover, even though the directive was pretty clear: undo the perm and make her look like someone living in the twenty-first century.

She found Fanny and Louise sipping tea at a lobby table. They were rarely together one-on-one, and Aimee was surprised to find them deep in conversation.

"Aimee," Louise said, spotting her. "Good morning! I told Diego we'd meet him in the salon at nine thirty, but no reason not to just head over there now."

Fanny powered up her wheelchair.

"You know what, gals? I think I'll join you in the salon. I could really use a manicure." A beat passed. "Don't look so shocked, Louise. Stuck in this chair, I've got to do what I can to make my top half look as good as it can."

"I think that's an excellent idea. A deep red would look great with your skin tone. Maybe Arabian Nights." Louise sounded giddy. Aimee would love it if Fanny could be her mother's project—anything to deflect attention from her. Making over Fanny Weingold wouldn't fill the gaping hole of Louise's widowhood, but it would certainly occupy some time.

The three of them headed toward the salon. It was on the lower level of the hotel, next to the gym. "The men *shvitz* while the ladies get *shain*," the older generation of women at the hotel used to joke, using the Yiddish word for "pretty." It was all so terribly outdated, Aimee thought now as they approached the beauty parlor. The women she knew worked out just as much as the men, and the men cared just as much about their hair as the ladies. Roger did, anyway. He would spend a good fifteen minutes working gel through his curls, "taming the beast," as he called his morning struggle with his aggressive cowlick.

Aimee was a few steps ahead of her mother and Fanny, who had fallen back into quiet conversation. When she reached the glass door of the salon, she froze momentarily before turning around.

"Maman, Fanny, you know what? I am not feeling great. Too much tagine last night. I need to lie down. Can we do this later? We really need to do this later." She moved to block their approach.

"Absolutely not, Aimee Delphine Goldman. Do you know how long it took Diego to get here? He rescheduled a vacation to help you. We cannot cancel on him. Imagine how he might retaliate with my hair color." Louise moved to push past her.

I think he's already having a vacation, Aimee thought, panic rising up the back of her neck like climbing ivy.

"Yes, Aimee, that really wouldn't be right," Fanny said, and edged her chair toward Aimee. Good grief, Fanny Weingold was going to run her over. Well, that was fine. This was worth losing a toe over.

"Aimee, turn yourself around and get into that salon."

"It's not open yet," she protested.

"I have a key," Louise said.

"Aimee, I haven't gotten a manicure in probably thirty years. I don't feel like waiting," Fanny said, and her wheelchair sped off before Aimee could stop her. She grabbed her mother's hand and rushed to Fanny's side. They reached the glass wall of the salon entrance at the same time. They looked in together. Three faces, eyes wide, watching.

There, in the tan leather reclining chair used to wash hair in the basin, a shirtless Diego was on his back. And on top of him, wearing only a salon cape, was Michael Weingold.

The paramedics arrived quickly, considering some kid in the next town over had blown off a finger with an electric saw at the same moment Fanny Weingold had seen her grandson making out with Louise Goldman's hairdresser.

And the worst part—well, not really, considering an entire family was breaking down and an old lady in a wheelchair was now hooked up to a respirator—was that Aimee's hair still looked like it had gone through a spiralizer.

"*Mon Dieu! Mon Dieu!*" Louise hadn't stopped with the French since they'd encountered Michael in flagrante delicto.

"Maman, you're not helping," Aimee snapped. "Amos, can I get you anything? Coffee? Wine? The rabbi?"

She couldn't stop thinking about the way Fanny's head had just rolled to the side. For a split second, Aimee had thought maybe she was dead. But then she'd started gasping, "How? How?" At least she had a pulse.

After the paramedics had cleared out, the families gathered

in the defunct roller rink to avoid the prying eyes of the hotel guests. Ambulances arriving on scene weren't anything too out of the ordinary at the Golden, considering the age group of the clientele. Usually it just sparked a round of gossip: *Who? How? Where will shiva be held? Is there an available widow/widower to fix up?* Still, the Goldmans and Weingolds decided to play it safe, and secreted themselves where nobody would find them.

Diego and Michael were huddled together on a bench next to the skate rental. Brian was kneeling by his mother's side. She still had the oxygen mask on her face, and Amos was silently stroking her hair. Phoebe and Zach were standing by the Pac-Man machine, holding hands. When exactly had that coupling happened, Aimee wondered, cursing Roger again for making her this insane and distracted. She took a deep breath and walked over to Diego and Michael. Someone had to be the grown-up.

"Hi, Aimee," Michael said sheepishly. "I'm sorry about all this."

"You have nothing to be sorry about, honey. I mean, I might suggest you find more private quarters next time, but everything will be okay."

Her heart broke for this young man. Her teenage and young adult years had been torturous, and she hadn't had to contend with coming out. Maybe that was why she'd married so early, to avoid the humiliations that came with entering adulthood. Surely it was easier nowadays, but a bit more complicated when your family owned one of the last bastions of traditional family values on earth and your grandparents referred to homosexuals as "the gays."

"Diego, I think you better go," she said. "This is a family matter."

He rose quickly, like she'd handed him a ticket out of hell.

"Do you need a ride to the bus station?" she asked.

"Thank you, Mrs. Glasser, but I'm all right." She could tell he wanted to hug Michael but instead gave him a meek wave. With his knapsack slung over his shoulder, Diego leaned toward Aimee's ear, and she tensed. She had no room for any more shocks. If anyone knew how incredibly fucked up her own life was, they would leave her alone.

"Apple cider vinegar. Two tablespoons. Apply to damp hair. Leave on for three hours under a shower cap. That should take most of the curl out. Then come see me at the salon. On the house."

Aimee nodded at him gratefully. Apple cider vinegar had better not be one of the perpetually out-of-stock items at the general store.

She felt her phone buzz.

I heard Michael was caught in a compromising position. I hope this doesn't derail the plans to sell, read Roger's text message.

How did . . . what the . . . ? Zach must have texted Scott, who'd texted Maddie, who'd texted Roger. The goddamn rumor mill at this place.

I wouldn't use terms like "compromising position" if I were you, she texted back, feeling smug as the three dots of Roger's reply appeared and disappeared several times. She slipped her phone into her back pocket.

"I think everyone could use a little breather," Brian announced just as the neon S in SKATE sizzled and burned out behind him. Jeez, it was like there was a film director following them around, cuing visuals to drive home the point that the Golden was finished. "Let's take the day off from meeting and reconvene at dinner. I think it's important we eat in the main dining room tonight. With the firemen storming the hotel and the paramedics today and the newspaper articles, it would be nice if our families made a strong showing."

Gentle nods of agreement circulated.

"Aimee, can I talk to you for a minute?" Brian asked as everyone else gathered to leave. He didn't look pleased, but then again, his nephew was ashen, his mother had an IV sticking out of her arm, and it was basically up to him to get their families to decide what to do with the hotel in three days.

"Me?" She felt her stomach drop. "Sure thing."

Chapter Seventeen

Brian

Well, he wasn't going to claim surprise that Michael was gay. Brian had eyes and ears, so yeah, he had been pretty damn certain. And he imagined his brother and sister-in-law knew, too. Peter was way too sharp, even if Michael had never said anything outright. Greeda was no dummy, either. Before she'd devoted her life to spin class and injectables, she'd been an executive at a top-notch advertising firm. His parents, though. Fanny had been blindsided by this—her near heart attack made that plain. The dots that Brian had yet to connect were how his nephew had managed to hook up with Louise Goldman's hairdresser. He'd delve into that later. He was still processing the real shock of the week.

Benny Goldman, his father's partner in crime—though not really, since Benny was the lone criminal—had defrauded them. The betrayal was staggering. He was certain Louise had no idea. She'd made enough comments over the years to indicate that she believed if there was any grifting, it was on the Weingold side of the equation.

It was one of the many things that had come out at that terrible July Fourth barbeque, when the two families had come dangerously close to a proper feud. Come to think of it, it had been Benny who had brokered a peace that night. After the last fire trucks had left the grounds, Benny had insisted all quarreling cease.

Now there was no Benny to confront. No Benny to ask: *How could you?* Brian wanted to know what had driven the man who had been like an uncle to him to steal from the business. Was it pure avarice? Had he felt pressure to provide for Louise and Aimee in a way beyond his means? Brian wanted answers. What the hell was he going to say to everyone about the buyer's cold feet? Everyone was expecting a decision to be made by Friday. If Howard pulled the offer, what would he say? Could Brian really conduct more meetings about the future of the hotel with this new drama looming?

Aimee.

He needed to talk to Aimee about this. Had his timing ever been worse? Maybe the day he'd come home early from work and found his wife straddling the contractor. But this was a close second. He'd slept with Aimee, and now he had to tell her that her deceased father was a crook. His life was a series of poor decisions and bad timing.

He led Aimee away from the roller rink, and they walked in silence to his office. The way she looked at him when the door closed behind them, expectation in her doe eyes, it made him think that in a different life, the kind only to be found in movies, he would sweep the papers off his desk and lay her down. Make love to her fast and furious. But this was to be a different kind of rendezvous entirely.

"Brian, hi," she said, taking the seat opposite his desk. "I wanted to say, well, I don't know what I wanted to say. I just don't want things to be weird between us. And I don't want you to think I'm a bad person."

Brian studied her face. Beneath the makeup and tidy outfit that conveyed composure, she was clearly struggling.

"I could never think you're a bad person. You're an amazing daughter, mother, wi—" He stopped himself.

"Some great wife I am, right?" she finished his sentence. Then she shocked him by pulling a cigarette from her purse. "Do you mind? I haven't had one of these in years, but I really need it," she said. "I know, wife of a doctor smoking. And after all the lectures I've given my kids about vaping. But, well, this has been a trying week."

Brian crumbled, watching her jittery fingers struggle with the matchbook. He had been so sure that he would tell Aimee about Benny. He had to tell *someone* on the Goldman side. After all, the buyer was combing through the title records with a microscope. A less charitable part of him *wanted* to tell Aimee. He was sick of the perception that the Weingolds were the less-thans. Just because Louise was beautiful and sophisticated and Benny had been the life of the party didn't make them the rightful owners of the Golden any more than his family. He wondered how many other acts of disloyalty Howard would discover. An hour ago, Howard had sent Brian an email asking for any knowledge he had of a mortgage taken out in 1982. He and Peter would have been about fourteen then. Which meant that was the year Aimee had had her bat mitzvah. The party had been over the top, beyond anything the Weingold twins had seen back on Long Island. Instead of holding the party at the Golden, like Fanny and Amos had done for him and Peter, the Goldmans had had Aimee's celebration at the Pierre Hotel in Manhattan. A famous opera singer had been flown in from Italy to serenade the guests. Brian remembered Aimee talking about going to Paris to get her dress. The party favor had been a sterling silver heart paperweight from Tiffany. "Can you imagine how much this shin-dig cost?" he remembered his father asking over and over while they careened back to the Island through the Midtown Tunnel.

"By all means, smoke. I get how trying this has been." He stood up, relieved her hands of the matchbook, and struck a flame he held near her chin. "The hotel means so much to all of us. And I know you feel responsible for your mother. And Scott's not here, and Roger isn't well, and we——"

"Stop right there," Aimee said, taking a long drag and ashing into a glass dish etched with the Golden logo. "This"—she pointed to the cigarette—"has nothing to do with the hotel. Not directly, anyway. It's Roger. He's not sick. You may recall that while we were both loaded the other night, I called him an ass-hole. Well, that was me being generous. I learned very recently that he's been way overprescribing opioids. It's what's been pay-ing for our lifestyle. He's basically——" Aimee broke off. She was obviously on the verge of tears. Brian shifted in his seat. He hated to see people cry. Especially women. It was why Debbie, the ho-tel's first manicurist, still had a job, even though she couldn't color inside the lines. And why Larry stood behind the concierge desk, handing out activity sheets from 1972. Why Brian had never broken up with Angela, even though his heart wasn't fully in it. The woman was lately tearing up at insurance commercials; getting dumped would bring on full waterworks.

"You don't have to say anything more," he said, searching through his desk and bookshelves for a box of tissues. He was em-barrassed by how his office must appear to her, shelves still hold-ing trophies from his youth, empty Lay's potato chip bags crumpled into balls. It was the workplace of a man-child.

"I want to," Aimee said, sitting up straight, forcing her posture into a collected stance. "Michael's going to have to be brave, and so am I. Roger is a drug dealer. He preys on people's addictions. The kids don't know. My mother doesn't know. Things could get ugly fast. He's under investigation. The police tossed our house when Zach was there. I made up some story to him about it all being a misunderstanding, but if there's one thing I've seen over the last few days, it's that he's cleverer than I gave him credit for. It'll just be a matter of time before he tells his siblings."

Brian came up behind Aimee and placed his hands on her shoulders. There were only two other people in the world who understood the Golden in the way he did. And she was one of them. He would always feel tenderness for her, no matter what Benny had done.

She turned and buried her face in his chest, now freely sobbing.

"It's going to be okay," he said. "It's going to be okay."

But he was lying. He honestly didn't know if things would work out. His mother and father were reeling from the Michael shock; his brother was grinding away his life at the office with a wife going off the rails; Louise was mourning a man with a dark secret; Aimee's marriage was in tatters. Everyone was lost. They were gathered together in their summer home, but the glory days were long gone. In their place were pain, lies, confusion, and uncertainty.

Aimee pulled away from him, wiping her runny eye makeup with the back of her hand.

"I made this all about me. I'm so sorry. What did you want to talk to me about?" she asked.

"Oh, it was nothing. Just wanted your opinion on some résumés that came in. Assuming we live to fight another day, we gotta get our seasonal staff in place."

To: Weingold and Goldman Families
From: Peter Weingold
Subject: IMPORTANT

I'M ON MY WAY.
—Peter

Chapter Eighteen

Zach

"Hello, Zachary," Greta said, reaching in to give him a hug. He was unsure how close to get to her, because half her face was covered in thick white bandages. From the neck up, she resembled a mummy. From the neck down, a really fancy lady. The kind his mom used to roll her eyes at during school events, saying things like, "Honestly? High heels to work a bake sale?"

"Um, hi, it's good to see you," he said. "How, um, was your drive?" Making conversation with adults had never been his strong suit.

Greta sank into a leather armchair in the lobby and put on oversized sunglasses. She might have looked glamourous wearing them indoors if the rest of her face hadn't been shrouded in gauze.

"My ride? Let's see. Peter was on a conference call the entire time. When I had to use the restroom and asked him to pull over, he told me to be quiet and that I could blow a multibillion-dollar deal. When we lost reception in Katterskill, I tried to speak to him about Michael, but he said he needed to focus on the road. Which really means he's thinking about work but doesn't want to admit it."

"Um, I'm sorry," he said. Why were adults so weird? He hated when they overshared. One of his professors used to do that. If Zach got to seminar early and said, "How you doing, Professor Baker?" the friendly teacher in a cardigan and bow tie would say things like, "To be honest, I think my wife is cheating on me." What was Zach supposed to do with that information?

"Phoebe's been really awesome this week," Zach said. "She came up with a ton of good ideas to make the hotel more modern. And the social media accounts she created have tens of thousands of followers already."

"Do me a favor, Zachary," Greta said. Had she heard a word he'd said? "Fish out my lipstick from my purse. I can barely see anything through these bandages."

He reached into a black leather bag and found at least eight different tubes.

"Which one do you want?"

"Whichever goes best with stress," she said, and Zachary handed over a red one called MIAMI BITCH. "So, I hear from my daughter that something's brewing between you two. A Weingold-Goldman romance. That should be interesting to watch." There was a cackle in her voice he didn't know how to unpack.

"Um, yeah. So, I'm going to look for my mom," Zach said, excited that his "thing" with Phoebe had risen to the level of parent sharing. Still, he didn't want to have a conversation about it with a mummified Greta. This was way too much crazy for one week.

"Sure, sure," she said, and motioned with the back of her hand for him to leave.

"Are you going to be okay?" he asked, hesitating. "Do you need anything?"

He made out a smile from behind the bandages and a glistening speck of moisture from the corner of her eye.

"Do you know that's the nicest thing anyone has said to me in ages? But my doctor said I'm not allowed to cry. It'll mess up the stitches. You're a nice boy, Zachary Glasser. And yes, I'll be fine. These were just routine procedures."

Routine procedures, Zachary learned later from Phoebe, was code for an eye job, a repeat rhinoplasty, and a chin implant. And they must have been routine for Greta Weingold, because when Zachary studied the photos of her hanging in Memory Lane, he realized that the Greta he recognized from as recently as his grandpa's funeral shared only a passing resemblance to the young woman in the early photographs. He couldn't imagine voluntarily going under the knife for any reason. He made his mother go along with him to get a flu shot. He really was an overgrown baby.

In the rec room fiddling with a billiard cue, he waited for Phoebe. She had texted that she needed time away from her family while they "processed Michael," and he was happy to avoid his own mother, whose anxiety could now be felt if she was within one hundred feet. The perm didn't help. She had been acting like her head was going to explode, and now it looked like it actually had.

"Hey, there," Phoebe said, sliding next to him on the buttery leather couch that spilled its filling from several of the seams. "I heard you saw Patient Zero."

"Who?"

"My mom. I call her Patient Zero because I think all these plastic surgeons experiment on her. She said you seem very nice and that she's happy we're . . . you know."

"Um, that's nice," he said. He didn't know what they were. Based on his deep dive into Phoebe's social media accounts, she always had a different guy hanging on her. He worried when she got back to New York, he'd be yesterday's news. The Golden Hotel of boyfriends. And he couldn't really blame her. She was a successful entrepreneur, and he was clocking eight hours a day on his parents' basement couch playing video games.

"You okay?" Phoebe asked. "I'm picking up on a stressed vibe." She circled her open palm in front of his face.

"Something's going on with my family," he said, lowering his voice.

"Join the club," Phoebe said, and threw some popcorn from a bowl into her mouth. "Eww! This is insanely stale."

"No," he said. "My family situation is like really, *really* bad."

"What is it?" Her brows crinkled in concern, and for a moment Zach was distracted by how utterly irresistible she was. Concern was a look she wore well, along with excited, amused, tired, and basically every other emotion.

He glanced around and saw only Otto on his break playing Ping-Pong with a guest. There was a baseball game on TV in the background, and Zach determined that, between the pinging balls and the announcer's voice, he was safe.

"The day before we came here, the police showed up at our

house in Scarsdale. They were doing a search. They ripped through our drawers, tossed our bookcases, even emptied my closets and stripped my bed."

Phoebe's jaw dropped. "What were they looking for?"

"That's the thing. I have no idea. My parents won't tell me. They said it was a mistake, just a misunderstanding, but, like— my dad's not here this week, and it was Father's Day and all."

"I thought he had a stomach thing," Phoebe said.

"Well, somebody was throwing up in the house, but I'm pretty sure it was my mom. The stomach thing is bullshit. I think my dad's in real trouble."

"Shit." Phoebe cocked her head to the side for a beat, contemplating. "What do Scott and Maddie say?"

"They don't know," he said. "Scott's away in school, and nobody ever wants to bother him because, you know, he's the smart one. And my mom specifically said I can't mention a word to Maddie, because she'll blab to her boyfriend."

"What are you going to do?" she asked. He could sense she genuinely wanted to help and wasn't just eager for gossip.

"I don't know. I talked to my dad, and he's, like, super fixated on the hotel getting sold. So maybe it has something to do with the Golden?"

Phoebe stood up and took a pool cue off the wall, twirling the felt tip between her fingers.

"Could be," she said. He rose to join her. It would feel good to smash a ball with a stick right now.

"I just feel like everything's happening so quickly. We might not have the hotel anymore. Maddie's going to get married. My parents, for all I know, are going to end up divorced or worse."

"That's a lot to handle," Phoebe said, sailing a red stripe into the corner pocket. "You have a lot on your plate."

"I don't, though. I'm stuck. No idea what I want to do with my life, living at home, basically the same person I was when I was fifteen." Why was he telling her this? He had literally zero game, though at the moment, he just didn't care.

"Don't say that. You were way less cute when you were fifteen." With that, she tipped the edge of her cue and jabbed him playfully in the ribs. "Whatever happens with the hotel and your family, you'll adapt. And maybe you'll come out better for it. Same goes for my family. My grandparents will accept Michael's news. Did you know my uncle Brian found his wife in bed with another man? He dealt. The hotel is floundering. We'll either sell or make changes. Nothing stays the same forever. Just be grateful things have been as good as they have been until now. I mean, how many kids can say they had their own hotel to rule every summer?"

She was wise, Zach was realizing. He had underestimated how smart she was just because she was also hot. That really made him a shit, didn't it?

"You're right. I wonder if I should try to find out, though, about my dad. I did a pretty extensive search on my computer but couldn't find anything."

"I don't know. I think sometimes our parents keep things from us for good reason. And vice versa. Secrets aren't always a bad thing. If eventually it comes out, you will adapt. Take a page from my mom."

"Patient zero?"

"Uh-huh. My mom doesn't like her wrinkles. She gets a new face. Too much cellulite in her thigh? Liposuction. It's Darwinian if you think about it."

Zach found himself shaking his head in amazement. "You're very clever, Phoebe Weingold."

"Can you repeat that for my Instagram story? If I don't post it, it'll be like it never happened."

He laughed.

"On that note, I gotta jet," Phoebe said, grabbing her hoodie and darting out mysteriously.

"I thought we were going to paddle—" he started to say, but Phoebe was already gone.

Zach didn't have much of an appetite, but he wasn't going to sit out this dinner.

If it was possible to appear both anxious and relieved at the same time, Michael Weingold had achieved it. He was avoiding everyone's gaze by staring at his plate, but his shoulders were finally down from their perpetual hunch. The rest of them were nibbling nervously at their potato knishes, waiting to see who would be the first to speak. At least Zach was. Greta and his mother were both wearing hats; Greta's a baseball hat pulled low to hide her bandages, his mother's a wide-brimmed straw hat that kept hitting him in the eye.

"I just don't understand," Fanny said, finally breaking the silence. "I thought you were dating that girl we met when we visited you at Harvard."

"Me too," Amos said. "We spent the whole ride home discussing how we'd handle a shiksa."

"Um, so many things wrong with what you just said," Phoebe said. "Keep it down about the shiksas. That's not very PC."

"Sorry," Fanny said. She didn't sound sorry.

"Gina is my acting partner," Michael said. "I have no idea why you thought she was my girlfriend. I certainly didn't tell you that. You're seeing what you want to see. Everyone in this family has the same problem."

"Michael, sweetheart, how in the world did you connect with Diego? My roots were overgrown in March, and it took me two weeks to track him down," Grandma Louise said. When everyone looked at her in shock, she said, "What? I'm curious."

"It's called Grindr," Michael said. "It's where men who want—"

"That's enough, Michael," Amos said, holding up his hand like a stop sign. "Where is George with the damn Manischewitz?"

"I'll have some, too," Fanny said.

"Mom, you don't drink," Peter said.

"Today feels like a good day to start," she said, so fiercely no one thought to say another word on the subject.

"What about this switch from being an economics major to drama?" Greta asked, her voice muffled by the layers of gauze covering her face. "Did you not think to mention that to your parents, the ones paying your tuition?"

"Oh, I'm sorry, did you want me to have a job like Dad, where he works all the time in some dumb office helping people who have a shit ton of money make more of it?" Michael crumpled up his napkin and threw it across the table, where it landed in Brian's soup, sending a splash into his eye.

"Jesus," Brian winced.

"That job pays for your Harvard education," Peter said. "And I don't work all the time."

"Actually, Peter, you do," Greta said. "We never see you. Did you even notice that I changed my hair color? Did you think that maybe I'd want you to come to the hospital benefit I chaired? Did you think rather than just pay for the kids' school, you should have taken an actual interest in it? Name a single teacher either of our children had."

"Maybe we should go," Aimee said, elbowing Zach and starting to rise. "This sounds like a family discussion."

"Our families are intertwined," Amos said. "Benny was a brother to me. Sit down."

"Not that we necessarily know everything about our brothers," Brian said, and took a long pull from his wineglass. Zach didn't know what he meant by that, but he sure said "brothers" in a strained voice.

"Honestly, I really don't understand how you guys can be so against the drama thing. All I heard growing up, over and over and over, was about all the great talents who performed on the Golden Stage. Bette Midler. Rodney Dangerfield. Jerry Seinfeld. Jackie Mason. Henny Youngman. Sammy Davis Jr. Mel Brooks. It was seeing those shows that made me *want* to be a performer. And now you guys are like, 'No, that job isn't good enough for me'? It's paying the best possible homage to the Golden Hotel. Grandpa, you feel like we don't honor tradition enough? Well, look at what I'm doing. As for the other stuff, with Diego, well—"

"There's something of a tradition there, too," Louise said, looking at Amos and Fanny pointedly.

"What do you mean?" Greta asked.

"Let's just say Mort Kaufman and Sol Bergman did a little more than compare scores in the golf clubhouse. And Shirley Abramowitz and Penny Silverstein—those two had their own interpretation of Bungalow Bunny."

"Interesting," Phoebe said. "I'd like to hear more about *that*. Garçon?" She lifted her empty glass. "I could use another tequila for this."

"Well, let's just say the men's locker room—" Louise started.

"Maman, I really don't think this is helping much," Aimee said, shooting off a fiery glare. "You're trading in idle gossip, and what we really need to discuss is what the hell we're doing with the offer from Diamond Enterprises. We have only two days left to—"

"Actually, something's come up," Brian said. "The buyer is rethinking a few—"

"What's this? Cold feet? That's not good. Not good at all," came a familiar voice from behind Zach's seat. "I knew I should have been here all along."

"Roger? What the hell are you doing here?" his mother asked, dropping her fork with a deafening clang.

"Dad?" Zach felt like he was seeing an apparition.

"Okay, everybody, fill me in," Roger said, taking his traditional seat at the owners' table and pushing up the sleeves of his shirt. "Let's get this baby sold for top dollar. And fast."

@GoldenHotelCatskills: Call your grandma and write your favorite Catskills memory in the comments below and enter to win a CatsKillMe T-shirt designed by @Free2BPhoebe #catskills #goldenhotel #retro #nostalgia #fashion #design #ontrend #memorylane #dirtydancing #mountains #memories #family #tradition #summer #vacation

@bubbetotherescue Winning the 4th of July pie-eating contest at Grossinger's with my husband Abe

@ajewgrowsinbrooklyn Bingo nights at the Golden

@sarahshwartzman Going to the beauty parlor with grandma when I was little to get manicures

@shirleystein Canoeing on Lake Winetka and beating Kutsher's in the race in 1968

@morrismeyer EVERYTHING. The Golden Hotel is the most special place on earth

@marisaweiner Eating all day long without stopping

@paulaweiss I've heard you might be selling. Please don't sell.

@laurencohen Winning the Gold Rush in 1987

@marilynsimon You did not win the Gold Rush in 1987 @laurencohen. My second cousin on my father's side @jeffreyrlevine66 won the Gold Rush that year

@jeffreyrlevine66 No @marilynsimon I didn't win the Gold Rush. I won the kugel-eating contest

@marilynsimon Sorry! @laurencohen

@stevenbaronphilly Searching for golden nuggets the night of the bonfire

@perrywinter singles mixer at the Golden because that's where I met my wife @sherrywinter

@houstonhipster I've never been to the Catskills but dying to go!

@mikeymikester You're so hot @Free2BPhoebe

@leilalevine Pheebs, you are the best BFF in the world and the cutest ever! Omg, I love this.

@MarktoMark Take off your shirt @Free2BPhoebe

@terry10075 Save the Catskills!

@coolleggings Follow my account to save 20% on the best exercise pants ever

@MrsMaiselWannbe I read that the hotel might be sold. NOOOOOOOOOO!!!!!

@catskillscutie Memorial Day BBQ, July 4th fireworks, the end of summer bonfire. I can't choose which one!

@angelaruggiero The best thing in the Catskills is Brian Weingold.

@larrylerman #savethegolden

@juicyjew #savethegolden

@fivetownsfamily #savethegolden

@morriszelkowitz #savethegolden

@mamabear212 #savethegolden

LOAD 1,293 MORE COMMENTS

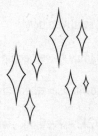

Chapter Nineteen

Louise

One look at her daughter's ashen face when Roger appeared at dinner and Louise knew things were worse than she'd conjectured. And it filled her with an unending feeling of dread and doom, because Aimee—and her happiness—were all that she lived for.

Over her lifetime, Louise had heard parents lament that they could only be as happy as their least happy child. Louise imagined there was truth to that, as there was to most aphorisms passed down generation to generation, but she believed that if you had a child going through tough times, you would still experience pockets of joy from your other children. For Louise, everything hinged on Aimee. More so for her than Benny, even though she knew him to be a devoted and loving father. But Benny had the hotel, which functioned as something of another child—Aimee's older brother, so to speak. He'd created it, nourished it, celebrated its successes, and mourned its failures. Louise loved the hotel, too, and felt a pride of ownership greeting the guests and singing her traditional anthem at the closing weekend; but the hotel was never the appendage to her that it was to Benny. She could return to their apartment in Manhattan and put it out of her mind for weeks at a time, but never did she stop thinking about Aimee. Aimee's face, and the faces of her grandchildren, were the first thing she saw when she woke up in the morning and what she imagined as she drifted off to sleep.

What had Roger done to her daughter? She would kill him for hurting her baby.

The only silver lining of Roger showing up was that it took the heat off Michael, who looked far more like an eight-year-old caught with his hand in the cookie jar than the scholar who had been admitted to all eight of the Ivy League schools. Fanny made sure everyone who passed through the Golden's threshold knew that detail, along with the fact that Michael was a Presidential Scholar, a National Merit Finalist, and a master-level chess player. Louise had always found it terribly tacky of the Weingolds to go around bragging about their grandchildren, which was another thing that had come up the night of the ugly Fourth of July barbeque. She hadn't meant to say "We all know that, Fanny" quite so emphatically when it was repeated for the tenth time that Michael had earned a 1600 on the SATs. "Fanny is just very proud, Louise," Amos had said, making her feel like a small child being scolded.

Louise was also tremendously proud of Aimee and her grandchildren. Her daughter was a kind person, putting others before herself to the point that she ran herself ragged trying to care for her family. While she sometimes couldn't help chiding Aimee for not wearing enough makeup or taking the time to pull together a flattering outfit, she admired that she wasn't caught up in superficial pursuits. But Louise knew better than to brag about it, which would only invite the evil eye anyway. Though based on the tension at last night's dinner, it seemed the evil eye might already have found the Glasser family. Louise would get to the bottom of it. She needed to.

She found Aimee eating breakfast alone the next morning.

"Your hair!" Louise gasped. Her daughter's curls had miraculously unwound, and she was sporting a chin-length bob.

Aimee cupped her newly shorn hair. She had to have chopped at least six inches. Louise wouldn't have thought her fuller face could take it, but it was extremely flattering.

"It turns out the Catskills are not totally without style," Aimee said. "I found a salon in Livingston Manor that opens early, and they saved me. Do you like it?"

"I love it," Louise said. She eyed the chair opposite Aimee. "Join you?"

"Sure," Aimee said.

Louise cleared her throat and pushed away the croissant Aimee put on her plate.

"Darling, I want to know what's going on. You looked like a ghost when your husband showed up. I know you're a grown woman and you don't have to tell me, but you might feel better if you do."

Aimee seemed to consider what she'd said. She could hardly be surprised at the inquiry. Even the waiters had sensed trouble last night and stayed away, as though their table had an electric fence around it.

Finally, Aimee nodded and whispered, "I'll tell you."

Louise breathed a sigh of relief.

Growing older was no picnic, but there were perks to the mother-daughter relationship maturing to the point where Aimee didn't immediately get defensive over everything Louise said, and Louise could turn to Aimee for advice as well. Louise could recall the exact turning point. It was August 1995, and the summer had been a relatively smooth one. Benny and Amos had staffed the place to the point that Louise's usual roles were quietly being usurped by paid employees. She'd gone to check on the menu, but there was now a "cuisine supervisor." She'd supervised the pool area to see that the towels were rolled into tight cylinders, but suddenly there was a "cabana captain" overseeing that. Louise had had all this free time materialize, and the prospect of an empty day had terrified her. She'd thought, with a modest degree of apprehension, that she should join the ladies card tables. But when she'd approached Fanny and her fearsome foursome to inquire about subbing into their canasta games, they'd exchanged quiet glances that told her everything she needed to know.

One of Fanny's cronies had cobbled together some excuse about how difficult it was to learn canasta ("So many rules! And they make no sense!"), as if Louise had been a birdbrain. She'd been the one who'd found out about the estate sale three towns over, where the hotel had picked up stunning display china. She'd figured out that by tracking where the big entertainers were performing in the area, she could invite them for the next day and avoid paying for their travel. Now she was supposed to buy some flimsy excuse that she couldn't pick up the rules of a card game? Dejected, she'd turned to Aimee, her pigtailed child who was now someone's wife. Aimee had said exactly what she'd needed to hear. That Fanny and her friends were just intimidated by Louise. She was chicer, more urbane, the darling of the hotel. Next to Louise, they'd feel frumpy and unaccomplished. From that point on, Louise frequently turned to her daughter. Had she done that to the exclusion of helping Aimee?

"But first let me ask you something," Aimee now said. "You were awfully chummy with Fanny yesterday. I didn't think she was your cup of tea."

"It's true, Fanny has never been my favorite. I think we both envied each other. She envied me for the reasons you and I both know. And I—"

"Yes?" Aimee said, leaning in closely. Her daughter's face was awash in surprise, thinking, *What could she possibly envy about Fanny?* Louise took a deep breath. She'd never spoken about this out loud to anyone but Benny and her own mother.

"I wanted more children. Now, Aimee, I never want you to think you weren't enough for me. I feel like the luckiest mother in the world to have you. But after everything I went through—years of infertility—seeing Fanny pop out two beautiful boys in one beat, it just unhinged me."

Aimee dropped her scone.

"What are you talking about? Whenever anyone at the hotel asked you about whether you wanted more children, you said, 'And risk losing this figure?'"

Louise was horrified. Had her child really believed that? What else had she overheard and not understood to be the way of adults speaking without saying the truth? She took Aimee's hand in her own. Her daughter was still wearing her wedding ring.

"Darling, I had three miscarriages before you, and five after." She didn't want to tear up and pile on to whatever Aimee was managing, which was clearly a far fresher wound than the disappointment of Louise's womb from decades ago. Nor did she want to risk opening up the spigot any more. Who knew what else would come tumbling out?

"I had no idea," Aimee said. "I'm so sorry."

"You've given me three incredible grandchildren. I wouldn't have it any other way."

"There's so much we don't know about each other, isn't there? Even though we've basically been trapped together at this hotel every summer since the dawn of time," Aimee said.

That was truer than her daughter realized.

"Goodness, did you feel trapped? I never thought that. To answer your question, Fanny and I were kidding around about Zach and Phoebe being an item," Louise said. It had shocked her how much pleasure she derived from seeing them together. A Weingold and a Goldman romantically involved. There was a certain inevitability to it.

"Now my turn. Tell me about Roger. And why Zach looks like the cat that swallowed the canary. My vision may be shot, but trust me, I still see things," Louise said. "That's another thing Fanny and I spoke about. She said even with Amos's macular degeneration and her floaters, it's like we can see things more clearly than ever. Metaphorically speaking, of course."

"You sure you want to hear?" Aimee said. "It's upsetting, and you have enough to deal with."

Louise nodded, willing her face to stay calm. Inside, she was trembling, but she needed to remain strong and composed for her daughter. It was like at Benny's funeral. The more Aimee had cried, the less Louise had. It was only in private moments she'd allowed herself to fully break down.

"Roger's been prescribing opioids in massive quantities. It's been going on for at least a decade, and I had no idea. I don't know if the pharmaceutical company courted him or whether he sought them out, but basically he's a pill pusher. They call him a 'whale,' because he makes so much money for them. And the company that makes the pills has been giving him huge bonuses, free vacations, even our cars."

Louise felt the ground fall out from underneath her. If she was hooked up to an EKG machine, the peaks would be off the charts. Roger? Her doctor son-in-law was a drug dealer? She'd seen a harrowing *60 Minutes* on those horrible doctors that preyed on people's addictions to enrich themselves. The show had scared her so much that she'd refused Percocet after her knee replacement.

"Please don't say I told you so," Aimee said.

Aimee used to say that Louise didn't approve of Roger, but that had never been the case. There was even a brief period where she'd thought Roger might be like another child to her, though quickly she'd realized the phrase "in-law" was part of the familial description so that you were reminded the person wasn't your flesh and blood; that a judge could dissolve the relationship with a signature. If she hadn't been as effusive as she should have been when Aimee had announced her engagement and the wedding plans had begun, it was because losing her daughter to marriage had been painful. She'd known Aimee would still make time for her, but it would never be the same. And as for Roger not being good enough? Well, no man was good enough for her daughter as far as she was concerned. Hotel guests joked about the Jewish mothers not thinking any of the young ladies were good enough for their perfect sons; well, Louise Goldman didn't see why it shouldn't cut both ways. Which raised some red flags about Maddie. Her granddaughter was awfully concerned about pleasing her boyfriend and his family, when really they should be courting her. Their son was marrying into a legendary family. It was why Aimee had hyphenated her name, even though Goldman-Glasser was a mouthful. When you introduced yourself with the Goldman name in certain places, it wasn't uncommon to be asked: *Are you the Goldman Sachs Goldmans? The Levi Strauss Goldmans? Or the Catskills Goldmans?* When they affirmed they were the Goldmans of the Golden, there was an outpouring of reverence.

Oh my God. Where was her head? Aimee was still talking.

"And now he needs money to pay legal fees. Which is why he was so pushy about selling the hotel last night," she was saying.

"What do you think?" Louise said, because it was easier to ask questions than to say anything substantive at this point.

"I think it's not fair to sell the hotel to keep my criminal husband out of jail. It's not fair to me and the kids, but it's also not fair to the Weingolds. This isn't their problem. On the other hand, the idea of having to see my children go through a metal detector to visit their father—it turns my stomach. But it's not like the money will guarantee he doesn't go to jail. I don't know what to do."

Louise's ache for her daughter was a throbbing in her chest that felt like a heart attack. What she would do for a return to the days when fixing Aimee's problems was as simple as slapping a

Band-Aid on a scrape and taking her to the toy store. The worst part of adulthood wasn't a creaky back or financial worries. It was facing problems for which there was no good answer, only the lesser of evils.

"And Zach? He knows?"

"No, but he was home when the police raided our house. So he's definitely worried something terrible is happening, though thankfully his obsession with Phoebe has distracted him. And the hotel business. I've never seen him so motivated and engaged. Silver linings, right?"

"Golden linings," Louise corrected. "Remember how Daddy used to say that? When something bad would happen at the hotel, he used to say, 'We need to find the golden lining.' Sometimes that's all we can do."

"True. Well, now you know my secret. It feels good to unburden myself," Aimee said.

Louise nodded as she thought: *Some secrets are meant to stay that way forever.*

The year was 1967. It was the Summer of Love on the West Coast, but at the Golden Hotel, it was the summer of Louise's anguish. She had had her third miscarriage, this time during opening weekend of the hotel. While it seemed like every other woman on property was pushing a pram or setting up baby blankets on the lawn, Louise was lying in bed with heavy sanitary napkins in her underwear. It had happened again. She knew the telltale signs the minute the cramps started.

"Take it easy," Benny said, kissing her on the forehead. "You call Larry if you need anything. And I promise, we will figure out what's wrong. We'll call Dr. Hamburger first thing Tuesday morning." He slipped into a linen sports coat and blew her another kiss from the doorway of their cottage. When he was gone, Louise let the tears go. Dr. Hamburger was her gynecologist. But what if the problem was with Benny? She tried to suggest as much many times, but he turned a deaf ear. Her mother urged her not to push it. "You can't attack his manhood," she said strongly.

By Sunday morning, Louise felt well enough to be out and about. She couldn't spend the entire weekend out of sight, or the rumors would be vicious.

"Hi, Louise," said Emily Fetcher, crossing the lawn with a baby in smocking perched on her hip. "The pickle man is here!" She gestured toward a cart set up near the flagpole. The ladies loved the black-haired, green-eyed pickle man most of all the vendors. Victor Cardino was by far the handsomest of all the men who came to peddle their goods, and he was a terrible flirt. "I'll take his pickle any day," the ladies would giggle, buying more pickles than anyone could safely consume.

"Did you know Victor has six children?" Emily said, linking an arm through Louise's. "I guess if I was Mrs. Cardino, I wouldn't mind getting on my back, either."

Six children? Louise went goggle-eyed. She hadn't known that about him. Victor was so young. How did he support such a big family selling pickles? Louise accompanied Emily to buy two pounds of half-sours. She couldn't get Victor and the image of his family out of her mind for the rest of the day.

A month passed, and Dr. Hamburger was kind enough to drive up to the hotel to examine Louise. Once again, he said everything checked out. "It'll happen for you," he said to Louise, as if Benny had nothing to do with the equation. Phil Hamburger was a golfing buddy of Benny's. Louise sensed the doctor treading cautiously.

"Got any dills?" Louise asked Victor the morning after the doctor's visit. She specifically sought out the pickle man while he was still setting up for the day and the guests were still finishing breakfast.

"Of course. And the most delicious butter pickles you ever tasted," Victor said. "Care to sample, Mrs. Goldman?"

Mrs. Goldman. Mrs. Goldman. Mrs. Goldman.

"Louise, please. Can I see inside your booth?" She gestured to the open door of his U-Haul.

"Sure," he said, looking confused.

When they were inside, Louise took a deep breath. It smelled strongly of brine. She could do this. She could. Louise pressed her lips to Victor's and slipped a hand into his jeans. Victor unbuckled his belt.

"We're going to do this once, Victor," Louise said. "And then you're not going to come back to the Golden Hotel ever again. You will sell your pickles elsewhere." She handed him a thousand dollars in cash. "This is to make up for lost wages." Victor was breathing hard in her ear, lost income the farthest thing from his mind.

Nine months later, Aimee was born. Louise slept with Benny at least ten times for the one time she was with Victor. Victor was tan; Aimee was pale. Benny had stubby fingers; so did Aimee. Victor wasn't the sharpest tool in the shed; Aimee was clever like Benny. But that cleft chin . . . Aimee's artistic talent . . . Where, oh where did those come from?

Chapter Twenty

Brian

The rain beat against Brian's window so hard, it roused him before dawn. He was disappointed that he wouldn't be able to go for his run if the rain kept up. Last night's dinner had stressed him out to no end, watching his nephew squirm while Fanny and Amos basically asked him to reconsider being gay, listening to Greeda disclose that her and Peter's marriage was dead, and then Roger—the drug dealer!—crashing and demanding an instantaneous sale of the hotel. And still all Brian could think while Roger tried to persuade the group was, *I slept with your wife. I am a bad man.*

He craved endorphins to restore his sense of well-being. He felt the need for fresh air like he was being suffocated. He needed not another goddamn thing to go wrong. Maybe he'd run through the rain. It might feel good, the pelting on his skin. But first he needed to reach Angela. Guilt had tugged at him since he'd been with Aimee. Angela hadn't responded to any of his texts from the night before. Had Paula the bartender spilled what she'd seen? That was unlikely. If the woman had loose lips, she'd have been out of a job ages ago. He decided to drive over to Angela's condo on his way to work. To say what, he wasn't sure.

There was no answer after several rings of the doorbell. Brian used the key she'd given him months ago in what was probably meant to be a significant moment, but which had ended up feeling more like a practical maneuver.

"Ange?" he called out, stepping farther into her home. He heard a flushing toilet. When it quieted, the sound of guttural retching sent him running toward the bathroom as the most selfish thought flitted through his mind. If Angela had the stomach bug and he caught it . . . well, the timing could literally not be worse. He had a call scheduled with Howard later in the day, and the families were meeting to do a walking tour of the grounds in an hour. Though with the rain and his mother in a wheelchair, he didn't see how that would work. The idea to canvass the property had been Aimee's—if the hotel were to stay open, they needed to assess how much it would cost to get it back into fighting shape. Brian had agreed because he didn't want to hurt Aimee's feelings. But he knew a face-lift was pure fantasy. Resurfacing the tennis courts alone came in at an estimated sixty grand.

"Angie, what happened?" He dropped to the ground and held his breath. The smell of vomit triggered his own urge to retch, which had been difficult growing up, since Peter had coped with his anxiety by throwing up his most recent meal.

Angela's face was ghostly white, except for the pools of yellowish-green under her eyes. But the weird thing was, she was smiling. And holding a bunch of markers or pens. Like, five of them. Good Lord, please let her not be sticking things down her throat. He really ought to have told her how much he loved her body. She was thin on top with a generous behind and could be self-conscious, hating the way the tie at the back of her apron rested on the shelf of her behind.

"I'm all right," she said weakly, and pulled herself to sitting by clutching the edge of the toilet.

"I'm sorry, babe. You look awful. Can I make you some tea?" *And can you please not get too close to me in case you're contagious?*

She put the markers under his nose. Except, up close, they weren't markers. They were pregnancy tests. And the symbols in the windows were all different, but they all pointed to the same answer. The pluses, the double lines, and then the one that was hard to misinterpret—PREGNANT. Wasn't he too old for this? Wasn't Angela too old? Two nights earlier he had been in bed with another woman. What did it say about his feelings for Angela that he'd slipped so easily under someone else's sheets? He hoped to chalk his poor judgment up to the stress of selling the hotel and having everyone on campus, but he couldn't be sure. Brian had already made up his mind that he wouldn't tell Angela about what had happened with Aimee. On a particularly slow day at the hotel, he'd joined some staffers in the break room and watched an episode of one of those daytime talk shows featuring a couples therapist who'd said coming clean about extramarital sex is for the cheater's benefit, not for the spouse's. Don't hurt someone just to clear your conscience.

Angela stood up and moved into the bedroom, sinking into the mattress. She began to cry what were unmistakably tears of joy.

He didn't know what to say. His mind was blank, his throat

dry. Brian could feel that this was going to be one of the defining moments of his life—that he could prove to himself his maturity and potential—and yet he couldn't see past his own foibles to say anything intelligible to Angela other than, "Oh my God."

"I know we didn't plan this," Angela said, wiping her eyes with the back of her hand. "And you don't have to do anything. But I'm so happy. I didn't think this would happen for me. I've always wanted to be a mother. Growing up around my dad at the hotel and working here myself, I've been obsessed with the idea of family. But it just didn't seem like it was in the cards. And now, when we weren't even trying. Don't worry—you can be involved as little or as much—"

He had to say something more. But what? He didn't know if he was happy or scared. He didn't know if he wanted to be a dad at this point in his life. It was something he'd desperately wanted as a younger man, when he'd been newly married and believed the blank page of his life thus far would fold into something beautiful like origami. When he looked up Melinda on Facebook, it was easy to imagine photoshopping himself into the Dad role.

He was certain of how he'd been raised; how lucky he was to have such devoted parents. Filling his father's shoes would be difficult, but it was a worthy thing to strive for. With so much out of his control, finally there was something he could do right.

"It's wonderful news," he said, and pulled Angela into a tight embrace.

The rain let up by late morning, and Shaggy led the pack of them as they set off on their stroll. Only twenty minutes into the walk, and Louise nearly combusted when she caught Shaggy digging up the rhododendron. Then his mother's wheelchair got stuck in a small ditch, and Zach had to hoist her out. Greta pleaded with Peter to pull out his AirPods as she trudged along in high heels. Phoebe constantly made everyone stop for pictures, and Roger shut down all suggestions with the phrase "lost cause."

"Where are the balls?" Michael asked when they reached the tennis courts. The baskets of balls used to line the courts; tossing balls from the baseline into the hopper was a favorite activity of all the kids.

"We had to lock them up because the guests were stealing them for their walkers," Brian explained.

Next they visited the roller rink—everyone silent, thinking about the scene with Michael and Diego—and then they moved on to the ice rink, the outdoor and indoor pools, the golf clubhouse, the rec room, the cabaret lounge, the card room, the dining room, and the auditorium. The "tour de force" concluded in one of the standard hotel guest rooms. The roller rink needed a new floor, the rec room had no working arcade games, the cabaret lounge reeked of Camels, the dining room's color palette could take away one's appetite (but mysteriously never did), and the guest rooms were tired. Brian tried his darnedest to focus, and he appreciated that he bore enough gravitas that everyone looked to him for direction, but all he could picture was the little seed sprouting inside Angela's womb. His seed. Good timing remained his Achilles' heel.

At every stop, his father brought up a Benny memory, and Louise would make everyone pause to hold a silent vigil for the man. "Remember when Benny decided to host the sixty-plus tennis tournament and half the men threw out their backs?" "Remember when Benny insisted on judging the Miss Golden Girl contest?" "Remember when Benny threw out that comic who made an anti-Semitic joke during his performance?" Brian felt his pulse quicken every time he heard the man's name. He had half a mind to chime in, "Remember the time Benny cheated my father? No, wait, you don't. Because only I know that, and I'm going to explode with the information."

After two hours of traversing the property, they called it quits. His mother's wheels were caked in mud, and Phoebe claimed her calves were sore from the goat yoga.

"I'll draw up some numbers on how much I think these renovations would cost. Without even doing the math, I know we won't be able to do everything. And Phoebe, the insurance costs alone that would be required for us to bring goats and llamas onto the property makes that a nonstarter. Also, no cryotherapy. Air-conditioning put the Catskills out of business decades ago—we're not making people any colder." Phoebe pouted but didn't verbalize a rebuttal. She would probably mount a social media campaign against him instead. Whatever. He had bigger fish to fry.

"Well, that sucks," Zach said bluntly. This generation didn't bother with artifice. It was refreshing, not unlike the way the old-timers were, freely speaking their minds no matter whom they offended. It was Brian's generation, bracketed by two impossibly tough-to-please age groups, that watched their words so carefully.

"But we can maybe explore some of your other ideas," Brian felt compelled to add. "I like the app check-in, which will reduce staffing costs. And a selfie station, we can handle." The truth was, it helped Brian to focus on work. The baby and Benny's deception were the boulders on his shoulders, but they didn't change the immediate situation. The owners had to decide whether to sell, assuming Diamond's offer was still on the table. If the buyer pulled out because of fishy financials—well, Brian would cross that bridge when he came to it. Hopefully Howard wouldn't unleash any new information on him later that day.

"Bri, I'd like to help," Peter said when they had stopped in front of the giant tire swing, hanging from one of the more formidable oaks on the property. It was the swing that Brian had fallen out of and broken his wrist when Peter had pushed him too hard. Fanny had nearly lost her mind that summer because Brian had refused to keep his cast dry, claiming dubiously that he'd "fallen" into the pool each and every time. "I can run numbers with you. We can shoot around ideas."

"I thought you were driving back tonight," Greta said, visibly in shock.

"I decided to stick around a bit longer," Peter said, and, quite uncharacteristically, sat down on the swing and started pumping his legs with reckless abandon. Neat black work socks rose to mid-calf, meeting pale skin that hadn't seen sunlight in who knew how many years. Greta slid her sunglasses up to her head because, like the rest of them, she clearly couldn't believe her eyes.

"I had another thought," Peter said, his voice practically giddy as he sailed through the air. "If there's a chance the Golden will be turned into a casino like what happened over at the Concord, shouldn't we check that out? The future of this spot matters. It's not just about getting top dollar from the buyer."

It's not? To hear a sentimental statement from Peter made everyone do a double take. It was startling, in the best possible way.

"Are you saying you want to go play blackjack?" Greta asked, fighting her bandages to smile.

"Roulette is more my thing, but yeah, let's gamble," Peter said.

"I'd like that," Michael said, and Phoebe and Zachary chimed in that they were game.

"Stupid waste of time," Roger called, but he pulled car keys from his pocket.

"I'm going to stay back," Louise said, exchanging a look with Aimee.

"Why? It's not like the slot machine is going to take a dump on you, Grandma," Zach said. "Just stay away from the craps table."

"Too soon, Zach," Michael said, hitting him on the arm. But even Louise smiled, and soon they were all doubled over.

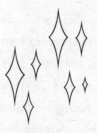

Chapter Twenty-One

Peter

So his son was gay? It wasn't like he hadn't known. Greta didn't seem bowled over by the news, either. The question was why they had never discussed it—with Michael or each other.

The answer was simple. He and his wife didn't talk about anything. Neither did he and his children. He could barely remember his last heart-to-heart with any of them. He worked until midnight on most nights, and Greta was lightly snoring when he entered their bedroom—could none of those plastic surgeons fix her deviated septum while they were operating? Then the weekends would come, and he'd disappear into his home office to continue working. There was no end to the work. It was like waves crashing on shore. The minute the tide seemed to settle, another wave came along.

It turned out that if you wanted to, you could fill every inch of your waking hours, and even the space of your dreams, with the minutiae of corporate takeovers and leveraged buyouts. You could serve the client while shampooing, riding in a taxi, while you pretended to listen to your child tell you about their day. It was all billable, too. Such was the beauty and curse of being a lawyer who charged $1,500 an hour for services.

In the beginning, his impulse to work hard had been to provide Greta with everything she wanted. Peter worried his in-laws were supportive of their marriage because they were under a false impression of just how full the Golden coffers were. Yes, his parents were comfortable, and the hotel netted a hefty profit at the time he started dating Greta Bauman, but outside of the family, the rumors of how much the hotel was worth were largely exaggerated. The truth was, Peter did nothing to clear up the misconception. He had pined for Aimee Goldman for as long as he could remember, and when it was clear that was never going to happen, he started asking out other women. Nobody sparked much interest, and he rarely made it past a second date. Then came Greta. She was funny, in a sarcastic way that kept him on his toes, and she was beautiful. Greta was at the University of Pennsylvania studying English at the time he met her. She was never without a book, and he loved that she used big words he pretended to understand and then looked up later. Her most appealing quality was that she liked him back. And unlike Aimee's parents, who acted superior to his own, the Baumans were thrilled with the match. Steven Bauman all but handed his eldest daughter to Peter on a silver platter he swiped from a waiter. If he could have rolled her down the aisle like a bowling ball, he would have. Peter vowed to himself never to let Greta or her parents down. He was so grateful to have met her—a woman who helped him get over Aimee and showed him it was possible to love more than one person in a lifetime.

But what had he gone and done with this purest of desires to please his wife? He'd infused their bank account with money beyond their wildest dreams while leaving her emotionally bankrupt. Peter hadn't felt particularly guilty about the nonstop working when the children were little and Greta didn't have a spare second to breathe. She was so busy shuttling Phoebe to soccer and Michael to tap (okay, there was their first clue), and then making sure the homework was done and correct and packed into the backpacks and the backpacks not forgotten, that he honestly thought if he tried to engage with her on any serious subject, she might implode.

Their problems had started in earnest when Phoebe had left for college. Greta, once too busy to take bathroom breaks, grew restless. She developed nervous tics, like tapping her suddenly always-polished fingernails on their glass kitchen table when they ate and tucking and retucking her highlighted hair behind a diamond-studded ear. She couldn't fall asleep without the television on to quiet her brain. Then Michael had left, and things had really taken a turn for the worse. It was then that Greta had started the process of replacing her children with new body parts.

That had been two years ago. Michael was only going to be a junior at Harvard. Maybe there was time to right the ship of his marriage. Being back at the hotel was crystallizing everything for him. He called Michael.

"Time for Ping-Pong?" he asked after his son picked up on the third ring.

"Are you serious?" Michael asked.

"Yes, why?"

"Um, we've never played Ping-Pong in my entire life. We never do anything together," Michael said.

Peter's stomach turned. He forged ahead, though a part of him was begging to retreat.

"Well, let's start now," he said.

Peter agonized while waiting for Michael to come to the rec room. It made Peter sick to think that his son had secreted a part of himself for so long. Should he or Greta have sat their son down to ask if there was anything he wanted to tell them? Was that what people did nowadays? These types of things weren't discussed at his law firm; even with all the diversity breakfasts and ally groups, no one actually gave out an instruction manual that explained how to broach certain topics. He and Greta had tiptoed around the question of their son's sexual orientation for years, with things like "Well, that's just Michael," or "You know Michael and his ways." How had two intelligent, worldly people been so capable of turning a blind eye? His parents had been truly clueless, arguably more excusable than he and Greta, who had known and chosen to ignore it.

It went without saying that they would accept their son, but had they considered how difficult it would be for Michael to come out to them? If they had, it had only been in private, fleeting moments. The dismissive attitude wasn't uniquely directed to his dealings with Michael. When he worried about the state of his marriage, it was only in passing while the elevator in his office tower climbed to his floor. When he realized he didn't really "get" his daughter, it was only to dwell on it for the brief second when someone at work would say "My kid loves @Free2BPhoebe" and he'd graciously nod.

When Michael arrived, Peter changed his mind.

"How about a walk instead?" he asked. They didn't need to volley a ball back and forth from ten feet apart. They needed to talk.

"Dad, we don't have to do this," Michael said as they set off toward the tennis pavilion. "I'm fine."

"I know you are. You're more than fine. I just wish you had talked to me more," Peter said.

Michael stopped abruptly.

"Talked to you more? When? While you were on a conference call? Should I have asked your assistant for fifteen minutes? You were never around," he said.

Peter flushed. Why had he done that? Made it Michael's fault that he'd never sought him out? That hadn't been his intention. Though he shouldn't be surprised. It was too much to assume he could go from walled-off absentee parent to Dr. Phil in minutes.

"You're right. I wasn't around. But I'm going to make an effort. Anything you need," Peter said.

"In that case, it's hot. Can we go back inside?" Michael asked, grinning for the first time since they'd met up.

"That I can do," Peter said, smiling in return.

"Is that you and Mom?" Michael asked when they approached Memory Lane. He was looking at a picture of a man attempting to put a bite of wedding cake into his new bride's mouth, but both were laughing too hard to connect.

"That's us," Peter said, and he watched his son's mind churning with surprise. "I was never very coordinated."

"And that's you and Uncle Brian?"

Peter nodded.

The picture Michael was staring at showed two boys running

wild by the kidney-shaped pool. Whoever had snapped the picture had captured the exact moment that Brian was about to push Peter in. The corners of their smiles stretched to their ears. Peter noticed Aimee in the background, hanging by the diving board, watching. Always Aimee near them. She was their shadow, their third musketeer, their forever friend. How was it that now he saw her at most once a year, the last time being at a funeral? He wondered what was happening between her and Roger. All married couples tangled. Greta could chew him out for something as simple as putting back a near-empty carton of orange juice. But the tension between the Glassers seemed of a different nature, a level beyond everyday bickering. He hoped Roger was treating Aimee well. She deserved it.

"Wow, Dad. You used to be fun," Michael observed.

"I guess I was," Peter said. "But never as much fun as your uncle. Sit with me a minute." He gestured toward a bench positioned under a photograph from the 1968 Gold Rush.

"Michael, I love you. Nothing you could say or do would ever change that. I hope you know that," Peter said, looking into his son's soulful eyes.

"I do know that, Dad," Michael said. "But it still feels good to hear it."

"I'll bet it does," Peter said. "I'm going to get better at saying a lot of things."

It's very bright in here," Peter said, squinting his eyes to adjust as their group entered Resort's World casino.

"It's also very loud," Greta said, sticking her fingers in her ears.

"It smells like Cheetos," Phoebe said, pursing her lips. She had a heart-shaped mouth, like Greta used to, before she'd filled her lips with injectables. "Dad, why are we here again?"

"I think it's kind of fabulous," Michael said, and shimmied to the background music.

"We are here because the Golden Hotel is a very special place," Brian said. "And if it's going to be turned into something else entirely, we should know what that thing is."

"Apparently it's a place for emphysema patients." Roger pointed at the row of oxygen tanks attached to wheelchairs. "And considering how musty it is in here, I'm not sure this is the best place for them."

"Nobody cares about your medical opinion," Aimee said, and everyone jumped. Aimee wasn't a gratuitously mean person. Quite the opposite, really. So if she was treating Roger this way, he must have done something pretty awful. An affair. It was the most obvious explanation for the chill between them. Peter couldn't imagine anyone cheating on Aimee Goldman. If he had ever had the chance to be with her, his fidelity would have been that of a sworn knight.

"Well, what do we think?" Amos asked, looking around in a daze. The flashing lights from a nearby slot machine were reflecting off his bald head. Peter tried to put himself in his father's shoes. Amos and Benny had built the hotel from the ground up; there wasn't a nail or a piece of plywood they couldn't tell you a story about. This wasn't like Peter's work at all. He dealt in paper. He served clients whose faces he sometimes didn't see in person. He didn't create anything. So he couldn't really understand what it was like to watch something you'd poured blood, sweat, and tears into ("BST," he and Brian would call it, because they needed a shorthand for how often they'd heard Amos say the phrase) go up in smoke.

An air of desperation hung in the casino. Lonely people sitting at slots, loading coins in the machines and pulling the levers on autopilot. There was no natural light, but an abundance of neon. It could have been 10 a.m. or midnight. Peter supposed that was the point. There was something inherently unsettling about a place that made more money the more its clients lost.

"I think it's not really a place where family memories will be made," Greta said. She was holding her handbag tightly to her chest, as if some in-over-his-head gambler would snatch it. Her observation was indisputable. It wasn't like a multigenerational family would come to the casino for vacation and then later reminisce... *Remember when Uncle Jack lost ten grand at the poker table?* or *Remember when Grandma Sally fell asleep at the slot machines?*

Greta fanned her nose for the dozenth time. The smell of the recirculated air really was unpleasant. "But I guess that guy looks happy," she said, pointing to a man with tattoo sleeves doing a silly touchdown dance.

"He's just drunk, Mom," Phoebe said. "I saw him pounding shots like two minutes ago. Speaking of, alcohol, anyone?"

"Yes, please," Zach said, and Michael moved to follow them. He was still underage, and Peter and Greta exchanged a quick glance but subliminally decided to let the bartender sort that one out.

"The one thing I do like about this place is that more people have motorized scooters than don't," Fanny said. "I usually feel so small. Now you guys just look giant." There was a very large percentage of the elderly and wheelchair-bound at the casino, undoubtedly due to the coach buses they'd seen upon arrival depositing nursing home residents.

"That just feels wrong," Zach had said when they'd seen the white hairs getting unloaded. "Can we make sure Diamond Enterprises doesn't do that kind of thing?"

"Afraid not," Peter had said. He had firsthand experience with these kinds of transactions. He specialized in private equity deals and had been down this road before. Business owners would sell and then have to watch their precious enterprise entirely rebuilt or sold off for parts. "It just doesn't work that way, kid."

"Fanny, care to scoot off with me to the blackjack table?" Amos asked. "I've set a two-hundred-dollar limit on myself, and I could use you for luck. Lord knows I can barely see the cards with my eyes."

"I was twenty-one when we got married," she said, squeezing Amos's arm. "That's got to be a good sign."

They set off together, and Peter took notice of how his father kept expert pace with the wheelchair. They were so naturally in sync. He studied Greta with gratitude. He owed this woman so much. If the measure of a woman was the children she'd raised, his wife was outstanding. She was looking better and better each day as she healed from whatever battery of procedures she'd subjected herself to. The purple bruises were fading to yellow, and she'd shed at least half of her bandages. Peter reached now for her hand.

"Roulette? Play with me?"

The surprise that registered on Greta's face when he asked for her company told him everything he needed to know about the magnitude of his neglect. He marveled at her shocked expression— the pinched forehead, the quizzical purse of her lips. It was a miraculous thing, considering how much Botox she'd had. He didn't know exactly how often Greta went, only that charges from Dr. Nussbaum appeared regularly on their credit card.

"I would love that," she said.

"How are you feeling about the hotel sale now that we're back here?" she asked him when they were alone, having left Brian, Aimee, and Roger in an awkward isosceles triangle, Roger positioned so far from Aimee that it looked like he was part of another group.

"Conflicted. I love the place, but we're hemorrhaging cash. It's hard to justify staying in business without any hopes of turning things around."

"Apparently Phoebe and Zach came up with a whole list of ways to make the place hip. Some of them are pretty out there."

"I heard. Whatever happens, it's nice that we're all here together. You, me, the kids." She leaned into him, and the weight of her head on his shoulder compounded the warm and fuzzy déjà vu he'd been experiencing in spades since being back in the Catskills.

For the next hour, he and Greta moved from roulette wheels to craps tables to slots, and then back for more roulette. They were down about three hundred bucks, but Peter couldn't remember feeling so up.

"You guys good?" Brian asked, approaching with a beer in his hand. He looked slightly more relaxed than he had when the day had started, but not by much. "I think we should pack it in soon. I have the call with Howard, and I want to take it back at the hotel. We got a sense of this place. Depressing, cheesy, but not gonna kill anybody. Agreed? At least they make the smokers stand outside."

"Agreed," Peter said. "Hey, listen, do you want me in on the call? No pressure either way." The last thing he wanted was to make his brother feel that he doubted his competence. Brian was just fragile in that way. Peter only wanted to be of use. Sure, he was a Johnny-come-lately, but he had valuable business skills to offer. And whatever decision was ultimately reached, somebody was going to be unhappy. Why should Brian shoulder all that on his own?

Brian seemed to consider his offer for a beat too long, but said, "Sure. That would be great."

"Well, well, well. If it isn't the Weingold boys, together again."

They spun around to find Horace Fielding, owner of the general store in Windsor, holding a bucket of chips.

"Hi, Horace," they responded in unison. Was Brian also thinking about their brief fixation with shoplifting in the summer between sixth and seventh grades? Horace had caught them, but instead of ratting them out to their parents, he'd made them scrub his toilets and floors until they gleamed.

"Peter, I can't remember seeing you in these parts in ages," Horace said. "I guess the rumors of a sale are true."

Peter felt heat rising to his cheeks. He was embarrassed to be called out for his abandonment of the hotel. He perceived the accusation as though he'd left his offspring in a bassinet on the steps of a firehouse.

"It's good to be back," he said simply. "How are things at the store?"

ELYSSA FRIEDLAND

Horace scratched at his white beard.

"Oh, you know, folks sure do seem to like Amazon. But we're surviving for now. Hey, it's amazing what people are doing for the Golden. That must feel real good."

"What do you mean?" Brian asked.

The scratchy reverberation of a loudspeaker announcement cut the conversation short.

"Attention, all Resort's World guests. For the next thirty minutes we are lowering the table limits on all poker tables to five dollars. Good luck!" The announcement sent gamblers off on a mad dash from all directions.

"Gotta go!" Horace said, rushing to join the others.

www.GOFUNDME.org
For: The Golden Hotel in Windsor, New York
Organized by: The 5B (Bring Back the Borscht Belt, Baby!)
Goal: $1,000,000
Raised So Far: $95,618

Update #1: Friends—The beloved Golden Hotel in Windsor, New York is struggling to survive. For those of you who have stayed at this magical resort, or have had friends or family stay there, you know how special this place is. It is believed that the hotel owners might need to sell the property to a casino operator. It would be a crime for a place so steeped in tradition, where families have bonded and romances have bloomed and children have been raised, to turn into a gambling establishment.

Catskills lovers—Who doesn't remember the joy of the blouse man arriving with his goods on Tuesdays? Who doesn't fondly recall bingo nights, trivia competitions, canoe races, the Gold Rush, the Labor Day bonfire, the Friday evening challah, the comedy shows, and the sing-alongs? Close your eyes and picture the Weingolds and Goldmans waving to the cars on the first day of the season. Smell the mountain air and picture yourself canoeing on Lake Winetka. Long live the Catskills! Long live the Golden Hotel!
Thank you for your support.
Fondly,
The 5B (Bring Back the Borscht Belt, Baby)

Chapter Twenty-Two

Brian

"Howard, Howard. Listen to me. I can assure you that my family and the Goldmans had nothing to do with that Go-FundMe campaign. I just learned about it myself a half hour ago."

Brian hit the mute button and looked at Peter. "He's pissed. And I don't blame him." He unmuted and transferred the call to speakerphone.

"Are you serious sellers, or what? I can't be having this nostalgia crap creeping into our negotiations, Brian. Don't waste my time."

"Howard, hi, this is Peter Weingold. I'm Brian's brother. I can assure you we have nothing to do with the GoFundMe page. I'm a partner at Minter and Logan in New York City. I'm sure you're familiar. I've just come up to campus to lend my brother a hand because we are very seriously considering your offer. I understand we have until Friday close of business to respond?"

"Well, yes. That is correct. I have shareholders breathing

down my neck, and I can't stand for any funny business. Our fiscal year is about to close. It seems your father and his partner ran more of a handshake business. Y'all know what I mean, figures scrawled on the backs of napkins. Not the way we run things at my shop. Whatever funny business went down over there—and I can assure you there was funny business—our offer stands."

"Understood, Howard. You will hear from us by Friday. You have my word," Brian said. He hung up the phone and looked at his brother. Now there were two of them in on this nasty business.

"What was he talking about? Funny business?" Peter was looking at him wide-eyed.

"I was going to tell you," Brian said. It was the easiest thing to say in the moment, though he hadn't actually decided what he planned to do with the information. The baby news had eclipsed everything else.

"I'm listening," Peter said. He was anxiously twirling a Golden Hotel pen between his fingers while his knee bounced up and down. Was this what his brother was like at his law firm, nervous and twitchy? Brian doubted it. Peter wouldn't have climbed so high up the corporate food chain if he was this on edge. It was something particular about being with family that made everyone a baseline level of anxious.

"Benny was cheating Dad. He was taking out loans against the property without Dad's knowledge. Who knows what else?"

"Jesus. Are you going to tell Dad?"

"No. Definitely not. It would break him. Do you see how weepy he gets every time he passes that portrait of him and Benny on the stairs?"

"You're right. And it's not really fair to assassinate the character of a man who's not here to defend himself. Louise, Aimee—they would be crushed, too," Peter said. "But still, it's awful. What a betrayal. I feel sick." He dropped the pen, and it rolled across the desk into Brian's lap and hit the floor. It was hard not to see everything as a sign. A crooked picture in the lobby, a hair in the food, a clogged toilet: They were all signs pointing in the same direction. *Sell, sell, sell . . .*

"Agreed. But this stays between us," Brian said. "When I talked to Howard earlier, he said he might pull the offer depending on what he found. We got lucky."

Peter rolled up his chair closer to the desk. The physical proximity to him made Brian realize how much he'd missed his twin. Spending holidays together and calling on birthdays didn't pass muster for a real relationship. Not with the person with whom you'd shared a womb, the person who for the first eighteen years of your life you couldn't go anywhere without and not have people ask, "Where's your other half?" When Peter cradled his chin in his hands, Brian studied his brother's grays and receding hairline. Corporate life did that, apparently. Your hair either lost its melanin or fell out—in his brother's case, both.

"Is that why you looked spooked earlier? I thought you were going to faint at the casino," Peter asked.

If only that were it, Brian thought. He took a sip of the bitter coffee on his desk, now cold. If they did implement some of his niece's suggestions, a coffee bar that served decent java would be chief among them. Even the Catskills fundamentalists would approve of a move away from Sanka and Lipton.

"You can tell me," Peter said. "It's not exactly like my life is perfect. My wife's plastic surgery bills rival Kim Kardashian's. Michael gave Mom a mini heart attack."

Brian felt not a shred of schadenfreude at his brother's family tension. He took a deep breath through his nose and let it out slowly through his mouth, buying time. Telling Peter about his night with Aimee would be cruel. Decades had passed since his brother's crush was at its peak, now they were both married with five children between them, but Peter still wistfully studied Aimee's sketches hanging around the hotel.

"Brian, it's okay," Peter said. "Let it out."

The baby. That's what really mattered.

"Angela's pregnant. My girlfriend. You met her during the shiva for Benny. She works at the hotel. I know, I know, don't shit where you eat."

Peter laughed before his face sank back into something more appropriate for Brian's revelation.

"Trust me, if you worked at my firm, you'd see very few people observe that rule. Is this good news? Phoebe and Michael think the world of you. You're a terrific uncle, and Greta's always said it was a shame you weren't a father."

"I am excited. I'm also petrified. And in shock. And feeling like if one more big thing happens in my life, I'm going into hibernation. I just don't know if I'm ready for this."

"There is literally no way to prepare for parenthood," Peter said. "You can read all the books and make a schedule and love that little person more than you ever thought possible, but being a parent will still gut you. Your kid will say they hate you, they'll projectile vomit in your face. They'll have friends you don't like, or they won't have enough friends and you'll worry. You'll never be sure if you should push them harder or whether you need to back off. You won't know whether to follow your instincts or do what everyone else is doing. You will never be fully relaxed again. All that is to say, I know you're going to be an incredible father."

Brian felt a dopey grin spread across his face. He remembered that many moons ago he'd been the only one who could get Phoebe to burp when she took her bottle. The baby nurse, Greta, Peter, they would try all different maneuvers. A little bounce. A gentle rub. A walk. Nothing worked. Finally they would hand over the baby to Brian, and instantly, she'd release the air bubble that everyone had been waiting for. He'd never told anyone his secret—a subtle, barely perceptible shake of his hips. Everyone thought you needed to move the baby up and down, but it was really a side-to-side motion that did the trick. He hadn't thought about the feel of his niece and nephew's baby skin for ages, the way they'd fit into the palm of his hand when they were infants. When they were born, the sting of Melinda's betrayal had still been fresh. Brian had pretty much sworn off love—and definitely marriage—for good. He'd resigned himself to the role of fun uncle, which in many ways suited him better than father. Brian was the type to give whoopee cushions as birthday gifts and to serve cupcakes for breakfast. He wasn't a rule follower himself and didn't imagine he'd particularly shine at making them for other people. But now, more than twenty years after resigning himself to the forever-uncle role, Brian was finding the idea of fatherhood exciting.

Yes, fatherhood. He could get behind that.

But what shape his family would take was the great unknown. He liked Angela very much. She was easygoing in so many respects. Choosing a movie, picking a restaurant—the decisions that could devolve into World War III with other women—were seamless with her. But were agreeability and compatibility in bed enough of a reason to get married? Assuming that was what Angela even wanted. He had a sudden, comical image of Angela's father, Vinny, a man Brian had known since childhood, taking him out back by the garbage dumps with a shotgun and demanding he marry his daughter—except, because he was a waiter, in Brian's vision, Vinny wielded a baguette.

"Want some unsolicited advice from your older brother?" Peter asked.

"How you got out first is a mystery to me. I'm so much more athletic than you," Brian said.

"Mom and Dad have medical records that prove otherwise. So, you want my advice or not?"

"I'm not in a position to refuse advice," Brian said. The ways in which his life was complicated and his future uncertain were myriad, and he'd sit for a fortune-teller if one were to pass by. Which reminded him . . . He had forgotten to book talent for the next evening. Maybe the local tarot lady would do readings.

"Be involved in the kid's life as much as you can. I missed so much working. It's very easy to tell yourself you're doing it all for the kids. I certainly made that excuse when I looked at my watch and decided to stay in the office instead of making it home for dinner. But now I look at them and realize how much I've missed. If I'd made more time, taken more vacations with them . . ."

"Like at the Golden," Brian said. He hadn't meant it to come out like an accusation, but it thudded like one.

"Yes. Like at the Golden. That's exactly what this place is all about. Family time. And you know what? I know my kids are giving you shit about the Wi-Fi being spotty. But frankly, I love it. I missed a video conference this morning and realized that the world didn't spontaneously combust. I sort of like the time-warp vibe. So does Greta. I mean, I'm sure she'd be happier if there was a Chanel store nearby, but she honestly seems more at ease than I've seen her in ages. You're doing really good stuff here, Bri."

"Not good enough." He heard the downtrodden tone in his voice. The hotel's demise was just a fact.

"This isn't your fault. Lots of people want new, bigger, better. And different. But clearly not everyone. What about that Go-FundMe? Think the kids are behind it?"

"No idea," Brian said. "Should we check it out?"

He pulled up the page on his computer and swiveled the monitor to face Peter.

"Jesus, my clients would die for returns like these," Peter said, shaking his head in disbelief.

Brian stared at the screen and rubbed his eyes to make sure he was seeing clearly. In the past hour, another thirty thousand dollars had been donated to keep the hotel afloat.

"I don't know who the 5B are, but they certainly don't mess around. I think we serve borscht tonight in their honor."

Chapter Twenty-Three

Aimee

Aimee, you can't avoid me forever," Roger said, which was technically true at the moment because he'd trapped her inside the costume closet at the back of the auditorium. It was raining, again, and this was the only place she could think of to smoke out of sight.

He discovered her seated with her knees hugged to her chest on the dusty linoleum floor, partially obscured by Joseph's Technicolor dream coat and Glinda's witch outfit, both of which looked highly flammable. The tradition of the guests mounting a Broadway show was not a ritual Aimee missed. Mrs. Hoffman's Gypsy Rose had sent half the audience in search of earplugs, and the Canasta League of Jericho's *42nd Street* costumes had sent the other half in search of blindfolds.

"You smoke now?" he asked, making a show of waving away the fumes.

"You deal Oxy now?" She blew a smoke ring right in his face.

Brian Weingold had taught her to blow rings back when they were teenagers and would smoke cigarettes and drink booze in the woods behind the staff housing. She remembered thinking his perfect clouds of white circles were the sexiest thing she'd ever seen. "How'd you find me here, anyway?"

"Larry saw you take the closet key. At first he thought I was asking about Amy Schwartz—remember the bridge teacher that your mom caught stealing office supplies?—but then I clarified that I was looking for my wife. Because, remember, we are still married."

"For now," she said flatly, fixing her gaze on a Cleopatra wig with synthetic black hairs she'd love to use to strangle Roger.

"Aimee, I am so sorry for what I've done." Roger dropped to the floor next to her. "I don't want to make excuses, but if you'll just hear me out. The drugmaker is relentless. I saw all these studies that convinced me that I was actually helping people. Remember after Maddie was born how horrible you felt?"

Of course she did. Her daughter had been over nine pounds. She'd labored with her for twenty hours, and when Maddie had finally emerged, it had felt like her insides had gone through a paper shredder. Not to mention the level four tear that had reached all the way up her backside. She'd had to sit on a donut for a month.

"Imagine if you'd had to endure that pain without the Percocet," Roger said.

"You and I both know that the police wouldn't have torn our home apart if you were prescribing drugs to people who actually needed them. And by the way, I still remember that pill bottle. I used to stare at it, waiting for eight hours to pass so I could have my next dose. What I remember the most about it was the all-caps NO REFILLS label slapped across it. Roger, you have to tell Scott. You have to tell each of them. I can't protect you from this. I have been a devoted wife to you since day one, but this isn't in my job description."

"You're absolutely right, Aimee. It's not. Can I just say something? Please." He looked pitiful. She nodded for him to proceed. Roger sucked in a deep breath. There wasn't much oxygen to be had in the closet, and Aimee felt her lungs getting desperate.

"Do you know what it's like to marry *the* Aimee Goldman? It was literally like marrying royalty. I could practically hear the guests whispering—*Why him? What makes him so special?* I actually did overhear one lady say that I was "just" an internist, not even a plastics guy or a surgeon. People tried to poke around to see if I came from money. It made me feel like a loser. I worried you felt that way, too. I wanted to prove I wasn't just any doctor—a dime a dozen in these parts—but a really successful one. Did I get there through shitty ways? Yes. Do I regret it? Yes. Aimee, my love, what are you thinking?"

She tried to squash the image of a naked Brian in her bed, but it was like playing Whac-A-Mole. No words came to her. She felt sympathy for Roger for the first time since he'd come clean. And the sympathy made her course with guilt.

"Aimee, listen. If we sell the hotel, we can use the money to get me the best legal defense possible. The fault lies with the pharmaceutical companies way more than the doctors. You should see the data. The carrots they dangle if we prescribe their so-called wonder drugs. If we could just get our hands on a hundred thousand—"

She squeezed her eyes shut and took a few deep breaths. He

was back to the money. Always with the money. She felt an urge to put her cigarette out on Roger's arm.

"I slept with Brian Weingold," she said, because it was the next best thing she could do to cause him pain.

"Huh? You did?" Roger looked surprised, but she wouldn't quite say he looked hurt. "It's okay. We can work through that. What did Brian say about how the Weingolds are leaning?"

His response to her confession said everything she needed to know. To have the worth of a thirty-year marriage reduced to a single wicked reaction gutted her, but it also gave her the clarity she'd been seeking.

She stood up abruptly, pushing past a sequined number from a poorly received *Cabaret* revival, and flung open the closet door.

"Tell the children as soon as we leave the hotel. You have one week. Or I will. And my version will not be as pretty."

She hadn't made it more than twenty steps from the theater when Maddie called. Aimee's stomach lurched. Had Roger already told their daughter? And if so, how had the conversation been that short? She imagined the text. **Dear Firstborn: I'm going to the clink. Will probably have to miss your wedding. Love, Dad.**

"Maddie, honey, how are you?" She was grateful Maddie couldn't see the throbbing vein in her neck.

"I'm fine," she said. "I mean, not really."

Oh, God. Oh, God. She wasn't ready for this.

"Dad called you?"

"What? No, why? Was he supposed to? Is he feeling better?"

Aimee felt like an IV of fluids had been jammed into her arm. She would live to fight another day.

"Yes, he is. He's joined us at the hotel, actually. What's wrong with you? What does 'not really' mean?" She was relieved that her daughter didn't know about Roger yet, but that also meant there was another problem to deal with. Whoever said God didn't give people more than they could handle was a moron.

"Andrew and I had a big fight last night," her daughter explained, and Aimee heard the sniffles and yearned to reach through the phone and wipe Maddie's tears.

"About?"

"Well, we were at dinner at the Hoffs' club, and his parents' terribly snobby friends were there. And Mrs. Hoff—I cannot believe I'm twenty-nine years old and have to call her that—said to her friend, 'Maddie's grandparents built one of those Catskills hotels. You know, those corny places where they teach polka lessons and play bingo. And there's endless food, but of course it's all terrible and ethnic.'"

"Oh no," Aimee said. She felt the blood drain from her face. "What did Andrew say?"

"He kind of said, 'Mom,' like he was a little annoyed, but that was it. I literally wanted to stab her with a fork. Then they all went back to talking about their yachts and jets, and then later on, Mrs. Hoff's friend said, 'Dear, does anyone still go to your family's hotel? It sounds dreadfully outdated.'" Maddie put on this haughty voice, and Aimee could imagine exactly what that must have felt like for her daughter. Her mama-bear instincts kicked into high gear. Could she find out who these awful friends were, and how quickly could she get a stink bomb into their mailbox?

"I'm really sorry, Maddie. That sounds terrible. We're lucky most people realize how special this place is. Did you know there's a GoFundMe to save the hotel? Zach told me one hundred thousand dollars has been raised so far."

"Really? That makes me happy. It actually gets even worse. Mr. Hoff said he read in the paper about how Diamond Enterprises was going to buy the place and rip it up, and that he was thinking about investing with them. Like, he'd actually be helping the people buying the hotel."

Worlds were colliding in the worst possible way. What was next? Roger dealing Oxy to hotel guests?

"So now what, honey? Where do things stand?"

"Actually, that's why I'm calling. I just landed at LaGuardia. I'm renting a car and should be at the hotel in two hours. I need you, Mom."

How Aimee craved hearing those four words. Maddie was normally so self-sufficient—the architect of a life plan that never seemed to include needing her mother—that this desperate cry for help came as a true shock.

"I'll have Chef Joe make all your favorites. Drive safely."

Chapter Twenty-Four

Zach

The casino excursion was way more fun than Zach had expected. He and Phoebe held hands as they roamed the casino floor. When he hit the jackpot on The Price Is Right, she jumped into his arms and snapped a selfie of them together, which was posted moments later with the hashtag #squeezingmymain-squeeze. So not only were they a couple away from the hotel, but also online, where tens of thousands of people would like, comment, and repost their status. It was like Phoebe had taken the largest megaphone and shouted, "I like Zach Glasser!"

After they had returned to the hotel, Phoebe disappeared again, and Zach had a text message from Wally. His roommate had come through with a weed connect not too far from the Golden. But something made Zach stop himself. He hadn't been stoned since last Friday, and he felt sharper than he had in ages. Why did he need to get high so often? He wasn't swearing off pot for good, but he decided to lay off at least until he got home.

"Hi, Zacky," his mother said, surprising him in the lobby. "You doing all right?"

"Yeah, I'm good," he said, and the relief in her eyes made it obvious that if he hadn't said he was okay, she might have collapsed.

"Your sister is coming. She'll be here in about two hours."

That was unexpected news, but Zach was pleased. Four days ago, Maddie had been making fun of his obsession with Phoebe Weingold, and now they were dating. He didn't know what would happen when the week at the hotel ended. It was hard to imagine bringing a girl as sophisticated as Phoebe to his parents' basement to watch Netflix and chill. Zach needed a job, and quickly. Maybe Maddie would hire him. He could be a real estate agent, couldn't he? He didn't understand mortgages and how to calculate square footage, but how hard could it be? Maybe he even had a flair for reinventing spaces. The brainstorming with Phoebe had awakened something in him. Maybe Phoebe would give him a shout-out on her social media account to jump-start his client roster.

And if he could get his act together and move out of his parents' house, maybe that would give them the space they needed to fix their problems. That was another reason he was happy Maddie was returning to the hotel. She wouldn't miss the tension between the 'rents. And then Zach could tell her about the police raid. Let Maddie ask questions and figure out what was up. She acted all mature and grown-up—let her fix this.

An hour later, Zach was seated in the dining room surrounded by family, hoping Maddie would appear before dinner concluded. The hotel was fuller than it had been the past four days, though still far from busting at the seams. He could remember a time as a young child when he would use his owner-brat status to cut the queues at the waterslide and at the driving range. At least the higher occupancy meant less talk at the owners' table and more schmoozing with the guests. An unfamiliar woman approached their table to ask his father to look at a rash on her arm; his mother was still hitting the wine hard, but looked a bit less homicidal.

The waiters were moving with more pep, though there still were too many of them idling near the kitchen. Another thing Zach had used to do when he was younger was practice balancing serving trays with Scott. A decent Golden waiter could handle thirty stacked plates. Now, even if they had such deep talent on the bench, it wouldn't be necessary.

"Borscht?" Michael said, pushing his soup bowl away. "What are we, peasants?"

George looked crestfallen as he continued ladling feebly.

"We are paying our respects to the people doing the fundraising campaign to keep the hotel open," Brian said. "They call themselves the 5B. Bring Back the Borscht Belt, Baby."

"Excuse me," Grandma Louise said, her spoon clattering to the table. "There are people trying to give us a bailout?"

"Yep," Zach said. "Apparently we're too big to fail."

Everyone looked at him.

"Andrew Ross Sorkin. His book on the 2008 financial crisis. Am I the only one who reads?"

Amos, returned from chatting up nearby tables, slapped down his napkin.

"We do not accept charity from anyone," he said. "Fanny, back me up."

"I agree. We will not accept a handout. This is so shameful. Who would do such a thing?"

"Grandma, it's people who love the hotel. They miss this place," Phoebe said. "It's a really generous thing. We're up to a hundred and fifty thousand dollars in donations now."

"If they missed it so much, why don't they book a room?" Louise asked.

"It is pretty remarkable," Peter said. "Mom, Dad, Louise—I think you should be flattered. You've created something that's very meaningful to people."

"But it's not supposed to be a charity. It's a business," Louise said. "I'm just glad Benny isn't around to see this."

"Louise, I couldn't agree with you more," Roger said. "If the hotel needs donations to stay afloat, it's time to sell."

The look Zach saw his grandmother give his father was possibly the most menacing he'd ever seen in his life. Everyone shifted uncomfortably.

"Hey all. What'd I miss?" Maddie appeared, a rolling suitcase in hand and a few crumpled tissues peeking out of her jeans pocket.

"Nice hair, Mom!" She kissed their father on the cheek.

"Welcome back, Madeline," Louise said, and motioned for her to sit alongside her.

His sister studied the bowl of purple liquid placed in front of her.

"Borscht, seriously? Did anyone ever think how much money we could save if we stopped serving this stuff? You can't get these stains out of the tablecloths. At least I assume you can't—my Lululemon hoodie is toast."

"Why do we even have tablecloths? It's so stuffy in here," Phoebe said.

"That's actually a really good point, sis," Michael said. "If you guys love beets so much, Chef Joe could try a beetroot cocktail. We make them at our cast parties and they're great. I mean, the signature drink of the Golden is an old-fashioned. The name kind of says it all."

"Beetroot rocks," Maddie said. "Actually, I did some thinking on the flight about other ideas that could be good for us. What if we did theme weekends? You know, get the fetishists excited. We could have, like, a *Star Trek* convention here, and then maybe a Scrabble tournament. Ooh, what about a murder mystery weekend?"

"We've done a murder mystery weekend before," Fanny said. "You kids wouldn't remember. Some of you weren't even born yet. We got the mustached inspector, the officer in uniform. Whole nine yards."

"And?" Phoebe said. "It sounds fun."

"And then Mrs. Taitz actually died. The actor who was supposed to die had just stumbled out of the kitchen with a knife stuck in his chest, fake blood everywhere. The guests were excited. The inspector had just arrived on the scene. And then out of nowhere, Sally Taitz had a heart attack and fell off her chair. Her body jerked around for a minute or two, and then she was perfectly still. Everyone was confused. Was she in on it? Was she playacting or improvising? But she was really dead. We were calling over to Riverside Memorial within the hour. Let's just say we didn't do any more theme weekends after that."

"Yikes," Zach said. Now seemed like a bad time to bring up his latest idea, a real-life Grand Theft Auto simulation.

ELYSSA FRIEDLAND

"I had an idea," Phoebe said. "Because of climate change and temperatures being higher, we could extend our high season all the way through Indigenous People's Day."

His grandma's hot tea sprayed from her mouth like a garden hose. Everyone else just looked confused.

"It's what they call Columbus Day now," Zach said quietly. "You know, because of the whole killing the Natives and ransacking their villages thing."

"Uh-huh," Amos said. "While they are renaming holidays, might I suggest changing World War II to The Time Six Million Jews Got Slaughtered."

"Amos, calm down," Fanny said, resting her hand on his elbow. "Let's focus on what matters. The hotel. Not what they call a holiday that we couldn't afford to stay open for anyway, no matter the name."

"Fine. Any other ideas?" Amos asked brusquely. "Or should we just let our online saviors take over?"

"Keep your voice down," Grandma Louise hissed. "We don't need all these people in our business." She did a grand sweep with her arm over the dining room, but it was a fact that all the tables in their immediate perimeter were empty.

"Amos, that's not fair," Aimee said. "The kids are trying. This week has been relatively civil. Let's try to keep it that way. We have to let Diamond know our answer tomorrow. I'm sure we can keep it together for the next twenty-four hours."

"Aimee's right. We need to focus on the offer. There's not much time left." Brian gazed slowly around the table. Zach looked down at his hands. What did he know about something this monumental? Sure, it was his birthright, his grandparents' legacy, but he still didn't feel like he should have an actual say. He was still a kid! All he knew about business were a few fancy terms to throw around that he'd learned in his mergers and acquisitions class—there were cool things called "bear hugs" and "poison pills," but he didn't remember what they were. And he hadn't even read the Andrew Ross Sorkin book that he'd name-dropped from the syllabus.

"The fairest way to do this is a simple vote, like the operating agreement specifies. There are six Weingolds—Mom, Dad, Peter, me, Phoebe, and Michael. There are only five Goldmans—" Brian said.

"Your point?" Louise snapped. "We're equal partners."

"My point, Louise, was that you should have a double vote. So that it's equal. Your vote counts twice, then Aimee, Maddie, Scott, and Zachary. A tie is a possibility, but we'll cross that bridge when we come to it."

"Why should the children have a say at all? I don't care what the damn operating agreement says," Amos asked. "Did they build this place? Are their names on the deed?"

"Darling, we're old," Fanny said gently. "At some point we have to recognize that what the children want matters more than us. Besides, if they don't want the hotel, they'll sell it the minute we're six feet under—and maybe not for as good a price."

"I believe the children are our future." Michael crooned the Whitney Houston song. Phoebe quickly joined him, making her fist into a pretend microphone. Everyone gaped.

Michael shrugged. "What? I thought it was apropos. Plus, hasn't my singing gotten way better since the karaoke competition last summer?"

"Not that you don't sound lovely, Michael, but can we just back up a second about the children voting? Scott's not even here," Aimee protested. "He hasn't been privy to all the discussions."

"Actually, Scott will be here tomorrow morning bright and early." Everyone whipped around to face Roger. Zach was excited to see his brother. He'd spent the afternoon wandering the premises, thinking about him. Tracing their footsteps like he was following a trail of breadcrumbs leading back to their childhood. An actual childhood, not the quasi-man-child life he was leading now. In the athletics shed, he'd found the sticks he and Scott had used for roller hockey, the foosball table with half the poles missing, the Frisbees, beach balls, Kadima paddles, and lots more detritus of their summers. When Zach had freed a soccer ball from a sack of sporting equipment, a cloud of dust mites had exploded. If Scott arrived early enough tomorrow, they could hit the basketball court or throw the Frisbee around. His brother could use a break from that stupid studying. Their differences were not unlike Peter and Brian's.

"Since when is Scott coming?" Clearly this was news to his mother as well, but her inquiry was overridden by Louise.

"I have a concern," she said. "I think my grandson Zachary is under the influence of Phoebe now that they're an item and that he will just vote whichever way she tells him to."

"We're not an item," Phoebe said. Zach didn't like her tone. He didn't know if she meant they weren't "an item" because nobody born after 1960 used that phrase, or if they'd somehow broken up in the intervening hours between the casino and dinner. Which would be weird, because of her Instagram post. "We're just having fun," she added.

"We are?" he asked.

"Yeah. What did you think this was?" Phoebe looked to be stifling a giggle. And fucking Maddie was swiveling her head between them like she was watching the U.S. Open.

"Excuse me, but do you think you're too good for my grandson?" Grandma Louise demanded, making that scary face all over again, this time directed at Phoebe.

"Grandma, stop, please," Zach begged. He wanted to crawl under the table and die. Could he die? Was that a viable option now? Run out to the tetherball court and wind himself up in the rope?

"Here we go again. A Goldman can't believe that a Weingold wouldn't be interested in them," Fanny said. "You've always thought you're better than us, Louise. Well, Phoebe doesn't want to date Zach. He doesn't do anything. He lives at home. Phoebe is a major inspirator."

"Influencer," Greta said. "Fanny, you're not helping things. Neither are you, Louise. The children should work this out themselves."

"Oh, shush, Greeda. You know that's what they call you when you're not around, right? Greeda. Because all you care about are designer labels," Louise said. She was wild-eyed. Even the waiters were standing down, the friction at their table mounting so quickly that it was lapping the dining room in concentric circles.

"Is that true?" Peter asked. "That's horrible. Greta is a wonderful person. She doesn't deserve that nickname. If she spends a lot of money, it's because that's all I've emphasized the last two decades, living at the office."

"You know, I don't care whether Phoebe is an inspirator, an

influencer, or an imitator, she should feel lucky that Zachary likes her so much. Benny carried this place with his innovation and charm, so if I think we're better than you, I have my reasons." Louise tossed her napkin onto the table and jutted her chin in the air.

Zach saw Peter and Brian exchange glances.

"Benny was wonderful. But it was a partnership through and through. We each had our strengths," Amos said, keeping remarkable composure.

"That's right. And everyone, keep your voices down," Aimee urged. "People are starting to eavesdrop."

"Well, we know why you wouldn't want that to happen," Phoebe sneered.

"Phoebe, don't," Amos warned. Zach looked at her in confusion. She must know what was happening with his parents. But how?

"What are you talking about, Phoebe?" Fanny asked.

"Well, now's as good a time as any to tell you all," Phoebe said. "Dr. Glasser's a drug lord."

Chapter Twenty-Five

Maddie

I'm not sure I like that phrasing," Roger said. "But while we're telling secrets, did you also know that Benny was stealing from Amos? So let's not anybody at this table get all high and mighty."

"How dare you?" Louise yelled. "You hurt my daughter, and now you assault the character of my late husband with your lies?"

Maddie's heart was pounding. What was everyone talking about? She couldn't follow anything. Phoebe had called her father a drug lord, and he hadn't denied it. And then he'd said her grandfather was a thief? She looked at Zach, who was staring at his lap, appearing on the verge of tears.

"Figures he was a crook," Fanny said. "Think you're better than us now?" She powered up her wheelchair, though Maddie didn't know if she was planning to charge or retreat.

"Louise, Roger, let's take a deep breath," Brian said. "There is no proof of anything."

"You knew about this?" Aimee asked.

"My brother doesn't know anything," Peter said. "And I would like to know where Roger goes making these accusations."

"Brian's emails," Roger said. "I read them while he was off pretending to manage this place. This family can't separate the memories from the reality. I just wanted to get a look at the financials, see how bad things actually were. And there, right on his desktop, was an email to you from someone named Howard that spelled it all out. 'Possible fraud . . . fishy financials . . . yada yada.'"

"Possible!" Louise said. "Possible! It's not possible, that's what it is."

"Dad? Why are they saying you had something to do with drugs?" Maddie asked, her voice coming out in a squeak.

"I'll explain everything," he said, cupping her chin. "I promise I will."

"This isn't right," Amos said. "Not right at all. We can't take back the things we say. And the children are here. There is no fraud of which I'm aware. And, Phoebe, you should be ashamed of yourself for airing other people's dirty laundry."

"So what do we do now?" Zach asked. Maddie got up from her chair and put her arms around her little brother.

"We sell this goddamn hotel," Roger muttered. "Oh, and Brian, by the way—congrats on the baby. The doctor confirmed your appointment for tomorrow. Nice work knocking up a staff member."

The next thing they heard was, "HELP! Call an ambulance!"

If Milton Green's defibrillator hadn't failed, Maddie couldn't imagine where the night would have taken them. But it did, and an ambulance came with sirens blaring, and everyone crowded around Milton as the medics strapped him to a gurney and piled him into the ambulance. Though everyone knew it was merely a perfunctory trip. Milton was DOA. And watching a human take his last breath—it did something to all of them. Shut them up.

While everyone fussed around Milton's wife, Maddie snuck outside the hotel to her favorite spot, the giant tire swing on the front lawn. She tried to unpack it all.

If the Hoffs thought the Glassers weren't good enough for them because they owned a shtetel-like resort in the Catskills, how in the world were they going to react to the news of her father being a criminal? She didn't *actually* wonder. She knew they would tell Andrew to break up with her. The question was whether he would listen. What Maddie hadn't told anyone yet, not even her mother or her best friend, was that she and Andrew had picked out the engagement ring two days earlier. It was a beautiful three-carat emerald-cut, excellent color and quality. And it was on hold at a jewelry store on Worth Avenue while they waited for Andrew to ask his parents to take money out of his trust to buy it. She acknowledged the weirdness of being old enough to get married but needing permission to get the money for the ring.

"Hey," Zach said, walking toward her with his hands jammed into his pockets. "Come back inside?"

"What the hell, Z? You knew about Dad? And how does Phoebe know?"

"I just found out same time as you. I told Phoebe about the police raiding our house—by the way, the police raided our house—but that I didn't know why. I guess she had this relationship with a hacker dude a few months ago. She asked him to get into the Scarsdale police records, which was apparently super easy."

"Well, she didn't have to go and announce it," Maddie said.

"No, she didn't. But it was going to come out eventually," Zach said. "Mad, everyone wants you back inside. C'mon."

She didn't have the strength to argue. The dining room had quieted since the paramedics had left, and miraculously the guests were digging into dessert as if nothing had happened.

"I'm sorry," Phoebe said when Maddie took her seat. "Everyone was being really cruel to each other, and I felt like the one person who really sucks in this group was getting away scot-free."

"You might want to mind your own business," Roger said sharply. "And nobody is Scott-free, because he'll be here in the morning. He will understand my situation is a whole lot more nuanced than you all realize."

"Shame on you for bringing Scott," Louise said. "He has enough on his plate."

"It's important for him to vote with the rest of us," Roger said, opening the top two buttons of his shirt. "Jesus, it's hot in here. Why the hell doesn't the air-conditioning work, Brian?"

"Leave Brian alone," Aimee said. "At least he runs an honest business. You're full of crap about Scott. You called him here to get him on your side. Scott rarely looked up from his textbooks when he was at the hotel. He wouldn't know how to get from the pool to the card room without directions. He doesn't care about this place. Sorry to say it, but it's true."

"None of the young people care about this place," Amos said. "They want to turn it into a hippie-dippie, goat farm, Indigenous People–loving pot factory."

"Grandpa, that's not true. This is just the future," Michael said. He tugged at his sweat-ringed T-shirt, which said THREE-DOLLAR BILL on it.

"The kids are right, Dad," Brian said. "But I think we need to cool it for tonight. Tomorrow we'll vote in the boardroom at lunchtime. Whatever our differences are, our squabbles, our complaints and gripes and hostilities, they will still be there after we vote. Can everyone agree to a truce until tomorrow at noon?"

"Can everyone agree that it's time for dessert?" George interrupted, wheeling over a giant trolley with wheels the size of a horse-drawn carriage. It was typically only brought out on special evenings at the hotel.

"Oh, thank God," Greta said. "Yes, we would all like dessert."

"You're going to eat sugar?" Phoebe asked. "Wow. The world really is coming to an end."

"Tell us what you have," Peter said, even though they knew Chef Joe's confections like the backs of their hands. Apple strudel, linzers, chocolate and cinnamon loaves, raspberry roll-ups, sponge cake, marble cake, and the hotel specialty: a pineapple-strawberry Jell-O mold. Everything available with a scoop of vanilla ice cream if you just said "ALM," hotel shorthand for à la mode.

Maddie had been avoiding desserts for the past few weeks. She had her eye on a red Alaïa dress that Andrew said he'd buy for her. It would be perfect for an engagement party. They had decided the party would be in New York City, so that it was easy for their friends to make it, and because the wedding would be at Andrew's family's club in Palm Beach. "Imagine exchanging vows with the waves crashing in the background," Andrew had whispered in her ear dreamily. This had been the night before his parents had acted so abominably, and so she'd just kissed him by way of agreement. In truth, she thought getting married on the sand would be terrible. Andrew was eight inches taller than her, and if she couldn't wear heels, she'd look like a dwarf bride. And they'd have to scream their vows to be heard over the ocean. Now she wasn't sure any wedding would be taking place. Which meant . . . carbs.

"George, I'll have the Golden Palette," Maddie said, and watched the waiter's face light up. It was his favorite thing to serve—tiny slices of everything on the trolley. He'd have to Edward Scissorhands the cakes and tarts to make it all fit on one plate. "And I want it all ALM."

"Me too," Greta said, and her order was followed by a whole chorus of requests for the same.

"Brian, can I speak to you for a moment?" Larry the concierge approached while George was doling out the sweets.

"Sure, Larry, what's up?"

"Guests are asking what the Saturday night entertainment is going to be. You still didn't let me know, and I'm printing up the schedules," the concierge said.

For a moment it looked like Brian was about to wave him off, but then his face darkened.

"You know what, Larry, you're right. I can't believe this. I don't think I've forgotten to book a Saturday night act in, well, ever. I don't know what we're going to do."

"More strudel?" came a female voice from behind Larry. It was a waitress Maddie had seen around the dining room. She was pretty, in a middle-aged, Katie Couric kind of way.

"Angela, hi," Brian said, and the angst on his face just deepened. "You shouldn't be working the dinner shift anymore. I'll make sure to change that."

It was then that Maddie noticed Brian look at the waitress's midsection with tenderness.

Oh dear, Maddie thought. Her father had said something about a baby, hadn't he?

Maddie blew air from her lips in a whistle. And so the plot thickened at the Golden Hotel . . .

Maddie woke up to the sounds of lawn mowers winding their way across the property, louder as they passed her window, then receding, then loud again when they zigzagged back around. The alarm clock read 7:00 a.m. Why would Brian have the grounds-keepers start this early? She thought about suggesting a change, but why bother if this was the hotel's final summer? Its swan song might as well be lawn mowers.

Before she slipped on her glasses, she reached for her cell phone and powered it on. Squinting, she saw what she had been dreading. Not a single text message had come through overnight. Which meant Andrew was firmly planted under his parents' thumbs.

She felt new tears springing from her eyes, even though she was sure she had dehydrated her body the night before. The revelation about her dad had slicked Maddie in a cold, relentless sweat. Her mother must be dying a thousand deaths. And poor Scott, her father's lackey, about to walk into a storm his worst nightmares couldn't portend. Everything was falling apart at once.

Incinerated by the empty green and white text app without the telltale red circle, Maddie's head thudded back to meet the pillow. How could he? Did their two years together mean nothing? She didn't know how the unraveling of their relationship would play itself out, only that its end was inevitable. She could text him that it was over—say that if he couldn't stand up to his parents while they maligned her family's heritage, they were finished. Or she could wait a bit longer, just to be sure Andrew didn't grow a pair. One thing she knew from staring at her vacant phone—Andrew was who she wanted in a crisis. She longed to curl into a ball on their sofa and have him stroke her hair, even as he was the one causing her pain.

Their breakup was going to be excruciating. And today was voting day.

Before she'd left for Florida, Maddie had been certain she was on the side of selling. The hotel depressed her, beyond the smell in the closets and the decrepit furniture. Everywhere she turned, she saw signs of disrepair: peeling paint, chipped plates, threadbare carpets, rusted faucets. And the guests were geriatric, moving like snails from the card room to the dining room in repetitive loops three times a day. One of them had gone and died last night! There was something unsustainable about a resort where half the guest conversations started with "Remember when."

But after that sour evening with the Hoffs and the last twelve hours at the hotel, Maddie felt her mind shifting. She'd licked her Golden Palette clean last night—there wasn't a better linzer cookie to be found in all of New York. Then Zach had convinced her to play midnight tetherball. It was the most innocent fun she'd had in ages, and she'd been able to put Andrew and her father out of her head as the ball whizzed by and the lake sparkled in the background. She was really freaking tempted to vote against the sale. *F U, Mrs. Hoff and your stupid friends. You think you're so much better than my family?* The way their crew gossiped was no different than the Golden guests, rating spousal potential like credit scores.

She dressed while checking her phone at least half a dozen more times in between mascara swipes and shoelace tying, then headed to the dining room for breakfast. If she ate early enough, she could hopefully avoid seeing any Goldmans, Glassers, or Weingolds.

The lobby was predictably empty, except for Larry, who appeared to have spent the night at the concierge station. He had his head down, and a shiny thread of drool ran from his mouth to the stack of daily activity schedules he had fashioned into a pillow. She eyed the coffee station with gratitude, even though it was sure to be prison-quality compared to the cold brew at Blue Bottle that she and Andrew picked up every morning before work. But it was fuel, and she needed it after a crappy night's sleep. A pink Post-it Note affixed to the coffee urn read: OUT OF ORDER. Jesus, seriously? Not even an apology!

She slumped onto one of the floral-patterned couches in the lobby and pulled her Kindle from her purse. She and Andrew had made joint New Year's Resolutions, which included reading more. Maddie was in the process of rereading the same page for the third time when she heard a rapping on the front door of the hotel. The door was kept locked overnight, a lesson she and her brothers had learned the hard way when they'd snuck out as teenagers to drink at a local pub, come back at 2 a.m., and were left to sleep outside. She looked up and startled, dropping her Kindle onto the floor. Behind the glass was Andrew with a bouquet of azaleas in his hand. Maddie ran to greet him.

"Hi!"

She thrust herself into his arms, and the bouquet fell to the ground in a soft landing. Petals flew in the wind, and Maddie heard an awake Larry saying: "He loves you, he loves you not."

"He loves you," Andrew said, taking a step back and looking around. "I'm so sorry. I hope this is okay that I showed up here."

"It's more than okay. I was getting whiplash from checking my phone so many times. I need a massage, but there's no spa here. Only a cosmetician who believes blush goes on in stripes."

Andrew made the adorable bewildered face he always did when she talked about anything feminine, where he furrowed his brow and cocked his chin to the right. It was the look he'd given her when she'd asked him if she should wear wedges or a kitten heel to their friend's Memorial Day barbeque in the Hamptons. "Kitten heel? As in a cat?" He'd started meowing, and she'd laughed hysterically, and they'd had really great sex before the party. Andrew could be such a goofball when he wasn't around his parents.

"I was going for the element of surprise. Listen, I've done a lot of thinking since you left Florida. It's absurd that I've never come with you to see the hotel. I know how important it is to you and your family. And I should have stood up to my parents at dinner. They're all about hotels on private islands and using the jet, but the truth is that they're miserable. I can't think of any trip we've ever taken where the memories remotely compare to what you've described here."

She stood on tiptoe and kissed him passionately, noticing how deep the circles under his eyes were. They were both sleep-deprived and in love.

"You look like you need coffee. Sadly, the machine's broken and breakfast doesn't open for twenty more minutes. Want to sit down?" She tugged him toward the couch where she'd been pretend-reading.

"I am tired," Andrew admitted. "But I'm too excited to sit. Show me around." He took her hand and gave it a gentle tug.

The early morning air was crisp, and the smell was the perfect mixture of freshly cut grass, mountain air, and wildflowers. They laughed when they got socked by the oscillating sprinkler.

She showed Andrew everything: the rec room, the card room, the auditorium, the dining room, the nightclub, the tennis courts, the golf clubhouse, the water sports area, Lake Winetka's rocky "beach," Roberta's salon, the lounge, and the iconic kidney-shaped pool, where Maddie had splashed away her childhood summers, blasting water pistols at Zach and Scott. Even though the rowboats were rusty, the clay courts full of potholes, and the pool water an unsettling shade of gray, Maddie felt a surge of pride taking Andrew around. They concluded their tour in Memory Lane.

"These pictures are incredible," Andrew said, his nose mere inches from the display. "So that was your grandpa when he was young? And that's the Gold Rush competition you've talked about? The trophies are huge. What's that picture?" He pointed to a photograph that looked to be from the sixties, based on Grandma Louise's full-skirted peach shift dress with a white leather belt around the waist.

"Oh, that's the talent show. That's one tradition everyone agrees was okay to retire."

"But what are they doing?"

Maddie came closer to the picture. "Oh dear. It looks like they're reenacting Marilyn Monroe's 'Happy Birthday Mr. President.' Except instead of Marilyn Monroe, it's Marilyn Moscowitz and her backup dancers, the Brooklyn Babes."

"Holy shit," Andrew said, his face mere inches from the photograph now. "Maddie, look." He pointed to one of the dancers, second to the end, wearing a skimpy two-piece, heels, and a sailor hat.

"What is it? You think she's hot?"

"Maddie, that's my grandmother."

To: Brian Weingold
From: Howard Williams
Subject: Sale of the Golden Hotel

Brian,

    This email is to confirm our understanding that your family and the Goldman family will respond to our offer to purchase the Golden Hotel by 5 pm EST today. Should we not hear a response by that time, we will proceed with alternate plans to buy an adjacent property.

    Kindly,

    HB

Winwood Holdings, a subsidiary of Diamond Enterprises

"Where everyone is a high roller"

Chapter Twenty-Six

Brian

Brian did not expect that on the day the future of the hotel was decided—and by extension his career either finished or furnished an extra life—he would be at a doctor's office with his girlfriend looking at a fuzzy sonogram image of his unborn child. Life had thrown him another curveball, and this one looked like a white alien wearing sneakers, gestational age nine weeks.

"Let me get that jelly off you," Dr. Leeds said, using a wad of paper towels to wipe the aqua goo off Angela's still taut belly. "Everything's looking good. Baby is the right size, the heartbeat is nice and strong, and despite the fact that this is technically a high-risk, geriatric pregnancy, I feel good about what I'm seeing."

Brian watched Angela's face. Was there not a more diplomatic way to speak to a mother over the age of forty? He wasn't sure Dr. Leeds was right for them as a long-term care doctor. In the towns surrounding the hotel, there weren't many options, and the ultrasound machine in Leeds's exam room looked like a personal computer from the 1980s.

"Thank you, Dr. Leeds," Brian said. "That's great to hear."

"Let me step out so you can get dressed," Dr. Leeds told Angela, who was struggling to stay covered underneath a paper-thin gown in a room that felt like a meat locker. "Congrats, Mom and Dad." He shut the door behind him and left the soon-to-be parents, their quivering fingers holding black-and-white images of their baby.

"It's not a Polaroid," Angela said. "Not sure why we're both shaking these so much."

The doctor had called him Dad. He wasn't a dad, though. Not yet. Amos Weingold was a dad. He'd taught his boys how to swim and fish and unclog a toilet and rewire an electrical circuit. He'd worked his ass off for decades to provide for his family. Was Brian capable of such things? To nurture and love someone without a trace of resentment, like his mother, who'd cooked dinner even when she had a headache, and his father, who'd stayed up to watch the Mets with his boys even though he needed to review the books? In hindsight, Brian wondered if Benny's chicanery had happened because Amos had been so distracted by his family. Aimee had been a less demanding child than him and Peter. Louise would say she could give her child a canvas and some paint and not hear a peep for hours.

Brian believed he had the capacity to be a good father, but would he really know until the baby came out wailing seven short months from now?

"Angela, I'm so impressed with you," he said, bending down to get the neat stack of her clothes piled on the spare chair.

She put a finger to his lips and the gown slipped off her shoulder. Brian adored the heart-shaped birthmark at the base of her neck. He would peck it repeatedly when he was tipsy. There was genuine affection between them. But he had felt something possibly stronger two nights ago.

"Brian, you and I have a lot to discuss. But not today. Today is about the hotel and your family."

"You're amazing, Angela. Truly." He felt gratitude for this woman warm his body like a vapor rub, and he bent down to kiss her stomach.

Brian walked into the final family meeting feeling about as nauseous as Angela seemed every morning. He was pregnant with stress, molecules multiplying inside him at such lightning speed, he worried he could vomit at any minute. Grave faces greeted him upon arrival. Nobody mentioned the baby—either they felt too awkward, or Mr. Green really had died at the perfect moment and they hadn't heard.

Shaggy was an unexpected attendee. The golden retriever was sitting on one of the chairs around the table, sniffing to a staccato beat and looking thoroughly unimpressed. An old girlfriend of Brian's had once said all men were like dogs, and he wondered if there was symbolism behind Aimee's choice of companion this morning. What an asshole Roger was, and stupid, too, to risk so much for greed. Aimee deserved so much better. Brian had never liked the guy. In fact, the doctor was generally disliked around the hotel. On more than one occasion, he'd had the audacity to send back wine, as if the Golden were the Ritz in Paris. The waiters used to make fun of him behind the barn doors leading to the kitchen, putting on a faux-French accent and saying, "Excuse me . . . I ordered ze 2016 Manischewitz and zis ees clearly ze 2017 Kedem." He was the kind of guy who flipped out if someone called him "Mister" instead of "Doctor." The only reason Brian was upset about what was coming to the guy was that Aimee and the kids would be collateral damage.

"Let us not speak of last night," Amos said, breaking the pin drop silence with a call for more silence. Brian agreed. Whatever had happened between Benny and Amos, whatever was going on with Roger, whatever long-standing resentments existed between the matriarchs, it all had to be set aside, at least for today. Nods intimated that the group agreed to a temporary moratorium. They had to vote. Fighting could happen later.

Brian wondered how many in the room were in the same place that he was: undecided. Until the voting cards were handed out (Phoebe had created nifty ballots on her laptop, with matching envelopes that would be stamped rather than hand-marked to preserve anonymity), Brian really didn't think he'd be able to make up his mind. He had been leaning toward selling at first. It was hard for him to ignore the numbers, especially as he was the most intimately acquainted with them. He watched the way the hotel bled money every month, paying a bloated staff, repairing essential equipment like the AC condenser and pool filter while the guests bellyached about cosmetic repairs though the carcass was rotting. But having everyone converge back on property, Brian felt his heart shifting. How could they lose their summer home? Would he and his parents be able to stomach the sight of the wrecking ball leveling their legacy? But was a legacy something enshrined in bricks and mortar, or could it live on in photographs and apocryphal stories? And now there was the baby and Angela to think about.

His indecision called his ex-wife to mind. When he and Melinda went out for dinner, she would say she couldn't choose an entrée until the waiter came with pad and pen. She needed the pressure. Well, that's exactly how he felt now. All night long he'd ventured guesses as to how everyone would vote. He was fairly certain of one thing: It was going to be a close one.

Brian looked over at Scott, who must have arrived just hours earlier. His clothes were rumpled, and dark circles made his eyes look like they were in deep sockets.

"How's med school?" Brian asked him.

"It's hard," Scott mumbled, and Brian was about to laud him for working so diligently, when he continued. "But I do have some news. I decided on the flight here to change my area of medicine. I was going to go into internal medicine like my—well, you know. But I actually really hated it. I'm going to do psychiatry instead."

"Are you, Scott?" Louise said, clearly shocked. "I had no idea you were interested in that." The "that" might as well have been "phony-baloney woo-woo medicine."

"Nobody knows anything about their grandchildren," Fanny said through thin, pursed lips.

"Well, I think that's great, Scott," Greta said. "Therapy has been a wonderful thing for me. Peter and I decided to see a couples' counselor when we get back."

"Seriously? What is with everyone?" Amos glared at his daughter-in-law. "Does nobody believe in privacy anymore? Benny and I used to sit around playing cards with the men until four o'clock in the morning. You think anyone said they weren't getting along with the old ball and chain? Hell, no. You think people shared about their business problems? Absolutely not. We talked about poker, sports, politics. Everything else is a family matter."

"Grandpa," Michael said, extending his hand toward Amos's. "We are family. All of us. The Goldmans and Weingolds and Glassers are closer than most blood-related people. And there's nothing wrong with talking about personal stuff."

If there was anyone among them who could make that statement with gravitas, it was him.

"I agree," Aimee said. "Scott, that sounds fantastic. I'll be your first patient." A nervous laugh escaped, swallowed by the sound of the air-conditioning kicking on.

"So, we ready?" Brian said. He eyed the ballots stacked at the center of the boardroom table.

"I don't think we'll ever be ready," Peter said. "But we don't have much choice."

Slowly, Phoebe circled the table, handing out the ballots. Amos put his eyedrops in. Aimee pulled out her reading glasses. Fanny adjusted her wheelchair. The kids fiddled with their cell phones. Brian pictured the sonogram image.

It took at most five minutes for everyone to vote and place their ballots into the shoebox that someone had intelligently thought to bring.

Brian took the box over to the corner of the room and went through the votes one by one.

He returned to the table moments later.

"A decision has been reached," he said.

"Yes?" everyone seemed to say all at once.

He looked back at the paper where he'd done his tally one more time to confirm his eyes weren't sending an incorrect signal to his brain. Then he scanned the faces of his family and the Goldmans one more time before making the announcement.

"This will be the last summer at the Golden Hotel."

Chapter Twenty-Seven

Amos

All at once, Amos felt the room spinning. The boardroom table lifted off the ground and tilted on its axis. He wanted to reach out and put it back in place, but it would be too unwieldy. The landscape paintings on the wall rattled, and everyone's voices garbled into one cacophonous stream. An invisible fist—whose was it?—grasped his heart and started to squeeze. And then all he saw was blackness.

"Dad? Dad? Are you okay?" Peter was on top of him. Or was that Brian? They looked different, but their voices had always been similar.

"Amos, drink some water." That was Fanny. He heard a motor buzz. Her chair. Fanny was coming closer to him. The sound of her approach throbbed in his ear.

"Someone get Roger," Aimee wailed. "He's upstairs packing. Maddie, Scott, Zach, get him fast. Tell him to bring his medical bag."

Amos heard the scrape of chairs and the thud of footsteps. They were getting Roger. Was it because of him? He wondered what a heart attack felt like. Fanny used to repeat the warning signs to him. Shoulder pain. Shortness of breath. He didn't know if he had either of those. Mostly he felt numb.

And then there was a bottle of water being lifted to his lips. He thought he recognized his granddaughter's hand, all those jangly bracelets she wore shooting laser beams at his pupils.

"Have a sip, Grandpa. It's important." He did as he was told.

The door to the boardroom opened.

"Caught him just as he was driving away," Scott said, panting.

"Amos, it's Roger. I'm going to ask you some questions. Is that all right?"

He nodded. What choice did he have, anyway? Amos was no longer calling the shots. He was old, and other people directed the course of his life.

"Can you see how many fingers I'm holding up?"

Three.

"What year were you born?"

Nineteen thirty-six.

"Are you seeing spots?"

"He has MD," Fanny shouted. But he wasn't seeing spots anyway. He was seeing everything clearly, but all at once. The day he and Benny had broken ground on the hotel. Peter's wedding. Phoebe's tiny hand in his at the hospital the day she was born. Fanny on the ground after her stroke. Bette Midler singing her heart out in the ballroom. Brian's face when he'd returned home after Melinda. Everything in stark relief but out of order, layered like tissue paper.

"All right, I'm going to take your vitals. Try to breathe normally."

Amos felt Roger's fingers on his wrists. Everyone quieted while his pulse was taken. A bright light shone in his eyes. Then his mouth was forced open. More instruments. Cold ones. Prodding that left him feeling less human than ever before. The quiet in the room broke, and a chorus of "What happened?" and "Will he be okay?" sounded.

"He's going to be okay," Roger said. "It was a panic attack. All vitals check out. Pulse is slowing. No signs of visual impairment. But he should rest for the remainder of the day."

"Thank you so much, Roger," Fanny said. "We really appreciate you rushing back to help."

"Of course. Is there anything else I can do?"

Amos saw everyone in the room look over to Aimee for direction.

"We've got this," Aimee said. "I saw Dr. Miller sign the guest book this morning. He'll help us with anything we need."

"Dr. Miller is a podiatrist, and he's deaf in both ears," Peter said.

"Doesn't that just make him deaf?" Michael asked.

"For some reason that's how his wife likes to describe it," Brian said.

"We'll manage without Roger," Aimee said, this time more firmly.

Amos saw his sons exchange glances and agree in their telepathic twin way not to argue.

"I'm feeling better," Amos said. "You should go. Thank you."

He watched Roger silently pack his medical bag and wave

feebly at his children. "Aimee," he said when he got to where she was standing. "We'll talk?"

She acquiesced with just the smallest movement of her chin, and Roger turned to leave.

"Drive safely," Aimee said quietly when his hand was already on the doorknob.

"Dad, you gave us quite a scare," Brian said, kneeling beside him. Something about what Brian said echoed in his head. *You gave us quite a scare . . .* But Amos was the one who felt scared. Scared about what would happen to Brian without the hotel. Scared about knowing how little time he had left. Yes, he was "retired," but was that an accurate description when he called Brian at least twice a week to check on things? When he still got to close out the season as the hotel's co-founder, guests shaking his hand and telling him what a special place he'd built? The sale of the hotel felt not so much like the shuttering of a business; it felt like the closing of a life. He imagined a SORRY, WE'RE CLOSED sign around his neck, strung with the heavy links of a metal chain.

"I'm all right," he said, looking at his boys' faces. In Peter's he saw a renewed hope. Something positive had transpired between him and Greta. Not since their courtship days at the Golden had he seen them hold hands and kiss on the lips. And Brian, he didn't look as crushed by the results of the vote as Amos would have predicted. If anything, he looked dazed. Hell, maybe he'd even voted to sell. Though he wasn't necessarily book smart like his brother, he probably could have gone further than balancing payroll and reordering housekeeping supplies. Brian didn't fit in this Podunk town, not all year round. But what was that last night he'd heard about a baby?

ELYSSA FRIEDLAND

"Do you want something to eat? I can get George to bring you a fruit plate." Fanny was next to him now, fussing. He was supposed to care for her after the stroke, not the other way around. But when he approached anything close to caretaking with her, she'd shoo him away. "With your eyes, it'd be the blind leading the blind." He knew she hated to feel helpless. Fanny had been a bustling, frenetic woman before the blood decided not to travel to her brain, and she must hate to be stripped of caretaking, her raison d'être. It was like how he felt impotent without his identity as the lovable innkeeper. He wondered if possibly Fanny had voted to sell. She had made comments in recent years like, "Who needs all that agita?" and "Wouldn't it be nice to stay in Florida full-time?" But no, it would be hard to imagine she'd vote to sell something so precious to him.

Aimee and Louise were wild cards. Aimee needed money—or rather Roger did, but they were tangled together, with children who hung in the balance. Louise loved the hotel dearly, but he knew without Benny it brought her more pain than pleasure. And the grandchildren. They had all sorts of lofty ideas about how to modernize, but many of them were impractical. Did that mean they'd voted to sell, or were they idealistic and hopeful like he'd once been? Amos simply didn't know, and with the decision made, it really didn't matter. The others had complicated lives in which the hotel played only a supporting role. For him, and for Benny if he'd still been here, the choice would have been a purer calculation. How he'd hated to hear Benny's name dragged through the mud last night. If they only knew the truth about the mortgages. Maybe one day he would share it. Or not.

"What do we do with the money raised by the 5B? Can we,

like, give it back? So far they've raised over two hundred thousand dollars," Phoebe said, flashing her phone around.

"I don't know," Brian said, scratching his chin. "We have to notify them that we're selling. And then I guess it's up to the organizers."

There was a knock on the door.

"Come in," Brian called out.

It was the intern. The girl with the ladder of earrings posted through her cartilage who'd called the fire department the other day.

"Yes, Lisa?" Amos wanted to assert his voice, to prove he wasn't going the way of Milton Green anytime soon.

"It's Lucy. I'm afraid there's a problem in the kitchen. Mrs. Lewison insisted on making her own challah for Friday night dinner. The staff tried to keep her out of the kitchen, but she pushed her way through. Anyway, she broke two ovens, went through three dozen eggs, and is screaming at Joe for buying the wrong yeast."

"Okay, okay. Tell Joe I'll be over there in a few minutes," Brian said.

With the hotel sold, they wouldn't have to deal with these kinds of issues anymore. Crazy guests, unhappy staff, broken kitchen equipment—it would eventually bundle into one faded memory. Before they knew it, they wouldn't recall whether the bed linens were white or ivory, or whether they did brisket or roast chicken for the first Friday night of the season. They wouldn't know where the tennis balls were kept hidden or what year the wild bear had gotten into the swimming pool. Mrs. Teitelbaum would get confused with Mrs. Turtletaub and nobody would remember the house rules for poker.

Lucy flashed a thumbs-up and took her leave.

"So now that we've reached a decision, when is everyone planning to leave? Not that we need your rooms vacated because of demand, obviously," Brian said, sheepish grin softening his chiseled jaw.

"Um, I don't know," Aimee said. "I guess I hadn't really decided. I suppose we can leave now, can't we? Kids, what do you think?"

The youngsters exchanged glances.

"I'll stay the rest of the weekend," Maddie said. "Andrew's just arrived, and I want him to get the full experience."

"I'm game," Zach said.

"I can access most of my study materials online, so sure, why not?" Scott said. "This beats the library."

"Well, if my kids are staying, then I am, too," Aimee said. "I can't believe I've been here a whole week and I haven't gone in the pool once."

"Peter, you must need to get back for work, no?" Fanny asked. It was shocking that Peter had made it up to the hotel at all, that he hadn't just tried to manage the Michael flare-up via Zoom. Surely one of his minions could have drafted an email on the matter of his child's sexuality.

As if on cue, Peter picked up his iPhone. The man's work was unrelenting.

"Actually, I'm just texting Greta. I think it might be nice to stay through the weekend."

"Wow, so we're all staying," Brian said. "That's really . . . I'm just . . . it's so . . . this is great. Although I still don't have any entertainment lined up for tomorrow night."

"Oh, I have a question," Maddie said. "Grandma, Amos, Fanny, do any of you remember a woman by the name of Estée Feinberg?"

"Do you mean Esther Feinberg?" Amos asked.

"That hussy!" Louise called out.

"Such trash," Fanny said, waving her hand dismissively.

"Who could forget Esther?" Amos said, laughing at the memory. He hadn't thought about her in decades. "She slept her way through the waitstaff at Grossinger's, Kutsher's, the Concord, and the Golden, and when she ran out of men there, she hit the bungalow colonies. Why do you ask about her? Not a classy broad, that one."

"Um, oh my God. This is insane," Maddie said, a wide grin taking over her face. "Esther—well, now Estée—Feinberg is Andrew's grandmother."

Chapter Twenty-Eight

Louise

When the ballots had been placed in front of her, Louise had been trembling. She'd hoped nobody had noticed the way her hands had shaken when she'd gone to stamp them. It was unbecoming of a woman her age to appear this uncertain. Maybe they would think she had Parkinson's with all that shaking. She'd looked to see if others were feeling similar distress, but it had been poker faces all around. Of course, only she had a vote that counted twice.

Benny, her love. The man who had lifted her when she was down, who had made her feel like a princess again after her father had lost everything. And he'd been good to her mother, too, welcoming Celine to the hotel every summer and describing her as a very renowned and influential woman in Montreal, even after she was forced to fire all the help and clean her own toilets. Never gossiping about Louise's father, even though the stories would have gotten a lot of traction in the card room. Benny would even buy jewelry for her mother and, knowing she'd be too proud to accept a gift, tell her these were unclaimed items left behind by the guests. Who cared what flirtations—or more—he'd dabbled in on the side? She had secrets, too, worse than his. A betrayal that would have slain him. How could she vote against him? A vote to sell was a vote against her late husband. It was that simple.

But then there was her daughter. Aimee needed the money from a sale. Whether she used it to help keep Roger out of prison or to support the kids—especially the grown-and-unflown Zacky—or both, it didn't really matter. Her daughter would benefit the most from a million or so dollars in her bank account, because the government would seize everything that could be traced to Roger's business. With these twin urges tugging her in opposite directions, when Brian had announced that everyone should keep their eyes on only their own ballot, Louise had stamped one ballot in support of the sale and one against.

The decision to sell had relieved her, though she'd tried to keep her face stoic when Brian had announced it. Keeping the hotel was a way to honor her husband, but he was six feet under. A decision to sell helped Aimee in the here and now. And life, as her own mother often remarked, was for the living.

But then Amos had nearly collapsed on them, and Louise had felt terrible all over again. What had she done? Was it her split vote that had tipped the scales? Only Brian knew the tally, and as CEO, he had made the decision not to share it. Everyone agreed with his decision to keep the final count private. It relieved them all of feeling their choice was the one that had summoned the wrecking ball.

After Amos had been declared well enough to go to his room, their group disbanded quickly. An urgency was setting in, to soak up every last thing the Golden had to offer before the title transferred. Aimee headed for a dip, Peter went to meet Greta for tennis, Brian needed to deal with the challah disaster, and the kids decided on an impromptu Ping-Pong tournament. Fanny suggested gin rummy to Louise, but she demurred. She knew where she wanted to be, and this was her best chance to get there alone. But first, a stop was needed at her cabin.

Louise pushed open the door and found a young gal from housekeeping inside, wiping down the countertops in the kitchenette.

"Mrs. Goldman, I'm so sorry," she said. Louise studied the young woman quickly gathering cleaning supplies and loading them onto her cart.

"It's no trouble," Louise said. "Though it would be better if you would come back a bit later. Tell me"—she squinted to read the name tag affixed to her uniform—"Carol, how long have you worked here?"

Carol looked flustered. Louise was always gracious to the help, but if she was honest with herself, there were few she'd gotten to know well.

"Ten years, madam," Carol said. "I love it here."

Louise smiled at her, because what else could she do? Tell her that she'd soon be out of a job, but that hopefully Brian could finagle employment at the casino? But even that was a long shot. By the time Diamond built their behemoth, it would be years that the Golden staff would be without income. There was a part of Louise that wanted to know the gory details—How many children did she have? Did her husband have a job?—but what would be the point? More heartache.

After Carol had left, Louise let out a shudder. So many livelihoods were about to be upended, though it could hardly come as a surprise. If Carol had friends on staff who had worked at the hotel longer than she, she would know it had once been a place where overbooked rooms meant working extra shifts and running out of clean towels and linens. She would know that she worked at a shadow of something once great.

Louise opened up the closet in the bedroom and pushed aside the matching pants and sweater sets she'd grown accustomed to wearing in recent years. They weren't sloppy, like the yoga outfits the mothers pushing strollers on the Upper West Side wore. Her outfits were neat, cashmere tops and narrow slacks fitted around her slender body. Still, the ensemble was a far cry from the silk dresses and linen trousers she used to wear, her handbag and shoes always a perfect match. Flexing her aching calves, Louise knew she needed to throw in the proverbial towel. She was growing older—no, she was old—and was a widow to boot. But for the next half hour, she would put that realization aside.

The mint green chiffon gown, with its lovely beaded bodice and lace trim at the neckline, hung pristinely preserved in a black garment bag, in which paper stuffing kept the dress's shape. Louise knew it would fit because she kept to a very strict diet. She never stepped on a scale, but if her pants ever felt snug, she simply abstained from her morning bagel until her waistline shrank back. It was hard to close the dress without Benny to help with the zipper, but a wire hanger eventually did the trick. She slipped into her matching heels, ignoring the protest from her arches, and draped a white fur stole over her shoulders. Now she just had to pray nobody saw her on the walk. Luckily, she knew a back trail that led to the theater. It was the same place Aimee and the Weingold boys used to smoke and drink, thinking they were being stealthy. But Louise knew their every move. Not that she ever punished her daughter or ratted out the twins. It had been her feeling—Benny's, too—that it was better for the kids to get into trouble at the Golden. Let them feel like rebels in their own backyard so they didn't seek out the sensation elsewhere.

She made it to the empty auditorium without detection, just a little mud on her shoes. She wished she could have called for a golf cart, but how would she explain this getup? Louise found the microphone and stand in its usual place and dragged it to the center of the stage. Feeling silly, she tapped the mike and said "Testing" in a soft voice. The reverberation, though expected, made her jump.

She closed her eyes and let a meditative silence take over. As her body relaxed and her diaphragm expanded, she imagined each empty seat filled with guests in their finest attire. The men were clutching Scotches, the women were gossiping amiably about who was wearing last year's fashion and who had gained weight. Celebrities filled the front row. Everyone was flush with excitement, ready and not ready to say goodbye to a fabulous summer at the Golden.

Louise cleared her throat and purred in French.

My friends. You all look fabulous this evening. Thank you for making this our best summer yet at the Golden Hotel. Now please join me in singing our beloved anthem.

Everyone cheered.

She began to sing, her voice wavering at first but growing stronger as she moved from stanza to stanza.

"Grandma, what are you doing?" Maddie's voice, high-pitched and giggly, broke through.

Louise's eyes flitted open.

At the back of the auditorium stood her three grandchildren, along with Phoebe and Michael Weingold and Andrew, Maddie's beau.

"You sound amazing, Mrs. Goldman," Andrew called out. "Keep going!"

Michael let out a wolf whistle.

"Maybe you should be the entertainment for tomorrow night?" Scott called out.

"Nah, nah, we've got that all worked out, remember?" Phoebe said.

Louise gathered the skirt of her gown in her hands and rushed stage left. What excuse could she give the children as to why she was all dressed up, singing her heart out to an empty auditorium?

Zach charged forward to help when he saw her struggle on the stairs. Aimee had done a lovely job with her children. They were mensches, each and every one of them.

"I was just checking on the—" she started to say, but Maddie interrupted.

"So cool you're singing up here, Grandma. We're also going around the hotel doing our favorite things for the last time."

"Speaking of which, we gotta go," Scott said apologetically. "We have a hot dog eating contest to start, a Gold Rush to reenact, and some other things that you're better off not hearing about."

Before she could ask any questions, the children were gone,

and Louise was left in the auditorium, alone once more. But now she felt a fullness in her heart. She looked again at the empty seats, but this time she didn't close her eyes.

"*Vous êtes tous beaux*," she murmured.

Hey, the kids told me you were in the auditorium all dressed up," Aimee said, spotting Louise seated on a rocking chair outside the main entrance. "You feeling all right?"

"Yes, yes," Louise said. "Just a little foolish. Want to have a cup of tea?" She rose from the chair, not liking how clumsy her movements were. Long gone were the days when she could pop up and down to greet guests.

"Sure," Aimee said, looking at her watch. "I've got time. I'm a little hungry, too."

They walked into the kitchen together. It wasn't a mealtime, so they went to help themselves to the pastries that Chef Joe always held back for staff.

"Shoot, I want Splenda," Aimee said. "I think there's some in there." She gestured with a raised hand to a cabinet above the fridge. As she did so, her tank top slid off her shoulder and revealed a constellation of bright red dots above her bra. Cherry angiomas.

"Aimee, you have those red dots, like your father. When did that happen?"

Aimee looked down at her chest.

"Ugh, those. All over my stomach, my chest. One of the pleasures of middle age. They've been sprouting like crazy," Aimee said. "My dermatologist said they're genetic, so I'm not surprised. Dad was covered in them."

"He certainly was," Louise said, her entire body tremoring. Clarity, after so many years. It ripped through her like an electroshock.

"Maman, you look like you've seen a ghost," Aimee said, facing her with a puzzled expression.

"It feels like I have, darling," Louise said. "In the best possible way. Now let's have tea, shall we?"

Chapter Twenty-Nine

Michael

On Saturday morning, Michael jumped out of bed and headed straight for the auditorium. The costume closet smelled like cigarette smoke, and Michael coughed his way through the metal racks stuffed wall-to-wall with costumes and props from decades of shows. The dangling fluorescent bulbs were causing him to sweat, but he simply couldn't part with Tevya's cap nor the red pleather Kinky Boots he had on. Finally, he found what he was looking for: a simple black bodysuit that had been worn for a production of *Cats* many years ago. Michael was going to kick off the evening's performance with "Memory."

He was almost done compiling everything he would need for the show when a stack of leather-bound albums caught his eye. Michael reached for the top book, and a single Polaroid fluttered to the ground. He picked it up and saw Jackie Mason standing in between his grandfather and Benny Goldman. On the flip side of the photo, someone—likely the comedian himself—had scrawled:

Money is not the most important thing in the world. Love is. Fortunately, I love money.

Michael tore open the book. There were at least a hundred photographs affixed to the pages. It was always an entertainer flanked by Benny and Amos; a Hollywood-meets-Catskills sandwich. Billy Crystal, Andy Kaufman, Henny Youngman, Sid Caesar; a who's who of entertainment spanning many decades. A young Jerry Seinfeld was pictured giving bunny ears to Benny; Joan Rivers was smooching his grandpa. He turned over every picture and found a handwritten note. Rodney Dangerfield had written, *You owe me dry cleaning money for the borscht spill.* The fighter Rocky Marciano, pictured shirtless in his boxing shorts and gloves, had written, *Chef Joe's babka is a TKO.*

A drop of water fell on a photograph of his grandfather sitting at the piano next to Sammy Davis Jr. Michael looked up at the ceiling, trying to spot the leak. This whole place was falling apart. He wouldn't be surprised to find a gaping hole in the roof of the playhouse. But he saw nothing other than yellowed paint on the popcorn ceiling. It took him a minute to realize he was crying.

Get it together, Michael. He used his shirt to dry his eyes and shimmied into the cat costume. He was a little worried about how his grandparents would feel seeing him pirouette to Andrew Lloyd Webber. He was the headliner, but Phoebe, Maddie, Scott, and Zach had agreed to be "backup." Zach had needed the most convincing, demurring that he'd help backstage, but once Phoebe had said "Don't be lame," Zach was stretching for the *Dirty Dancing* lift reenactment. They'd apparently patched up from Phoebe's dismissive comment about their relationship at dinner Thursday night. When he asked his sister about it, she said, "I dunno. I like the whole Capulet and Montague thing we have going on." Which reminded Michael . . . he might throw a little *Midsummer Night's Dream* action into his performance.

Michael's professional goals were born of summers spent sitting front row, goggle-eyed, at the Golden's performances. Watching a singer captivate an audience, a comedian bring on laughter, a musician tickle the ivories—Michael had longed to leap onto the stage and join them. When his acceptance to Harvard had come via email and actually brought his father home from work midday to celebrate, other people's ideas about his future had started to take shape. Acceptable paths were law, medicine, or business. Slightly more offbeat detours that were still acceptable were variants of the above—not-for-profit law, public sector medical research. When Michael had secretly switched majors a few months earlier, he had channeled courage from the very performers who had graced the stages of the Golden. How upset could his parents be when he was simply honoring a tradition their family had fostered for so long? And they weren't. His parents were adjusting.

"Michael, we need to practice," came his sister's voice through the closet door. He heard the giggles of the Glassers. "What are you still doing in there?"

He opened the door and watched with glee as everyone took in the sight of him in the cat costume.

"You're right. I'm done being in the closet."

Thunderous applause followed the performance, even a standing ovation from the more spry audience members.

"You were really amazing," Fanny said, kissing him on both cheeks. "Who knew such talent from our family? Though I had an uncle who could really tell jokes." She was beaming, buzzing around in her wheelchair and stopping at every table to accept congratulations on behalf of her grandson.

But when she got to the Cullmans, things got a little dicey.

Mrs. Cullman, an old-timer guest of the hotel who had once dated Benny briefly before he'd met Louise, asked Fanny about Michael. "You know I have that pretty granddaughter at Brown. Thin, sweet, studying to be an economist if you can believe it. And yours goes to Harvard, I know. Could be a nice match. What do you say, Fan?"

"I'm seeing someone," Michael said, saving his grandmother the discomfort.

Mrs. Cullman looked disappointed.

"Well, if it doesn't work out, don't forget my Julie."

Once the guests had cleared out, the Weingolds and Goldmans collapsed into chairs.

"That went well," Brian said. The ice in his Scotch clinked as he took a sip.

"Considering we had half a day to rehearse, I'd say yes," Scott said. "I was forced into singing with the UltraSounds by someone in med school. Well, the someone is actually my girlfriend, Bella. I wanted to bring her here."

"You still can," Aimee said. "We're open through Colum— Indigenous People's Day. I'd love to meet her."

"What happened at the end?" Phoebe asked, looking at Grandpa Amos. "I thought you were going to announce the sale once our performance was over."

ELYSSA FRIEDLAND

"I just wanted to enjoy tonight. There's always time for that. Rumors swirl like flies around here. I'll tell Shirley Cohen in the morning, and she'll get on the horn and everyone from Brooklyn to Miami Beach will know by the end of the day," he said.

"On that note, Andrew and I have a little announcement," Maddie said. She unwound her hand from Andrew's and revealed a sparkly diamond.

"Oh my God," Aimee exclaimed, jumping up from her seat and swallowing Maddie and Andrew whole. "You're engaged!"

"Let me get champagne from the kitchen," Brian said, popping up.

"Well, more than engaged, technically." Maddie pulled her other hand from her pocket, where a thin metal band circled her ring finger.

"What? When? How?" Louise asked. "Are you crazy?"

"Maman, stop," Aimee said. "Let's enjoy this moment."

Louise stood up and kissed Aimee on the forehead. She cupped her daughter's chin.

"You're so much like him, you know? Your father. Benny would have focused on the positive as well."

"We figured there's no time like the present," Andrew said with a modest shrug. "With Maddie's dad and—well, you know. So we went to a justice of the peace this morning. And, if it's all right with you all, we'd like to celebrate our marriage here. At the Golden."

"If the Catskills were good enough for Elizabeth Taylor, then they're good enough for me," Maddie said.

"And she only got married at Grossinger's," Louise said. "Wait until you see what we put on for you here."

@GoldenHotelCatskills FRIENZ . . . Sad, sad news
😢 😢 😢 After nearly sixty years of continuous
operation, the Golden Hotel will be closing its doors at
the end of this summer. The hotel and surrounding land
has been purchased by Diamond Enterprises, which will
build a casino and resort on the premises. Everyone at
the Golden Hotel, in particular the Goldman and
Weingold families, thanks our thousands of guests for
their many years of loyalty. Together we built something
incredibly special that will forever be a part of history.
The hotel will be gone, but the memories will last
forever. With love and gratitude, Louise, Amos, Fanny,
Benny (of blessed memory), Aimee, Peter, Brian,
Maddie, Scott, Zachary, Phoebe, and Michael
#borschtbelt #movingon #hotel #resort #jewishalps
#thanksforthememories

@GoldenHotelCatskills Due to the outpouring
of love and support upon the announcement of our
closure, the management of the Golden Hotel has
two important announcements. The first is that we
hereby declare May 15, the date the Golden Hotel
opened its doors, National Catskills Day. We encourage
all Catskills lovers to share their memories on social
media using the hashtag #natlcatskillsday. Second, we
have received a tremendous volume of inquiries about
what we will be doing with the furniture, signage,

and other mementos from the hotel. We will be holding an auction for these items in the fall. Please check our social media channels over the next month for more information. XO, the Goldmans and Weingolds

Chapter Thirty

Aimee

She forced herself to log out of Facebook, though it was harder than expected, considering she'd been rereading posts and comments for an hour already. Tightening her robe around her and rising for a coffee refill—the drive ahead of her would require caffeine—she wondered why she was suddenly a glutton for punishment. It was hard to explain the urge to read hateful comments like *Roger Glasser should be locked up for life* and *I can't believe I ever let Dr. Glasser treat me* and *What a horrible thing for our own lovely town.* The Facebook group, Scarsdale Citizens, was more often a place to post a listing for a housekeeper whose services were no longer needed or to inquire if anyone knew the nearest Goodwill to deliver old clothing. But since the news had broken about her husband, the group had been a cauldron of gossip and mean-spirited comments, speculation, and lies. Someone named West-chesterMommy had suggested the Glassers move out of town. Aimee knew the person hiding behind that innocent handle was her next-door neighbor, Betsy Lehman, the same woman who had delighted in Zach's lack of ambition and Aimee's unsuccessful attempt at a rose garden on the front lawn.

"Zach, you almost ready?" she called upstairs, a knot in the back of her throat. "We're leaving soon. It'll be chilly; dress warmly." She checked her phone. It was typical November weather in Scarsdale—midfifties—but in Windsor the temperature would be closer to forty.

There was no answer.

She called her youngest's name again.

"Zacky?"

Aimee looked at the staircase hopelessly. She felt so weak lately; all the emotional distress that had started back in June had had a funny way of atrophying her muscles over the past five months. Maybe she'd have time for a jog once she and Zach reached the Golden. It was time to get her life back in order, and that would start with fixing things from the inside out. Exercise, eating healthier. Things she could control, because Lord knew, if there was anything she'd learned this year, it was that so much was out of her hands.

When there was still no answer, she climbed the steps to Zach's bedroom. The empty shelves and stripped bed startled her. Zach had been packing up his room for at least a week, but she hadn't made it upstairs to see his progress until now. Aimee couldn't believe he was moving out, and seeing boxes with his belongings was too much to face. Suddenly the house felt entirely too big for her without Zach's hoodies strewn all over the sofas and the tangle of his computer and phone chargers making her stumble. And then there was Roger's absence, looming in every closet and cupboard. His Italian coffee gone; dress shirts banished; toothbrush trashed. Her lawyer had suggested it. Not as a legal maneuver, but as a friend. "You don't want to see bits of your ex-husband every time you turn around." *Ex-husband.* The word still felt thick and unfamiliar on her tongue. And it wasn't even accurate yet. She and Roger wouldn't officially be divorced for at least another year. The hotel had sold faster than her marriage could be unwound. Which went to show, as much as the hotel felt like a character in their lives, it was still an inanimate object. And humans were a heck of a lot more complicated than things.

"Mom, were you calling me?" Zach asked, appearing in the doorway behind her.

Her boy. A flop of dark hair covered one of his eyes. His shirt, a University of Vermont tee, was wrinkled and shrunken, but still looked great on him. He was a handsome boy—no, a handsome man. Zach looked like Roger, down to the gap between his front teeth. At least her future ex had been good for something. He'd given Maddie athleticism, Scott a penchant for science, and Zach his striking good looks. And he'd given her things, too. Thirty happy years. It was important to remember the good times, not to let a drop of ink poison an entire well of memories. That advice had come from her therapist. It was Dr. Wind who had analogized the end of her marriage to the sale of the hotel. "Just because it failed in the end doesn't mean it wasn't wonderful while it lasted."

"I was calling you. We should really leave by ten. The auction is called for two, and I want to see the items before the crowds arrive. Where were you, by the way?"

"I was outside. Mrs. Lehman asked me to bring the giant pumpkin on her front porch to the curb for garbage collection. That thing was gross and rotting."

She could explain to Zach that Mrs. Lehman was a nasty bitch who was maligning their family online, but what was the point? Aimee was proud to have raised a kind and helpful child. She was proud of all of her children. Maddie and Andrew's celebration was coming up; they still hadn't quite figured out whether Roger should be in attendance. Formal charges had just been filed, but a trial was months away. Andrew's grandmother—the hussy from the photos in Memory Lane—had been rather embarrassed to be outed as a Catskills dweller, and a less than reputable one, no less; but it had certainly gone a long way toward changing the Hoffs' snooty attitude about the Borscht Belt. Scott was thriving in medical school. Since he'd changed his focus of study and emerged from his father's shadow, Aimee had seen a whole new side of her middle child. And his girlfriend, Bella, was simply lovely. It turned out she had contributed $200 to the 5B's fundraiser without even realizing her boyfriend's connection to the place. "My grandfather was a busboy at the Nevele for two summers during law school," she explained. "He was famous for never dropping a plate."

And Zach. Her directionless wonder. He had found an apartment on the Lower East Side that he would share with a few roommates. He claimed to have professional plans, though he wasn't ready to share them yet. Maybe she'd get some details out of him on the ride to the Catskills. Or maybe not. She saw his Beats poking out of his knapsack.

"Is there really going to be a crowd?" Zach asked, heeding her advice and layering on a sweatshirt. Just that action was a sign that her children were now fully formed adults. As teenagers, if she'd told them to wear warm jackets and hats, they specifically wouldn't to prove they knew better. Of course, when their inevitable colds had come, she'd still run out for lozenges and made chicken soup with a very specific carrot-to-celery ratio. She hoped that even in adulthood, her children would always still need her, like she needed Louise. Her mother had been her rock during the divorce proceedings. Aimee could call her at 2 a.m. and Louise would always claim to have been awake.

"Maddie said there will definitely be a crowd. She and Andrew got up to the hotel a few days ago to meet with the party planner, and apparently all sorts of strangers have been poking around."

"Is Joe making the Thanksgiving dinner?" Zach was always focused on his next meal. Aimee would miss feeding him, spontaneously leaving out snacks on the kitchen counter that he'd devour within minutes. But she needed to grow up, too. She would always be a mother, even if she wasn't grocery shopping for her kids and doing their laundry.

"He is," Aimee said. "It's been too many years since we've all done a holiday meal together. Brian called me to ask if we had any specific food requests."

She had frozen when Brian's cell phone number had appeared on her screen a few days earlier. They hadn't spoken since Labor Day, and even that weekend, it had just been friendly snippets when they'd passed each other in the lobby and in the dining room. Aimee had tried to find Angela on social media, but it was a dead end.

"I'm really looking forward to seeing you at Thanksgiving," Brian had said after she'd listed off Zach's ten dietary requests, emphasizing the marshmallow and sweet potato hash as the highest priority. Something in his tone had made Aimee's heart race, though she'd chastised herself after they'd hung up. He was having a baby with another woman! *Don't be a loser, Aimee Gold-*

man. She was also no longer a hyphenated woman. She'd chopped the Glasser off the moment she'd finished reading the indictment against her husband. The numbers were staggering. In the past year alone, he had written 2,500 OxyContin prescriptions. His low-income "clinic" was a drug den, operating under the cover of darkness. She saw pictures of strung-out patients waiting in a line half a block long to see Roger. Most heartbreaking of all, he had called in several Oxy prescriptions to the local pharmacy in Windsor.

"Nice," Zach said. "Hopefully we all get along. I'd hate to have to . . ."

"Hate to have to what?" Aimee asked.

"I need to come clean about something. Remember the fire that broke out on July Fourth, the one where—"

"Where the Weingolds and us almost stopped speaking. Yes, of course I remember."

"I did that. I couldn't stand the fighting. Of course, I had no idea there would be so much damage. I just wanted to cause a diversion. Grandpa Benny would have killed me if he knew. I heard the insurance didn't cover half of it."

Aimee was shocked. And weirdly proud. She went over to kiss Zach on the forehead.

"I don't suggest that method of conflict resolution in the future. But I think we can keep this as our little secret. Shall we go?"

She wondered how things with Phoebe were going, but didn't ask. She knew they were in frequent touch, "P" coming up on Zach's screens often whenever Aimee could sneak a glance.

"Sure," Zach said. "Scott texted his train is ten minutes from the station, by the way." She and Zach stepped outside the house, and Aimee locked the front door behind her without a backward glance.

THE WINDSOR WORD

HISTORIC GOLDEN HOTEL
TO AUCTION OFF ITEMS TODAY

*Everything from dishes to sofas
to first aid kits will be up for grabs*

By George Matsoukis

Windsor, NY—Nostalgia lovers will be living it up on the grounds of the Golden Hotel for the start of a two-day auction in which management will be selling off virtually everything from the hotel, from the rafters to the floorboards.

As was reported in June, the Golden Hotel entered into a sale agreement with casino operator Diamond Enterprises. The title will transfer in January of next year, after a family wedding in December.

Insiders at the hotel say that among the items being auctioned off are photographs from the hotel's "Memory Lane," featuring guests throughout the years, the famous sign on Route 87 that indicated the hotel was three miles ahead, and a baseball signed by Jackie Robinson, who stayed at the hotel for several weeks every summer in the 1960s.

"I hope they don't auction off my uniform," longtime concierge Larry Levine said. "Then I will have nothing to wear home."

ELYSSA FRIEDLAND

An auctioneer from the well-heeled Sotheby's, based in New York City, will run the auction. Many of the items feature autographs from celebrities who performed on the stages of the Golden. A more unusual lot is the bathrobe Joan Rivers wore when she went to the Golden Hotel to recover from plastic surgery.

"I want that painting behind the check-in desk. The one that the daughter painted with the backwards G," said one former guest of the hotel, who wished not to be identified. "I'd pay top dollar for that."

When the sale is complete, there will be no remaining hotels or bungalows left from the so-called Jewish Alps, so it is not surprising that folks will be lining up to collect memorabilia. At one point there were more than five hundred hotels and five hundred bungalow colonies in the area, but today all that remains are ghostly vestiges of a different era.

All owners are expected to be on the premises for the sale.

Chapter Thirty-One

Brian

The last time parking had been a problem at the hotel was back in the late 1990s, and that was because a water main had burst and flooded half the parking lot. But today, for the auction of the Golden's vessels, cars were lined up for at least two miles down the road in each direction. Somehow word had spread that people coming up to the hotel should dress "classic Catskills," and so the bodies dotting the endless front lawn were outfitted in pedal pushers and plaid shorts with socks hiked to the knee, despite the November chill. Many of the women had embellished their looks with jaunty hats and cat-eyed sunglasses. Brian was grateful he'd asked Angela's brother, a talented photographer, to document the scene.

He spied the curve that was now Angela's defining feature from across the lawn. She was directing traffic and passing out auction paddles, even though Brian had insisted she rest. She was in her sixth month already, and backaches, swollen feet, and the urge to pee every ten minutes were plaguing her. Brian would often marvel at the injustice. He was getting a kid, too—a boy, they'd learned at the twenty-week anatomy scan—but he felt totally fine. And since he and Angela had decided that they would raise the child together, but not as a couple, he wasn't even around in the evenings to rub her feet or bring her pickles and ice cream, if that was really a thing. He had offered to spend the night on the couch in her condo many times, but she'd declined. Sensibly, she'd say that their lives were going to be complicated enough; there was no need to intensify them.

"I don't think you're in love with me." That's what Angela had said to him after the first trimester had passed, plain and straightforward and wildly brave. He had told her he was open to trying anything: together, apart—he'd even thrown the word "marriage" on the table. But Angela had been firm. She wanted more than he could give her, and she demanded more for herself.

The arrangement they'd worked out—for Angela to care for the baby during the week, Brian to have three weekends a month, both of them to have access when they wanted it—meant that he was now free to lay down roots outside Windsor. But that also meant facing hard choices. Selling the hotel was a choice, but he didn't have to make it alone. Next steps, where to settle, what to do: They were on him alone. His parents had offered to reach out to longtime guests of the hotel to pursue job leads. It was a gracious offer, but with his fiftieth birthday looming, he fought off the urge to accept. Maybe once a child, always a child. He'd find out eventually with his own.

"Can you believe this turnout?" Peter asked, approaching with his arm around Greta. She, too, had gotten the memo and was wearing a mustard yellow swing dress topped with a brown felt cape, looking like a sixties superhero.

"It's wonderful to see," Greta said, lightly touching Brian on the arm. "But not surprising. You did a remarkable job organizing all of this." Her face looked less taut than usual, like a balloon with a bit of air let out. Since the week in June when the family had gathered, there had been new life breathed into his brother's marriage. He and Greta had sat on a blanket together during the Labor Day weekend fireworks show, and when, predictably, the Wi-Fi had gone out for the day, Peter had stayed. "The office will manage without me" were actually the words he'd uttered, which had cued a number of jokes about a secret lobotomy.

"Thank you, Greta. You look great," Brian said. Greata. That could be her new nickname, replacing Greeda, which it turned out she'd never really deserved. If you had a certain opinion about someone, anything they said or did confirmed it. Change that opinion, and suddenly their actions could be viewed in a whole new light. "Mind if I steal my brother away for a few minutes?"

She motioned for them to go on.

"I want to talk up the tea service platter anyway," Greta said. "I heard Lucille Ball used it every morning when she stayed at the hotel, and I think the reserve price is too low."

"What's up?" Peter asked after his wife had sauntered away.

"This is kind of delicate," Brian said. "But I really want to be honest and transparent. You know the painting behind the check-in that—"

"Aimee's picture. Of course," Peter said. "I was surprised she didn't claim it when we did the family walk-through."

"Yeah, well, I think she felt guilty. It's going to fetch a pretty high price, and she needs the money. And she didn't want to take it away from us. She may have drawn it, but you and I know it's as much a part of the hotel as the banister, the pool, the nightclub—it's steeped in a lot of history."

"So what are you saying?" Peter asked. He could be overly analytical at times, missing an emotional gene. Brian had hoped his brother would have already connected the dots.

"I'd like to buy it for her, if that's all right with you. I know it's one of our more desirable lots, and I don't want people to get upset that an owner is taking it back, so I've spoken to Otto. He has a cousin in Loch Sheldrake who will come over and bid in my place."

"Why are you doing this?" Peter asked, but before Brian could respond, his twin's face changed, his expression finally washed with understanding.

"Yes, what you're thinking is true. I have feelings for Aimee. She's going through a divorce. I'm having a kid. It is possibly the worst time in history to even think about a relationship, but it's like what Chef Joe says when he brings out the dessert trolley."

"You think you don't have room for another bite, but you still can't resist," Peter said. "Does she know?"

"We were intimate. Back in June. I wanted to tell you back then, but I was a coward. I know how you used to feel about her for so long . . ."

"'Used to' is the operative phrase," Peter said. "I love Aimee. I always will. But Greta is my wife. And more than that, she's my life." He put a solid hand on Brian's shoulder. "Go for it. Seriously."

"Thanks, Peter. Speaking of other auction items, I was think-ing we should go through Amos and Benny's desks before the auction starts. Sotheby's sent along some fancy locksmith to open up the locked drawers and cabinets without damage."

Man, our father was a mess," Brian said when, ten minutes later, he was bent over Amos's desk. At first Brian had been surprised when his parents had said they would arrive after the auction, just in time for Thanksgiving dinner. "Your mother loves the sun," Amos had said. "And I should get to the eye doctor before I head north."

He'd mentioned their parents' absence to his brother, and Peter, showing a rare surge of EQ, had said, "I think Pops doesn't want to watch his baby gefilted like a carp."

Their mother had called Brian later, when Amos wasn't around, and told him to lay off his father. "Brian, he doesn't need to be there when the vultures circle the entrails." Peter had been spot on. Brian hoped the shock of arriving in a few days to an empty shell wouldn't be too much for either of his parents. He still felt numb remembering when his father had nearly lost consciousness in the boardroom.

"Benny was so neat," Peter remarked. They had just finished checking over his desk. Everything was spick and span, organized hotel brochures and copies of activity and payroll schedules in neat files.

"I feel like their desks were versions of themselves. Benny's, polished and shiny, perfect for show. Dad's sloppy, literally covered in elbow grease," Peter said.

"Yeah, but Benny was the greasy one," Brian said. "Sometimes I think I shouldn't even try with Aimee. With all that muck between our families. You know, I tried to ask Dad about it after that dinner, but he's just so freaking protective of Benny."

"They were brothers," Peter said, looking at Brian. "About Aimee, why don't you first worry about whether she'd be willing to have coffee with you?"

"Good plan," Brian said.

"Got it!" Peter exclaimed, yanking open Amos's top drawer. "Junk drawer. Paper clips, nonworking pens. Wait a second. I feel something weird."

"What?" Brian asked.

"It's like a false back. Hang on, I'm getting it."

Brian moved next to his brother. "Let me," he said. "I'll use a key to shimmy it out." He tinkered with what was clearly a fake back of the drawer until he pried the board loose. Cold metal greeted his hand as he groped in the dark.

"What the—" he said when he pulled out a pair of furry handcuffs. They dropped to the floor in a clank. Brian reached back and retrieved another pair of handcuffs and a leather whip.

"Is this a joke?" Peter asked, studying the handcuffs. "Was Dad a fetishist?"

"Not just Dad," Brian said. "Mom's name is stitched into this whip. Oh my fucking God. I really want to unsee this."

"Didn't you just assume Mom was a big prude?" Peter asked.

"No, because I tried to never think about their sex life, period. I need Purell. We can never mention that we found this to anyone."

"Obviously," Peter said, already stuffing the sex toys into a shopping bag. "I'll drop this into the garbage dump ASAP."

"Do we dare look in the second drawer?" Brian asked. "I guess we don't have a choice."

He dropped to his knees and opened the unlocked lower drawer, combing through a jumble of yellowed papers and file folders.

"Peter, come over here," Brian said. His brother joined him in a huddle underneath the giant mahogany mass of their father's desk, as if it was up to them to literally shoulder the weight of his legacy.

"Is this what I—am I seeing this right?"

They were looking at scraps of loose-leaf paper, where figures had been scrawled in both Benny's and Amos's handwriting.

"Jeez, this is what happened," Brian said. "Benny didn't steal from Dad. They had an arrangement."

"Why the secrecy? Why was Benny borrowing a hundred thousand dollars from Dad? This promissory note looks like a kid's homework assignment. And if he was already borrowing money from Dad, why did he also take out loans against the hotel without Dad knowing?"

Brian was as bewildered as Peter. Never in any conversations about the hotel had Amos intimated any side arrangements.

"We could call him," Brian suggested.

"I want to," Peter said. "If there's one thing the closing of the hotel has shown me, it's that time doesn't stand still. Who knows how many more opportunities we'll have to ask him things?"

Brian took his cell phone out of his pocket and called Amos on speaker.

"Let me guess," their father said when he picked up the call.

"Every housewife from Roslyn to Cherry Hill wants the dessert trolley cart?"

"Um, hi, Dad. I don't think 'housewife' is really the term these days. But the auction hasn't started yet anyway. I'm here with Peter, and we were just cleaning out your desk before it goes up for sale. We found some papers. Some kind of agreement between you and Benny. He borrowed an awful lot of money from you, Dad. And we see that Howard was right about the property liens."

The twins could hear their father's jaw clenching. He was old school in so many ways, one of them being that children were on a need-to-know basis, even when those children were past middle age. When it came to the private sphere that he and Benny had shared as best friends and business partners for decades, Amos did not welcome visitors.

"All right," he said, offering no more.

"Dad, after Roger accused Benny of fraud, you said he didn't do it, but didn't explain anything. Why? Louise was always so haughty. The Goldmans moved to Manhattan, we stayed on Long Island. Louise went to Paris to buy clothes, Mom was all about Loehmann's. How many years did we listen to that crap? And here he was the one borrowing from you."

"Louise didn't go to Europe to buy clothes. And she didn't go to Paris. She went to Switzerland. Geneva, to be precise." He paused for a long beat. Peter looked like he was about to press, but Brian held up his hand to stop him.

"I suppose it's all right for me to tell you this story now. There was a medical clinic there—maybe it still exists, maybe not. She desperately wanted another child. But it was so expensive—

these drug therapies and procedures, all experimental—and Benny didn't want Louise to worry about the money. She had Fifth Avenue tastes—I think a part of her channeled what she was missing from her life into her appearance and reaching a certain station."

"I think I can appreciate that dynamic," Peter said knowingly.

"One of the loans is from the same year as Aimee's bat mitzvah," Brian said. "That over-the-top party. Mom couldn't stop talking about it."

"That's right," Amos said. "Another thing to keep Louise happy and busy and distracted from the disappointment."

"Amos! We're needed at the Harrisons' for bridge. You're always the one making me late." Their mother's voice, loud and clear, could be heard summoning their father.

"The boss beckons," Amos said. "I'll see you boys in a few days. Good luck with the sharks out there. Tell them Sammy Davis Jr. used all the toilets in the hotel—maybe we can sell those, too."

W ell, that was a smashing success," Aimee said, rubbing the soles of her feet. All the furniture had been tagged and carted away, and the Weingolds and Goldmans were perched on the steps, exhausted.

"The Sotheby's guy has no idea what happened to the driveway sign. That thing weighs at least forty pounds and is staked eight feet into the grass," Peter said. "I checked with the guard at the main gate, and he swears he didn't see anyone take it. It's a shame, because I think that might have fetched the highest price."

"Nothing we can do," Brian said. "I had a feeling some townies would snag a few things with all the chaos here today."

"Did they leave any tables in the dining room for us?" Scott asked. "I'm hungry. I tried to get one of Chef Joe's chocolate chip cookies, but they were gone in two seconds. One lady wrapped up at least a dozen and put them in her purse."

"The pocketbooks are bottomless at the Golden," Brian said. "And yes, there are tables. And chairs, too. We're donating them all to a food pantry nearby. After Maddie's wedding—I mean marriage celebration."

"Actually, we're going to rent furniture. There's, um, a lot more choice out there now. We thought lucite chairs might be cool. And instead of round tables, we're thinking of just bringing in a bunch of cocktail tables and couches."

"It was the party planner's idea," Andrew said.

"I don't understand. We're going to have to bend over to get our food? And who ever heard of couches at a wedding?" Louise, plainly flummoxed, let her nostrils flare.

"Maman," Aimee said firmly, shooting her a look.

"Fine, fine. Who am I, other than the person who decorated most of this place? I agree with Scott, though. Let's eat."

"Let me help you up, Grandma," Zach said, extending a hand to Louise.

"Such a good boy," Phoebe teased, and Brian watched Zach's face redden. *What is happening with those two?* Brian wondered. Normally he wouldn't meddle in the affairs of young adults, but it could be awkward if he were to date Aimee and his niece was dating Aimee's son. There he went again, getting ahead of himself.

"Yes, let's eat," Brian said, and everyone rose. As long as the kitchen was in operation, the Golden was still the Golden.

@GoldenMotelLES After nearly fourteen months of construction, we are ready to open our doors. Tonight, join us for bites and booze. #thecatskillsredefined #lowereastside #whereitallstarted #thenextchapter #exclusive #hospitality

@hipsterdipster This is the coolest thing ever

@AvenueBbaby I'll be there!

@Jessie212 Major FOMO

@ParkSloper Sick

@theLouiseGoldman HOW DO WE MAKE RESERVATIONS? THERE IS NO PHONE NUMBER

@FannyWeingold THERE IS NO PHONE NUMBER. AM I DOING THIS RIGHT?

Load 1,321 more comments

Chapter Thirty-Two

Phoebe

The four of them were sitting in a velvet banquette in the newly built Golden Motel, Fanny and Louise stirring loose-leaf teas and Zach and Phoebe nervously sipping Lavender Collinses in skinny, tall glasses. Opening night was only an hour away.

Above their heads, affixed to an exposed redbrick wall, was a sign that read THE GOLDEN MOTEL. It was the same sign that Amos and Benny had hammered into the ground themselves in 1960, the letters of the hotel in a loopy green script—all but the letter M, which was in neon blue.

"So *you* stole the sign?" Louise said. "We all drove the security guard crazy about it."

"Guilty," she said, tapping Zach on the arm. "But I had some help. Needed muscle, of course."

"It looks nice here," Fanny said. "Though why didn't you match the letters? I don't understand. What's with the blue? And why would you call a nice place like this a motel?"

"Maddie kept talking about how the H was missing in the sign and how someone really ought to fix it," Zach explained. "And Phoebe and I both kind of hit on the idea at the same time. We'd been discussing the idea for the hotel—I mean motel—for a while, and then it was like we had this mind meld: Let's use the sign with the missing H and change it to an M."

"But still, why a motel?" Louise asked, as confused as Fanny.

"It's ironic," Phoebe explained. "Like, it's cool because it's not cool."

Fanny and Louise exchanged bewildered glances. It had taken a rather frustrated explanation from the waitress to understand how the tea strainer worked. When she'd asked them if they preferred Darjeeling or rooibos, they'd stared back blankly until Phoebe had muttered they would take mint.

"What I don't understand is why there is no website or phone number. You're going to be sitting with a ton of empty rooms," Fanny said. "Phoebe, you're good with the computer. You set up my Instapicture account. I bet you could fix that quickly." She held the bar menu askew and adjusted her reading glasses, as if understanding the offerings were a matter of eyesight.

"What is folk kale topped with massaged fig? How do you massage a fig?" Fanny pointed out the item to Louise.

"With olive oil, I suppose," Louise said.

"Good one, Grandma," Zach said.

"You should try the reimagined borscht," Phoebe said. "Our chef got the original recipe from Joe, and he added parsnip puree and changed the sour cream to vegan nut cheese. It's amazing. And we don't have to worry about all the purple stains on the tablecloths because—see—we have none!"

"Phoebe, Zach, we're being serious with you. We are very proud of what you've done. Being an entrepreneur takes a lot of guts. But you need to update the reservation system. I heard from Marcia Winter that her grandson tried to book a room, and all he got was a busy signal for three hours and an email that said no bookings available." Louise looked up at the sign above her head. "You've got a legacy to uphold here."

Phoebe felt her insides surge with pleasure. She had been waiting for this moment.

"As a matter of fact, we're entirely booked solid for the first year. And there is a three-hundred-person waitlist to come to tonight's opening." She winked at her grandma, so cute in the hot pink dress that Phoebe had gotten a designer friend to loan her. "You're lucky you know the right people." And here she playfully jabbed at Zach again, though she was careful not to be overly friendly. If they were going to succeed as business partners, a romance was off the table. Besides, one Weingold-Goldman romance was enough. Speaking of, Phoebe checked her phone.

"My parents are arriving any minute, and they said Uncle Brian and Aimee are just a few minutes behind."

"I have a guest to add to the list," Louise said. "A Walter Cole will be joining me. Do I tell her?" She pointed at a hostess in a skimpy black dress, fishnets, and Doc Martens approaching their table.

"We've got you covered, Gram," Zach said.

"Phoebe, Zach, the *New York Post* would like a word with one of you. I took a message." The hostess handed Phoebe a slip of paper.

"The *Post* is going to run a big story on us tomorrow," Phoebe said. "We're going to play up the museum a lot in the interview."

After the families had made the hotel sale public, the 5B had taken to social media to decide what to do with the money raised. It was decided that a museum paying homage to the Borscht Belt would be opened in the Catskills, though a location hadn't been chosen yet. Amos, Fanny, and Louise would be the honorary chairs of the museum, but the operation would be left to the younger generation. Phoebe had so far received over two thousand photographs from Catskills vacationers and was in the process of culling them down. The 5B had a very active Facebook page.

"Maybe our problem all along was exclusivity," Grandma Fanny mused. "If we had only not picked up the phone, imagine how busy we'd be."

Phoebe laughed. She knew her grandmother would never grasp the vision behind the Golden Motel, much like Phoebe couldn't comprehend what made people so eager to sit on I-87 for up to nine hours every Friday to get to the Catskills.

"This place has more to offer than just exclusivity," she said. "We have virtual check-in, room service available via iPhone, a silent disco every Saturday night, a meditation class every morning—"

"Why bother coming at all?" Louise said, though she wasn't being mean-spirited. "If you're just going to be quiet, you can stay home for free."

"What else does this place offer?" Fanny asked. "Will you be bringing in goats?"

"Oh my God, I wish," Phoebe said, realizing a moment later

that her grandmother had been joking. She looked over at Louise, whose face indicated she was still not over the poop incident.

"We have some stuff you guys had at the hotel. We have Ping-Pong. Bingo. Billiards. Even a shuffleboard set up on the roof," Zach said.

"If those things are still popular, why did the hotel fail?" Fanny asked.

"Because now it's not just about playing shuffleboard for the sake of playing shuffleboard. It's playing shuffleboard so you can post a picture of yourself playing shuffleboard. It's posting about the experience instead of living it," Louise said, judgment in every syllable.

Phoebe wanted to protest, to explain it was all more nuanced than that. But Louise was probably right. Behind her was a jumbo magnetic poetry board that screamed, *Tag me!*

"Oh, look, Peter and Greta just walked in," Fanny said, waving them over.

Her father swept Phoebe into a bear hug of the kind he hadn't given her since she was a small child.

"You've done an incredible job," he said, standing back from her to look around. "The sign!"

"There's more . . ." she said, handing her parents the drink of the evening from a nearby tray. It was an updated grasshopper, a nod to the insects that provided the evening soundtrack in Windsor. "Upstairs in the lounge we hung the portrait of Grandpa and Benny."

"You and Zach are truly impressive," her mother said, air-kissing her. "Oh, screw it, I can touch up," she said, smacking her lips on Phoebe's cheek.

"We couldn't have done any of this without Uncle Brian," Phoebe said truthfully. While Phoebe had an idea a minute, it was Brian who grounded her. He'd shown them how to set up a proper payroll, how to link up with the right employment agencies, where to get liquor at a better cost. The list of ways he'd helped her and Zach realize their dream was immeasurable, which was why they'd named the best suite in the place the Brian.

"Speaking of the devil," Zach said, pointing to the door, which was opened by a smartly dressed attendant in jeans and a tight-fitting blazer, holding a clipboard and wearing an earpiece.

Aimee and Uncle Brian entered, holding hands. Phoebe surreptitiously snapped a photo to post on the motel's feed.

"Congratulations, Zachy," Aimee gushed, enveloping him the way Phoebe's father had swallowed her moments earlier. Phoebe had to laugh a little bit at the outpouring of support and admiration from both sets of parents and grandparents. It was obvious how little confidence they'd had in the youngest generation before they'd pulled this off. "You too, Phoebe. You look stunning."

Phoebe beamed. So much of her life up until this point had been about appearances, the pressure to look good while selling another person's product driving her to the gym every morning and causing her to agonize over filters. Finally, she was promoting her own product, and how she appeared wasn't just about what would look good on camera and cropped into a square. Not that she hadn't specifically chosen a navy jumpsuit that looked insanely hot in photographs. But there was something infinitely more exciting about the lineup of actual people that would soon form outside the building, waiting to offer congratulations to her face rather than comment on her posts—though there'd be plenty of that, too.

"Uncle Brian, you were beyond helpful," she gushed, standing on tiptoe to hug him.

"Well, I come by hospitality honestly," he said in a modest tone. "Oh my God, the freaking sign. You guys had it all along!"

"We did," she said. "The maintenance guys just hung it up this morning. Couldn't spoil the surprise."

"Kids, did you know that your grandfathers grew up not two blocks from here?" Louise said.

"Of course we knew that," Phoebe said. "Sunrise, sunset, baby. Back to where it all began. Where is Grandpa, by the way?"

"Sweetheart, he's not feeling great. He wanted to be here so badly to see this, but the doctor thought he should stay in Florida. But I even learned how to do the FaceTime for him for tonight."

Phoebe felt herself sinking. She had never imagined that her entire family wouldn't be here for opening night. Michael was driving from Cambridge and was due to arrive momentarily. Her parents and uncle were already there. Grandma Fanny was in true form. But Amos—the man who'd breathed the hospitality gene into their bones, whose portrait hung upstairs—was going to miss it.

"We'll send him a ton of pictures," Zach said, coming up from behind and putting a supportive hand on her back. "Plus, the FaceTime. And the Twitter. And the Instapic." He squeezed her elbow playfully. The grasshoppers were working their magic, and she was reconsidering if a little romance on opening night might not be the end of the world.

"Well, well, well, sis, aren't you fabulous," Michael said, sweeping inside the hotel with the cold air behind him. He wasn't alone.

A striking Asian guy, in dark slacks and a slim sweater, followed a step behind him.

"Phoebe, this is Troy," Michael said. "He's an engineering major at MIT. And he's my—"

"Michael, give me a hug," Fanny said, rolling up to them. Michael bent down. Phoebe felt her insides tensing.

"This is my friend Troy," Michael said to their grandmother. His mechanical speech made it obvious her brother and Troy had rehearsed this introduction.

"Michael, sweetheart, I know who this is." Fanny extended her hand. "Fanny Weingold. It's a pleasure to meet you."

"Phoebe, the bartender wants to have a quick chat," Uncle Brian said. "He said the tequila isn't tasting right. And the bathroom attendant just slipped, so we need to get her an ambulance. And the heat broke in the Borscht suite."

Her eyes widened and she felt a strong impulse to run for the door. There was a cool spot on Avenue C where she could look cute at the bar, flirt her way to free drinks, and go back to living her life online. But no. She could do this. It was in her blood.

"Welcome to hotel management," Brian said.

She looked from her uncle to her grandmother to her parents, and said to no one in particular, "I got this."

Chapter Thirty-Three

Aimee

I think that's the last of them," Aimee said, handing over a generous tip to the head of the moving crew, a muscly, tattooed guy who had been surprisingly familiar and cautious with her rare book collection.

"Good luck in your new place, ma'am," the mover said, pocketing the money. "Can't believe we fit it all in." He looked around, as if struck for the first time by how small the apartment was. Aimee acknowledged how odd it must seem—a middle-aged woman moving from a sprawling Westchester McMansion with nine bathrooms and a swimming pool to a fifteen-hundred-square-foot apartment with a view of mostly brick walls. But she didn't care. A fresh start was what she needed, and that was what she was getting. All her children were out of the house. She didn't need a large backyard and a basement with a hundred-inch television.

Brian crossed paths with the mover on his way out. He was carrying something large, wrapped in brown paper. He was sweet to insist on helping with the move. She liked the sight of him with sweat rolling down the back of his neck, the way he was handy with tools and took the back stairs two at a time when the elevator was too slow.

"What's that?" She pointed at the package.

"A move-in gift," Brian said. "Open it."

She couldn't imagine what it was. Giving someone art for a new home was a bold move. He didn't know her style or how she planned to decorate. Aimee didn't even know her own taste yet. Most of their belongings had been picked out when she was practically still a child bride, updated along the way with pricier and flashier versions of the same. But she'd never had a chance to create a home de novo, without input from a husband or the considerations of small children.

She reached for the brown paper and gave a downward tug that ripped it apart.

"My picture!" she gasped. It was the painting she'd made as a little girl that had hung behind the reception at the hotel. "I thought this sold at the auction?"

"It did. To me," Brian said. "I waited a while to give it to you because I didn't want you to think I was some crazy stalker."

"And you had just gotten another woman pregnant," she added, but in a friendly tone.

"And that," Brian said, and flashed his dimpled smile.

"I'm so touched, Brian," Aimee said, rubbing her fingertips against the inside of his elbow. "Where should I hang it?"

Brian looked around.

"I know, not many options. But I don't need more than this apartment for now. I'm kind of happy to be out of the big house.

It was scary sleeping there alone, and everything was breaking. I had no one to kill spiders anymore."

"I'll kill your spiders," Brian said, resting the painting against the wall. His cell phone rang. "It's Phoebe. I should take this."

One week had passed since the opening party of the Golden Motel. Phoebe and Zach called Brian constantly with questions. He was a good sport about it, though Aimee urged him to let them figure out some things for themselves. How she wished she'd had more independence and faith in her abilities when she was their age. Brian stepped into the bedroom to take the call, and Aimee collapsed onto the still-wrapped couch in the living room.

She and Brian had been dating for three months now. He was applying for management jobs at several hotel chains, but nothing had panned out yet. Maddie was pregnant, which meant Aimee was going to be a newly divorced grandmother. It was as unlikely a thought as the Golden Hotel no longer being in existence. Aimee, who had never been one for spontaneity, was slowly learning to expect the unexpected.

A knock on her door interrupted her thoughts. She thought it might be the movers, having left something behind. But it was Louise, a bottle of champagne and a bouquet of flowers in her hands. Aimee's new apartment was only five blocks from her mother's. She was moving on with her life, but also moving back. Life was always going to have some tension between the familiar and the new.

"Maman," Aimee said, motioning her inside. "You didn't have to bring anything."

Louise furrowed her brow. "I hope I taught you better than that. You never show up at someone's home empty-handed. Now show me around." She walked toward the fireplace and stopped short. "The painting!"

"Brian bought it for me. From the auction," Aimee said. "He's in the other room, on the phone with Phoebe. I'm not sure those kids realize what they've gotten themselves into."

"Neither did your father. Or Amos. Or any of us. But that's part of the magic. They will build something wonderful. It's in their blood," Louise said, admiring the painting.

Aimee looked poignantly at her mother, then to Brian, who had joined them, then set her eyes back on the painting of her creation.

"It certainly is."

Epilogue

F ollow me," Ben said in a whisper. "I cracked the code to the padlock on the office. Let's check it out."

"What was it?" Charlie asked, picking at a scab on his knee that he'd gotten from a scrape when he and Benny had been climbing the fire escape at the motel two weeks earlier.

"The street address of the Golden Hotel. Phoebe and Zach do not have much imagination."

It was after 11 p.m. at the Golden Motel, and Ben Hoff and Charlie Weingold, sixth and seventh graders respectively, were supposed to be sleeping in the room they were sharing for the weekend. But why would these best friends, who were more like cousins—siblings even—sleep, when they could be causing mischief at the hotel owned by their uncle and cousin respectively?

It was Labor Day weekend, and the Weingolds, Goldmans, Glassers, and Weingold-Glassers were planning to spend the weekend at the Golden Motel, as was turning into tradition. The motel had seen its highs and lows over its twelve-year existence—

it turned out having a website and a phone number *was* a good idea—and Phoebe and Zach had also realized that reading the comment cards (not technically cards because they were submitted electronically) could be very useful, even if the complaints stung.

Favorites at the motel, if the TripAdvisor reviews were any indication, were the thoughtful offerings of nostalgia. The most popular activities were the cha-cha lessons, bingo, and karaoke. But for Ben and Charlie, the best things to do at the hotel were to hide in its many seductive crevices, steal desserts from the freezer, and prank call the hotel guests after midnight.

"Well, if it isn't the tiresome twosome," Brian called when the boys slipped into the locked office. The lights had been out, but Brian's face was illuminated by a single bulb in a desk lamp. "Tell me, you boys looking for something?"

They both reddened. It was one thing to bend the rules and get caught by Phoebe or Zach, who were definitely grown-ups but still cool and with more recent memories of what it was like to be young. But Brian, whose hair was gray and who chastised them in a deep voice, was a whole different story.

"Um, we were just . . . I thought I left my—" Ben started to say, attempting to save Charlie from a punishment.

"Save it, kid. You are just like your great-grandfather. He always had that mischievous glint in his eyes. It's what made all the guests love him so dearly."

"What was Grandpa Amos like?" Charlie asked. Even if his son was trying to steer the conversation away from the boys breaking the rules, Brian was willing to oblige. He missed his father every day and insisted that Phoebe and Zach put bags of Famous Amos cookies in all the guest rooms to pay homage. Amos had died shortly after the Golden Motel opened, and, to everyone's grave disappointment, had never gotten to see the second iteration of his legacy. Among the family, they called the motel "Golden 2.0."

"Your grandfather was a wonderful man. Hardworking, smart, a devoted husband. And most of all, he was a loyal friend. Like the way you boys are to each other."

"Can we hear more?" Ben asked.

"Yes," Brian said. "Tomorrow. And the day after. And the day after that. But not now. Now you both go to bed, and try not to get into any trouble on the way upstairs. Ben—don't make me rat you out to your grandma." He gestured to the framed picture of Aimee on his desk.

"We got it, Dad," Charlie said. "Before we go, Ben and I have some ideas for the hotel. We were thinking a skate park in the garden, and also, could you tell Phoebe and Zach to put in a gaming room, and—"

Brian put up his hand to stop them. This was how it started, wasn't it? Traditions uprooted by the energetic voices of the young. He would hear them out. He'd make sure the co-CEOs did, too, his niece and his wife's son. But not tonight. Tonight, he was tired.

The boys saw that he meant business.

"Good night! Night!" they called out, and scrambled out of the office.

When they were gone, Brian swiveled his chair around to look at the portrait of Amos and Benny, which had been moved into the office to keep it from getting damaged by the many inebriated guests of the Golden Motel.

"Good night, gentlemen," he said softly, and he could swear they answered him back.

Acknowledgments

What a year! I started writing this book on a high from publishing *The Floating Feldmans* and finished writing it during a worldwide pandemic. As I write these acknowledgments, I have no idea if I'll be sharing the Golden Hotel with readers virtually or in person, or to use the phrase du jour, in a "hybrid model." But boy, do I hope I can hug my dear readers and celebrate with them in person.

Kerry Donovan is my supportive, brilliant, and patient editor. We are a true team. I deliver material that will make Kerry smile, and she indulges my requests for eleventh-hour plot changes. My agent, Stefanie Lieberman, calms my neuroses better than anyone, and is a savvy and thoughtful advocate for me always. On Stefanie's team, I am also grateful to the wonderful Molly Steinblatt and Adam Hobbins. Fareeda Bullert and Loren Jaggers make up my stellar team at Berkley, marketing and publicizing my work tirelessly so that I can reach the broadest possible audience. Ann-Marie Nieves, I am thrilled to partner with such a clever, dedicated, and hardworking publicist. Adam Auerbach, thank you for another stunning cover. Muriel Smith is the talented artist who created the stunning illustration of the Golden Hotel in the front of the book.

There is one incredibly special lady—and she is a lady, indeed—to whom I owe a major debt of gratitude. Bunny Grossinger, daughter-in-law of the famous Jennie Grossinger of Grossinger's Catskill Resort Hotel in Liberty, New York, provided me with numerous stories about the Catskills and gave me an insider's look at running a hotel in the "Jewish Alps." I met Bunny at Pilates and visited her in her apartment for interviews, where she received more phone calls from friends and family in an hour than I receive in a day. She is a one-of-a-kind treasure.

For research, I relied on the following books: *The Catskills: Its History and How It Changed America* by Stephen M. Silverman and Raphael D. Silver; *The Borscht Belt: Revisiting the Remains of America's Jewish Vacationland* by Marisa Scheinfeld with essays by Stefan Kanfer and Jenna Weissman; and *A Summer World: The Astonishing History of the Jews in the Catskills—the Borscht Belt—from the 18th Century to the Present Day* by Stefan Kanfer. The documentary *Welcome to Kutsher's* was a great resource, and of course, the movies *Dirty Dancing* and *A Walk on the Moon* were very inspiring. I'm in debt to Marc Chodock, owner of the super-hip Scribner's Catskill Lodge in Hunter, NY, for his insights on the Catskills of yesteryear versus today.

Andrea Katz, what can I say? I finished this book more quickly and had a blast doing it because you read installments of it every day and gave me invaluable feedback along the way. Love our texting.

My wonderful mother, Rochelle Folk, grew up spending her summers in various bungalow colonies in the Catskills. She had many colorful anecdotes that enriched this book. I appreciate her keen editing and suggestions for improvement, as always.

Author/book world friends Leigh Abramson, Lisa Barr, Jenna Blum, Jamie Brenner, Fiona Davis, Liz Fento, Laurie Gelman, Emily Giffin, Brenda Janowitz, Pam Jenoff, Lauren Margolin, Courtney Marzilli, Susie Orman Shnall, Amy Poeppel, Kim Roosevelt, Maureen Sherry, Lauren Smith Brody, Randy Susan Meyers, Rochelle Weinstein, and Allison Winn Scotch are incredibly supportive and "get it" like only fellow book people can. A special shout-out to Catherine McKenzie for everything and beyond.

My extended family continues to support me and be cheerleaders and ambassadors for my work, and I am truly grateful. My children, Charlie, Lila, and Sam, are very proud of their mommy and get more excited about bookstore sightings than I do. They make me laugh and experience pure joy every day. William, you are a prince among men. I love you.

Readers, thank you times ten billion. I love my job!

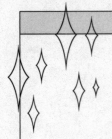

Last Summer at the Golden Hotel

ELYSSA FRIEDLAND

Questions for Discussion

1. Many characters in the novel are struggling with feelings of aimlessness or a lack of direction. What do you think is at the core of these feelings for each of them? Is there a character who deals with these feelings better than the others? Does anyone deal with these feelings particularly badly?

2. At many points during the novel, children learn that their parents are imperfect humans. Do you think the generations are sufficiently forgiving of one another? Are they able to learn from one another's mistakes, or are they stuck thinking about their differences?

3. The secrets uncovered during the novel often structure the characters' lives before they know about them. Have you ever learned something about your own life that you were not aware of? How did you react, and do you think the characters at the Golden Hotel reacted productively?

4. How does age/generation play a role in the relationships formed and kept at the Golden Hotel?

5. What does the hotel represent to the owners? To the middle generation? To the younger generation?

6. What do you think about family businesses? What are the advantages and disadvantages of working with family and friends?

7. While reading, did you find yourself wanting the Goldmans and Weingolds to keep the hotel? Why or why not?

8. Where does the tension between Louise and Fanny stem from?

9. How does the sibling dynamic between Brian and Peter as they're growing up shape who they become as adults?

10. Why does Brian manage the Golden Hotel? Where do his attachment and commitment to the hotel come from?

11. What do you think the Golden Hotel says about tradition versus change? How are we to balance these values or realities in our own lives?

12. What is lost when the Goldmans and Weingolds reach a decision about the future of the hotel? What is gained?

Keep reading for a preview of Elyssa Friedland's new book

MOST LIKELY

Available in summer 2022

Prologue

Westport, Connecticut
1998

T he smart-but-social table in the lunchroom was in the back corner, underneath a row of wall-mounted pennants (boasting first place in swimming, wrestling, and football) and kitty-corner from the hot-and-popular table, which was next to the cafeteria line. This ensured the jocks could get their food first. Scattered in between were the artsy types, the nerds, the stoners, the goths, and the milquetoasts who defied classification.

Holland Altman, Suki Hammer, Prisha Chowdhury, and Gemma Taylor had taken over the smart-but-social table during their sophomore year. Staples High School, the public school in their hometown of Westport, Connecticut, had the usual Anytown, USA groupings. Holland, Suki, Prisha, and Gemma had been best friends since the eighth grade, a convenient time to fortify a social group. They had agreed upon entering high school that they wouldn't attempt to penetrate the popular crowd, but they wouldn't fall in with the geeks, either. Instead they'd dwell in the precious milieus of the honor roll students who got invited to parties, though were never the ones to throw them. They wouldn't necessarily be trendsetters, but they wouldn't be followers, either.

The four of them stuck together through high school, earning high marks and carrying enough social currency that the jocks and cheerleaders at least knew their names, and the nerds knew better than to ask them to study together. And now they were seniors. Graduation was only a month away. Today was the day they'd been dreading, anticipating, awaiting, stressing over, and picturing, all at once.

It was yearbook day.

Yearbook day meant finding out if their efforts had paid off. Having the right clothes, avoiding the calories in the vending machine, joining the extracurriculars, maintaining GPAs above 3.5. College admissions season, which was arguably the more important barometer of success in high school, had already come and gone. But the four friends felt just as anxious, if not more, to find out what their senior superlatives would be.

There were fifty superlatives each year, and approximately two hundred and twenty graduating seniors. The entire class voted. Some were obvious. Kim Konner would get Most Popular; Lulu Anderson would clinch Most Fashionable. Charlie Rice would get Most Athletic, and class clown Byron Cox would get Most Likely to Win the Lottery and Lose the Ticket. Suki, Prisha, Holland, and Gemma each had agonized over what they'd get, silently fearing how it would affect their dynamic if they didn't all win something.

Holland was head of virtually every extracurricular club except for yearbook, so they had no special insight into what lay inside the book's pages before it was released. Holland had spoken chair-to-chair with David Gross, the head of the yearbook committee, but he wouldn't breach his oath of secrecy. She couldn't imagine getting skipped over in the superlative section. Holland had made her mark on the school. Treasurer of the Glee Club. Editor in chief of the school newspaper. Honor roll every term.

Suki was also feeling confident. She wasn't Holland, a student government professional with a list of extracurriculars on her college application that required an addendum. But she was well-known around the school. For starters, she was half-Japanese. And in a lily-white school community, her background made it so every freshman through senior knew her name. Her mother was Japanese, a former model in Tokyo turned accessory designer, married to a white engineer who had promised the good life in America but had ended up laid off more times than it seemed he'd been hired. She was a solid student, cursed in Japanese when she wanted attention, and was rumored to have dated a college boy for the past year. She'd started the rumor, but only Holland, Gemma, and Prisha knew that.

Then there was Prisha. Repressed, overworked, brilliant Prisha Chowdhury. Another student of color in the community, but somehow it didn't ring the bells that Suki's roots did. Prisha's father, Dr. Chowdhury, was one of the most popular pediatricians in town. In middle school, the boys used to joke about Dr. Chowdhury grabbing their junk when he examined them. Prisha had brushed it off. It was easy to do when her nose was always in a book. She was on a path: Harvard, Harvard Medical School, then a fellowship in orthopedics. She'd always loved the intricacies of the human body, studying the skeletons strung as Halloween decorations around the neighborhood while the others were just fisting candy.

Last but not least, there was Gemma. She'd had stars in her eyes since starring as Pilgrim Number Three in the fifth grade Thanksgiving play. Gemma had begged her parents to get her an agent (they'd finally relented in middle school), and since then she'd appeared in six commercials. Of their foursome, Gemma was the most fearless. She'd broken into the drama director's office to sneak a peek at the cast list for *Chicago* before it was posted. She'd scored copies of the math test from their teacher's locked drawer. Nothing she did ever got her in serious trouble, because the principal relied on her wealthy parents for generous donations to support the Fall Fair and Spring Fling. As the only member of the graduating class to ever appear on TV, Gemma had little chance of being overlooked in the yearbook.

"Oh my God, he's here!" Holland said, jumping out of her seat. She pointed to where David Gross had entered the cafeteria, pushing a hand truck stacked with cartons of books. As if he was tossing hundred-dollar bills in the air, everyone rose at once and charged at him.

"He's walking toward us," Holland gasped. She was white as a sheet. None of them wanted to be around her if she got something that she deemed beneath her.

"Just like I told him to," Gemma said, grinning. She popped a French fry into her mouth with obvious satisfaction. "I said he could squeeze my right boob if he brought the yearbooks here first."

"Gemma!" Prisha clapped a hand to her mouth.

"We'll see if I actually follow through. I think he'll be satisfied with a look."

David Gross had raging acne that hadn't quit since the ninth grade. There was little chance he'd ever seen a live breast.

"Why the right one?" Suki asked, clearly amused.

"Saving the left one to find out who the prom king and queen are going to be."

Holland threw a crumpled napkin at Gemma, but she was clearly grateful for the first look.

"Oh, hey, there's Josh," Prisha said, pointing straight ahead. "Right behind David."

Josh Levine had been Holland's boyfriend since sophomore year. They were an under-the-radar couple, hardly the sort worthy of gossip. Josh wasn't a looker, but he was sweet and dependable and put up with Holland's exhausting schedule of extracurriculars.

"Hot off the presses, ladies," David said when he reached their table. Four hands grabbed at the top box on the pile, ripping into the packing tape.

"Got one," Suki announced, the first to pry a book free. She flipped ferociously until she reached the superlatives double spread.

Gemma grabbed it from her hands and laid it flat on the table so they could all see at once.

"Most Likely to Cure Cancer . . . Prisha Chowdhury!" Suki announced. "Very nice."

Prisha burned with pride. Her parents would like that. They would probably frame it next to her older sister's valedictorian plaque on the mantel.

Holland cheered when she saw hers.

"Most Likely to be President," she said, giddiness bringing her to her tiptoes.

"Nice job, babe," Josh said, throwing an arm around her while scanning the spread for his own name, which wasn't there.

"Suki Hammer . . . Most Likely to be a CEO." Suki read her own aloud. Her mind raced to make sense of it. She had turned the school bake sale into a lucrative event with gourmet treats. And she'd gotten the student newspaper to take on advertising from local businesses. Yeah, it was starting to fall into place. She was happy with her honorific, and at least it had nothing to do with being Japanese, like Most Exotic.

"And Gemma Taylor gets Most Likely to Win an Oscar," David Gross said, his eyes fixed on Gemma's right boob.

"I'll take it," Gemma said grandly, in a voice that sounded like she was already onstage clutching her statuette, about to thank her family, friends, and agent.

"We did good, kids," Holland said.

"You did," David said. "Gemma, I'll see you later." He gave her a wink that made them all cringe. He and Josh walked off together.

"Think any of these things will actually come true?" Prisha asked. They had their heads huddled together, studying the rest of the superlatives now that they'd found their own.

"Obviously," Suki said. "We're going to light the world on fire."

Chapter One

Holland

Westport, Connecticut
2023

M om, there's a fire in the kitchen!"

Cameron, Holland's teenage daughter, was calling upstairs at the top of her lungs.

In her bedroom, Holland Levine quickly shut her laptop. She was in the midst of emailing with a promising guy she'd matched with on one of those dumb apps her daughter had insisted she download. She'd let Cameron do the technical work of setting up her profile, but she didn't need her know-it-all, attitude-plus teenager getting involved with the correspondence. Besides, all she'd written to CTguy77 was, "Would luv to meet up." Overly colloquial for a man who claimed in his profile to be an English professor, though nothing was for certain behind the curtain of the internet.

Holland ambled down the stairs, not exactly in a rush. Cameron was prone to hyperbole and drama, a trait that emerged around the time of her parents' divorce. Holland took a moment to study the crack in the bottom stair, and then let her eyes rove over to the peeling wallpaper. Their house was showing its age, not unlike her. Getting the place shaped up would mean calling her ex, Josh. She'd rather live with the imperfections.

"Holy shit, Cam," Holland exploded when she reached the kitchen. This time her daughter had not been exaggerating. Bluish flames were shooting into the air, and a cloud of smoke was quickly filling the room. "What the hell happened? Get the fire extinguisher."

Cameron pointed to a tray of charred brownies. Holland went to tamp down the flames with a dish towel while her daughter rushed to the pantry, returning with the fire extinguisher.

Holland stared at the red canister. She had no idea how to use it. It was one of the things she'd bought after Josh moved out, along with a pole to change out-of-reach lightbulbs.

"Forget it," Holland said, resting the fire extinguisher on the floor. "I think it's dying down. Why are you baking, anyway?" Holland hoped she didn't sound judgmental. Cameron had been hitting the sweets pretty heavily lately, and the results showed in her midsection, the same spot Holland wore every extra cookie.

"For the senior class bake sale," Cameron explained.

Though her daughter was a senior at the same school Holland had attended, observing many of the same rituals and learning from a handful of the same teachers, the years felt like a hazy memory to Holland. She wished she could convey to Cameron how utterly insignificant anything that happened in high school was in the grand scheme of things. She wanted to reassure Cam that one day she'd barely be able to recall the details of a fight that made her bawl for hours, or the name of a boy she'd obsessed over.

"I totally forgot it was tomorrow."

Because you're not organized, Holland thought, but held her tongue. She didn't want to say anything that could unleash one of their *Get over it, I'm not you* fights. After she and Josh had split, arguments between Holland and Cameron had grown more severe. "I want to spend the night at Dad's" was one of Cam's crueler retorts. But nothing hurt as badly as "Kelly would never say that to me." Kelly was Holland's replacement, fifteen years younger and with tits four inches higher.

"All right, let's clean up this mess. Then we'll swing by Bridget's Bakery, buy some lemon squares, ugly them up a little so they seem homemade, and call it a day." Holland reached for a wad of paper towels and started wiping away the mess.

"I love you, Mom. You're the best!" Cameron said, wrapping her mother in a rare hug. Holland's flesh prickled with goose bumps. She so rarely experienced physical affection these days. Not from men. Not from her daughter. Not even from friends, who were few and far between. After the divorce, many of the women in her orbit had sworn they'd stick by her. Her closest mom-friend, Stacey, the mother of Cameron's best friend Laurie, promised that she was eager for a third wheel for date nights. But after one trip out to a Mexican restaurant followed by a movie, Stacey never reached out to Holland to tag along again.

"Should we go now?" Holland asked, looking at her watch. It was only 5:30 p.m. She could race over to the bakery with Cameron and make it back in time to start dinner, then turn back to the work she'd brought home with her. She was one of two marketing managers at the local radio station, and her counterpart, Annie, was on maternity leave. If only the work was a bit more interesting, maybe she wouldn't mind the second helping of it.

When Holland looked up, Cameron was already halfway out the front door.

"Don't worry, Mom. I'll just go myself. I'll probably meet up with Laurie after."

Not going to the bakery meant Holland had more time to herself. Cam would probably end up eating dinner at Laurie's house, so she could even skip cooking. But as the allure of a quiet evening revealed itself to Holland, a sadness dogged her.

Holland sat down at the kitchen desk and opened her email. There was a message from Cameron's guidance counselor. Cameron wasn't nearly the student that Holland had been, so if Ms. Lafferty was reaching out, it wasn't to alert her that Cameron had won one of the numerous prizes that Holland had collected back in her day. At least Cameron wasn't a troublemaker, not beyond the typical teenage boundary pushing—some light vaping and a skipped class or two.

She clicked the email open, but fortunately it was just a reminder about an upcoming college prep meeting. Below that email was a message from Dr. Giffords, the school principal.

Dear Holland,

It's hard to believe it's already May! We are so proud of Camryn and all she has accomplished at Staples!

Holland blanched at the misspelling of her daughter's name.

As I'm sure you noted from the Save the Date sent in the fall, your
25th reunion is around the corner. We are looking for some volunteers
from the Class of 1998 to help make this weekend back on campus
very special. Of course, you were the first person to come to mind,
what with your exemplary record of leadership positions during your
time here. And of course, your track record as the longest-serving PTA
president speaks volumes.

Dr. Henry Giffords had been a first-year principal when Holland was a ninth grader. He'd come from an inner-city school
where most of the homes were single parent and a sizable chunk
of the student body relied on the public school for breakfast and
lunch. It was culture shock when he arrived at Staples to find a
parent body in a tizzy that the parking lot didn't have sufficient
spots for the seniors and that AP Mandarin wasn't offered, two
details that were quickly rectified.

Please let me know if you can find the time in your busy schedule
to chair the reunion weekend. I can't imagine anyone doing a better job.
Yours,
HG

Holland blushed, though she was alone. Flattery was her
Achilles' heel. It was the reason she'd taken on the thankless job
of PTA president for the past eight years, chasing down parents
who didn't pay their teacher gift dues and never signed up for
safety patrol slots. She loved the accolades at the end of the year,

the moment when the student government president handed her a bouquet of roses at graduation in gratitude for her service. She loved sitting on the dais at school functions, sandwiched between the superintendent and the principal.

Holland had certainly not forgotten about the reunion. She just hadn't decided whether to attend. It was yet another event where she risked being in the same room as her ex-husband and his new wife. Holland preferred to call Kelly a second wife rather than a new one, because it implied there would be a third.

Now, with Dr. Giffords's offer, Holland felt certain she would go. She could attend the reunion with her head held high as reunion chair, making sure Josh and Kelly were seated nowhere near her but with a perfect view of the stage as she mounted the platform to welcome everyone. Fuck! She would need to start a diet. She looked down at her waist, where a roll of extra skin spilled inelegantly over the waistband of her jeans. Maybe she and Cameron could diet together.

Holland eyed the photograph tacked to the corkboard in the kitchen showing Suki, Gemma, Prisha, and her in Napa Valley. It had been taken seven years ago. Her high school friends had not disappointed her, unlike so many others, in rallying around her after the divorce. It didn't hurt that Suki had offered to fly them all to the Auberge du Soleil resort for a long weekend of drinking, spa time, and fine dining. She'd picked up the tab for all of them, which had made the weekend too tempting to miss, even though it had been hard for Gemma to leave her new business and for Prisha to leave work and the kids. There were talks of making it an annual girls' trip, and it had happened the following year, Suki bringing them all that time to a charming village in Colorado for skiing and rounds of après-ski cocktails. But the trips had fallen by the wayside as Suki's star burned even brighter and her commitments grew in tandem. The rest of them were also burdened with obligations of their own, which made carving out the time to get away more effort than it was worth. Their friendship now existed mainly in the ether—monthly check-ins on group text.

Unpinning the photo, Holland brought it closer to her face and studied Prisha's rare smile. Prisha was the most serious of their foursome. She'd been the kind of student who could be overlooked by a teacher because she rarely raised her hand, but when her perfect tests had piled up, she'd caught the attention she deserved. Her parents had also been the strictest of their group. Prisha had rarely gone to parties, had had to be pressured by friends into finally wearing a skirt above her knees (which she'd had to change into at school), and had been mincemeat if she'd missed curfew. Of all of them, her life had unfolded most predictably. Still, something always seemed missing. When she smiled, her eyes lacked a corresponding twinkle.

Holland decided to start her asks with the good doctor. She lived in New Haven, only forty-five minutes from Staples. It ought to be easy enough to convince her to come.

Prisha answered after three rings.

"Hang on a sec," she said, and Holland heard her firing instructions at a nurse.

"You sound busy," Holland said when Prisha returned.

"Always," Prisha said. "What's up?"

"Well, I've been asked to chair the twenty-fifth reunion," Holland said. While moments earlier she had felt proud, saying it out loud made her feel childish.

"Of course you have," Prisha said.

"Dr. Chowdhury, you need to sign some discharge papers before you leave," a female voice said, and Prisha put Holland on hold again. It was easy to picture her friend at the hospital, looking the picture of calm and competence in her white coat as gurneys flew by. She kept her cool always, even when the mean kids in school had started calling her Clam Chowdhury.

"Ok, I'm back," Prisha said. "So, what's the plan for this reunion weekend? I put the date in my calendar ages ago, but I don't know if I'll be able to make it."

"P, I need you there. Please, please. I can't face Josh and the bimbo without my girls around me."

Prisha sighed. Holland could hear her gears cranking, thinking who could watch the kids, how many days it would mean taking off of work.

"Isn't Kelly a yoga teacher?"

Holland bristled. Bimbo, yoga teacher. Tomato, tomahto. "Whatever."

"I'm just saying that Kelly might not be that bad of an influence on Cam. If nothing else, she should have good posture."

"She doesn't," Holland said sharply. Her daughter slumped; her head was permanently rounded forward because of her cell phone addiction. "Well, please try to be there if you can. Even if you only drive for one night."

"I have to talk to Dev," Prisha said predictably. Dev was her husband, an orthopedic surgeon with an ego that barely fit in the operating room.

"I understand. I'll follow up," Holland said, trying to sound breezy, when really her heart was pounding.

"I know you will," Prisha said, and they both giggled. Holland was tenacious. A dog with a bone when she set her mind to something.

"Love you," Holland said. "Say hi to—"

"Wait," Prisha interrupted. "Is Suki going?"

Would Suki come? It wasn't like Holland hadn't already been wondering about it off and on since the moment the Save the Date had arrived.

"I don't know yet," Holland said. "But you know I'm gonna try."

She hung up the phone and replaced the photo on the corkboard, next to one of Cameron's elementary school drawings that she couldn't bear to take down. It was a family portrait—her, Josh, and Cameron depicted as colorful stick figures. Instead of putting herself in the middle, Cam had drawn her parents side by side and put herself to the left, next to Josh. It was an unusual setup—Cam's kindergarten teacher had even commented on it. "She must really love seeing you two together."

Reaching again for her cell phone, she thought of how best to phrase the ask to Gemma. It would be the hardest for her, of everyone, to return to campus after what had happened at the twentieth.

Holland opted for the truth, tapping out a text.

Gem . . . I miss you. Our 25th reunion is a month away and I've been asked to chair the weekend. I cannot fathom doing this without you by my side. And I think you facing everyone would prove that everything that was said about you was a total lie. Your absence would speak louder than your presence. Besides, we can get wasted at the bar together. Lmk. XOXO

The three dots of a reply flashed on her screen immediately.

Hm. Tempting, but no. Miss you too. X

Holland flinched. She hadn't even gotten Gemma to consider it. What could bend her mind?

Suki is coming.

The three dots returned, disappeared, and then came again.

Really? Maybe I can make it.

Holland smiled to herself. It was a harmless lie. Besides, maybe she'd succeed in convincing Suki to come. It wasn't like getting there from Palo Alto was that difficult when she could fly in and out on her private jet.

Her email dinged. Had Prisha already made up her mind? But the message was from CTguy77, the man she'd been corresponding with from the dating app. He was awfully handsome. Maybe if things went well between them, she could bring him as her date to the reunion.

Holland opened the message, feeling a flutter in her belly.

Dear Holland,

　　I'd really like to meet up soon. Might you be free for dinner this Saturday night? I can come to Westport and we can eat at one of the places on the water. Let me know if that's convenient for you.

　　Fondly, Mike

Oh, she liked Professor Mike. She was about to respond when she noticed there was an attachment to the email. It was titled "Something Extra." Odd.

She clicked it open and gasped when she was greeted by a close-up of Professor Mike's penis, flanked by two hairy balls.

Photo by Brian Marcus

Elyssa Friedland is the acclaimed author of *Last Summer at the Golden Hotel, The Floating Feldmans, The Intermission,* and *Love and Miss Communication.* Elyssa is a graduate of Yale University and Columbia Law School and currently teaches novel writing at Yale. She lives with her husband and three children in New York City, the best place on earth.

CONNECT ONLINE

ElyssaFriedland.com
ElyssaFriedland
AuthorElyssaFriedland
ElyssaFriedland